Honor Bound

The Honor Series
By Robert N. Macomber

Honor Bound

A Novel of
Cmdr. Peter Wake, U.S.N.
(ninth in the Honor Series)

Robert N. Macomber

Pineapple Press, Inc.
Sarasota, Florida

Inquiries should be addressed to:

Pineapple Press, Inc.
P.O. Box 3889
Sarasota, Florida 34230

www.pineapplepress.com

Library of Congress Cataloging-in-Publication Data

Macomber, Robert N., 1953-
Honor bound : a novel of Cmdr. Peter Wake, U.S.N. / Robert N. Macomber. -- 1st ed.
     p. cm. -- (Honor series ; 9)
ISBN 978-1-56164-493-3 (alk. paper)
1. Wake, Peter (Fictitious character)--Fiction. 2. United States. Navy--Officers--Fiction. 3. United States--History, Naval--19th century--Fiction. I. Title.
PS3613.A28H65 2011
813'.6--dc22
                              2010053164

First Edition
10 9 8 7 6 5 4 3 2 1

Design by Shé Hicks
Printed in the United States of America

This novel is dedicated to four friends of mine,
people who have actually *lived* their faith,
saved thousands of lives,
and made one sad part of the world
a much better place

Donald D. DeHart
(1935–2006)

Eva DeHart

Rosaline Présumé

Racine Présumé

An introductory word with my readers about the Honor Series and this novel

I believe some background on the fictional hero of the Honor Series, Peter Wake, might be helpful for both new and long-time readers. Wake was born just east of Mattapoisett, Massachusetts, on 26 June 1839, to a family in the coastal schooner trade. Going to sea full-time at age sixteen, he worked his way up to command a lumber schooner by twenty-one. In 1863, at the height of the Civil War, Wake became a volunteer officer in the U.S. Navy. His naval career lasted until 1908.

Stationed on the blockade of Florida's coast, he married a Southern girl, Linda Donahue, at Key West in 1864. The couple's daughter Useppa was born at Useppa Island, Florida, in 1865; son Sean at Pensacola in 1867. Unlike many volunteer officers, Wake remained in the navy following the war, hoping to make a career out of it.

After serving as a deck officer for sixteen years, he began his intelligence work while observing the War of the Pacific on South America's west coast in 1879–1881. He then joined the newly formed Office of Naval Intelligence (ONI) in 1882. As one of the few officers who did not graduate from the U.S. Naval Academy, his career path was without major ship commands or fame, and he remained in ONI for the next twenty-six years. Most of his intelligence work was in the clandestine Special Assignments Section (SAS), which worked directly for the Chief of the Bureau of Navigation (parent command of ONI) until 1889. After that he reported directly to the office of the assistant secretary of the navy. There has never been any record of the SAS's existence.

The first six novels of the Honor Series were in the "third person." But in the 2009 novel, *The Honored Dead*, a fascinating discovery was described: in 2007, Wake's collection of memoirs were found inside a one-hundred-twenty-four-year-old ornately engraved trunk, a gift from the emperor of Vietnam to Peter Wake, that was hidden away in the attic of a bungalow on Peacon Lane, in Key West. It was owned by Agnes Whitehead, who had recently died at age ninety-seven. There has been much speculation among Honor Series aficionados about Agnes Whitehead, her relationship to the Wake family, and how she came to possess that special trunk. With each novel after *The Honored Dead*, another facet of that puzzle is revealed.

The individual accounts in the trunk (more than a dozen were found) were typed by Wake himself in the 1890s and early 1900s, usually a few years after the events within occurred. Each contained an explanatory letter to his naval officer son or Christian missionary daughter. Wake did all this because he wanted his children and their descendants to understand what he endured and accomplished in his career, since the official records on most of it were sequestered in the ONI vault at the State, War, and Navy building, now known as the Eisenhower Executive Office Building. A note in the trunk requested that none of the material be made public by the family until fifty years after the death of his two children, Sean and Useppa. Sean died in 1942 and Useppa in 1947. To my uncertain knowledge, no current *direct* lineal family heirs are known.

Sean Rork, an Irish-born boatswain in the U.S. Navy and lifelong best friend of Wake, served with him in the naval service until 1908 and shared ownership of Patricio Island, on the lower Gulf coast of Florida. He was eight years older than Peter, and it was for him that Wake named his son.

It must be explained here that Wake was a product of his times, and his descriptions of people and events may not be considered "politically correct" in a modern context. However, he was also remarkably tolerant and culturally astute, and his military and political observations were usually proven accurate. Much of his rather arcane academic knowledge was gained through an international network of intriguing individuals met during his assignments, with whom he kept a lasting correspondence. Few military men of the period had as diverse a selection of intelligence sources as Peter Wake. I have corrected only the most egregious mistakes in Wake's grammar, and kept his spelling for foreign words, though they may be debated by twenty-first-century scholars.

IMPORTANT NOTE: I strongly suggest that after finishing each chapter, readers peruse the chapter's endnotes at the back of the book, where they will find interesting background details I've discovered while researching this project.

Thus, my friends, with the Honor Series, of which *Honor Bound* is the ninth, we have the unique opportunity to see inside the events and personalities of a critical period of history, through the eyes of a man who was there, and secretly helped make much of it happen.

Onward and upward…
Robert N. Macomber
Twin Palm Cottage
Matlacha Island
Florida

The Preparation

The Saint Francis Inn
Saint George Street
Saint Augustine, Florida
Saturday, 30 June 1888

My nerves were dangerously raw that morning.

It had taken a lot of effort to get to that moment. Lives were in jeopardy, national policies were in the balance, time and treasure had been expended, my reputation was at stake. Such is the way of my profession, immersed in the grayer shade of a deniable but very real war between nations, fought by men in civilian attire, employing tactics usually thought criminal by the more prominent social circles of the Christian world. The fact that I was within my own country, made it all even more peculiar, almost unreal.

A noonday rain shower hadn't defeated the June heat. It was not heavy enough to cool off the place; its anemic effort just left puddles and a steaming atmosphere. The sort that rapidly saps one's patience. I sat there in sweat-soaked clothes, watching and waiting, expecting the worst. Thus, I was less than tolerant of the naïve—stupid, really—question posed to me by the junior member of my detachment while I was intently occupied in trying to spot any counter-intelligence surveillance, or an assassination attempt, by Spanish government agents.

"What d'ya suppose they'll do, if they find out about him, sir?" asked Ensign Jefferson, while leaning out the window to the balcony where I sat, ostensibly relaxing with a book. His young face showed genuine concern for a man he'd never met and knew nothing about.

"The same damned thing we'd do, if he was one of ours—only without the prerequisite formalities," I snapped back as Jefferson recoiled in surprise. Seeing his reaction, I vowed to not lose composure again. It was happening too frequently lately.

Jefferson's question took me back two years. I didn't have to *suppose* what would happen. From my own gruesome memories, I knew precisely what the Spanish would do if they found out about what their man was doing with us. I'd been a prisoner in the very dungeon in Havana, the dreaded Audiencia, where the Spanish interrogated their enemies. I'd met the dead-eyed men who did those interrogations, enjoying their prisoners' agony. After their work was done, they cleaned off and neatly stowed the instruments of their trade on the table beside the victim's chair—a surgical display immediately visible to the next client who entered the room. The lamp-lit scene in that dungeon, complete with condensation-dripping walls carved from coral rock, was permanently seared in my mind.

No, Jefferson didn't need to know the mechanics of our informant's fate if things went badly. Though, if the ensign had actually known the man and his proclivities, I dare say he wouldn't have cared.

"Ah, there he is," I said, calmer now. "Get into position, Mr. Jefferson."

The ensign mumbled "Aye, aye, sir," and ducked back inside,

glad to be away from me. I heard the hallway door close and his heavy frame clumping down the stairs.

From my vantage point on the balcony, I could see the subject of Jefferson's inquiry coming farther into view. A hundred yards away, an older man—old enough to be my father—approached my position, right on time. If you didn't know him, and what he was about to do, you'd think him some grandfather making his way through the quaint old town. Clad in a faded black suit from the fashions of Europe forty years earlier, gray hair comically disarrayed by the breeze, he desperately clutched a large brown valise while trudging south on the uneven stone footpath beside Saint George Street. Even at that range, I could sense his anxiety by the cautious gait, his downward gaze.

The disturbed manner indicated he was going about some disagreeable duty, which he most certainly was. A passerby might think it an unpleasant chore for his elderly wife, but they would be wrong. There was no wife. Never had been. I knew what that duty was, for it was my idea. Six months of considerable effort on the part of half a dozen men in three countries had been expended to get that old man to this rendezvous.

So he could betray his king and empire.

Just past the Presbyterian Church, the man stopped to admire a vine of purple flowers cascading over a crumbling whitewashed wall of oyster shells, lime, and sand. I knew he wasn't the type to appreciate flowers. No, he was taking an opportunity to look around for anyone following him. Slowly he swiveled his head, trying to seem nonchalant. He wasn't very good at it and hesitated for a moment, staring at the wall. Leaves floated down around him like green snow from a gust of wind through the oak trees canopying the street. He ran his fingers over the exposed shells along the top of the wall. It was a relic from the original Spanish days—the wooden house behind the wall had decomposed a century earlier.

The old man seemed pensive for a moment, and I wondered

if he'd had ancestors living in the town back in those terrible days. Or was his mind weighted down with the enormity of the task at hand? Would he place national honor over personal humiliation and worse, and back out at the last minute? The hand stayed on the wall another few seconds, as if somehow communing with it.

There were remnants of a lot of ancient walled courtyards in the area. Some were two or three hundred years old, each one built not for aesthetics but for last-ditch defense. In those days, you did not want to lose the battle. Especially if you were still alive. Prisoners didn't live long after their capture. Most didn't want to.

Actually, that concept wasn't such an antiquated idea, I thought, watching the man glimpse nervously around one more time before resuming his journey. There'd be no niceties observed if he was caught by Colonel Marrón's counter-intelligence operatives. No procedural protection. No opportunity for defense or mitigation. No compassion for his predicament. He'd be dead within hours, *after* they extracted all he knew about his foreign contact—me. Ah, yes, and that particular bit of information would greatly incense the Spanish imperial authorities in Havana. They already had substantial reason to hate me, but far less than I had against them.

Behind the old man, another figure came into sight, sauntering around the corner of a private entryway onto Saint George Street. Tall and lanky, with salt-and-pepper hair twisted into a sailor's short tail, he wore a light blue cotton shirt and dark trousers. This second man walked with the confident rolling pace of one who'd spent decades standing on swaying decks. He was a son of Eire named Sean Rork, officially a senior boatswain in the United States Navy, and more particularly, my assistant and dearest friend. A newspaper—that day's *St. Augustine Press*—was carried loosely in his right hand.

Well, to be more accurate, the right was his *only* hand. He'd lost the other to a sniper one August night in '83, at the Forbidden Purple City, inside the Citadel at Hue, capital of the Empire of Viet

Nam. The shooter was trying to kill me, but instead he hit Rork with that lump of lead. It's something he occasionally reminds me of when in need of some libation and lacking sufficient funds. Since that wound, Rork's had a stump just below his left elbow, courtesy of a French naval surgeon. But our friends in the French Navy didn't stop there. Oh, no, they went on to create a veritable masterpiece of malevolent art.

A carpenter's mate fashioned a false hand made of flesh-painted India rubber, carved into an opened fist, the fingers able to grip a bottle, a cutlass, or an oar. It even has fingernails and wrinkles painted on it, and one has to be close, indeed, to discern its true counterfeit nature.

A French gunner's mate did the rest. Underneath that apparently benign façade of a rubber left hand is a wicked-looking sailor's marline spike, mounted securely on the base of the underlying appliance. The rubber hand fits over it quite nicely, but can be removed in an instant to reveal the device beneath. Beside its nautical uses as a tool, the spike is quite handy in our line of work—quiet, lethal, concealable. Its unveiled appearance is an excellent attention-getter and motivator in dialogues. And, of course, Rork being Rork, the whole contraption is a source of great pride to him. In fact, the mere thought of his spike, and its various uses, makes my friend smile, a sign of that rather dark Gaelic soul lurking within.

The appearance of the newspaper in his right hand was a good sign to me. It meant there was no counter-surveillance by the Spanish government. That we were in Saint Augustine, the oldest city in America, was no guarantee of protection against foreign operatives. The Spanish had intelligence agents all over Key West, Tampa, Jacksonville, New Orleans, and New York. They were, and continue to be, even now in 1896, fully engaged in a dirty little war against rebel Cuban insurgents, most of whom are funded by people in this country. If the Spanish knew, or even had an inkling, of what the old man was delivering to me inside that valise, they most certainly would be following him. If they knew I was involved, my fate would duplicate the old man's.

My second-story balcony jutted out from the south and west walls of the century-old Saint Francis Inn. The inn stands at the southern terminus of Saint George Street, a narrow lane running down from the town's central plaza. It ends at the cross street of Saint Francis. My perch was on the northeast corner of that intersection. The balcony was a perfect platform for observing activity on both streets.

The old man crossed Saint George Street obliquely, his course shaped for the front door of the inn. Leathered creases were visible now on his worried face, as his step quickened. Shielding his eyes from the afternoon sun, he glanced up at me, then quickly looked away when a loud double pop exploded behind him.

Dropping the novel I appeared to be reading—Admiral David Dixon Porter's *The Adventures of Harry Marline*—I reached inside my coat for the Merwin-Hulbert forty-four-caliber revolver I had at the ready. Following the old man's frightened stare up the street, I saw a wagon straining under a load of turpentine barrels. The driver was snapping a whip into a pair of mules. Its crack made a sound exactly like the report of a small-caliber revolver.

Rork was already partially behind the trunk of an oak, his back to me, facing the wagon. That good right hand of his had dropped the newspaper and was inside the right trouser pocket, no doubt gripping his navy-issued Colt. He turned and nodded toward me before retrieving the newspaper and resuming his walk. I allowed myself to breathe again, stowed my pistol, and picked up the book.

Admiral Porter came to mind. He had approved this mission, but I doubted whether his superior, the secretary of the navy—or *his* superior—knew of it. Porter was quite good at that sort of thing. *Devious* might be a more apt descriptor of his machinations. In unguarded moments, he called it "executive protection, from their tendencies toward idiocy."

Porter was a legend in those days. Some said he was arrogant, especially when faced with dissenting views, but no one denied his power. And not a soul on Capitol Hill, or over in the Presidential Mansion, crossed him. The irascible seventy-five-year-old had been the senior admiral commanding the United States Navy for almost two decades. Porter had seen a lot of secretaries of the navy and presidents come and go, and he knew where all the political bones were buried.

In the last few years he'd even had the leisure to apply himself to his long-submerged passion, writing books about the navy. Porter had already penned eight books—naval histories and novels—and was pretty good at it, though I thought some of his reminiscences on the late Southern rebellion were a bit self-serving. His sales were assured, of course. Every naval officer on active duty prominently displayed copies of Porter's books, for the obvious reasons. I myself found them valuable for doorstops, chart weights, and as an accoutrement for surveillance. But, just like the others, I admit to having his *Naval History of the Civil War* on my desk at the Office of Naval Intelligence.

My mind returned to the situation at hand. I watched the informant enter the Saint Francis Inn's garden courtyard. Seconds later, Rork followed him in from the street. Ensign Jefferson and Lieutenant Singer were in their positions at separate tables in the courtyard, scanning for any strangers. Their duty was to prevent interference, by force if need be. After a final check of the streets, I vacated the balcony, went into my room, and made a last-minute survey of our preparations. All was ready.

The two chairs and a coffee table were arranged just inside the west window. In the southwest corner, behind my chair, stood a table, atop which were two potted geraniums. Between them was a new Kodak box camera—precisely six feet, six inches away from the chair across from mine. Maximum effective range for this scenario. The camera's lens was aimed exactly at the far chair, which would be the informant's. At that moment of the day, a shaft of sunlight focused on the chair as if one of Mr. Edison's electric searchlights had been trained upon it.

Draped over a table in the background of the Spaniard's chair was a vividly new American flag, surrounded by red, white, and blue flowers. It was displayed artfully as a patriotic commemoration of the upcoming one hundred and twelfth anniversary of our nation's declaration of independence, to be celebrated in five days. It was also nicely within the view of the camera. I wanted there to be no doubt as to the location of the transaction.

A new-fangled photographic device, the Kodak is an amazing implement, a true wonder of our age. The thing can record one hundred pictures on a length of papered film rolled up inside the boxlike apparatus. It requires no tripod and hood, no wet plates dripping in chemicals, and no complicated development process.

One simply depresses a button to capture the scene. When you desire to make another photograph, you merely turn a tiny crank to advance a new section of film to the aperture. When you reach the end of the roll, you send the box off to the company in the mail. In a few days they send you the photographs and the box with a new roll of film. No longer is photography the realm of the few. In fact, the designer, an energetic young man named George Eastman, touts it as a camera for the general citizenry and sells his invention for twenty-five dollars each.

I'd met Eastman when he came to Washington a month earlier, in May, to present one of the first of his Kodaks to President Cleveland. Commodore John Grimes Walker, chief of the Bureau of Navigation, and thus of the operations at the Office of Naval Intelligence, was with me at the time. After hearing Eastman's explanation of how the camera worked, the commodore turned to me and quietly said, "Get one of those for us. ONI could use it."

I did, and now was using it clandestinely for the first time, in a role I'm sure its creator never imagined. To make sure it would work properly, a week earlier I had photographed Rork sitting in that same chair, illuminated solely by the sunlight at the exact moment of its maximum intensity. It had come out a bit darker than optimum, but was recognizable enough for our purposes.

Most importantly, we'd heard just the tiniest click from the trigger button, which had been modified by Eastman before we'd left Washington to make it smoother. He didn't know the camera was being used for cloak-and-dagger purposes by the intelligence service—Rork told him it was for his elderly grandmother in Boston who lacked the strength to depress the standard button. A shameless lie. Rork's grandmother died in Ireland thirty years ago.

Everything in the room appeared ready, but my insides were churned up like a bilge in a storm. This scenario was the culmination of dangerous work in Havana, Nassau, and now, Saint Augustine. In five minutes, it would finally be done. The contents of the valise would be in my hands. By the next morning, they would be in a sealed navy envelope guarded by Jefferson and Singer aboard a train heading for the Office of Naval Intelligence in Washington.

In two days, Commodore Walker and Admiral Porter would be reading the material. I would be on a well-deserved annual leave at my island in southern Florida. I should have been contented by the situation, but I wasn't.

So far, everything was going much too well.

2

The Coup de Grâce

The Saint Francis Inn
Saint George Street
Saint Augustine, Florida
Saturday, 30 June 1888

I'd chosen the Saint Francis Inn because it was small and away from the center of town, but close enough to the army barracks on the waterfront two blocks away, if things got deadly. Not that we told the army about any of this. They didn't need to know, and would only complicate it if they did.

As far as civilians in the area were concerned, by June tourists were gone and there was little other activity. I was lucky the inn was still open this late into the summer. My informant might have been noticed, or even worse, recognized, if he'd stayed at the more aristocratic Ponce de Leon or Alcazar hotels.

He'd done exactly as told, contriving a furlough and trip to New York to see a distant relative and the opera, a passion of his. Taking the Ward Line steamer from Havana to New York, he'd gone ashore at her first port of call in Nassau and there met with one of my network. Then, instead of continuing onward with the Ward ship to Charleston and New York the next morning, he'd quietly boarded the weekly steamer from Nassau to Jacksonville that carried the highly prized roses of New Providence Island to the American market.

It was a journey calculated to deceive any of his compatriots who doubted his reasons for departing Havana, and to facilitate an alert to my operatives if the Spanish had men following him. Neither had evidently occurred. The ruse had worked.

Inside the valise was supposed to be the 1888–89 repair schedule of the Havana naval yard for the Spanish navy's squadron in the West Indies, along with the naval coal depot reports from Havana and Santiago de Cuba. With it in our possession, we could see dramatic proof of the true state of readiness of our potential enemies, instead of relying on rumor or anecdotal third-hand indicators. Periodic war scares with Spain over the previous fifteen years had engendered the need for such factual intelligence. Rather than basing decisions upon what the press blathered or the diplomats simpered, real knowledge of an adversary's capabilities is invaluable in planning political responses, or naval actions. The endeavor to obtain such knowledge was judged to be worth the risk.

Three solemn knocks sounded on my room door—Rork's signal. I opened it and ushered the two of them inside. Closing the door, Rork remained there, arms folded as he glared ominously at our guest. The Spaniard hesitated, his eyes on Rork's imposing form, then crossed the room and slowly sat in the chair I indicated.

I kept my voice firm, the volume low, to better set the atmosphere. I wanted him intimidated, not terrified. Intimidated men perform as expected. Terrified men do not.

"Señor Paloma, please enjoy some orange juice after your long journey. This won't take long, and then you'll be on your way. Did you bring what we discussed?"

Paloma's eyes lingered on the American flag arrayed behind him, then quietly answered, "Yes."

He ignored the pitcher of juice on the table between us and handed over the valise, which I opened, withdrawing three files. Over the next ten minutes, I read each of them twice as he sat there fidgeting. The files confirmed what I'd suspected, but hadn't been able to prove to my commanders until then.

The Spanish fleet was not in a state of preparation for war. It was, in fact, in dire need of maintenance and replacement of its ships and equipment. The schedule at Havana's naval arsenal had been prioritized to work on ships in the worst shape, allowing the others to lapse into a state of decrepitude. The marine railway was inadequate to handle anything more than a small gunboat and the floating dry dock was down for repairs. Incredibly, there was no way the Spanish Navy could work on their hulls in the Western Hemisphere.

I noted that the time allocated for repairs on a ship was three times longer than a similar period at one of our naval facilities, suggesting that the Havana base's tool, iron, and boiler shops were in need of upgrading also. Some of Spain's ships based in the West Indies were relatively new and powerful, but they, like all modern machines of war, required constant skilled attention to remain ready for battle. According to what I was reading, that attention wasn't available.

The files on naval coal stocks at both Havana and Santiago de Cuba showed they were too low to fuel the entire squadron simultaneously on a war sortie. No more bituminous or anthracite coal was scheduled to be deposited at either depot for another six months. The loading rate for Havana was only 500 tons a day, for Santiago it was even less, at 100 tons.

This was telling information that no country would want public. But we already knew the approximate coal reserves through another source—I used it as a check on the accuracy of Paloma's repair yard data, to ascertain if we were being given false information. We weren't. Paloma had not been turned into a double agent against us.

All in all, what I held in my hand was an extraordinary intelligence coup.

I looked up at him and willed my tone to be unimpressed. His English was halting, but he could understand well enough. "This appears to be what was expected. Señor Casas has explained what you are to do next, now that this is delivered to me, correct?"

After a resentful sigh, he mumbled, "Yes."

I didn't care if he was upset. I needed to be certain he knew what to do. His life, and far more importantly, the future of the operation, depended on it.

"Then explain it to me."

He spoke slowly. "This afternoon, I am to take the train north to Jacksonville, just as I took it down to this place. At the station in Jacksonville, I take another to the city of Charleston. There, I take the . . . the Atlantic Coast Line train to Richmond, in Virginia. At that place, I take the . . . the Richmond . . . Fredericksburg, and Potomac train to Washington. There, I get on the Pennsylvania Railroad train to New York. I will be in New York on the morning of . . . Tuesday, the third day of July."

"And Casas advised you what would happen if you did not fulfill your future obligations to me?"

He looked at the floor. "Yes. If I fail to do what is expected, my superiors will know of my . . . personal life."

"Very good. You understand. And now I will give you your expense money, Señor Paloma. One hundred dollars, as agreed." I took out a wad of five-dollar greenbacks and laid it on the table.

He looked at it for a time, then put the wad in his pocket, his body slumping as he did so. Paloma was resigned to his fate— assisting the despised *norteamericano gringos*. Good, it was time to let him know what was coming next.

"In November, you will get Casas a job at the naval arsenal in Havana. It will be a foreman's job, with access everywhere. We will be in touch as to exactly how and when."

He barely moved his head in assent. When he spoke it was a whisper. "You said you would give me my photographs back."

Paloma fancied himself an artist with the camera, developing his own plates at his home. But his artwork was nothing that would appeal to the public. It was for his own private use. "Yes, I did, Señor Paloma. Here are your photographs. And I want you to count that money in my presence right now—just to show that I have not cheated you."

The Spaniard brought out the bills and began counting them as I shoved three photographs across to him. In the background, Rork had quietly moved across the room to the corner table behind me. He yawned and stretched his arm out over the table, then coughed just as Paloma finished counting and picked up the photographs.

Money in one hand, photographs in the other, with the American flag in the background—an instantaneous fragment of time that would incriminate the Spaniard beyond any plausible explanation. Rork timed it perfectly. I heard the Kodak click faintly. Preoccupied, the Spaniard didn't.

He looked at one of the photographs I'd given him, then put them all inside the valise, his hands trembling.

"I am not a bad person, Commander Wake."

"I never said you were, Señor Paloma. But I doubt whether your superiors would share my tolerance. Mere homosexuality goes against the teachings of the Church. But your sexual preference is sometimes known as a *crime against innocence*. You might want to destroy those pictures."

He was shaking, about to cry. A very different deportment from the first time I saw him, arrogantly berating a waiter at the Hotel Inglaterra in Havana for failure to display proper respect to a senior official.

It was time to end this, before he lost all self-control—and ability to function as he was expected. I stood up. "Mr. Rork will escort you to your train. Good luck, Señor Paloma. Until we meet again. Don't forget to destroy those photographs."

He lifted himself out of the chair, but the attitude suddenly changed. No longer were his eyes timid. Now they smoldered at me. The old Paloma was emerging. Humiliation had reached its limits. Now he was fighting to retain his dignity, his power.

The rising tone had an edge to it. "I *will* destroy them, Commander, so *you* cannot use them against me in the future. And for your information, Fernando is gone, out of my life."

Obviously, my intimidation needed some reinforcement. I'd anticipated that he would destroy the photographs, of course, and had copies of them made. But I also had something else for him as motivation to continue to assist us. Something with considerably more weight. I'd held it in reserve until now. The moment had come to end Ignacio Paloma's sudden cockiness and preclude any future notions of double-dealing.

"Oh, yes, we know that Fernando got away from you," I said pleasantly, lowering the dialogue back down to a conversational level. I didn't want others in the hotel to hear a row in the room and start asking questions. "Fernando left you a month ago—after you beat him almost to death. A thin little seventeen-year-old boy, who now has a disfigured face. He had to flee Havana . . ." I counted out two seconds and added, "for the safety of *America*. You wondered where he'd gone to, didn't you?"

Paloma's jaw lowered, now realizing we knew far more about him than he'd thought. I let that sink in for a few more seconds, then delivered the *coup de grâce*.

"But it turns out that poor little Fernando was not the only one, as you originally claimed to me in April. In fact, we have a sworn statement from Pedrito Arena about *his* love affair with you last year. I understand he was even younger at the time than Fernando is."

Rork had shifted position to stand beside Paloma, looming over him as I continued. "Señor Paloma, young Pedrito wasn't appreciative at all of the way you treated him. No, he was very angry, though we made sure to let Pedrito know that he was actually very lucky—you didn't beat *him* senseless. And when Pedrito saw a photograph of Fernando's face after you were done with it, he understood just how fortunate he'd been to escape your wrath."

From my coat pocket I pulled out the photograph of Fernando and put it on the table in front of Paloma. His eyes grew panicked, then looked away.

I continued. "For such a young boy, Pedrito became very resolute, realizing what a victim he'd become at your hands. Very resolute, indeed, for a fifteen-year-old. His testament included *everything* you did with him."

That hit the target. I thought Paloma was going to collapse. Pedrito Arena was the nephew of the social secretary to the Captain General of His Most Catholic Majesty's Ever Faithful Isle of Cuba—the personal representative of the king of Spain on the island.

"No . . ."

"Oh, yes, Señor Paloma. I think you need to reflect somberly upon your personal deficiencies and resolve upon ending them— if you want to stay alive. Perhaps a confession with your priest would be a good start. No? Well, that's your choice. But for now, it is time for you to go. And by the way, you should fervently hope that Pedrito Arena does not become even mildly ill, or someone would suspect you have harmed him. You do *not* want anyone to think that, do you?"

"No."

I pointed at the door. Rork allowed his heavy left hand to fall on Paloma's shoulder as I said, "Do what is expected of you. We will be in touch."

Thus was the manner in which I obtained the Spanish Navy's most sensitive information about its readiness from the number-two man in charge of their naval repairs in the Americas. The method I employed did not make me feel proud of myself and my profession. The revulsion went beyond the use of blackmail. In the past, I have had to consort with the lower forms of humanity in order to accomplish assignments, but never someone as squalid as Paloma.

After Rork guided the stunned Spaniard out of the room, the sickening photograph of Fernando's face caught my attention. I wondered how long I could play this foul game. Up in Washington, the operation had seemed grim but academic—a perception that quickly disappeared when looking into Paloma's evil eyes, knowing what he had done and wondering how many victims there really were.

And so I ended up spiritually weakened at precisely the place and time where my distant past could confront me. Was it God giving me a chance to redeem my self-worth with a life-saving quest?

I will let those who read this account form their own opinions.

3

God's Will

Grace Methodist Episcopal Church
Carrera and Cordoba streets
St. Augustine, Florida
Sunday, 1 July 1888

The next day was when my post-mission leave was to begin.
I'd kept the plan simple and flexible.

After Paloma had headed north to New York, and Jefferson
and Singer had departed for Washington, Rork and I would be
officially on annual leave for two months and free to enjoy life for
a while. On that Monday, some friends of mine were due into St.
Augustine on the train from Washington, and all hands would
then board the weekly passenger train later that day and head south
down the peninsula. It would take all day to reach Punta Gorda,
then the next day get to Patricio Island, a little tropical refuge to
which Rork and I escape when freed from our naval duties. It is
on the lower Gulf coast of Florida, a locale made famous in recent
years by Northern sporting fishermen's fascination with one of our
aquatic species.

The object of their interest is the tarpon fish, a bony six-foot-long predatory creature no one actually eats, but which gives a tremendous fight in its efforts to stay alive. It is quite active in those waters in June and July, rolling and jumping among the islands in an ecstasy of eating other fish. My Washington friends wanted to try their hand at this activity and I had invited them down. Unlike Rork, I am not a fisherman, but can row and sail a small boat as well as any, and would act as guide.

Now we had a day to rest before their arrival, but I was unable to do so. I was consumed by worries over how the Havana mission would evolve, and disgust over how it had already developed into using such a repugnant informer. There was nothing more for me to do at the moment, except wait until the next step in the mission, which was planned for early October, three months away. Until then we would not contact Paloma.

Since it was a Sunday morning, Rork, seeing my state of mind, insisted I go to services at a church for some quiet contemplation, or perhaps some inspiration, regarding my work. Or maybe he just wanted some time away from my glum behavior. In any event, my old friend understands my ridiculous idiosyncrasies better than anyone and knew I would further descend into melancholia without an infusion of positive morale.

"Peter, methinks ye're needin' to reprovision that heretical soul o' yours," he said. "So get thee to a church."

Well, that made sense to me, and so I decided to follow his advice. A professed and sincere Christian, I am not the dogmatically pious sort, but do draw solace from my faith. Of course, Rork, being Irish Catholic, does not step so much as a toe inside a Protestant church, so my attendance would be a solo affair. Should the truth be told, Rork rarely steps into a Catholic church anymore, but in a noble effort to provide leadership by example, he announced that he would go to the Roman Church's cathedral in the town while I went to my denomination's sanctuary, the Methodist church.

We would meet afterward, he announced, for a "wee dram

o' rum," sweetening the idea by graciously offering to buy, a rare event. I reminded him that Saint John's County, in which we were located, was as dry as a bone on Sundays, so his kind offer would be unfortunately impossible to fulfill. He countered with a sad shrug, as only an Irishman can do, and that sly smile that the ladies adore. He really is incorrigible. And so, the rarity of Rork actually buying *me* a drink was maintained.

It was sweltering under the sun as we walked up Saint George Street to the central plaza, a treeless commons over which brooded the ancient Spanish cathedral. Along with the surrounding area, it had suffered through a serious fire the year before, but was well on the way to recovery with a magnificent new tower. I bid him farewell and made my way another two and a half blocks up to the new Methodist place on Carrera Street. Opened on New Year's Day of 1888, it looked as Catholic as the cathedral, a very unusual architecture for heretical Protestants. I later found out why.

It seems that Henry Flagler, the wealthy railroad man, spent the incredible sum of eighty-five thousand dollars building the extraordinary church for the town's Methodist population in the notable span of less than a year. He insisted its design match that of his newly finished resort, the Ponce de Leon Hotel, which sprawled across several blocks two hundred feet to the south.

The Ponce de Leon is a replica of the palaces of Andalusian Spain. It immediately reminded me of the Alcazar in Sevilla, a place I unfortunately associate to this day with my near death—but that is another story. I will digress enough, however, to explain the reason for the rich man's munificence. Flagler is not a Methodist and did not do all this from the kindness of his heart toward the teachings of John Wesley.

The Methodists had been worshipping in a simple little wooden affair across King Street from the Ponce de Leon's majestic entryway. Some called the structure crude, saying it marred the view for the rather swanky hotel guests who had paid a lot of money to travel to an American version of the Costa del Sol.

Flagler offered to buy the church, but the Methodists had insufficient funds to buy new land in town and build another, so they declined—something he was not used to hearing. Needing that land for an expansion of his properties, he now made the Methodists an offer it was impossible to decline or even ignore. If they would vacate the property he wanted, he would build them a beautiful new church, downtown, that was big enough for the natural expansion of their congregation and ornate enough to be the envy of every flock everywhere. That offer was accepted.

The day I attended, Reverend Charles McLean, a man with a naturally easy smile, preached a sermon from the carved flying pulpit jutting out from a front corner of the sanctuary's altar space, high above the worshippers. Fanning ourselves in the heat, we heard a message centering on the twenty-third Psalm and the trials and tribulations of mortal life. McLean added a local touch with admonishments to remain steady in the face of yellow fever being reported in Jacksonville, a mere forty miles up the coast. The subject resonated heavily in my heart, for that dreaded curse of a disease had touched my life many times. The good reverend did not dwell on abject fear of that menace, however.

Instead, he concentrated on the ability of Christians to remain calm in the face of adversity, using the strength of their faith and hope to make it through the dark times and emerge in the light of grace. His words imprinted themselves in my memory.

"You do not get immunity from disease or evildoers as a Christian, for disease and evil are all around us and we have to deal with them. Storms and disease and suffering are constant. Human nature is flawed and there are those around us whose behavior is destructive. We cannot ignore all these adversities, we must face them," he intoned, eerily speaking directly to my personal condition. "But fear not, for you have the certainty that no matter what you face here, you will see a better day, a day where there is no more evil to mar your eternal life. Jesus already took care of that for each of us, a long time ago. So, my beloved, carry on in life and work, and look not to the left or to the right at those dangers and depressions that assail us, but do what you know to be the will of God."

After the service, my soul "reprovisioned" as Rork put it, I joined the end of the line of people greeting the pastor at the doorway, in order to offer my own heartfelt congratulations on a job well done. Yes, I'd had to deal with the Palomas of the world, but I just may have saved the lives of many men, Spanish, Cuban, and American, by preventing a miscalculation into war. And yes, life was good and getting better. In the morning, I would meet my friends at the train station and be en route to the island. Two months of leave, away from the personalities and politics of Washington—some of which was almost as disgusting as dealing with Paloma. It would be bliss. I might even try *my* hand at this tarpon fishing phenomenon.

Last to speak to him, I met McLean just inside the shadow of the heavy mahogany doors. He thrust out a hand and a cheerful greeting.

"Hello, sir. I'm Charles McLean. I believe we haven't had the pleasure of your company in our church before. Hopefully, you can come again, Mr. . . . ?"

"Wake, Peter Wake. I don't live here, Pastor. I'm just passing through on my way south, down to my home in the islands by Fort Myers."

"A long journey. Very nice to meet you, Peter. A good namesake, that," he said with a chuckle. "I presume you're named after the saint. Sorry you can't attend more often, but you're always welcome here whenever you are in town."

His infectious sincerity got me to regretting there was no church near my island, and that the church I did attend when in Washington did not have a man like this in command.

"Thank you. I enjoyed your message, Pastor. It picked up my spirits, which have been a bit low lately due to some work stress." I suddenly realized I sounded like some whining simpleton and immediately bucked up my attitude. "But that's in the past, for I'm on leave now—my first in two years—and I'm looking forward to a couple of months of relaxation."

Why I babbled on, I have no idea. But I did and thus opened a door I usually keep closed. The pastor inquired what type of work would preclude me from rest for such an extended length of time. Tired of the layers of falsities in my life, I decided to be straightforward. After all, there was no need to be guarded with a preacher.

"I suppose the best explanation is to introduce myself properly, Reverend. Commander Peter Wake, United States Navy."

He gave me a slight bow of respect.

"Well, well . . . a navy man. How very interesting! Say, while I have you here, please tell me something, Peter. What do you think of the efficacy of the naval chaplains? Many years ago, I had a friend who applied to that position of service and was refused admittance. Before passing onward to the afterlife recently, he confided to me that the failure to go to sea as a bearer of the word of the Lord was his greatest regret. I think he would have made a good chaplain. But what is your opinion of them? Do they make a difference? Do the sailors care?"

I'll profess here that I have not been a staunch supporter of *most* of the chaplains I have known, but must heartily admit that some of them have displayed the right sort of character needed to minister to men of war. Those particular clergymen have earned my respect and that of the sailors, who are a very tough breed to impress. So, since I had the time and he had the interest, I passed along some sea stories of parsons at sea, both good and bad, but concentrating on the good. As I progressed, he asked insightful questions and I answered frankly. We were getting along splendidly and he invited me to a luncheon with his visiting bishop that was to take place in an hour. I accepted, asking if Rork could join us after he did his duty as a Catholic, which was readily granted.

I shared another of my recollections. It was of a chaplain in a boat full of sailors going on liberty ashore in Key West. While standing up in the boat and stridently exhorting against the sin the lads were about to face, the preacher managed to fall overboard. The sailors kept on rowing for shore, later explaining with straight faces that after his fiery exhortation they honestly figured the cleric could walk to shore on top of the water. McLean's laugh was genuine.

"Yes, I've known the same type," he said, about to close the church's door.

Outside, the summer sky was filled with a blinding glare so intense that I didn't see the figure rapidly approaching us. In fact, it was the voice that I first noticed.

It was a voice from my past, so unique, with such vivid memories, that I instantly recognized it.

4
Déjà Vu

Grace Methodist Episcopal Church
Carrera and Cordoba streets
St. Augustine, Florida
Sunday, 1 July 1888

"*Please wait!* Can't you leave the church open a little bit longer?"

I'd first heard that dulcet drawl twenty-four years before, on the middle Gulf coast of Florida during the war, when I'd rescued her family and liberated her slaves. I'd last heard it fifteen years earlier, in '73, at San Juan, on the Spanish island of Puerto Rico. That was when I discovered she'd married one of my former enemies in the war, a man who'd subsequently become a dear friend of mine.

The lady was Cynthia Denaud Saunders. Cynda was the childhood nickname that she still went by. She paused demurely in front of McLean, who was instantaneously captivated by her charm—clergymen are, after all, only male. Seeing his reaction, I smiled. Cynda didn't even have to try, she just naturally had that effect. I'd seen it happen to other men before. It'd happened to me once. But this time it was different. Still strikingly beautiful, at what I calculated to be forty-three years of age, with a figure that was impossible to ignore, she was dressed differently than I'd ever seen her.

Cynda was clad in somber black bombazine silk from neck to toe. Even her wavy blond hair was gathered up in black mesh. She was obviously in mourning and had a look of despondency in her face—so much so that she did not register my presence, much less my identity.

For my part, I stood there in dumb shock while Reverend McLean recovered enough to reply. "Why yes, of course, madam. The church is always available to those in need. Can I be of assistance to you in some way, madam?"

She was about to cry. I'd seen her do that, too, but this time it looked real.

"Oh, pardon me, sir. My name is Saunders. Cynda Saunders. I wanted to pray, sir. Pray for the soul of my husband and the life of my son."

Motioning for me to wait, McLean led her to the front pew and withdrew to the rear of the sanctuary to allow her privacy. I didn't wait and instead headed for Cynda. In the corner, the minister, ignorant of my intentions, looked askance at me as I sat down beside her.

"Cynda, it's Peter Wake. Is something wrong?"

She turned and noticed me for the first time, her expression transforming from abject distress to joyful surprise. Raising her hands in supplication to the altar, she let out a shriek.

"Thank you, God!"

Well, to say the least, *that* disconcerted me.

"Cynda, what's happened?"

Another shriek to heaven. "Thank you, God, for sending my protector!"

This was becoming bizarre. McLean rapidly made his way toward us as I tried again to ascertain her problem, which I was beginning to suspect had a mental component.

"Cynda, please tell me what has happened."

Her eyes glistened as she spoke. "It's ordained in heaven. The Lord sent you here to help me, Peter. My husband Jonathan is dead and my son Luke is missing at sea. You can't help Jonathan, but you can find Luke. They say he is dead and gone, but you will find him, Peter. I know that. You will find him and save him!"

It was too much to assimilate quickly. Jonathan had been a blockade-runner during the war. He had settled with other former Confederates in western Puerto Rico after the South's surrender. A foe I'd tried to kill during the war, he saved my life from a rabid ex-rebel when I went to assess the ex-Confederate settlement for the U.S. government. We became friends, last seeing each other in San Juan for lunch, years later. That was when I found out Cynda had married him. I hadn't even realized she'd known him.

"Please calm down, Cynda. What happened to Jonathan?"

"He died at the beginning of the year. Inspecting the sugar cane fields, he just fell down, dead, Peter. They say his heart failed."

I'd always thought of Jonathan Saunders as a fit and strong man. But then I remembered that he was nine years older than I. The tropics can make a man old beyond his years.

"And you have a son?"

"Yes. Luke. He's fourteen and the joy of my life, Peter. We have to find him!"

The minister sat down on her other side, listening as she continued her tale.

"Luke wanted to go to sea like his father. Why this strange urge in certain men, I just don't know. But he kept badgering Jonathan the last couple of years. His father tried to humor him, Peter, and said he could go to sea for a month when he turned fourteen. Just to get a taste—but only for a month, as a cabin boy or steward, or something like that. Of course, Luke remembered his father's words, and when he turned fourteen in March he turned those same words against me, demanding I honor his father's promise. Oh, Peter, by then Jonathan wasn't there anymore. I was weak and I gave in to Luke. I let him go to sea."

The tears overwhelmed her. I held her hand, trying to steady her nerves.

"How do you know your son's missing at sea?"

Through wracking sobs she said, "It's been months since he left on the schooner in April and not a word. I wrote the owner in Philadelphia and his reply said the schooner was reported missing somewhere in the Bahamas, presumed lost in a storm. He wrote that he'd not pay a cent to me for my son's life. What a wretched thing to tell a mother . . .

"Peter, I never even asked for that type of thing from the horrid man. He thought I wanted money. I only want my son. Then the owner stopped answering my letters."

"How did Luke get a berth aboard that schooner?"

She was regaining her poise now, trying to help me understand. "Jonathan knew the captain, Frederick Kingston, for years. He'd hauled our molasses and sugar many times. Jonathan and the captain placated Luke with the notion he could sail aboard when he got older. In March, Kingston delivered some supplies to us and told me he had a rich charter party he was to take on a pleasure cruise to the Bahamas. He would take them aboard in Key West."

She sighed. "Luke wanted to go so badly. Somehow, I thought that a pleasure cruise would be safer for Luke. That he would be exposed to some quality people and after a month, he'd come home to our place in Puerto Rico with some good sea stories. Get it out of his system, I thought. Then he could continue with a *normal* life."

Cynda shook her head. "It was those stories he'd heard as a boy. His father, as you well know, told some wild tales from his years at sea. Luke wanted to experience that."

I smiled while remembering Jonathan's accounts of his life

as a sea captain. He was a good spinner of yarns. But sailors' sea stories are rarely realistic, omitting the privations and boredom and uncertainty. Naval life is even more difficult. Many a man and boy has gone to sea to learn, far too late, that the life of a sailor is nothing like what they'd heard around the fire on a cold winter's night.

The reverend asked, "How did you find your way to Saint Augustine, Mrs. Saunders?"

"Trying to get to Washington. I got a steamer to Havana, then a Plant company steamer to Tampa, where I boarded the train to go up north. My plan was to head to Washington," she turned back to me, "—to find *you*, Peter. I knew you would help me. You're the only man I know in the States that can help me find my baby."

She paused, staring at me with awe. "But I never dreamed you'd be *here*. The train stopped at Palatka on the St. Johns River—some sort of trouble with the engine—and they brought the passengers here to find lodging for the night while they repair it."

"You can stay with my wife and me, Mrs. Saunders," offered McLean.

Cynda never heard him. She was still looking intently at me, unnerving me with those blue eyes I remembered so well. "Did you move to St. Augustine, Peter? Your last letter years ago said you had an island down on the Gulf coast. I almost tried to find that, but you wrote that you were only there when on furlough, so I thought I'd find you at Washington. Didn't you get my letter? I never got a reply."

"For the last four months Rork and I have been in transit, Cynda. My private mail hasn't caught up to me yet."

"Rork! Is he here too?"

When I nodded in the affirmative, she let go another shriek toward the altar. "Thank you, dear Lord, for sending them *both* to me in my hour of need!"

McLean tried again. "Madam, my wife and I would like you

to stay with us for however long you may be in our area."

She nodded to him. "Yes, I will. Thank you so much, Pastor."

Then she turned back to me. There were no more tears, no weakness in the voice. It was the Cynda I'd known, a woman who wasn't frail or afraid of anything, the female who could turn grown men into devotees with a single glance.

"Luke is not dead. I know that absolutely, Peter, as only a mother can. And Divine guidance has brought you and me together, here in this church. You will help me find him."

The last wasn't said as a request, but as an assumption of fact. After what seemed a long time, I heard myself say, "Yes, Cynda. We'll find him . . ."

Her eyes softened and she slid her hand delicately over mine. "Peter, I must apologize for my self-absorption. I haven't asked about *your* current life. You're not in uniform—have you left the navy? And have you found a lady to share your life? It must be, what, six years since your dearest Linda passed on. And your children! How are Useppa and little Sean?"

So much had changed. "Well, yes, I'm still in Uncle Sam's Navy, Cynda. In fact, I've got twenty-five years in now. I do special assignments, keep pretty busy. Useppa is twenty-three now and headmistress of the school for black children in Key West. Little Sean isn't so little anymore. He's at the naval academy and due to graduate in two years."

Holding the worst until last, I tried to hide the ache inside. "And it's been seven years now since Linda passed on."

Those words were so hard to say, even after all that time. "No, there isn't a special woman in my life. I've occasionally gotten to know some nice ladies, but nothing lasted—usually because I had to leave to go somewhere and that angered them. I guess Rork and I are resigned to our fate as bachelors."

I shook my head in wonderment at my friend. "Although, Sean Rork still never ceases to amaze me. He finds female companionship wherever we go on assignment. That Irish rogue has the gift of attractiveness to your fairer sex. Ladies simply adore him. One told me once that he makes them want to cuddle and protect him. Imagine that, cuddling up with a big brute like him."

"I can, indeed, Peter. And I imagine they think the same of you, but you probably don't even notice. You're not open to them. You can be very distant, Peter Wake. Like your mind is far away. That scares women."

"Really? Well, I never got that impression. How so?"

She cast me that look I remembered so well. A combination of sultry jest and innocent interest. "Because they know that if your mind is far away, they can't hold you under their spell. Women don't like that sort of competition—the kind they can't see to defeat."

"Cynda, I don't think of companionship on adversarial terms."

It dawned on me that she was free now, as I'd been for seven years. She slowly patted my hand, or was she caressing it? The blue eyes had deepened to indigo in the dark church, and no longer looked so innocent. "I know you don't, Peter. That's why women like you. You're a good decent man, and you deserve to be happy."

Hearing someone clear his throat, I realized the pastor was still beside us. Reverend McLean sat there, visibly perplexed by the two strangers who'd entered his life on a quiet summer Sunday. I understood his confusion completely. My best laid plans had just crumbled, replaced by a commitment to accomplish what I knew was a daunting, probably impossible, task. With a woman who always made me feel uneasy.

I never doubted that Rork would support my decision and join the endeavor. Cynda joined us for lunch and explained the situation to him as the preacher and bishop looked on. Rork sounded far more confident than I had when he looked at her and said, "Aye, we'll find the lad. An' no worries 'bout *that,* me dear."

Over dinner that evening at the parsonage, the chief topic was how to go about the search. It was decided that we would begin at the last place Luke was known to be, Key West, and go on from there by whatever means available. The search would be expensive. I found myself insisting on sharing the cost with Cynda.

Another unpleasant aspect was that the next day my friends from Washington would arrive in Saint Augustine, happily bound for their fishing holiday in southwestern Florida. They were en route already and out of communication. At the station depot, I would have to tell them the grand expedition was cancelled and they should turn around and head north.

Walking back to the Saint Francis Inn later that night in the patter of soft rain, Rork asked, "You're thinkin' that poor lad's dead an' bleached by now, ain't ye?"

Remembering the scene when Cynda had poured out her dilemma to McLean and me, I shook my head with misgiving. Rork was right, that's precisely what I thought, but I couldn't say those words.

"Not sure. I just know we're honor bound to find out, Sean."

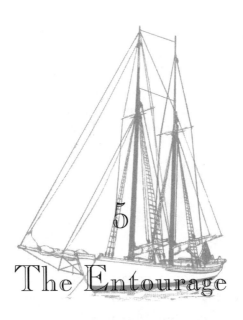

5
The Entourage

Railroad Depot of the
Saint Augustine & North Beach Railway
East Orange Street
Saint Augustine, Florida
Monday, 2 July 1888

The whistle sounded while the train was still a half mile out, eliciting whinnies from the dray horses of the St. Augustine Transfer Company, who knew they'd be working soon. Mr. Colee, owner of the company, sat atop a small cargo wagon that was loaded down with four steamer trunks, two hat boxes, a portmanteau, and two seabags. The seabags belonged to Rork and me. Everything else was Cynda's.

Colee thought it amusing. Since I was paying for his services, I didn't. It was hard to fathom what might be in all that baggage, or why Cynda would need it. However, I knew enough about women not to ask.

The train was short, only three passenger cars, and those only half-full with local people from Jacksonville, the northern tourist season being long over. My associates trooped off together, disheveled but happy to be nearing their ultimate destination. It was, as the novels of Mr. Twain might describe: a motley crew, unfettered by the latest fashions of attire or comportment.

Dr. Cornelius Rathburn, or Corny, as his friends called him, was a fifty-two-year-old ethnologist for the Smithsonian Institution. He'd worked with Clay MacCauley, the well-known Indian ethnologist who had recently documented the culture of the Seminole people still living in the Everglades. Corny was an amiable fellow, slightly rotund, doubled-chinned, balding, bespectacled. Always ready with a laugh. A *bon vivant,* especially with the ladies, who loved his courtly manner and smooth French sayings. He held his own in men's company too, the sort who could tell a good tale of danger around a campfire.

His easy-going appearance belied considerable endurance. He'd been with Major John Wesley Powell on several expeditions through the rugged territory of the Colorado River. Rumor had it that he'd killed a man in Nevada.

Corny bounded over and slapped a handshake on me and Rork, one eye taking in the lovely but sad-eyed form of Cynda, who watched from five paces.

"Powell says hello, Peter. Hey, the boys in the office want a tarpon fish stuffed and brought back!"

Then he said, *sotto voce,* "And just who is the fetching lady, Peter?"

Before I could say a word in reply, George Brown Goode loped on over. George, an accomplished ichthyologist, was the chief administrator of the United States National Museum and had been, until the previous January, the chief commissioner of the U.S. Fishery Commission. He had the gentle eyes and quiet manner of an administrator, but there was another side to him as well.

I'd met him in Washington back in seventy-nine, after his arduous scientific research journey through the islands of my coast. It had been an extensive assignment to ascertain the seasonal mullet fisheries of the islands, several of which were run by Cubans, the rest by Key Westers. While there in the worst season of the year, early autumn, he battled tropical storms, heat, and incessant biting insects. His report that year, and a subsequent one in eighty-five, were the first of their kind about Florida, and had generated serious attention in Washington, for they documented that the mullet fisheries made considerable money.

That first meeting with him was four years before I bought Patricio Island, but I'd known the coast well during the war, so we'd had some pleasant discussions of the area. In fact, it was those conversations with George that had planted the seed in my mind of returning to the islands and building a place there. Now, at thirty-eight years of age, he was nearing the top of his profession, but he still loved going off into the unknown on field trips. George was the de-facto leader of the fishing mission to capture a record-sized tarpon.

Shaking my hand, he said, "Cushing says that he wants to visit your islands someday, Peter. Says no one's done a decent study on those pre-Columbians you mentioned to him. I told him what I'd seen, the mounds and such, and he's definitely interested."

George referred to Frank Cushing, another ethnologist I'd met in Washington who worked with the Smithsonian. We'd spoken about the Calusa, a highly sophisticated native empire that had already occupied Florida's Gulf coast for a thousand years by the time the Spanish arrived.

"He should've come on this trip, George," I said, forgetting for a moment the bad news I was about to announce.

"No, he's busy now. Heading off next month for a survey."

The oldest of my comrades came forward. At fifty-eight, Daniel Horloft, naval architect for the government, still had a sailor's face tanned the color of driftwood, with pale green eyes narrowed by decades of squinting into an ocean sun. A small set of trimmed side-whiskers descended from long gray hair. Lanky and tall, Dan was the physical opposite of Corny.

He was a recent acquaintance. He did work in warship design and construction for the navy. A man of few words, Dan was a product of growing up as a fisherman on the coast of Maine. He kept his flinty attitude when he left the sea and entered the academic world. His hard work and inherent abilities led him to graduate with distinction from the Lawrence Scientific School at Harvard University. Dan Horloft was nationally known as a brilliant engineer, specializing in hydrodynamics and its effect upon ships.

He and the others shared a common bond that I did not— they were all members of the Theoretical Society of Washington, an intellectual organization of accomplished leaders in their fields, who met monthly at the Celestial Club, on Lafayette Square by the Executive Mansion, and discussed topics of the day. A heady group, to say the least. Occasionally, I had been invited to share a meal or a drink with them at the club and our friendship had deepened. Now they had come almost a thousand miles in response to my depiction of the islands and sport fishing on the southwestern coast of Florida.

Horloft put a callused hand out and locked mine in his grip. "Where do we go to get a decent washup and meal? It's like a Turkish bath down here. And what time tomorrow do we get under way for this island of yours, Peter?"

"Very good to see you, too, Dan," I said, mocking his stolid mien. He, as usual, didn't appreciate the satire and grunted something back.

I forwent any further humor and addressed his queries. "The washup will have to wait, the meal will be a picnic lunch, and we get under way in an hour."

Now was the time to give everyone the bad news, so I spoke up so all could hear amidst the commotion on the platform. "Well, gentlemen, please give me your attention. The plans have changed. Regrettably, Rork and I can't go fishing with you. We must head south to Key West right now. We're taking this train. It leaves in an hour and will take us back to the main line at Palatka, on the Saint John's River. You can come with us to the main line and head north now, or stay the night and head north tomorrow. I'm sorry for the last-minute change, but Rork and I have been advised of a tragedy and must decline the fishing expedition. We're badly needed to help a long-time friend."

No one spoke, but their expressions said it all. Corny studied Cynda again, this time suspiciously. George sent me a quizzical look. Dan scowled.

I introduced Cynda and briefly explained her plight. My friends' attitude moderated, then transformed into sympathy while I elucidated the situation. I then offered them my island if they wished to use it in my absence. They could stay there and still go after their tarpon, but Rork and I would have to leave, bound ultimately for the Bahamas to search for Luke Saunders.

"Bahamas, you say?" asked Corny.

"Yes. Luke was supposedly lost somewhere there."

"Always wanted to go there. Studied the West Indian culture. Did some poking about a few years ago, but never made it to the Bahamas—it's so removed from the main West Indies. Do you need an extra hand in this effort? I've got the time."

I didn't hesitate. Corny would be good to have along. "Yes. Thank you."

George held up a hand. "Peter, I wouldn't mind helping the lady too, but I needed to get back before everyone else anyway. So I'll go to your island, get the fish, and ride the train back to Washington. Please cable me an update on your efforts when I get back to my office."

Before I could say anything in reply, Dan grumbled in a low tone, "I'll go on that search party too. I've sailed through some of those islands. I can wait for the tarpon fish, but we need to find that boy, Peter. Especially since it sounds like no one's done a proper search yet." He cast a faint smile at Cynda. "I know the weight upon your heart, ma'am. My brother was aboard a whaler lost in the South Sea, and no proper search was ever done among those islands."

I was grateful. "Thank you for your understanding and your help. I'm very appreciative and I know Mrs. Saunders appreciates your understanding too. George, please use my island as long as you need and, yes, I'll send you a telegram as soon as we know something. Dan and Corny, thank you for volunteering to come along on the search."

I gestured at the mound of baggage. "Now folks, Mr. Colee advises that the southbound train has steam up, so let's get our gear aboard this train so we can get to Palatka and catch the main one. We also have a basket of food for all hands and some real orange juice to rejuvenate your health."

The route south had improved over the past few years, both in physical ease and speed. Modern passenger cars with improved springs were available, and the time needed for a run from Palatka in upper Florida to Punta Gorda on the lower Gulf coast had been trimmed to a mere nine hours. At the depot on the west side of Palatka, we joined Henry Plant's misnamed Jacksonville, Tampa, and Key West Railway and sped south through the rolling oak-forested hills of upper Florida's lovely heartland.

Since the carriage was new, all of the windows could be opened, a huge blessing during a Floridian summer. Once the train began moving, a gentle breeze swept through the interior and took away the growing heat of the day, making the passage comfortable, even pleasant. I suspect my companion also had something to do with that impression.

Cynda and I sat together on a double seat, she at the window, quietly watching the passing greenery. Her face had aged, but gracefully. Lines around her eyes reflected her life, sadness and laughter, and I found myself surreptitiously studying her, still fascinated by this most unusual woman.

Beyond the usual pleasantries about the vistas going by us, we didn't say much, each lost in our thoughts. Mine turned to assessing what might lie ahead. The appeal of my surroundings faded when I began to ruminate on the various scenarios that could account for the disappearance of Luke Saunders. Most of them ended in heartbreak. While I was thus soberly engaged, a sideways glance showed me that my seatmate was revisiting her past. Cynda's face was drawn, with none of the brightness I remembered so well. She'd seen more than a fair share of misfortune in her years, but I knew she also had an uncanny knack for landing on her feet after all was said and done. I hoped she could now.

Swaying along, the train lurched frequently and we occasionally touched, glancing shyly at each other—a silly reaction at our age. Neither of us was innocent anymore about the natural attraction between men and women. However, our behavior was more than timidity. It was as if we were going out of our way to preserve our emotional defenses, not let down our guard, lest something happen that could endanger our quest. In candor, I suppose I was the one most reticent, a feeling born of my memories regarding the lady beside me.

When I, newly married, first met Cynda Denaud Williams and her little sister Mary Alice, it was along the middle Florida Gulf coast during the latter stages of the war. I commanded a gunboat, and was ashore on a reconnaissance to ascertain the likelihood of Floridians joining the national Union cause. Though that rumor was well established among politicos in Washington, in reality I found very few inhabitants of the state that would even entertain the idea, fewer still who would act upon it.

Cynda was an enemy noncombatant, wife of a Rebel planter who had scandalously absconded for the Bahamas when the fortunes of war changed against his side. Left behind, she was the beleaguered mistress of their estate. That plantation was part of the enemy's structure of sustenance, a legitimate target of war, and a subject of my interest.

Well understanding the effect she had on men, she'd used her Machiavellian scheming and feminine charm on me to gain her own purposes. It was a common enough tactic by women near the end of that long ugly event, but disappointing to see in one who had such intelligence and beauty and sophisticated upbringing. For a flickering moment one evening it worked, and my innate defenses were lowered. Then, quite fortunately, my sense of honor, and more likely my suspicion, prevailed. Still, she'd gotten what she wanted—transport out of the danger area for herself and her sister. Rork was there through it all, a steady hand in a very unsteady situation.

Though I couldn't help admiring Cynda, both her appearance and her internal strength, I never again fully trusted her after that. There was something about her, a chameleonlike ability to adapt to prevailing situations after determining what role and route would be most advantageous to her. I had seen the flash of predatory guile emerge from behind the demure damsel's façade. While I empathized with the concept of self-preservation, I didn't like her methods.

Then, sitting there in the warm carriage car rattling through central Florida, I thought about the hypocrisy in that judgment. My methods with Paloma hadn't been of the highest character either. Maybe Cynda and I did share a certain ruthless trait. Was my justification of saving future lives from war as thin-sounding as her goal of self-preservation during the war?

That little realization didn't improve my morale. And in the back of my mind, as the train took us south toward an uncertain future, I wondered about her present honesty and motives. It was obvious she had retained that captivating beauty—every man aboard watched her every move, not withstanding her mourning attire. But had the years dulled her cunning? Probably not. If anything, life experience would have increased her astuteness.

No matter, I told myself abruptly. It was time to center my attention on the problem at hand. I needed to understand the subject of our effort, and by understanding him more fully, perhaps I would grasp Cynda's intentions. So I asked her to describe her son—in appearance, intellect, and manner. I found her explanation revealing in more ways than one.

She described Luke Saunders as five feet, seven inches tall; with wavy blonde hair to his collar; and of medium weight, probably a hundred thirty pounds. He had blue eyes like his mother, but the prominent jaw and nose of his father. Raised on the family's sugar plantation in the west of Puerto Rico, he was strong but played no American sports. He was an avid fisherman and had confidence on the water—sailing his father's small boat single-handed considerable distances along the beach. His academics had been initially home-taught by father and mother, but he had attended the local Catholic school for boys since he was ten. Luke was bilingual and loved reading books, particularly those in English about the sea. He was very loyal to his parents and their Por Fin Plantation, and was devastated when his father died.

I replied that her recital contained absolutely nothing negative, as one would expect from a mother, but that every teenaged boy had another side. Mine certainly had at that age. Her eyes dropped.

"Tell me the rest, Cynda. It could very well be important to our success."

There was the beginning of a quiver in her chin. "Yes, I suppose you do need to know. Well . . . he wasn't perfect. There were tensions. Bad tensions."

"Such as . . ."

Her eyes filled. "Actually, Peter . . . well, actually Luke hated me. He hated his life at Por Fin. I think he felt stifled. Imprisoned. Especially after Jonathan died and he had only me for company."

"There's more to this than you've told me, Cynda. What is it?"

She took a breath. "He may not come back with me when we find him. I think he felt I was too . . . overbearing. He has this restless urge, this rebellious core. I'm afraid that Luke can be . . . cruel with his words. Very cruel. That's not how Jonathan and I tried to bring him up, Peter. Not at all."

Her son was large for his age. "Did Luke ever try to hurt you?"

"No. He never struck me, but he would become enraged when I said no to a request. His temper was short. After his father died it got worse. I don't know how I became the enemy . . ."

"When Luke left you to go on the schooner, what was his attitude?"

She looked at me with a sadness that laid open my heart for her.

"Luke said he hated our home so much that he just might not come back."

Rather dire sentiment for a fourteen-year-old boy. And one that had the potential to get Luke into far more trouble than his young mind could anticipate. Cynda shut down at that point, the grief too much, and I decided not to ask the big question in my mind: what would she do if and when we found him? Or better yet—what would *he* do?

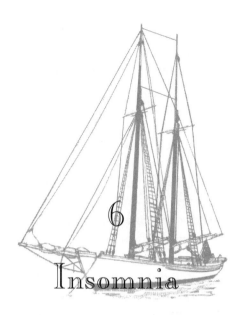

6

Insomnia

En route south by train
Central Florida
Monday, 2 July 1888

Our route was like a tunnel through the dense forests, stopping momentarily at the shady villages along the route. There was DeLand, with its newly founded college; Benson Junction, where we crossed the bucolic St. Johns River and changed to the South Florida Line, thereafter emerging from the close confines of the oak and pine forests to the vista of Lake Monroe, a vast inland sea. Sanford came next, a busy little port on the south shore of Monroe; then we chugged further south to Longwood; Maitland; Winter Park; Orlando, with its dappled ponds amidst small orange-tree-covered hills; and finally Kissimmee, a moss-lined burgh on the edge of a large marshy lake with the exotic moniker of Tohopekaliga.

At each stop, passengers were afforded an opportunity to stroll for ten minutes and see the incredible changes a railroad can bring to a community. Where five years prior those places had been backwoods crossroads, they now began sporting the signs of modernity, including small facilities to entice the growing winter tourist trade—hotels, eateries, taverns, health sanatoriums, fishing guides, land brokers.

Though there were few passengers on our train, the townspeople made sure every one of us knew what their locale had to offer. It was amusing in a way, inspiring laughs from those of us who knew Florida, and great interest in my friends who were visiting for the first time. Cynda took interest in the places, probably as much to displace the depressing thoughts in her mind as to see how her native state had changed. She listened intently as locals would proudly explain their town's amenities and advantages, asking kind questions designed to boost their egos. It was a masterful performance on her part, and instructive for me as I watched her.

We disembarked—no easy task with all that gear—at Bartow Junction in the middle of the peninsula, where the traveler had a decision to make: continue west to Tampa or south toward my coast. We chose the latter and changed to Henry Plant's Florida Southern Railroad, a far less comfortable affair. Most of these windows were stuck shut.

Proceeding south through Winter Haven, we came to the dusty mining and cattle town of Bartow proper, located on a small plateau overlooking a lake. Corny, whose active mind was always alert to opportunities for *bon vivance* or scientific gain, suggested that perhaps we might find ancient fossils in the phosphate mine excavations. Failing to excite any interest among his overheated companions, he ultimately decided that, "it's too damn hot to dig for bones, but maybe I'll come back in the decent season. Do they even have one down here?"

Down the spine of Florida we wobbled on the tracks, now along the sandy banks of the Peace River. The real hill country was gone now, and as we chugged southward we saw more cypress swamp and bog. The river level was still low, for the summer rains had not completely arrived yet. It wouldn't be long, however. Soon the skies would unload tons of the stuff and every river and stream would overflow with water, and along with the rain would come southern Florida's greatest nemesis, mosquitoes.

Cynda began conversing with me again. She asked if I still knew people in Key West who might know Captain Kingston or the schooner. When I said yes, she delved into the mechanics of how we would proceed from there. It was what we had already discussed, but I was glad her mind focused on the search, not the sorrow. You could see her mind and body strengthen. I resolved to do my best to keep her attention concentrated to that effect.

We entered frontier country, where life was rustic and more than a few of the inhabitants were trying to hide from society or authority farther north. Fort Meade, Stonewall Jackson's last post for the U.S. Army; the tiny hamlets of Zolfo Springs, Arcadia, Nocatee, Fort Ogden—we saw them all. I explained to my friends a little of the history of the places. No grand, or even modest, tourist resorts here. Cattle, mining for phosphate rocks, citrus, and vegetable farming dominated. These were rough backwoods places, some of the citizenry made up of violent men and crude women. They would grudgingly assist you, but weren't impressed at all by what you wore or how you spoke. Some of them might even take offense at it.

Once beyond the pine woods, the undulating of the rails became more pronounced, sinking down alarmingly into a rail bed set into the sand and mud, making the car slow down and wallow back and forth like a waterlogged vessel. Past Fort Ogden, the end of the line until two years earlier, the terrain became flat-land salt marsh and mangrove, the people more ragged, and the sense of isolation more palpable.

We were nearing the coast, and the new end of the railroad at Punta Gorda. A rudimentary fishing village of a couple hundred souls who harbored rather grandiose hopes for the future, it was the reason for the railroad's extension to the salt water, the destination for anyone venturing all that way through the swamps. We rolled to a stop in front of the newly built Punta Gorda Hotel at seven o'clock that evening—my entire band of travelers hot, tired, sore, sooty, and hungry. The hotel, a three-story frame structure fronting the mile-wide Peace River, housed fishing tourists in the winter and spring seasons. It was closed now for the summer.

The last of the day's sea breeze was dying, allowing a humid malaise to fill the air. Thunder rolled off to the east. I looked around for the man who took care of Patricio Island in our absence. He was known only as Whidden, a common surname in those parts. But he was nowhere in sight.

As we unloaded the mound of trunks, boxes, and bags, Rork and I exchanged glances—would Whidden be there to pick us up and sail us to the island, twenty-two miles away? Rork went searching for him and returned ten minutes later with a shrug.

Whidden wasn't around. We'd informed him of our intentions by telegram three weeks ahead of time. Something must have come up. It frequently did with Whidden. Time is a relative concept on the coast. The others cast expectant looks toward me. Very well, we'd have to find lodging for the night, hopefully before the bugs and rain attacked.

Requesting my friends to remain at the trackside platform, for there was no depot then, I dispatched Rork to the vacant resort hotel on the chance the summer caretaker was around. Those would be by far the most comfortable accommodations in Punta Gorda. Meanwhile, I headed for Tom Hector's place a block away, in which I spied a lantern glowing. Probably a billiard challenge going on, I surmised. Inside the place I found Tom, and three others I knew, gathered around the faded green affair which served as the sole billiard table in that region. In the normal manner of the locals, their greeting was a muted one.

Colonel Isaac Trabue greeted me with a nonchalant wave from the corner. A Union man in Louisville, Kentucky, during the war, he was still lean and handsome, with a confident air and one of those Kentucky goatees I associate with actors and lawyers. He was one of those fellows who are a bundle of energetic action, just waiting for release. A man who takes charge—even when nobody wants him to—and gets things done.

Trabue arrived on the coast in 1885. Within three years he'd bought up hundreds of acres, built a community hall, platted out a town named for himself, and thereafter promised and expected great things to come. He'd even persuaded Henry Plant to run that rail line down to the new town, with the prospect of creating a splendid resort, which came somewhat true in the form of the hotel.

But there was trouble in paradise. Trabue's vigor, civic efforts, and egalitarian views on blacks, were not fully appreciated by some of the hard-eyed natives, and when it came time to petition the government to officially incorporate the town in '87, they knocked him down a peg or two by voting to name it Punta Gorda, the old Spanish designation for the place. I thought that a slap in the face of a man who had done a lot for them.

The other two men didn't have Trabue's money or deportment. Albert Gilchrist was a pleasant-faced surveyor for Plant's railroad. A good man, and by all appearances quite smart, but for some reason, I've never been able to relax in the few times I'd been around him.

The third man was a close friend of Whidden. Daniel Smith was as black as a man could get, and as decent, too. He worked for Gilchrist on the survey crew, which also did repair work, new construction, and other assorted odd jobs in the area. Punta Gorda was unique in that the whites' racial prejudice was kept under the surface and an air of civility reigned in the town, with black and white working together.

Smith grinned at me, and said, "Hello there, Mr. Wake, sir. I didn't know you'd be down this time a' year. Lookin' for Mr. Whidden?"

"Hello, Daniel. Yes, I'm looking for Whidden. Do you know where he is? He was supposed to pick us up with the *Nancy Ann*."

Trabue shook his head. Gilchrist chuckled. Smith sighed with compassion for his wayward friend. "Oh, *Nancy Ann*'s over at the long dock. But Whidden, well, he's in the jail for drinkin', sir. Drinkin' bad, down at Big Six's place, tryin' to impress Miss Henrietta. Shoulda' known better than that, but you know how it is with him. Ol' Whidden's been in jail last night and this. Supposed to let him out in the morn, I think."

Big Six's establishment was a makeshift rotgut rum and beer joint, as coarse as the man himself, set up in an abandoned feed shed down on the cattle trail south of town. Big Six was a giant Florida swamp dweller who sold *anything* to anybody, including fools like Whidden. No one knew Big Six's name for certain and most figured he had a warrant outstanding from up north. I imagined Henrietta to be the latest down-and-out trollop passing through who'd decided to work for Six. The "Punta Gorda Jail" was a padlocked cattle car kept on a rail siding. We'd passed it coming into town. In that heat, it would've been hell inside.

I moaned aloud, which brought forth another chuckle from Gilchrist, who offered an unsolicited opinion. "Wake, I don't know why you employ that idiot. He's drunk most of the time you're not around. No telling what he does out on that island of yours when you're gone."

"Just another ne'er-do-well we've got to convince to leave this coast," said Trabue. "It's time to make this place civilized."

"He ain't drunk *all* the time, Colonel," said Smith, a religious teetotaler, defending his friend. Then he admitted, "Oh, my, but when he *do*, he sure do it up big."

Ignoring Trabue and Gilchrist, I continued with the black man. "All right, I'll get him out in the morning. Is he hurt?"

"Yessir, he's banged up a might. Big Six didn't hurt him too bad, though."

Whidden was a drunk, but he was a tough drunk. He'd

survive. "Good. Now, gentlemen, since we're not taking my sloop out in that approaching storm even if Whidden wasn't in jail, I need several rooms for the night. I've got Rork and four other friends with me, including a lady. Hotel caretaker around?" Wagging heads were the answer. "No? Well, what about boarding at Kelly Harvey's."

Gilchrist shook his head again. "Nope, they're gone to Tampa. So's R. B. Smith."

Trabue quietly said, "Sorry, Wake, but I've got no room either."

Thunder chose that moment to rumble louder. It was nearby. Outside, the wind was piping up. Not much time before it hit. Right about then, Smith solved my problem.

"Cap'n Brown's got two rooms, Mr. Wake. It'll be crowded, but dry." He glanced outside. Thunder sounded again, closer this time. "Well, sorta dry."

By their expressions, it was obvious the colonel and Gilchrist thought that inappropriate, but I didn't particularly care. I appreciated the help. "That's better than nothing. Thank you, Daniel."

I left to round up my troops. Smith went on ahead and sought permission for my entourage to spend the night from Captain George Brown, a black ship-builder who lived east of the main town. That was the poor part of town. I'd met him before and knew him to be an honest hard-working man, like Smith.

Smith and Captain Brown showed up with a rickety wagon at the rail depot, just as the first solid gust of wind hit. The sky to the east was a dense cliff of bluish-purple racing toward us, evil-looking in the yellowed dusk. Lightning sizzled white streaks, the thunder detonating exactly like a navy ten-inch gun. It was going to be a bad one.

Fortunately, by the time the clouds unloaded their cargo of water on us we'd made it to Brown's home. Shoving the baggage under the thatched roof, we staggered with exhaustion inside, to the obvious amazement of his wife and children—they'd never had whites visit, much less stay the night. The gentlemen of my party were assigned to the sand floor of the back room. Cynda slept with Mrs. Brown on the cot in the lone bedroom. Captain Brown and the children slept in the "parlor."

Through the night the dwelling was filled with the sound of hands slapping away bugs, for the windows had no cheesecloth for barriers. For the first two hours, rain cascaded off the edge of the thatch roof. A dozen leaks in the fronds hosed down among us to form puddles in the hard-packed floor. "Sorta dry" was an exaggeration, to say the least.

The Washington contingent said not a word about their hardship. Cynda, to her credit and my relief, accepted her fate without comment. Rork shook his head and grinned. He'd seen far worse.

I simply lay there, staring out at the staccato flashes, unable to sleep, wondering what I'd gotten into.

7
Lightning Strikes

Patricio Island
Pine Island Sound
Lower Gulf coast of Florida
Tuesday, 3 July 1888

The next day we made it to the island. The seven of us—our number now included a very sore and repentant Whidden—were grouped on the verandah of my simple bungalow. It sits atop the shell ridge centered along the narrowest part of Patricio Island. Everyone was quiet, not only from the exertions required to reach the island, but from the utter tranquility of the scene around us.

The sun, having lowered to about three fingers above the horizon, had shed its intensity and was now fading away through the orange phase. Next would be tomato red. Around the sun, the sky was transforming too. Gone was the deep blue, replaced by faint pastels of powdery pink and blue and wisps of even fainter green. This celestial canvas formed the backdrop for hundreds of birds who were returning to their island homes in the bay around us. Brown pelicans, gray ospreys, black cormorants, green ducks, pink roseate spoonbills, blue herons, white gulls.

The sky was a mass of movement, with a symphony of attending bird songs. It was as dynamic as the bay below, where the daily sea breeze formed a pattern of waves marching east, wrapping around islets and rearing up against the ebb tide. Two dolphins whooshed air from their blowholes fifty feet off our dock, while an otter rippled through the water after diving from a mangrove tree. The waters were dark now, no longer the jade green of high day.

Sunset is a magical time at these islands, even in the summer. The shadows of the gumbo limbo and coconut palms lengthen, the heat dissipates, and the moist sweet scent of jasmine flowers, swamp detritus, bananas and citrus, and fish roasting for dinner mingles and wafts everywhere.

Behind us, over the mainland, charcoal piles of clouds roiled like an angry phalanx about to descend on us. The daily thunderstorm approached, but it was still hours away from the coastal islands. We had time to relax.

The sun reddened. It wouldn't be long. Each person had a small glass of my best, Matusalem rum from Cuba, sitting in front of them. Rork held a large conch shell and stood, facing the sun. The low hum of whispered conversation among my guests stopped. They knew something was about to happen.

Rork glanced at me, then announced, "Madam, an' gentlemen, we have a bit o' a tradition in these islands at sunset. When the sun's down to a finger—ten minutes time—from touchin' the horizon, all hands take a wee moment to appreciate God's good work all 'round us, His daily display o' beauty, an' our blessin's for bein' here to enjoy it all."

My friends' faces glowed as they faced the last rays of the sun. As it settled onto the far horizon in the Gulf of Mexico, Rork sounded the time-honored three long wails from the conch shell. At the same time, islanders around the bay echoed the plaintive signal on their shells. I listened for them, each as different as the conch they blew. Nearby Useppa, Palmetto, Mondongo. Faint echoes from distant Captiva and Lacosta to the west. Bokeelia to the east. Reassuring sounds. Another day was done.

I proposed a toast, one I'd learned during pleasanter times in Cuba. "Health, wealth, and love—and all the time to enjoy them."

Everyone joined in, clinking glasses. I noticed Cynda studying me, like a doctor with a patient. Then Whidden declared the dinner he'd been preparing for two hours was ready. We sat at the table in my place. Crab cakes, fillets of grouper, coconut rice with seagrape jelly, followed by a simple orange and lime mash pie. Whidden may well be a hopeless drunk, but he's also a damned good seaman and cook.

It had been a very long day, starting at dawn when I managed to convince the local Manatee County deputy sheriff that Whidden should be remanded to my custody. Then we had set sail on my very overloaded—seven people and a mountain of baggage—thirty-one-foot sloop in light winds down the Peace River, and south through the vast bay of Charlotte Harbor, finally arriving at Patricio Island at four in the afternoon.

Due to Cynda's presence, our accommodation arrangements had been altered. Cynda was given the sole use of my bungalow, the three Washington guests and I were billeted in Rork's bungalow, and Rork bunked in with Whidden at his tiny place on the north end of the island.

The next day we'd get under way early in *Nancy Ann* for Key West. There were no dissenters when Rork stood after dinner and announced he was tired and turning in. He and Whidden headed off, the Washington trio departed and collapsed into slumber next door, while Cynda and I remained to wash up the dishes. I look back now with hindsight, and realize that the others may have sensed something, may have allowed Cynda and me that time together. Rork has since denied it, but not too strenuously.

I have the luxury of cheesecloth covering for the windows of my bungalow, to guard against mosquitoes and no-see-ums in the summer. I also have netting over the bed. So do Rork's and Whidden's dwellings. The cloths and nets are lowered an hour before sunset.

Most of my islander neighbors aren't as fortunate. They don't have such devices and have to keep a smudge fire going inside their homes. It literally smokes out the bugs. That fills my lungs and is a condition I abhor, so I paid the money for the cheesecloth. It inhibits air flow, but that's a minor annoyance compared to the alternative. In any event, the cheesecloth also provides some privacy, for one cannot see through it clearly enough to discern shapes or people.

By the light of an oil lamp, Cynda and I were putting away the dishes when snoring from next door punctuated the rumbling from the approaching storm, making us laugh. I felt the breeze pick up out of the east, straining the window cloths as it rushed through. "Time to batten down," I told Cynda and walked out onto the verandah.

Just as I finished dashing around closing the heavy storm shutters, a bolt of lightning struck a mile away near Mondongo Island, the flash of white showing bent trees whipping around in the night and Cynda standing in the front doorway, watching me. The wind caught her dress, making it flutter around her.

She looked so free, her blond hair flowing away from her. For the tenth time that day I thought about how beautiful she was, but how sad her situation. Seconds later we were at the back door when the rain arrived, riding that wind, lashing the place and soaking that dress against her figure—showing the woman underneath. I tried not to stare, but Cynda saw me watching her. She smiled, as if to convey that she understood.

We staggered inside and I pushed the door closed, but it was too late. A gust opened the door and swept into the kitchen, blowing out the lamp. I felt electricity in the air, an acrid smell mixed with a tingling sensation, then an explosion of light burst around us as lightning hit the island. Cynda screamed and leaped to

Cynda and I had endured personal tragedies of the most searing kind, and that they were all happy we were sharing affection.

In celebration of the day—it was July Fourth—the morning's meal was done with special effort. Rork ran up our largest flag on the bamboo pole and announced in one of his strident foc's'le bellows that breakfast was ready. It consisted of the standard island fare, but lots of it. Smoked mullet, grits with melted cheese, rum and orange juice—a fisherman's repast.

Cynda, the new hostess of the place, and wearing a blue cotton dress, was positively beautiful in the morning light. Radiant would be a better descriptor, her manner bright and cheerful as she assisted Whidden in preparing and dishing out the food. I must admit, it felt wonderful to have a woman on the island again. To hear a lilting tone, see a graceful form, feel gentle touches. It made the old place seem civilized.

At the table, talk centered around the latest copy—five days old—of the Fort Myers Press. Whidden had a pile of them for us he got from the mail boat. It seemed that the newspaper had recently been sold to a temperance lady named Olive Stout, who was running the operation with her husband Frank. Rork thought that worrying, for the temperance people were trying to dry up the new county that had been formed the year prior, when the area of the coast around Fort Myers had seceded from Monroe County to the south. It was named Lee County, after the famous general, since three of the five newly installed county commissioners had served in the Confederate forces.

My guests opined on the issue of the temperance movement in the nation, with a unanimous verdict of disapproval. "Un-American," said Rork, the Irishman. "Dull-witted," suggested Corny. "Un-enforceable," opined George. "Damned busybodies," grumbled Dan. "Those temperance people are bored," said Cynda with a sly wink at me. Whidden kept his mouth shut.

We then switched conversational targets to that of George Goode's effort to land the tarpon and the search mission to the

Bahamas. Whidden would stay behind with George, guide him in the island's small rowing skiff to catch a large tarpon. He knew a place near Gasparilla Island that he swore would produce an eight-footer—probably the biggest in the area. Then he'd boat George over to Useppa Island where they'd flag down the coastal steamer for Punta Gorda. There, as soon as the fish was stuffed, he would board the train for the long journey north, back to Washington. Rork asked with deadpan innocence if George would require a separate seat and ticket for the fish, to which the scientist replied, "That depends on how big a fish Whidden finds me!"

I brought up the search. The rest of us would head south aboard the Nancy Ann for Key West, where Luke Saunders and the schooner were last known to be. After inquiring among my contacts at that island, we would determine the next step. It might be the Bimini Islands, or the Abacos, or Nassau.

By nine that morning, our baggage and gear was aboard. As usual, Rork and I had only a seabag each. Due to the nature of our endeavor, we'd included our personal weapons. Rork favored the standard Navy-issue Colt revolver and his new Winchester model 1887 five-round lever-action shotgun, which he had amputated slightly—his description—to a shorter barrel. I brought along my personal choices: the Merwin-Hulbert .44-caliber six-shot revolver with the "Skull Crusher" grip and my 1882 model Spencer pump-action shotgun. Two years earlier, I'd made an almost fatal error and not brought weapons with me on a trip. I vowed then not to repeat that omission in the future. One never knows in our line of work.

After we all waved farewell to George Goode and Whidden on the dock, Rork set the mains'l and jib and I steered the sloop south past Useppa Island, scene of so many memories for me. It was already hot, but the wind was steady from the east southeast, and Nancy Ann pounded through the short chop at six knots under all plain sail. Two hours later we passed York Island and close hauled for Point Ybel's lighthouse on Sanibel Island.

Rork was on watch and steering, while the rest lounged on the windward deck, listening to me describe the places we passed—St.

James-on-the-Gulf with its massive new tourist hotel and little fishing shacks, Tarpon Bay's thatched huts, Point Ybel's spindly lighthouse structure, Punta Rassa's fishing lodge and telegraph station, Estero Island's crescent-shaped beach. Cynda sat next to me, every now and then holding on to me when we hit a bigger wave. I think Rork began steering for them at one point, and I didn't mind a bit.

By outward appearance it seemed a pleasure outing. I suppose to Dan and Corny it was, but below the gaiety I could tell that Rork and Cynda sensed the enormity of what we were starting. We were well out to sea in the Gulf of Mexico, with no land in sight, when the sun set in fiery splendor that evening.

Cynda held my arm tightly as she gazed westward. "He's waiting out there for us, somewhere."

"We'll find him, " I reassured her.

Her body relaxed as she turned to me. "We have to. It's up to us."

In the tropics there is no prolonged twilight. Darkness descends quickly, transforming the sea into another space and form. That night was remarkably uncommon, and very special.

I can remember it so plainly, even now. There was no storm, unusual for that time of year, and our light-wind passage under the stars was magical, entrancing. In the moonless night the horizon disappeared. The stars glittered mirrorlike on the water, appearing so clear and so close, it was as if we were steering a course right up through them, able to reach out and touch them as we slid by. Cynda and I sat on the cabintop for hours, speaking in reverential whispers about the beauty of the world around us, of our lives' loves, our dreams when young, our hopes deferred. It was a strangely mystical beginning, I thought at the time, for a voyage bound to a place that none of us could foresee.

In retrospect, I think it very wise that mortals are denied the ability to peer into the future and know what lies ahead. We just aren't strong enough to cope with it.

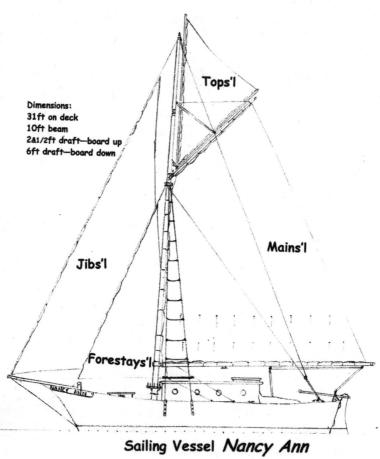

Dimensions:
31ft on deck
10ft beam
2&1/2ft draft—board up
6ft draft—board down

Tops'l

Jibs'l

Mains'l

Forestays'l

NANCY ANN

Sailing Vessel *Nancy Ann*

8

In Flagrante Delicto

Pinder's Wharf
Caroline and William streets
Key West, Florida
Thursday, 5 July 1888

M y crew couldn't resist the temptation. Key West has been known for fifty years as one of the greatest liberty ports for sailors. During the war, that reputation soared to new heights. After the catastrophic fire of 1886, an event I knew painfully well, Key West rebuilt itself with a considerably more genteel view in mind, trying to alter its reputation. Gone was the long row of bawdy taverns on Front Street. There were still some "watering holes" though, and Rork knew them all.

During the overnight voyage, the fellows from Washington, neither of whom had been to Key West, eagerly drank in all the stories Rork could tell. And may I here state that he has more than a few about that port—so many stories and so great their embellishment, that by the time we arrived at the island, the lads were more than ready for some entertainment ashore.

Once we secured ourselves at the dock, Rork led his party off to the local purveyors of pleasure to ascertain if any of them had intelligence regarding the missing boy and his ship. That worked out fine with me, for I had other things to do. Chief among them was to contact my acquaintances—a different social strata than those my crew was bound for—and see what they knew about our chief quarry, Captain Frederick Kingston, of the schooner *Condor*. I wanted to know about him, the vessel, the charterers, the crew, the destination, and if anyone had seen or heard of a cabin boy named Luke.

Leaving Cynda aboard *Nancy Ann*, where she wanted to nap after a sleepless night, I started out on my investigation. It began forty feet away, with Mr. Theodore Pinder, who owned the store and dock at the foot of William Street, where we moored the boat. Pinder was a long-standing Key Wester and knew much of the trade between the port and the islands of the Bahamas. He also supplied many of the vessels operating from Key West.

I informed him of the circumstances of Luke's disappearance and saw a spark of empathy. Pinder stated that he did, indeed, know of Kingston and the *Condor*. Kingston occasionally came into port, ordinarily carrying bulk cargo from the West Indies or from Charleston. The schooner anchored out, being too large for the dock, so Pinder hadn't actually seen her, but he got the impression she was a well-found vessel by the attention the captain paid to supplies. Kingston used him to provision the schooner most recently in late April. The provisions consisted of fruits, rum, vegetables, canned meats and butter, cognac and wines.

Pinder recalled it all immediately because the order was so unusual—much more expensive fare than the usual stuff most vessels purchased. Pinder said Kingston told him some rich Northerners were coming to Key West by steamer to charter his schooner. That once aboard, they were headed for the Bahamas on a pleasure excursion. Kingston told the store owner that he'd altered the cargo hold to provide additional accommodations aboard, as plush as could be done locally. The merchant couldn't recall anything else.

I was about to take my leave when Pinder's hand went up. "Wait! I just remembered that a letter came for him. I hold letters for ship captains all the time. I was holding it for his return. Should still have it somewhere."

Rummaging through several pigeon holes filled with mail he pulled out a small envelope. "Hmm, no return address, but it's stamped in Nassau," he said while handing it to me. "Take a look for yourself, Peter."

Scratchy, smeared handwriting—no woman wrote it. Cheap note paper that folded up into an envelope. It was addressed to "Kingston, schooner *Condor*, care of Pinder's Provisions and Supply, Key West." Stamps from Nassau on May fifth and the post office at Key West on May twelfth.

I nodded to Pinder. "I'll take it for you and deliver it when I find him."

"Well . . . I don't know about that sort of thing, Peter. Ship captains trust me to hold their mail for them."

"You're doing better than holding it for them—you're delivering it to Captain Kingston, through me. I promise you, he won't complain."

Thirty seconds after leaving the store I dashed around a corner on Caroline Street and carefully pried open the envelope, not a demanding task since the shoddy glue was barely holding anyway. The note within was simple, but confusing.

K

The O is heading to Nassau. Be careful, but continue.

W

That was it. No sender, no addressee. Same handwriting as the outside of the envelope. Who or what was O? And why would this O be a problem for Kingston. What kind of problem? A creditor? Jealous husband? Cheated business partner? And who was W? What was his connection to Kingston?

I stuffed the envelope in a pocket and made my way toward Duval Street to see a friend who usually knew what was going on in Key West, and even more importantly, who was doing it. Charles Merrill had owned the best hotel in town, the Russell House, before the fire of '86 destroyed it. Merrill was well ensconced in Key West's society circles. I found him at the Curry place on Front Street and asked if he had heard of any Northerners in town in late April who chartered a schooner named *Condor*. He did recall something of that sort, but had no details. He would ask around his friends and get with me.

Cogitating on what I'd learned so far, I realized that if Kingston had altered the vessel's interior into habitation fit for wealthy gentlemen, he'd probably used a shore carpenter, so I went to one with which I was acquainted. He was a man who knew a lot about what happened in the colored communities of Key West, among whom a high percentage were black Bahamian.

Charles DuPont was an interesting character, a black man whose family had been on the island for years. A carpenter, he was campaigning that year, against all odds, for the office of Monroe County Sheriff. I found him on Petronia Street in the Bahamian quarter of town, south of Jackson Square, working on a church.

DuPont greeted me cordially. We were not close friends, but the description of my reasons for imposing upon him moved the man. My premonition was correct. He readily explained that yes, he did do some work on a schooner named *Condor* a few months earlier, knocking out the after bulkhead of the aftermost hold so that there was a connection with it and the existing accommodation spaces. He then had put in some bunks, shelves, and lockers within the cargo hold, making it as smart as he could. Kingston insisted on quality finish carpentry, followed by varnish work, for which he paid in Spanish gold dollars from Puerto Rico.

DuPont remembered a boy of that description, and seven other crewmen, none of whom appeared to be doing much work. He thought it quite a large complement for a sixty-foot schooner, and upon registering his curiosity with Kingston, was told that three of the crew men were actually stewards. DuPont told me they didn't look or act like any ships' stewards he'd ever seen. Several of them hesitated when things were to be done aboard, more like landsmen.

I asked him about Kingston, what sort of man was he?

He rubbed his chin, searching for the right word. "Adaptable, Peter. Too adaptable, for my comfort. He'd do anything that would bring him money, including cutting up his cargo hold. Don't see *that* often."

"Anything else about him that seemed odd?"

"Well, one other thing seemed mighty queer to me. I saw a book lying out in his cabin. Only book there. Can't forget that title and author: *History of the Lives and Bloody Exploits of the Most Noted Pirates; Their Trials and Executions.* Written by 'Anonymous.' Now why would anyone like Kingston have a thing like that? Didn't impress me as the literary sort."

Why, indeed. "Did you see any weaponry?"

"Nothing large or out in the open. I've got to be going now, good luck on your search, Peter."

I thanked DuPont and bade him farewell, all the time wondering if my sense of suspicion was getting the best of me. Perhaps I was making more of all this than was warranted. Walking out of the black quarter I decided that I wasn't. There was something beyond merely unusual about Kingston and *Condor.* The signs were worrying.

In midafternoon, I was heading back to our boat when Merrill happened upon me.

"Peter!" he called out. "I've some news for you."

We stopped in the shade and he explained. "I was able to find some things for you. A group of four Northern businessmen arrived on the Plant Line steamer *Olivette* on Saturday, April twenty-eighth, from Tampa. They didn't stay in any of the nice hotels. They also didn't depart within the next three weeks aboard any Morgan or Plant steamer. And lastly, they haven't been seen since, so they might very well be the tourists that went aboard that schooner you're looking for."

He didn't offer, and I didn't ask, how he learned the information, but I surmised he'd somehow gotten a look at the steamer passenger manifests. "Excellent work, Charles. Thank you, sir. You wouldn't happen to have the names, by any chance?"

Merrill beamed. "As a matter of fact, I do." He pulled out a slip of paper. "Jason Hobart Vanderburgh, age sixty-two. G. Arthur Geldring, age fifty-nine. Julius Exeter, age fifty-six. And Monroe Archmont, age sixty-eight. All from New York City."

"My friend, you've been a great help. Another piece of this puzzle is potentially solved. Thank you. I'll let you know how this turns out."

"You're quite welcome, Peter. I hope you find the boy and the others. One more thing. There's no clearance record for the *Condor* leaving port. Unusual, don't you think?"

"Yes, it is. She should've cleared with customs."

He raised an eyebrow. "Unless Kingston didn't want the authorities to know his destination. You said earlier you thought it somewhere in the Bahamas. Do you know where?"

"No. I was hoping someone here would know. I suppose we'll start with the Bimini Islands. Also check at Nassau."

Merrill headed off, calling over his shoulder, "Well, I wish you good luck, Peter. Oh, and please say hello to Useppa for me. I haven't had occasion to see her lately. I fear I've missed church services due to work the last two Sundays."

He referred to my daughter, the assistant headmistress at the Frederick Douglass School in Key West. Useppa became a Methodist missionary in Key West, working with the island's black children, when only twenty years old. By the time of the great fire in '86, she was a teacher at the island's black school and working with both the white Methodist church and the black African Methodist Episcopal church.

Now, after a hiatus following the death of her fiancé in that fire, a traumatic event aggravated by its Cuban revolutionary connection, she was back teaching at the school in Key West again. She loved the island where her mother had been born and raised and had later married me during the war. The place was part of her heart, and she couldn't stay away.

From Pinder's store, I'd sent a note to the school, letting her know I was briefly on the island and wanted to invite her to dinner that evening. I hadn't seen her in five months and was looking forward to introducing her to Cynda and my other friends. We would meet at Curry's establishment on Front Street, at seven o'clock. A return confirmation note was requested.

Armed with my new knowledge about *Condor* and Kingston, I made my way back to Pinder's dock to give Cynda the good news that we finally had some solid information to use in formulating our plans. Walking down Fleming Street, close upon Duval, I passed the scene where the great fire had started—and I nearly died—two years earlier. That memory brought to mind the more suspicious side of my character and I began to mentally assess the current situation.

Questions arose about Kingston and his unusual crew. The O connection in Nassau. The piracy book. Those New York businessmen. And why had *Condor* departed quietly, bypassing the authorities, if she was only on a pleasure excursion? The questions had no answers yet and only led to more questions.

Were they really businessmen? Was O another businessman from New York? A rival of the passengers aboard *Condor*? How did the New Yorkers come to charter Kingston? Or even know of him? It was done in advance—Kingston altered his vessel before they arrived. Why did they choose *Condor*? There were real yachts available that were far more comfortable. Why would the captain carve up his ship like that, an expensive undertaking, for a single voyage? A seven-man crew? Why a crew that large? Most importantly, where did they go, and what was their purpose? Fishing? Sightseeing? Leisurely voyaging? Or perhaps an extended business meeting, a company retreat of sorts?

As I went by the tavern at Southard and Duval, a familiar shout interrupted my cogitation. It was Corny, well oiled by that time, calling me into the barroom. The lads were canvassing the island, pub by pub, and so far reported no luck, but declared that perseverance was their virtue. Even Dan Horloft, the stoic mariner and engineer from Maine, was smiling—a significant indicator of their level of intoxication.

Rork, who was marginally less under the influence than his shipmates but carried it better, told me they'd meet us at Curry's for dinner at seven, three and one half hours away. He also advised me that he had a potential witness he was tracking down. Hopefully, by dinner he'd have something to report. I reminded my dear friend of Useppa's serious aversion to alcohol and those under its sway. I further suggested that everyone slow down their rate of consumption considerably, so I'd be spared one of my daughter's frequent lectures on the evils of rum.

Useppa—like every other female who'd met the Gaelic rascal—adored Sean Rork and, of course, wouldn't dream of lecturing *him*. Oh, no, it would be I who'd be the object of her ire and recipient of her wisdom. Rork laughed and said that yes, he'd see that the boys would, "behave as gentlemen most certainly should at a proper dinner, an' nary a *drop* more than a final *pint* o' liquor should pass our lips between now an' then."

I was less than convinced, but what could I do at that point? Onward I proceeded to *Nancy Ann* and my opportunity to give Cynda notice of some positive progress in our search for answers.

The sloop had her sun awnings set up fore and aft and all hatches open for the air. The shadows and openings created a pleasant draft through the cabin, making it fully ten degrees cooler than shore. Cynda was seated at the tiny table in the cabin's main salon, reading a pocket book of poetry she'd brought along. I slid down the ladder in my zeal, kissed her cheek, and immediately gave her the latest intelligence gained.

She expressed her joy at my progress by embracing me, the first physical affection since the night of the storm in my bungalow. Before I knew it, and without any planned effort, I found myself on the adjacent bunk, entwined with her body and entranced by those captivating blue eyes. A natural progression ensued, soft caresses making time fade away until I lost all sense of place, except the overwhelming urge to please this woman who had brought long-dormant needs and abilities back to life for me.

Afterward, secure in the knowledge that our companions were well ensconced far away ashore, we lay there basking in the glow of complete repose, both of us depleted of energy and recovering our breath. Holding her beside me on the gently swaying vessel, I felt as carefree as I'd ever been and lay there savoring the sensation for a long time. There was no bed cover and none was needed in that tropic climate. Besides, we had privacy and several hours until we were expected for dinner. The rest of the sleepy afternoon was ours to laze away. Within minutes, we were deep in slumber, oblivious to the world. Our bliss ended abruptly, however, with an indignant shriek from the companionway.

"Daddy . . . *Good Lord!* What in the world are you *doing!*"

Useppa, my darling daughter and staunch defender of Christian morals, stood on the ladder a mere five feet away. Her father and a strange woman lay tangled before her, both as *au natural* as the day they were born. It was not my best paternal moment.

While we hastily gathered up our clothes, Useppa stormed up the ladder and waited on deck. Cynda was perplexed, I embarrassed, and my daughter madder than I've ever seen her. When the lady and I had assumed an appearance of better propriety, we ascended the ladder to confront our ethical superior.

I feel it incumbent upon me to explain at this juncture that

Linda and I had always attempted to instill in our children a sense of social and religious responsibility, for both their sakes and for the country. We wanted them to have a foundation on which to build good character, thus they were taught Christian values and behavior, with Linda and me serving as the primary examples. Hence, perhaps, the level of shock to my daughter's sensibilities.

Then, to compound the issue, I made the tactical error to treat the episode with humor, in an attempt to defuse it, so to speak. In my defense, I must say that this situation was never covered in Useppa's upbringing or my own anticipation. I had no earthly idea what to say, so unsurprisingly, I chose the wrong thing to say.

"Useppa, you seem to have me at a unique disadvantage, but may I have the honor to introduce you to Mrs. Cynda Saunders. Cynda, this is my daughter Useppa."

More blood drained from Useppa's face.

"A *married* woman! Oh, Daddy, how could you? And you're being so facetious about it. I just don't know what to say."

I immediately realized I shouldn't have used either the humor or Cynda's marital title. It was time to retreat. "No, no, dear. She's just a widow. And a friend."

Well, that didn't help at all, and only got me a cocked eyebrow from Mrs. Saunders. This wasn't going well, so I decided upon a strong counterattack. Two could play at etiquette.

"And just why didn't you announce your presence from the dock and request permission to come on board? I raised you to show proper manners on a vessel!"

"I did," she said, leveling those green eyes at me. "But evidently you were too tired out to hear me."

Touché.

"Well, I'm sorry you blundered into this, dear. Cynda and I are very close—"

"I noticed that, Daddy. And I am trying very hard not to judge you harshly because of your behavior, but I do not want to hear anymore. I will leave you now to your . . ." She stammered a moment then blurted out, "your *friend.*"

With that said, Useppa stomped off the sloop and down the dock, leaving me far behind in the scruples department. It was ridiculous but definitely not comical, being chastised by my *daughter* over ethics. This was so much worse than her diatribes against me drinking rum. I felt like some perverted lecherous cad.

Meanwhile my lover stood there, slowly fuming with indignation herself.

"Yes, it was nice to meet you, too, Useppa," muttered Cynda to the figure marching off. Then she turned to me. "So I'm *just* a widow?"

"You know I didn't mean it that way."

"Never mind, Peter. Just never mind. And don't worry, your precious daughter's not a child. Not chronologically, anyway. She'll calm down and be at the dinner."

Cynda didn't know Useppa.

9

A Motley Crew, Indeed

Curry's Saloon and Dining Room
Duval and Wall streets
Key West, Florida
Thursday, 5 July 1888

Rork and the crew met Cynda and me for dinner. Improbably, considering their condition, they were right on time. They had three extra men in tow. Drunk as he was, the ethnologist in Corny emerged and he proudly began introducing our additional diners.

The first of them was oddly attired, with bright clothing topped by a hair arrangement bordering on frightening when he removed his turban. His head was completed shaved bald except for a fringe across the front, from sideburn to sideburn; and a ridge fore and aft along the top, that dangled a double tail off the back. Corny solemnly introduced him as Hotal-kiha, also known as "Key West Billy" Fewell, of the powerful Wind Clan in the Kan-yuk-sa Is-ti-tca-ti, or Big Cypress Swamp Seminoles.

I knew of the man. Years earlier, Key West Billy became known in southern Florida for being the only Seminole in the region to live in both the white and Indian worlds. It was a lifestyle adopted out of necessity, for he was in sad exile from his own people after fulfilling tribal orders in 1870 to execute his own father for committing a capital crime. A crime which they later discovered his father did not commit. Billy was devastated and canoed to Key West, staying away from the clan for years. Recently he was back in the fold, but was still sometimes seen in the white settlements, representing his people in trading deals or disagreements.

My friend Clay MacCauley had interviewed Key West Billy during his survey of the Seminoles in 1884 and came away greatly impressed by the man's stature and dignity. True to his reputation, forty-two-year-old Billy sat there regally as Corny—Clay's colleague at the Smithsonian, who was clearly thrilled to meet such a personality—described him, his clan, and the legend of how the Seminole clans originated.

A young dark-skinned fellow, with prominent cheek bones and shiny straight black hair, was our second addition. He sat deferentially next to Billy and shyly acknowledged his introduction by Corny. He was Absalom Bowlegs, of the Bahamian Seminole clan that lived in a remote village in northern Andros Island, the largest and most unexplored island of that archipelago. I asked Corny to repeat that, for I hadn't even known there were any Seminoles in the Bahamas.

Absalom, or Ab as he was known by friends, had recently been a guest of the Big Cypress Seminoles, courtesy of Billy, who had met him in Key West several months earlier. It seemed that Ab was a deckhand on the *Delilah*, a schooner out of Green Turtle Cay in the Abaco Islands in the northern Bahamas. *Delilah* had put into Key West to discharge pineapples, when Ab met Billy.

The young man asked to know more of his Indian heritage, for the Bahamian Seminoles were former half-Seminole, half-black slaves who'd fled Florida in the 1820s for freedom in the predominately black Bahamas, where slavery had been abolished.

Their skin was African, but Indian facial features still showed through after several generations. Billy took him inland to meet his clan and learn about the Seminole culture.

After several months ashore, Ab now needed passage back to his islands and Billy had taken him to Key West to find a schooner for employment. It was added that Absalom knew the Bahamas like the back of his hand, having sailed that area on his grandfather's schooner when younger. I noted that his language was particularly articulate, not using the abbreviated patois garble usually heard from Bahamians. When I inquired, he explained that he'd been fortunate in attending a school in Nassau for a while, where he'd learned to speak proper English. He then demonstrated that he could effortlessly revert to island talk, a show that got a laugh from everyone.

Providentially for Ab, *Delilah* happened to be in the port at that very moment, hence the appearance of our third guest, a thirtyish man in simple clothes who walked with a roll and had squinted eyes and large callused hands. A seaman if ever there was one.

Rork, the most sober *appearing* of my three crew, did the honors for this man, presenting him to us Reginald Dunbarton, mate of none other than the *Delilah*. Then Rork, with a not so slight self-congratulating smile, enlightened me as to how these three men were of interest to our enterprise. It was but another of those twists of fate that dictated my life throughout the summer of 1888.

It transpired that Dunbarton was looking for a captain for *Delilah*. The schooner's master, Basil Nolles, was currently lodged in the jail on Whitehead Street on charges revolving around drinking and bloodshed. He wasn't getting out anytime soon and the schooner's crew was losing money just sitting at anchor in the harbor with a full load of canned meats and fancy goods from up north that were expected in Nassau.

As good a seaman as he was, like many mates Dunbarton

did not fully possess the skills of navigation, so the ship needed a captain. The telegraph cable from Key West northward was out of order at the moment, thus the mate was incommunicado with the owner of the ship in England. Dunbarton asked if I would fill the billet of master so they could get the cargo to Nassau.

I thought all this more than ironic. Earlier, Rork and I had discussed transferring at Key West to a larger vessel for the ocean voyage. We'd talked of chartering a ketch or schooner, but few were in harbor right then.

I regarded Dunbarton again. The man appeared squared-away in manner and thinking. The fact the ship's master was an alcoholic did not mean the vessel and crew were not seaworthy. But I had a legal question. "Has Captain Nolles left you in command, Mr. Dunbarton, with authority over the ship's affairs?"

"Captain Nolles is incoherently drunk, sir. I cannot offer you a company contract as master, but I need a captain to navigate and you need a ship. 'Tis a short voyage and you can pick up a ship at Nassau, or charter dear *Delilah* from there once we're offloaded. What say you, sir?"

Before I could reply, Rork jumped in with an energetic summation of the entire situation: "Sir, it seems to me that the luck o' the Irish is supplyin' the needs o' us all. For we'll be needin' a stouter vessel than dear wee *Nancy Ann* for our work abroad the seas to the Bahamas. This schooner *Delilah* is needin' a captain to get to the Bahamas. We're also in need o' a guide for the reefs an' islands, an' this lad Absalom is a bit o' an expert in that department, an' needin' passage back to the Bahamas." He proudly ended with, "So, the whole o' the situation has come together nicely for us by the grace o' God above."

It looked like a *fait accompli*, but I still had a point for Rork. He was energetic, but still, he was also inebriated.

"Who owns *Delilah*? Is she well-found?"

Rork said he'd had the same concern. "I've been aboard her, no more 'n thirty minutes ago—she's in good shape. Her owner is

English an' absent in Portsmouth, but he insists on good upkeep. The crew just wants out o' Key West an' away from their captain, who was a bit o' a tyro by all accounts. If we want to charter her once we're at Nassau an' the cargo's discharged, then a cable to the owner from there an' she's ours from then onward."

Everyone looked at me with expectant faces. I decided to go ahead with the idea. *Carpe diem.* "You're right, Sean. Like we've talked about, we'll need a bigger vessel than the sloop. *Nancy Ann* can stay at Pinder's until we get back. Very well, gentlemen, and madam, tomorrow at the start of the ebb, we set sail for the Bahamas. First we'll check in at Bimini and see if anyone saw *Condor*, then we'll stop at Nassau while we do the same and offload the cargo."

I thought of an additional legal point.

"I'll send a letter from here, countersigned by Mr. Dunbarton, explaining things to the owner."

A toast was drunk to our success and all hands present proceeded, courtesy of my funds, of course, to enjoy a pleasant evening. Except me, however. One distressing deficiency prevented me from taking full pleasure in the company of my friends— Useppa never arrived that evening.

When Rork quietly inquired about her absence during the party, I told him what had happened at the boat and how terrible I felt about it.

"Ooh, well, what's done is done, an' what's said is said, me friend. She'll come round in her own time. Don't waste time in the past, for we've enough to do with a strange ship, an' an even stranger voyage ahead o' us, not to mention a motley crew, indeed."

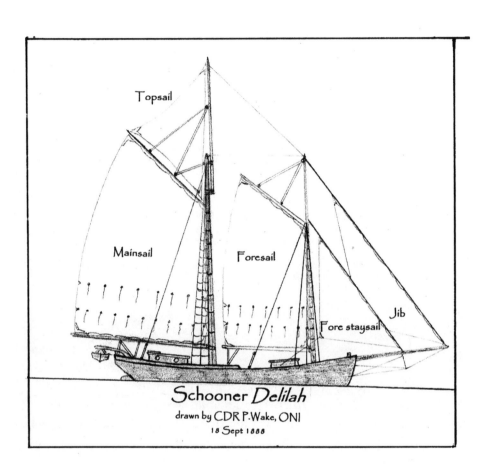

Topsail

Mainsail

Foresail

Jib

Fore staysail

Schooner *Delilah*
drawn by CDR P. Wake, ONI
18 Sept 1888

10

Rumors on a Glassy Sea

In the Straits of Florida
Off the Florida Keys
Friday, 6 July 1888

*D*elilah was stout, as one would expect from an Abaconian built and manned vessel. Fifty-three feet on deck, she carried the normal rig for a two-master: mains'l, tops'l, fores'l, forestays'l, and jib. The two cargo holds were generous for her size. Her most useful feature was her draft. She had a full-length keel that required only six feet of water aft—a crucial factor in sailing the shallow Bahamian islands, where uncharted reefs and shoals were everywhere.

There were eight souls aboard. I served as captain; Dunbarton continued on as mate—a generous offer from Rork, who could've served that function easily, but decided to be ship's bosun. Connerly Blackstone, a white Bahamian from Green Turtle Key, was the cook, who wasted no time in explaining to Cynda that she would stay out of the galley. Absalom Bowlegs was deck seaman and island guide. Dan Horloft and Corny Rathburn volunteered to work the deck.

Though they surely enjoyed her loveliness, Cynda's presence was not appreciated by the regular crew, which didn't surprise me. Females are regarded as trouble on a ship by many sailors— especially some of the more old-fashioned Bahamians. But aboard she was, and her role was expected to be that of a lady of leisure.

It was a bit crowded, for *Delilah* was built with accommodations for only a captain and three crewmen. After I conducted a thorough cleaning out of rum bottles and other trash, I took the small master's cabin at the very stern, for it had the chart table and necessary navigational accoutrements. Immediately forward of that on the port side was the mate's cabin, which Dunbarton surrendered to Cynda. Across from her was the galley storeroom. Forward of Cynda and the galley provisions was the galley itself, with an adjoining mess table, barely big enough to seat six men. Then came a bulkhead and the main hold. Continuing forward was a 'tween decks stowage space around the mainmast, then the forward hold.

The fo'c'sle in the bow of the ship was separated by a theoretically watertight bulkhead at the forward end of the forward hold. The cook and one or two seamen normally lived in the fo'c'sle. Now, the cook, and the two older gentlemen, Corny and Dan, lived there. Dunbarton, Rork, and Absalom Bowlegs, rested upon the main deck when off watch. I thought that far better than the cramped fo'c'sle myself, especially when shared with the fat and rather malodorous cook, but my two Northern friends proclaimed themselves happy with the arrangements for their lodging.

My stateroom was diminutive but functionally adequate, with a pleasant stern window—rare in Abaco ships. Cynda, to my surprise, didn't flinch at the cramped space of her cabin, the second largest aboard, but the size of an average house's cupboard. Quite the contrary, she allowed the faintest smile to show when she learned our cabins were next to each other, with the other shipmates far away, up forward.

In an attempt to maintain the dignity of my office, and the fiction of our relationship, I showed no such glee in front of the others. Privately, however, I wondered how long the illusion could be publicly continued, particularly with the mate, cook, and deckhand. And in the back of my mind, I still harbored lingering doubts as to the wisdom of such an arrangement, as gratifying as it was to my libido. However, wisdom, as I well knew after twenty-five years of commanding men in the navy, is frequently in short supply among seafarers when decisions are required regarding females.

Dunbarton and Blackstone topped off the galley provisions—on my account at Pinder's, which account had gained prodigious size—while Rork and I inspected the rig and the cargo. The stays and shrouds were taut, the running rigging undeteriorated, the blocks and spars strongly built, and her canvas as well as could be expected in the tropics. The cargo of canned goods was stowed tight and low. Dunbarton was obviously good at his job.

Once the supplies were aboard, we sailed with the ebb tide at four p.m. on Friday, the sixth of July, 1888, ignoring the traditional superstition of embarking on a long voyage on a Friday. Rork, as suspicious as they come at sea—he is Irish, as you know—reminded me of that violation later on, when things got distinctly uncomfortable.

The work of the ship quickly settled into the ordinary routines sailors know at sea. I scheduled three sets of watches of four hours each: Corny and I, Dunbarton and Dan, Rork and Bowlegs, with the cook, as is the norm, not standing deck duty. I took the first watch, the entirety of which was occupied in getting us out to sea, beyond the dangers of the deadly reefs surrounding Key West.

The wind was light as we slowly passed Fort Taylor under

plain sail, then rounded Whitehead Spit, and close-hauled for Western Sambo Reef, eight miles distant to the southeast. Once there, we took our departure from the Florida Reefs into deep water and tried to point easterly toward the Bahamian banks and islands, but to no avail. As it was, the nearest we could steer into the fading wind was southeast, toward Cardenas in Cuba. But, fortunately, the mighty Gulf Stream was fair for our purposes and we slid east southeast over the bottom at a little over two nautical miles each hour.

That area was one I had close memories of from the war, so I knew the geography and weather patterns and was confident the summer trades would pick up after our dreary beginning. At the end of my watch, I went below to maintain the logbook and chart our position.

I was greeted in my cabin by the lady of the ship. She persuaded me, as only she could, that navigation and record keeping were matters secondary to an intimate celebration of her appreciation for my assistance thus to date. Succumbing gladly to the shirking of my duties, I promised myself not to do it again in daytime in the future, as such behavior compromised the privacy of our relationship. That, as will be no surprise to the reader by now, was a pledge I found impossible to keep.

Upon returning to the main deck several hours later to ascertain how things were progressing, it was plainly evident that I had deceived myself on two important accounts: that the wind would pick up, and that my personal affairs were not generally known among my new Bahamian acquaintances.

The former was obvious. The barometer remained high, with a calm sea and a sky veiled with high wispy clouds. The schooner's reflection showed in the water, mocking our intentions and progress, and the only propulsion over the ground far below us was furnished by our present friend, the Stream.

The latter deduction was a bit more subtle and gleaned from the knowing glances and quickly ended conversation when

I showed myself to Dunbarton and Corny. All being well with the ship's equipment aft, I proceeded forward to inspect the sheet lines.

By the sampson post at the bow, I was taken aside by Rork, who whispered, "Ooh, ye're not bein' discreet, me friend. Nay—not when you're dallyin' in the middle o' broad daylight. Peter, kindly save that till the night watches. Dan an' Corny are your friends, but these others're not. Especially that dark-souled villain o' a cook."

Hmm. Sound advice, thought I, but more than a bit incongruous coming from a rogue like Rork. Usually it was I providing that category of counsel to him. I thanked my friend and returned to my cabin, there to ponder where *Delilah* was heading on the sea, and where I was heading with a certain lady. Neither seemed easy to determine.

Delilah's rate of advancement eastward remained tied to the current, a situation that became more anxious the longer it went on, particularly since we were in one of the primary steamer lanes of the world. We tacked ship, with considerable effort on the rudder, in the middle of the Straits of Florida and steered for Bahia Honda Key on the Florida reefs, still without much air to fill our sails.

The schooner slatted and banged about in the low swells, requiring constant attention to prevent damage from chafe. Maintaining sharp lookout against collision with the steamers and navigating with some semblance of accuracy under the incessantly blistering concentration of the sun's rays, all conspired to irritate our nerves. Heated words were exchanged at the least annoyance. This friction went on for three long days, without even the excitement of an afternoon thunderstorm. Everyone was on edge—I most of all.

The rumors began on the second day. As one would expect, they were not promulgated in my presence, but the ship's company heard them clear enough. Gloomy stuff at first, then sinister. Initially they centered on my navigational abilities, implying that had we stayed nearer the Florida reefs we would have had more wind from the coastal sea breeze effect. Then speculation turned to Cynda. By the third day, it shifted to our search for Luke and whether we really were taking the ship to Nassau.

Rork informed me the source of all this discontent was Connerly Blackstone, whom he'd despised from the start, labeling him a "snivelin' sea-lawyer an' a failure as a cook, who can nary even boil water."

Then, a day later, Rork added that Dunbarton, whom I'd previously thought a squared-away professional, was agreeing with the cook as the scurrilous talk continued. Dan, Corny, and Ab were listening, I was told, but not participating.

"If ye wants me opinion, sir," recommended Rork, " 'tis time to put those two scalawags ashore at the first opportunity. O' better yet, let me dump the bastards overboard now. Let 'em swim for Muertos Cay at Cay Sal Bank."

Both options were tempting, but I knew my own behavior was probably the instigating factor and might be the subject of an inquiry should an official complaint be made against me. My defense was meager.

I *had* been spending a lot of time below decks with Cynda, and though we'd thought our trysts were more discreet, by then it was a moot point. I'd lost the moral high ground.

Blackstone and Dunbarton thought me as ethically bankrupt as their previous captain. They also had signed ship's papers, a formal merchant marine contract, and had done nothing *overt* to negate them, thus the potential for an inquiry should I choose to end their contracts and set them ashore. Not to mention my own standing was a bit shaky, since I'd not had a formal contract myself. I resolved to watch them carefully and to remove my own behavior as a source of contention.

Therefore, over breakfast in my cabin on the morning of the fourth day, I broached it to Cynda, still clad in a peignoir. "We need to cease the amorous recreation, darling. This has gotten out of hand, and though I dearly love the affection, and fear I have become an addict, it has interfered with my command of the ship."

"Oh, my goodness, we mustn't let *that* happen now," she quipped, while passing a playful hand over me. Between the peignoir's charms and the skill of her hand, I was losing ground fast. Another thirty seconds and we would be back in the bunk.

"I'm serious. I've already told you what they're saying."

She laughed. "Two white-trash Bahamians gossiping like old ladies? That scares you?"

I didn't care much for her tone. "You're not *listening*, Cynda. I am in command and they need to respect me, not for my rank, but for my abilities and actions. Lately, my behavior hasn't been worthy of inspiring respect."

"You sounded so stilted just then, Peter." She caressed my face. "This isn't a navy ship. Let yourself enjoy life a little. Let *us* enjoy life. We both need and deserve it."

I'd never faced this. A temptress at sea. "Cynda, please. You know the power you have over me. We need to slow down."

Cynda's face froze into stone, her eyes losing their softness. The change was quick and dramatic. And disconcerting. The temptress instantly turned tigress as she huskily said, "Ignore them, Peter. All they have to do is follow orders. And don't worry about your friends. They're probably happy for us."

I wasn't confident of that. At the start of our odyssey, Corny and Dan had expressed admiration for Cynda's tenacity in finding her son and tactfully offered congratulations on my budding relationship, but lately praise for the lady had been missing. The tension I sensed aboard extended to them also.

"Cynda, this discussion has come to an end. From now on, we'll concentrate all of our energy on the search."

That did it. She said not a word, but studied me for several seconds, then rose and silently retired to her own cabin. Looking out the stern window at the glassy sea, I found myself wishing Reverend McClean had not delayed me that day at the church in St. Augustine.

11

Brown's Cut

The Florida Straits
Off the Great Bahama Bank
Wednesday, 11 July 1888

It took us five days to go the distance habitually covered in two. After drifting north with the current for days along the fanged wall of coral that guards the western edge of the Great Bahama Bank, the wind finally arrived.

As stated before, the weather was out of the norm for that time of year, when gentle breezes would be interrupted by brief afternoon thunderstorms. The disturbed aspect of the atmosphere made everyone increasingly edgy, the seasoned sailors among us worried that it portended a major storm lurking about somewhere to our east.

Shouts of joy rang out among the novices when a wind did come out of the northwest quadrant, at first a wonderful assistance to us. It turned up at dawn on the eleventh, soft in the beginning but steadily rising until the tops'l and jib were brought in.

Dunbarton, who knew his weather, looked at me warily and said, "Northwest at this time of year?" He shook his head and growled, "I expect things to get worse, much worse. Would have been better if we'd been over to the west when this came up, instead of this far east, with a reef to our leeward."

The clear implication was that I had put us in the situation. I let it go, judging the topic and man not worth furthering the acrimony aboard by addressing his borderline insubordination. *Delilah* was, after all, but a small island trading vessel and not sailing under naval discipline. Besides, the man was right.

Within two hours we were surging along at seven knots under easy sail on a broad reach to the northeast. I was steering for Gun Cay. It was just south of the Bimini Islands on the edge of the Bahama Banks, where I wanted to inquire after *Condor*, before heading east toward Nassau.

But the conditions changed. Rapidly. By noon, I knew for certain what Dunbarton had implied and I had feared—we were on the fringes of an approaching tropical storm. Squall lines, dark and full of brutal energy, appeared on the northwestern horizon, being borne down upon us by an increasing Force 6 wind. Using the old Florida sailors' trick, I faced the wind and held my right arm out perpendicular to it. My hand pointed northeast. I guessed the center of the storm was somewhere north and east of Grand Bahama Island, heading west to the Florida mainland. I hoped very much that I was right, and that the center of the tempest was not heading our way.

All of this meant that time was of the essence. A strong westerly wind kicks up frightening seas on the reef in those parts, seas that take over command of your vessel, lifting it high and smashing it down into the gaping maws of coral. The Bahamians say the reef is in a "rage." Quite an appropriate description.

We had to get to Gun Cay and anchor behind the island before the storm closed the entrance channel and we became trapped on a lee shore, unable to claw to windward, away from our destruction.

If we tacked and headed out into the Stream away from the Bahamas, we would run into monstrous and unpredictable seas, created by the opposing current and rising wind. That was not an option.

The weather got worse. The squalls joined together within the next hour, making a solid indigo-colored wall of cloud completely across the western horizon. The front edge was thousands of feet high, clouds cascading down like a waterfall before turning into rain that flayed the sea below. In front of that malevolent wall, the seas were pushed up in ridges topped with white foam, blowing off in streaks horizontally through the air.

I estimated the velocity of the storm's approach to be at least forty knots. The wind inside the storm would be at least Force 9, gusting much higher. It would be a race to safety, balanced with the need to reduce the area of our canvas so that we would not be blown down and capsized. The wind shifted from nor'west to westerly, right on our beam. We doused all sail except the fores'l and triple reefed that. Even then, *Delilah* raced through the water, heeled hard over, lee deck under water, bound north to Gun Cay. Only nine miles to go. An hour and a half at the most. But it was too late.

Fifteen minutes later that wall of wind hit us.

The outer forestay parted with a crack, the ends streaming off to leeward from the masthead and the end of the bowsprit. Seconds later, the wind whipped the foretopmast right off at the trestle where the upper windward shrouds broke. That cast loose the peak halyard of the reefed fores'l, allowing it to rattle like a Gatling gun as the gaff swung down and off to leeward. Then the fores'l sheet somehow got loose.

Dunbarton was standing near the starboard foreshrouds when that gaff went amok and the fores'l boom began sweeping the deck looking for victims. He yelled for Ab, who was clinging to the butt of the bowsprit, to come aft and help gain control of that vicious boom, but it was too late. The boom slammed into Dunbarton's head, turning his face into mush and launching his body like a rag doll out over the water to leeward. His body instantly disappeared in the froth.

Rork leaped forward with a bight of line and lassoed the end of the boom, binding it down to a ringbolt, just as the sail ripped along a seam across its width. I don't know how he did it on that leaping deck. We were without much sail at that point and being driven quickly downwind to the east. There I saw giant waves already smashing into the coral two miles away, a line of watery explosions erupting all up and down the reefs like a warship's broadside. It was a horrifying scene. To the west, visibility was swallowed by the wall of rainwater. To the east, death awaited, plainly seen.

Any thought of making Gun Cay ended, for we weren't heading north anymore. *Delilah* was heading east on her own, a piece of storm-tossed flotsam, determined to commit suicide. Dan and I struggled at the wheel, but we couldn't turn her away, for she wasn't answering her helm without enough canvas to assist.

The rigging howled up and down the sound scale, shrieking above a background of roaring wind and growling seas, making an onslaught of noise too great to shout orders over. The rain, flung at gale speed, pelted our bodies like birdshot. You could not look anywhere close to the west without being blinded by that damned rain.

Thank the Almighty that Rork was a veteran seaman and knew what to do up forward. He and Ab, their arms battered by the thrashing canvas, managed to hoist a reefed forestays'l—just enough sail to give steerageway to the rudder. I felt *Delilah* respond to my efforts at the wheel. All our eyes were on the windward lower foreshrouds, now under immense pressure. They held. A miracle.

Rork and Ab made their way aft, where Ab put his mouth to

my ear and screamed, "Let me take her through Brown's Cut! It's our only hope!"

I'd never heard of such an entrance through the reef, but these were his native waters. Rork yelled something, vigorously nodding the affirmative. I grabbed Ab and put his hands on the wheel. Seconds later I wished I hadn't.

He turned her away to the southeast, wearing the schooner around *downwind* to the east. The forestays'l thundered in protest but held together as it banged over to the port side and filled. In mid-turn a wave washed over *Delilah*'s stern, plunging us knee deep in water. We then collided with a wave in front, stopping us abruptly and enabling the next large following wave to completely inundate our main deck. The water was fully four feet deep where we stood at the wheel, as *Delilah* sank under the horrendous weight of that moving mountain of water that fell down on us. We'd broached, a deadly mistake.

Cynda, Corny, and Blackstone were below, the hatch secured, but not watertight. I knew it must be chaos down there, everything that had been stowed in shelves and lockers coming loose, water flooding down the hatchways, lanterns extinguishing, the whole effect surely panicking them in the dark as they worked the pumps in a desperate effort to keep the ship afloat.

Somehow, against all logic, that schooner rose back out of the sea and came around, shedding tons of water overboard. We were no more than half a mile from the chaos along the reef now. Ab stood up higher, trying to see through the rain, his eyes stark white against glistening black skin. I saw him bob his head in confirmation—he'd seen the cut, though I could see nothing. Rork pointed ahead. Then I understood.

There *was* a gap, an impossibly tiny space, in the line of surf explosions. *Delilah* slewed and surged down the waves. We all helped Ab steer for the gap—four men putting their muscles into it and barely keeping her from rounding up. Then another mountain of water lifted us up and we slid off to leeward, far short of our course to the gap.

Straining at the wheel, we sailed with the wind abeam, every wave raising us up and washing us closer to leeward and that razor-sharp coral. We frantically forced the helm back to windward, trying to get southing enough to make that gap.

I felt the sea bottom rising up under us, making the seas crest into surf. We were seconds from losing control. The reef was less than a hundred yards away—mere seconds in that maelstrom. Spray from the exploding surf filled the air, the deck vibrating with the power of those breaking seas.

Ab shouted, "Now!" and we put our weight on the spokes to turn her to port.

There was no time to think, to communicate, to do anything but instinctually steer *Delilah* down those twenty-foot waves washing through a corridor perhaps a hundred feet wide, crashing with thundering detonations against the coral on either side. *Delilah* hit bottom just once, a momentary thud during the trough of one of those monster waves, the resultant shudder shaking the masts and almost knocking us off our feet.

And then we were in calm water. I say calm, but the seas were still five or six feet and the wind was the same. But at least it was an easier task to man the helm. Rork got the leadline out and reported from the foreshrouds by hand signals that we had two fathoms showing. I ordered the anchor to be cast. It bit hard and swung us with a lurch bow-first into the wind as Rork paid out the rode off the Sampson post. We laid back on three hundred fifty feet of chain and line, our anchorage half a mile to leeward of that rumbling line of death. The reef sounded angry that we'd made it through, as if it would cross that half mile and grind us into pieces for our temerity.

Dan and Ab collapsed on the foredeck. Rork limped around the deck inspecting the rigging. I went below to check the hull. When I opened the hatch and looked down into the main cabin, three haggard faces looked up at me, water sloshing around their ankles. I descended, asking Blackstone if the pump still worked. He mumbled that it did, then fell down onto the bench seat at the table.

Corny looked bad. A gash was open from his right eyebrow to his hairline, and his hands were trembling. Cynda didn't look like the same woman. A grim visage lined her face as she said in a thin voice, "We've been pumping nonstop, Peter. We thought we'd die down here."

Finding a match in the waterproof oilskin pouch by the companionway, I lit the table lamp. "All right everyone, listen to me. We are safely anchored, well past the reef. We just need to keep the pumps working until the storm goes by. Rork and I are going to fother a sail around the hull and that should help stem the worst of the leaks in the seams." I turned to the cook. "Now, do you know if it's a hole, or is it the seams?"

"No hole . . . I think . . . her seams have . . . opened," gasped Blackstone.

I'd rather it'd been a hole or two, as that would have been easier to plug. Opened seams meant the entire hull was leaking. The pumping would have to continue, and my crew was exhausted.

"I'll send some men down to the pump. You all rest now."

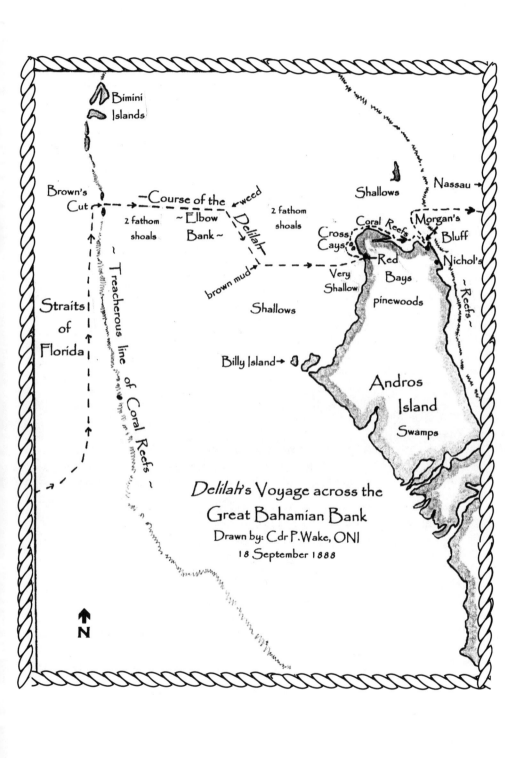

Bimini
Islands

Brown's
Cut

— Course of the — weed
~ Elbow
Bank ~
Delilah

2 fathom
shoals

2 fathom
shoals

brown mud →

Shallows

Nassau →

Coral Reefs

Morgan's
Bluff

Cross
Cays

Red
Bays

Nichol's
~ Reefs ~

Very
Shallow

pinewoods

Shallows

~ Treacherous line of Coral Reefs ~

Straits
of
Florida

Billy Island →

Andros
Island

Swamps

Delilah's Voyage across the
Great Bahamian Bank
Drawn by: Cdr P. Wake, ONI
18 September 1888

↑
N

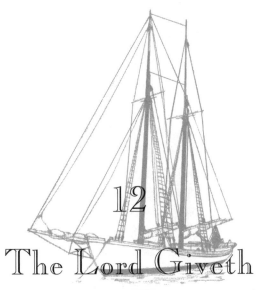

12

The Lord Giveth
and the Lord Taketh Away

Brown's Cut
South of Gun Cay, Bahama Banks
Wednesday, 11 July 1888

Rork and I spread the spare jib around the forward half of the hull, which was taking the brunt of the seas, then went below for the first hour at the pump. It was a two-man contraption that reached down into the main bilge, just forward of the galley spaces. There wasn't much room in the tight space to work the pump, and my elbows kept hitting the bulkhead. As I pulled and pushed that handle up and down, I tried to calculate the volume of water in the hull, but gave up. My mind just couldn't function anymore. Fifteen minutes later neither could my body, and I lay down on the galley table bench as Ab and Dan took over pumping.

When I regained awareness, Corny and Blackstone were pumping. The wind's howl had decreased outside and *Delilah* was riding discernibly easier. I tottered up to the main deck, the muscles of my legs and arms protesting every step. It was dark except for the binnacle light, which showed a form sitting against the main boom crutch.

Rork was on anchor watch. He gave me a weak smile and said, "Well, me boyo, we've been through worse, but not much worse."

I smiled back. Rork was opening a game we'd played for decades whenever things looked bleak. "South China Sea was worse," I offered.

"Ooh, that time in Africa was far worse'n that," he countered.

"Which time in Africa?" I asked, and we both laughed. The African mission in '74 had been dismal, indeed, for a while.

He held up his left arm. "Aye, sir—but Indochina topped it all. Damned dicey, that was."

"Got me there, Rork. Anything to report?"

"Aye, sir. Wind an' seas've laid down a bit. Visibility picked up an' I could see two keys o'er to the west while we still had light. We must've come through 'em in that wee bitty cut young Absalom knew. Anchor's holdin' fine, but I fear the heavy devil's done dug in halfway to Haytees by now." He sighed at the thought. "We'll have one helluva time gettin' that bastard back up."

I asked the important question. "Leaks?"

"Hull's no longer flexin' so we've gotten even with 'em, maybe gainin' by now. Not sure how long we can go like this, though. The lads are done in by it, sir."

"Any sign of Dunbarton?"

"No. His body's probably over in the mangroves on Andros Island by now. By the way, I told Blackstone about Dunbarton, since he was down below when it happened."

"And he blamed me, no doubt . . ."

"Well, did ye expect anythin' else? Blackstone's useless for a cook or a sailor, but he's been workin' away on that pump. I'll give him that. Self-preservation can truly inspire even the Blackstones o' the world."

I exhaled and leaned back on the cabin top. "So what do we do now? Suggestions?"

A voice came out of the darkness up forward. "I've an idea, sir." Our young black sailor appeared out of the gloom.

"Then I'm listening, Ab. You did very good work today, son. Saved our lives. Thank you."

Ab sat on the deck. "I think we need to get repairs as soon as possible—right, sir? Get Delilah careened and caulked and re-rigged."

"Yes, Ab, we do. But it's going to be a tough voyage. Key West is at least a week or more of upwind tacking—against that current—assuming we'd even make it that far, which is assuming a lot with this hull and rig. Nassau's closer, but still no less than four days' sail in our condition. We'll have to exit that cut, get back out into the ocean, sail up to the Bimini Islands. Then we'll use the deep-water channel to cross the Great Bahama Bank from there to Northwest Channel. Head onward to Nassau from there."

The young man shook his head. "Begging your pardon, sir, but I can get us through Elbow Bank and Sandy Ridge Shoals to Lowes Sound at Andros Island by tomorrow night, if the wind holds steady and fair enough to send us downwind. We don't have to go north. We can go east from here. Downwind, with less strain on the rig. Once there we can careen the ship and repair her ourselves. They'll help us there."

It was a tempting thought, but it wouldn't work. "Delilah draws six feet, probably more with this water in her, Ab. There's no channel across the banks for her draft south of Gun Cay."

Ab shook his head. "That's what I'm saying, Captain. There is a way, one you outsiders—even folks from other island groups—don't know. Just us Red Bays people know the way."

He was referring to the Bahamian Seminoles, on the isolated upper west coast of Andros. It was how they'd stayed hidden for the previous six decades.

"Sounds good to me, lad," said Rork. "An' if we do go down,

it'll be in shallow water."

"You sure you know the way, Absalom?" I asked, studying him by the dim glow of the binnacle.

"Aye, sir. That's how I got us through that cut in the reef back there—Brown's Cut. My grandfather showed me the way. He was one of the original people that came here from Florida sixty years ago."

Never look a gift horse in the mouth, I've been told. "Then you're just the man to lead us through, son. We weigh anchor at dawn. Now go get some rest until your spell at the pump."

"One more thing, sir. Could we have a service tonight for Mr. Dunbarton? You, being the captain, you could run it. It'd be the Christian thing."

"That we can."

All hands met on deck. The reef still rumbled, but the wind had lightened to twenty knots and I could see stars shining through holes in the clouds. That meant the storm was past—continuing west to Florida and thankfully not south, toward us.

There was no Bible aboard, so I extemporized as best I could to the bedraggled crowd assembled on the after deck. "The Lord giveth and the Lord taketh away. Dear Lord, please take care of the soul of James Dunbarton, a sailorman upon the mighty sea, which rose up and took him away today, to go and dwell with You in Your house, never to feel pain again."

I was about to finish with "Amen" when Rork interjected, his head bent down but his eyes squarely on the cook. "An' dear Lord above, please help us poor sailor lads still alive down here, that we may pull together an' find young Luke, to return him to his ever lovin' mother."

To which all of us, even a reluctant Connerly Blackstone, said "Amen."

Seconds later, following Blackstone's frightened gaze, I noticed that Rork had unsheathed that false left hand, letting his wicked marlinespike reflect the light from the binnacle. He'd kept it covered for the entire voyage until then.

When everyone had gone back below, Rork winked at me.

"Thought it were time to air out me spike. We've a long way to go."

13

A Most Interesting Time

Village of Red Bays
Northern Andros Island
Islands of the Bahamas
Friday, 13 July 1888

Delilah, waterlogged and sluggish, began her journey to Andros Island, a most anxious transit of the Great Bahama Bank. The day was devoid of sunshine, negating the usual practice in the islands of "eyeball navigation" by spotting the shoals and reefs from the colors of the water ahead. The water was a uniform slate gray. We proceeded anyway and subordinated ourselves to the innate judgments of Absalom, who had learned navigation from generations of his family.

Undaunted by the conditions, that young worthy, for whom my respect was growing considerably, set us on an easterly course from the southern point of Brown's Key, one of the two islands Absalom pointed out the morning after the storm. Brown's Cut separated them, the southernmost being called Beach Key. Our departure was attended by much effort in dragging in all that scope of chain and weighing anchor. I'd estimated it would take an hour. In reality, the struggle took three and a half. The damned thing was dug in like the Devil himself was holding it.

The wind had backed southerly, the last of the rain bands visiting us intermittently, further indication the swirling storm was westbound to our north. Conditions remained steady at twenty knots until mid-afternoon, when the strength left it. By our arrival at Andros, it was a normal afternoon sea breeze. Setting the triple-reefed mains'l and the full forestays'l, the only canvas we could support with our diminished rig, Delilah managed to make four or five knots as she barged her way on a broad reach across the banks toward an unseen destination.

Rork and I were quite worried about the stirred-up state of the water—reading the bottom was impossible, even for Absalom. But he used a technique I'd learned as a boy in the New England coaster trades, another way to read the bottom beyond seeing it in clear water. If you know its composition, then you can read it through a leadline.

Rork and Dan took turns in constantly swinging the lead, a cylinder of the namesake metal with tallow slathered in its concave end. With each cast and recovery, they showed Absalom what it had picked up from the bottom, two or three fathoms below us. He examined it closely, then would stare at the sky for a moment, conjuring up memories from the past as to what type bottom should be where on the banks. An Oriental oracle would have nothing on this lad. Scanning the horizon and pouting his mouth, our guide would then solemnly announce a continuation of our course, or a change in direction.

Forty miles along our way, the black Seminole saw weed imbedded in the tallow for the first time. Checking the wind and our decreased ability to sail close to it, he declared we should steer southeast right then, a bit earlier than normal, so that our leeway would compensate and we would be on the correct course for a place called Cross Cay. Mind you, there was no land, nor beacon, in sight. Sailing southeasterly for two hours, we picked up a brownish mud, which made our young navigator smile.

The sun was setting at the time, a diffused gauzy light to the west, and I thought Absalom would recommend anchoring for the night. But no, he said to bear off and steer due east again. Fifteen minutes later, in the final light of dusk, he spied a ridge topped by pine trees on the horizon and nonchalantly stated that we were home. Red Bays, the village of the lost Seminoles, was dead ahead.

We anchored with only a foot under the keel, fully a mile off the beach, the shoals extending that far out on the shallow coast. In the rapidly falling dark there was no light from the village, but Absalom said, "They know we're here. They've known we've been coming for some time. Since noon at least. And they know that a local man has piloted you here. They'll expect him to come ashore directly."

He then assured us of the natives' amity and asked permission to row ashore in the dinghy, suggesting that I accompany him to present our respects and explain our quest. I would return to Delilah in the morning.

Well, truth be told, I wasn't keen on leaving my ship in the dark on a strange shore with a disgruntled cook still aboard, but Rork, touching his false left hand, assured me there would be no mischief in my absence. Delilah's condition was the primary thing, he said, and the sooner we could get some assistance in repairing her, the better. Sound advice, thought I, so off Absalom Bowlegs and I went, into the murky night.

The bugs received us warmly some distance from land. My companion seemed oblivious as he rowed, but I filled the time with slapping the tiny creatures. They were even worse than ours in Florida, a distinction I had previously thought impossible. Feeling the dinghy touch the sand, Absalom and I waded ashore the final hundred yards, then walked up from the beach through a pine and mangrove forest to a group of thatched huts.

"It's a poor but proud community. Mostly spongers and fishermen," my guide said, "and whale oil is expensive." That explained the lack of lamp light.

I sensed we were being watched, though no one was visible. Then a match flared thirty feet ahead and a pile of cordwood, evidently full of pine resin, flared up in a sheet of yellow flame, immediately illuminating a crowd around us. Shouts of glee erupted, directed at Absalom. As his shipmate, I was instantly treated as a dear friend by the populace.

Poor in pecuniary terms they might have been, but I've seen fewer people richer in confidence and conviviality. We were gaily conveyed to the center of the place, the church, where the preacher, a Pastor Newton, who was head man in those parts, gathered all hands for a prayer of thanks at the return of one of their beloved sons.

Afterward, over a dinner of crab, redfish, and pineapple, concocted by the good reverend's wife, I explained to Pastor Newton the purpose of our voyage. In a deep bass voice, he expressed sympathy for the mother, concern for the boy, and admiration for the group of men who had taken on the challenge.

As for the wounded status of the schooner, he said there were shoals nearby where the vessel could be careened. If additional labor was required for the job, he would ask for volunteers, a gracious act that I explained wouldn't be needed. His suggestion of local pine tar pitch and lumber for a new topmast, I did accept, however. Northern Andros Island is full of pinewoods, like Florida, with a fair amount of good lumber for spars and good resin for caulking pitch.

It was quite apparent to me that heavenly intervention was involved in our arrival at this out-of-the-way but intriguing place. I was itching—literally—to learn more about their fascinating heritage, but thought it impolite to delve into that topic right then. Better to wait until my friend Corny, the Smithsonian ethnologist, was ashore. I knew he would be delighted with the opportunity.

And so, after an eventful and exhausting journey that ended in such an unusual burg of Christian tranquility, I yielded to slumber in a corner of the Bowlegs family's hut. In this instance, I gratefully breathed that smudge pot smoke in exchange for a reduced number of mosquitoes and no-see-ums draining my blood.

After rowing myself back to the schooner in the morning—Absalom stayed ashore with his family—I gathered the crew and briefed them on what I'd discovered and what we would then set about doing.

Corny Rathburn was almost delirious with joy. "They really are the descendants of Bowlegs and the Seminoles of the eighteen-twenties? I thought Absalom was jesting, or maybe mistaken about his history. Peter, this is astounding. Clay McCauley should be here to see this. The Institution will want to know of it. Obviously, I need to document everything. When can I go ashore?"

"The ship always comes first, my friend. So we'll we repair the vessel, then attend to academic matters ashore."

Dan Horloft and Rork, being practical seamen, asked where the careenage was and when they could get the material to caulk the hull seams. Cynda quietly asked for someplace to get a decent bath. I wanted to hug her right then, she was so pitiable. Blackstone said nothing, sullenly returning to his galley where I heard pots slamming around. The man was aggravating my patience. It was all I could do to not go down there and slam one of them on his head.

Seeing my reaction to the sounds from below, Rork whispered to me after the others had dispersed, "That scoundrel of a cook's not fancyin' this place at all. Thought we'd get to an island like Bimini, where he could jump ship, like the rodent he is, an' find a cozy hole. Aye, he knows this place ain't for him. Too far away from grog an' women—an' another vessel to ship aboard when he gets hungry. Ooh, that evil sod's not a happy lad right about now, sir. Keep a weather eye out for 'im."

My thoughts exactly.

The work started later that day, which fortunately saw the sun return to our lives after several long days of gloom. First job would be repairing the hull. Delilah was careened at high tide on a bar near Cross Cay, and Ab rowed a dory full of heated pitch and flayed oakum made from shredded palm fronds out to us. He then took Cynda to the village, where she was treated royally by the ladies. Not quite the spa at Monaco, but very welcome by my dear lady, who was a rejuvenated soul when she returned to the ship later that afternoon.

Detailed inspection of the hull by Dan and I revealed that most of the opened seams were along the waterline, below the main and forward shroud chainplates, where the hull planking had proved itself the most flexible in the storm. Dan pronounced it not as bad as he'd feared and suggested we attack the problem areas straight away. Corny, Blackstone, and I worked in knee-deep water at stripping the seams of the old worn-out caulking, while Rork and Dan followed along behind, paying in new caulking and pitch, an art with which they had experience.

The work went steadily, one seam at a time, each at least twenty feet long. Corny pleasantly regaled us with the delight he would have in presenting his paper on the Bahamian Seminoles to the Smithsonian annual meeting. I spoke of the Abaco boat builders I'd met during the war, an enterprising lot who'd made a bundle in gold coin building blockade runners. Dan compared New England and Bahamian ship designs, and Rork provided us with some tales from his homeland, of which he was always in good supply.

Blackstone continued his dour manner—most sea cooks regard themselves as a station above the seamen aboard a ship—barely keeping up with the productivity of the rest of us. At one point, I caught him eyeing me with undisguised contempt while holding the knife in an unfriendly position. That was enough for me.

Heartily ready to settle accounts, I asked, "Is there something you want to say, Blackstone?"

He mumbled, "Nay," and grudgingly returned to his work, which went even slower thereafter. Rork, who saw the exchange, gave me his cocked eyebrow look, meaning "I told you so." I rethought his idea of dumping Blackstone overboard. Unfortunately, that option was no longer viable, as we were now in shallow water.

Later that evening the cook made his move, but in keeping with his culinary skills, he botched the attempt. Having somewhere secured some rotgut on which to screw up his courage, Blackstone cornered me alone in the passageway by Cynda's cabin. He spoke with that unique manner of the white-inhabited islands in the northern Abacos—a mixture of Scots, Irish, and English from the middle seventeen hundreds.

"When're we gettin' to a real port, like Nassau?" he asked, pointedly omitting the customary "sir."

I recoiled from the stench emanating from his mouth. "When we repair the ship, Blackstone. Probably another few days, maybe a week." I tried to move past him, but he wasn't budging.

"A week in this bug-infested hellhole? Gawd, what a mess

we've gotten into."

Interesting assessment. I thought it far better than the other fate we'd faced. "We were lucky to survive that storm, Blackstone. You should be thankful."

"Thankful? For what? This is all your fault, an' so was the end of poor Dunbarton. He warn't lucky, was he? Yer a lousy sailor an' even worse navigator. We'll be lucky, all right, to live till we see Nassau."

It was time to end this charade. "Move aside, Blackstone. And take yourself forward right now, where you can sober yourself up."

He stood there, a leer spreading across his pudgy face. "What, so you an' your trollop can dance the dance o' delight, while the rest of us work our arses off? Not anymore Wa—"

I must be honest here and report that Blackstone never got the chance to complete his sentence, for his ample belly had my right fist rammed into it to the depth of about six inches. As he bent from the blow, the cook pulled his knife in response, but was far too sluggish. I had anticipated that little maneuver on his part.

My right hand was already withdrawn from his gut and swung up above the cook's head as he doubled over. I then brought my right elbow down into the side of his neck where it meets the collarbone. It's an effective move when done quickly with all your weight against a slower opponent, which Blackstone most certainly was that night.

Ordinarily, as Rork well knows, I do not indulge in violence. Nor do I enjoy it. But I will admit that Blackstone's actions and comments, from the very beginning of our voyage, made my efforts in the passageway especially gratifying. The big loudmouth was stunned by that elbow and went down to his knees, falling into the cabin door.

I have discovered over the years that chivalry in combat is an excellent way to die a ridiculous death. When one has an opponent staggered, that is not when kindness is a virtue. Quite the contrary—that is precisely the moment to definitively end all opposition and the ability to mount any future aggression. My right knee drove into the center mass of the cook's gasping face. Blackstone's head snapped backward, knocking a melon-sized hole in the thin veneer of the cabin door. Splinters flew everywhere, and through the dim light of the lamp inside I saw Cynda peering out at me with a horrified expression.

Rork and the others arrived about then. They carried the cook up to the main deck, where the bosun asked if he should lash the miscreant to the foremast. I thought that an eminently sensible thing to do and announced that come dawn, I would adjudicate the matter of the cook's insubordination.

In the final event, there was no verdict the next morning, for the defendant was gone. During the night he absconded, an act I surmised was abetted by young Absalom, who had a sympathetic streak in him. All hands denied collusion, except the young Bahamian, who stood mute. No doubt the prisoner played upon the lad's common nationality as well, though the white cook looked down on darker-skinned peoples.

After reflection, I thought it just as well, for Blackstone had, through the catalyst of his inebriation, already received sufficient physical punishment and humiliation for his defiance during the previous week. I supposed he had run off through the wooded interior of the island to a more trafficked port on the eastern shore, there to ship out for parts unknown. I had no inclination to pursue.

And, as I've already explained, there was the not so little matter of the legality of my authority over Blackstone and the others in the original crew. Sans documentation of the legitimacy of my command, the cook could have eventually made a point in Her

Majesty's colonial court at Nassau that I was actually something of a pirate who had taken over the ship by fraud or guile in Key West, then sailed her through international waters—hence the pirate moniker—to the Bahamas with the ultimate result of one British subject, Dunbarton, dead, and another, Blackstone, maimed.

I inwardly breathed a sigh of relief the whole damned thing was over.

"Good riddance to a bad character," muttered Rork. "An' now, me boyos, let's get the old girl fixed up right and proper-like, so we can get on with what we came to do—discharge the cargo at Nassau an' then get on with findin' young Saunders."

Corny, amused by it all, cheerfully summed up the first leg of our voyage. "What a most interesting time you've provided, Peter. Much more exciting than just trying to catch a tarpon fish. I can't wait till the fellows at the Smithsonian Institution hear of this adventure!"

Even with all the assistance and material furnished us, it had taken far longer than I anticipated to get Delilah in seaworthy shape again. To condense the explanation, the seams needed extra caulking in that summer heat, for the home-made pitch liquefied and drooled out; and the tree selected for the topmast replacement had to be specially chosen and worked by the Red Bays men, who seemed to know every pine tree in their area. So, a week after we started work, we hadn't finished.

During this time, several events came to pass that were of salient interest to us. First, following our initial meeting on the thirteenth of July, Pastor Newton sent word by boat and jungle trail to the surrounding villages of northern Andros that we were searching for a lost boy seaman from the schooner Condor. This I considered to be a polite pro forma, for why would Condor put in at Andros, a poor island with no amenities for tourists? However,

I was wrong. The good parson's efforts yielded results.

On Tuesday, the seventeenth, he received word from a pastor at Morgan's Bluff that a schooner called Condor had been at that place in mid-May. It was a memorable incident for the inhabitants, for the Americans aboard the schooner went ashore and asked about the location of Henry Morgan's lost treasure, offering money for information. Condor stayed a few days, the islanders only too happy to provide paid guides for the rich Americans. After a predictably fruitless hunt, the schooner departed, heading east, probably for Nassau.

Pastor Newton said Morgan's Bluff was a day's sail along a shallow channel around the top of Andros Island. The village was named after the famous pirate, who supposedly buried some of his loot in the area. Outsiders coming in to look for Morgan's treasure were not uncommon. In the two centuries since Morgan may have sailed by those waters, every possible site had been dug up, with no attending success. Only British and American tourists still believed in the legend, but as long as they brought currency, the locals were supportive of their dreams.

I determined to go there at once and follow up on the Condor's visit. Nassau, and the discharge of our cargo, could wait. With detailed inquiries, perhaps some indication of the schooner's fate could be gleaned from the villagers there. I needed to know more about the intent of Condor's voyage through the Bahamian islands in order to predict where they would've gone and why.

Treasure hunting? It sounded right for a pleasure excursion and explained the unusual book my friend DuPont had seen in Kingston's cabin, but I had a growing sense of unease with what I was hearing. Kingston, a veteran sailor of the area, would've known the stories of treasure at Andros were all bunk. Was he a fraud or confidence man, bilking the Yankees with a romantic notion?

14

Of Buccaneers
and Monsters

Morgan's Bluff
Northern Andros Island
Islands of the Bahamas
Friday, 20 July 1888

Defying Rork's superstition yet again, we left Red Bays on a Friday morning. Our departure waited until the dazzling Bahamian sun was high enough to send shafts of light directly down into the aqua and indigo waters, the better to illuminate the way ahead. Absalom stood high up at the foremast's spreaders to peer down into the water.

This passage was far more intricate than the one across the Banks, and it required constant attention. Calling out the positions of brown coral heads and white sandbars from his bird's-eye perch, Absalom led us, slowly short tacking—always an exhausting exercise for a schooner—against an easterly breeze through the maze of coral-studded shoals many miles long. I wouldn't have tried this gauntlet of nature without him.

The night prior to our departure another item of news came in from the island's gossip. No one had heard or seen Blackstone since his flight several nights earlier, and no one aboard *Delilah* had displayed much concern. But on the night of the nineteenth, Absalom reported that Blackstone had been seen in the woods, trudging east along a trail, trying to get to the more inhabited east side of Andros. He was said to look gaunt-faced and frightened and trailed by two Chickchannies.

Absalom looked pretty upset himself as he passed this along to all of us around the dinner table. Our resident ethnologist, Corny, was the only American who knew about Chickchannies. He enlightened the rest of us.

"Ah, yes, the Chickchannies of Andros. They're mythical birdlike beasts who roam the interior of the island and prey upon humans who behave badly to other humans." He thought them, "vaguely related to the legendary Irish leprechauns, since there had been Irish overseers in the days of slave plantations of the islands. The overseers used the myth to frighten and threaten the slaves."

Absalom corrected him. "Oh, no, they're not mythical, Mr. Corny. They're real, and they go after good people too, not just people like Blackstone. Even Christians like me. That's why so few of us walk about in the bush after dark. Blackstone is out there, among them. They have taken him into their midst."

"Perhaps," I said, trying to lighten the mood, "they might've recognized a kindred soul in him and will make him their king."

The islander didn't like my satire and huffed, "This is a bad sign. Just wait and see, Captain. Blackstone will come back to haunt us."

That was greeted with guffaws by me and the others, but then I glanced at Rork. He wasn't laughing. "Aye, boyo. I understand what ye're sayin', Absalom, me friend. I know there's things out there that no man can explain. Seen it in me home county o' Wexford, in the sainted island o' Eire. Let's just hope those Chickchannies hate that poxied cook as much as we do."

Dan Horloft growled, "Primitive nonsense, Rork. You Irish are as full of that foolishness as these natives. Stop being silly."

Absalom Bowlegs wasn't mollified. "You don't know, Mr. Horloft. We're in waters where we may just see the Bosee-Amasee if we can't get through the channel tomorrow and have to anchor for the night. 'Tis a half-man, half-fish, who will rise up and snatch a man off the deck."

"Oh for goodness' sake," Dan retorted. "Absalom, that sounds like some African mumbo-jumbo."

Corny held up a hand. "You're correct, Dan. Obeah, the locals' naturistical beliefs, which includes the Bosee-Amasee, does come from Africa. The slaves brought it over generations ago. The descendants of those slaves still use obeah in bush medicine among these islands. And Rork is also correct. There are some things science—even we at the Smithsonian, can't explain."

The discussion was becoming maudlin, and its effect upon Cynda apparent. She was frightened for her son and didn't need to hear any more about African beasts, mythical or real, in the islands where her son might be waiting for rescue. We needed our spirits and courage lifted, so I made fun of such difficulties.

"All right, let me understand this clearly. In addition to tropical storms, disruptive crew, and a leaking vessel, now I have to think about ancient buccaneers and mythical monsters?'

Put that way, even Absalom laughed, and the tension was relieved, if only for the moment. But I registered that Rork laughed in a perfunctory manner, more to support me than out of true mirth. He was worried.

I always pay attention when Rork is worried.

The anchorage at Morgan's Bluff is over a sandy bottom in three fathoms on the eastern side of a small bay indented into the northeastern end of Andros Island. Protected by a thin peninsula on the east side, the bay is wide open to the north, a perilous place to be when the winter northwesters came through. The peninsula contained the "bluff," more of a knoll to northern eyes. The village was tiny, perhaps fifty people in huts, and clustered under coconut palms on the southeast corner along a white sandy beach. A more substantial community named Nichols lay two miles away, down the island's east coast.

The sun had fallen into its lower altitudes when we made our final tack at Goulding Cay. *Delilah* broad reached south through the deep water behind the menacing reefs that sprawled between Andros Island and the Tongue of the Ocean, a bottomless deep to the east. Soon we were at the village of Morgan's Bluff.

After letting go the anchor and securing the ship, I exhaled all the strains of the intricate passage we'd just completed. Cynda, who had taken on the duties of cook with far more success than her predecessor, served our dinner up on the main deck. It was one of those magical settings that make the tropics famous, a glorious scene that would do credit to a romantic novelist like my friend Pierre Loti.

The thundering surf from the windward beaches, scents of warm moist earth and cooking fires, and a vast panorama of coco palms silhouetted by skyward brush strokes of rose and pale blue to the west, all served to relax everyone aboard *Delilah*. We were safe for the night, with a pleasant meal and trusted companions. The change in temperaments was immediate.

After dinner I took the first anchor watch, while Absalom went ashore in the dinghy to nose around for information and Dan and Corny washed the dishes. Cynda, Rork, and I sat on the afterdeck, saying nothing, just appreciating the sedative vista of awakening stars in the sky where a pitiless sun had broiled a few hours before.

We were about half an hour into the reverie when I heard the splash of oars and Ab calling out from the dark, "Captain! He's coming!"

He surged alongside, tied off the painter, and fairly leaped up to the deck.

"Captain Wake, I just saw Blackstone, in the woods south of the village. I was coming back from visiting a friend when I saw the cook. He came out of the forest onto the road and I know he saw me. I ran as fast as I could to get to the dinghy and row to the ship." Then, eyes wide with fear, he added, "He was heading to the beach here. And he's got something with him!"

Absalom, the sailor who had calmly guided us through a labyrinth of deadly reefs hours earlier, the young man who professed a strong Christian faith, was beside himself in panic.

"What does he have with him?" I asked.

"A ghost. A white ghost. It was big and looked like a man."

Hearing the commotion, the rest of the crew gathered around. Corny inquired in a professorial tone, "Did it have the body of a beast, Ab? Or was it all human?"

"A human, I think. All in white robes. But the hands . . . I think maybe they weren't hands. I think they were claws."

Rork stepped up. "Like a Chickchannie?"

Ab nodded vigorously. Corny rubbed his chin. Dan harrumphed, echoing my sentiments. Cynda, who heretofore had remained silent in discussions on legendary island creatures, proposed, "Maybe it's one of those native monsters, and they are guarding the treasure of the buccaneers."

Whereupon Rork, my dearest friend in the world, who at times can be exasperating with his superstitious Gaelic gullibility, wagged his head thoughtfully. "Exactly me own thoughts, Cynda," he intoned. "Aye, mark me words an' best beware. There're things, ancient things, happenin' here we don't understand . . ."

Intelligent readers of this account will agree that the issue had progressed beyond credence by this point. I determined to end such harebrained ideas right then and there, before it got worse.

"Very well, I've heard enough of this. Everyone get hold of yourselves, right now. We'll arm those men standing anchor watch tonight with a cutlass and belaying pin—" I dared not give them one of my firearms, lest they'd shoot some innocent person while in the grip of imagined terror. "—with orders to sound the ship's bell should they see anyone approaching in the dark. Then we'll all muster aft and repel whoever, or whatever, comes alongside. And may I remind all hands that this is a Christian ship visiting a crown colony of Her Majesty Queen Victoria, not some barge of terrified paganistic fools in the middle of the Congo River."

I meant to chastise them out of their trepidation, but they merely bobbed their heads in acknowledgment of orders. Except for Dan, I could see that they were still worried, which I deemed simply stupid. A week in the islands and my crew was already going native, falling under the sway of crazy local beliefs.

Little did I know then just how far we would *all* eventually descend into the mysteries of ancient Africa.

15
Curious Intelligence

Morgan's Bluff
Andros Island
Islands of the Bahamas
Saturday, 21 July 1888

The night yielded no attack by beast, human, or spirit, and the next morning saw me ashore at the district office in Nichols. I was there to press inquiries about *Condor* to the officialdom of the island. Rork and Absalom accompanied me on the walk, while Dan and Cynda stayed aboard, lounging under the deck awnings. Corny roamed the village of Morgan's Bluff. Ostensibly he was noting the cultural structure, as he did at Red Bays, but I suspected there may have been a bit of treasure hunting involved too. In spite of his scientific brain, he was a quixotic fellow at heart.

At Nichol's government house, a ramshackle cottage that had seen far better days, we learned that the man in charge of northern Andros Island was in that day, a rare good fortune. Sitting on the verandah were a dozen residents waiting for the district commissioner, none of whom looked very happy at seeing my arrival, since they knew that we would be taken care of first, a consequence of my skin's color. They weren't wrong on that either, for as soon as we took our place to wait outside, we were soon ushered within. Absalom insisted on remaining outside with his fellow islanders.

It turned out the commissioner and magistrate, a former sea captain named Ceruti, knew of our presence at Andros, and also of the altercation with the cook. With Ceruti was a Mr. Bode, a narrow-eyed sponge broker from Golden Cay and friend of the commissioner. Both were dressed informally. Ceruti greeted us cordially and offered Rork and me chairs arranged around a table covered with paperwork, where Bode was already seated.

My intention was to inquire as to the onward destination of the *Condor*, but Ceruti wasted no time in opening the conversation himself.

"Captain Wake, I have some criminal complaints against you—five to be exact—filed by the cook, one Connerly Blackstone, of the schooner *Delilah*."

Hmm. As has been described, this development was not totally unexpected by me, though it did unfold faster than anticipated. I judged it a good time to assume the mantel of captain's authority.

"And what do these complaints consist of?"

Ceruti picked up a lengthy document of three pages and regarded me carefully.

"Mr. Blackstone charges first, that you are guilty of theft, for being illegally in command of said schooner *Delilah*, which sails under the registry and protection of Her Majesty, our gracious Queen Victoria, and that you have no waiver of succession from the previous master and no authority from the vessel's owners in England.

"Secondly, he charges you with gross professional negligence in navigation and seamanship for placing said vessel in peril at the reef south of Bimini. Thirdly, he charges you with manslaughter for the death of the mate, a Mr. Dunbarton, whom you placed in mortal jeopardy at that same location and who succumbed from that jeopardy.

"Fourthly, he charges you with criminal aggravated assault upon his person, as a result of which he is crippled for life and unable to practice his profession of . . . *chef*.

"And lastly, he charges you with false imprisonment by lashing him to the mast of the said vessel in a humiliating and painful manner."

Ceruti raised an eyebrow and looked over at me. "Any comments, sir?"

The trade winds outside were picking up for the day, making the palm fronds swish and the surf line rumble, but inside that room it was deathly quiet as I spoke.

"Commissioner, those are the rantings of an incompetent seaman masquerading as a cook, who was more fond of drink than work and who constantly shirked his duty and degraded the efficiency of the crew by derogatory rumor mongering. When he provoked the altercation between us, I controlled my temper and mitigated my efforts at self-defense, allowing him to escape his just rewards with only the most superficial mementos of the occasion. I'm beginning to reevaluate that decision."

Ceruti nodded noncommittally. "Yes, well, you understand, Captain Wake, that I must take such charges seriously."

"I do, sir."

"And investigate them thoroughly."

"I do, sir."

He cleared his throat, then spoke slowly. "And I am sure you will appreciate that an investigation of this magnitude will consume . . . more than the usual amount of time . . . in order for me to ascertain whether the matter should be judged here, or remanded to the Queen's Court in Nassau."

There was something in his tone that told me to stay silent. I nodded respectfully.

"Therefore," he continued, "I must advise you that for the

aforementioned reasons this case may linger in litigation for some while. Even *after* you have departed this port."

Ceruti laid the document down and gazed at us. Rork's boot nudged mine under the table, but I already understood the point of the statement. The commissioner, a former ship's master, agreed with my view of the issue, but had to follow form for appearance's sake. In the meantime, we were being allowed to leave—or escape, to use a more accurate term.

"I strongly disagree with Blackstone's version and intend to lodge a civil suit for defamation of my character should he persist, sir. In the interim, I and my crew stand ready to assist you in any manner."

"Very good, Captain Wake."

"Sir, if I may? I have some questions about a schooner that passed through here in May—*Condor* is her name The boy seaman on her is the son of the lady aboard *Delilah*. *Condor* and her people are missing and presumed dead. We are searching for them, for the lady is convinced her son is alive. Do you have any information about that schooner, sir?"

He rubbed his chin while thinking. "*Condor*, you say? Yes, I remember hearing of her. Nothing of a specific nature. Only that she was here at Andros, anchored where you are, and something of a yacht, I believe. No cargo, only passengers. I wasn't here at the time, but upon my return I was told that her passengers secured the services of local men to act as guides on an exploration for Morgan's treasure. The inevitable happened and they left for Nassau empty-handed."

"Nassau? What about the captain, crew, or passengers? Any news of them, sir?"

"No. They didn't have any reason to come to this office's attention, Captain Wake. Most of our visitors don't."

A not so veiled reference to me.

He went on. "And I fear that your continued presence at this place will only make your situation, and my official position, more *uncomfortable*, if you understand my meaning."

Rork's boot again. He was getting on my nerves with the boot nudging. I replied to Ceruti, "Understood very well, sir. There doesn't appear to be a reason to delay our departure then. We are anxious to find young Luke, so we'll be under way tomorrow for Nassau, if the wind serves."

"An excellent decision, Captain Wake. But I think it won't. This easterly wind usually holds for a few days."

"Then as soon as it does, sir."

Bode was quiet until this point, when he mused aloud, "Amazing, is it not, Commissioner? The few yachting parties who visit us don't typically excite this much attention around here. They come, they go, and nobody cares—except this one aboard *Condor*. It surely has received some rather . . . diverse . . . interest lately."

Ceruti shot him a severe look, which raised my curiosity. Had someone else inquired about *Condor*? I turned to the commissioner's friend. "Mr. Bode, you have me at a disadvantage, sir. What interest are you speaking of?"

Ceruti pursed his lips as Bode answered. "Oh, some French fellow was here a week ago, asking the same questions. Came over on the mail boat from Nassau. It's well after the tourist season at Nassau, so naturally I thought he was an investor, here about Chamberlain's planned sisal plantation. That's beginning to attract some notice. Then I worried that he was a new sponge concern's envoy, but it turned out I was wrong on both accounts. He wasn't here for trade purposes at all, but to ask about some silly tourists chasing down hidden gold a couple of months ago. The commissioner wasn't here at the time, but I was, so the Frenchman came to me."

The commissioner's tone was dismissive. "Bode, really, we don't need this sort of thing."

His friend wasn't daunted. "Oh, don't worry, Number One. This tourist stuff isn't going to affect the sisal enterprise and you know it. Chamberlain will still bring his money here."

"Who?" I asked, totally confused now.

Ceruti answered. "Joseph Chamberlain, of Her Majesty's foreign office, a diplomacy fellow back home in England. He is setting up a large sisal plantation here, which everyone over the age of three knows about. The island could use the investment. It will bring employment, since the sponging has been off lately. But we do *not* need foreign inquiries into unexplained disappearances of tourists. Bad image for us. I worry that investors might be deterred."

I returned my attention to Bode. "What did the Frenchman ask?"

"He mainly wanted to know if there were any Russians on *Condor*. Kept asking about that in various ways. *Russians?* At Andros Island? Can you imagine? Well, there weren't any that we knew about. Just a typical mongrel crew from around the various islands and a Yankee captain. Plus, some New York City swells, out for a lark. Pretty innocent, actually."

Innocent? I wondered. "Where was the Frenchman from, sir? Why was he asking about Russians?"

"I don't know where he was from. France, I suppose. Passed himself off as a potential charterer, checking out the schooner— what type of skipper, crew, clientele, that sort of thing. But mainly he was interested in the Russian thing. Seemed quite odd. Not your usual charter client at all. Left the next day on the mail boat."

Odd, indeed. Was the 'O' in the letter to Kingston from Nassau referring to the Frenchman? Or did 'O' refer to this Russian connection? Or perhaps W, the sender of the letter, was the Frenchman?

"What was his name? His description?"

"Let me see . . . It was one of those long French names that they garble while saying. You know how they are. No, I cannot recall it. But wait! I do remember his first name—it was Pierre. Maybe forty years old, moneyed, smooth talker. Fluent in English.

Trim moustache and thin goatee, long hair. Debonair sort of Frenchman. I think he mentioned something about Paris, now that I think of it."

"And he headed back to Nassau? When was this?"

He grinned, knowing he was intriguing me and aggravating Ceruti. "About the time you arrived at Red Bays. Curious, ain't it?"

Ceruti wasn't done, though. He stood, the signal for us to exit, and issued his parting shot. "Much ado about nothing. We have no information about your missing ship and crew, sir. I wish you fair weather for your voyage. And by the way, what is your *regular* profession, Mr. Wake? You don't seem the typical schooner master."

He knew. I could tell by his eyes, which had grown colder. Blackstone probably told him. "I'm a U.S. naval officer, on leave."

Ceruti spoke deliberately, savoring each word. "*Really?* Well, I do hope you aren't receiving any remuneration for your services as master of *Delilah*. We don't allow foreign naval officers to operate on a private or a governmental basis within the colony without Crown permission. Especially when out of uniform. Gives a bad impression, you know. Makes government people nervous."

Touché. He was calling me a spy.

"I'm certainly not doing this for pay, sir. I am on holiday, helping the lady find her son. I am *not* operating in my professional capacity."

"I see," said the commissioner.

Rork coughed and moved his chair back, preparing to stand.

I stood first and said, "Thank you for the conversation, gentlemen. We won't be a bother to you anymore."

Absalom joined us for the walk back to Morgan's Bluff. As Rork and I discussed the intelligence we'd just obtained, the islander, clearly disturbed, asked, "Captain, excuse me, sir. Did the cook make a charge on you?"

"Yes, he did, Absalom. Several, in fact."

"I knew it. I should have left him tied up that night, but I let him go. He promised he would just go home to Abaco. I believed him. I am sorry, sir."

"I understand, Absalom. Don't worry about it. We can handle the likes of him."

Rork cut in. "Aye, lad. Not to worry 'bout that devil. At least *he*'s the devil we know. There's other things stewin' now." He shook his head pensively. "Methinks we're into somethin' far worse with that boy on board *Condor*. Froggie Frenchmen involved? Rooskies? I don't fathom that a bit. Oy, an' now me blasted foot's actin' up, sir—an' you know what *that* means."

I did, indeed. Rork's superstitions weren't limited to bizarre fables from local tales. His right foot was a weather vane for impending strife. And as idiotic as it sounds to our modern nineteenth-century minds, whenever my friend's foot acted up, we unfailingly would soon find ourselves immersed in trouble. Perilous trouble. It had happened on four continents.

I hate it when Rork says his foot hurts.

16

Nassau

Nassau
New Providence Island
Islands of the Bahamas
Tuesday, 31 July 1888

We gained our freedom from Morgan's Bluff on the thirtieth day of July. The strong easterlies at last abated and swung to the south southeast point of the compass. An overnight broad reach allowed us to fetch the western point of New Providence Island, where the schooner close-reached along the reef-bound northern coast as the sun rose over the central hills.

Twenty-five very long days after departing Key West for Nassau, we arrived at our destination. Normally that journey— without doldrums, hurricanes, or sinking vessels—would've taken four or five days. In the late afternoon our tired crew sailed the schooner between the old lighthouse on Hog Cay and the sprawl of Fort Charlotte on the main island. We anchored *Delilah* among other vessels in transit off Vendue Wharf, at the foot of George Street, and afterward all aboard sighed with relief. Our repairs to hull and rig had held.

Nassau is a delightful little place, pleasant to the eye and nose. Filled with native island boats and ocean steamers, the water is a luminescent jade green. You can see the bottom thirty feet down. From the harbor front, a whitewashed and pastel-painted town spreads up a gentle slope to the ninety-foot-high ridge dominating the island. Here and there church spires poke up, none higher than the Anglican cathedral's squared-off tower. A cornucopia of fruit trees fills the gardens, while almond, cork, palm, and mahogany trees give shade along the streets. And everywhere there are flowers: roses, hibiscus, bougainvillea, gardenia, jasmine—each scenting the air.

Above it all stands the white-columned, pink-walled, two-storied governor's mansion known as Government House, bastion of British imperial authority and justice in the Bahamas. Its solemn position on the highest part of the ridgeline ensures that every day, every person in Nassau is reminded about who is in charge. From our anchorage, we had an impressive view straight up George Street to the statue of Columbus and lawn of the governor's mansion. The scenery was familiar to me, for I remembered Nassau well from the war, when it was an openly pro-Rebel port, barely civil to visiting U.S. Navy warships.

Preparation for liberty in the town was the happy focus of the crew, who began taking great pains to improve their appearance for the occasion. Their task was to ask around the sailors' haunts for information on *Condor*, as they had at Key West. I could not join in that effort, for I had other duties to perform ashore. Accordingly, I took the dinghy in first and reported our appearance to the port captain's office in Vendue House. Rork went with me and struck out on his chore while I attended to my own.

After an hour of searching in the heat, I located the shipping broker at a nondescript hovel in an alley off the eastern portion of Bay Street. The broker, a Brit too long in the islands, was visibly disconcerted by the peculiar manner in which I was in command of *Delilah*. I ignored his bad attitude and informed him that the next day we would be ready to offload his consignment. One of those sorts who are devoted to a comfortably lackadaisical routine, he only laughed at me in reply.

I thought that a bit much. Upon my protesting his demeanor, he retorted, "Oh, mind your knickers. I'll get to your schooner when I find some boys to offload her and the space to store the shipment securely, Captain. And *that* might take a couple of weeks, so relax. This is the bloody Bahamas, get used to it."

This development was totally unacceptable. I'd planned on a twenty-four-hour stay in Nassau. "No," said I. "If it's not properly unloaded by three p.m. tomorrow, sir—then it will be unloaded across the harbor, onto the beach at Hog Island, by my crew and at *your* financial peril. We have endured storm, death, and contrary winds and have still delivered the cargo intact to this port. Our responsibilities end tomorrow at three o'clock."

"Tomorrow is Emancipation Day, Yank," he retorted smugly. "Nobody, *especially* the blackies, works on Emancipation Day."

Damn. I'd forgotten about the biggest holiday in the Bahamas outside of Christmas. It commemorated the freeing of the slaves at midnight on 31 July 1834 and was celebrated annually across the Bahamas on the first day of August. Our stay would be stretched.

"Very well, the day *after* tomorrow at three p.m. then. Unload it yourself or hope it stays unmolested at Hog Island Beach. Either way, it's yours at that point. I will so notify the ship's owner by correspondence that he should expect your payment draft immediately."

I didn't wait for further reply from the haughty little functionary and left him sitting there at his table, slack-jawed and dumbfounded as I strode out. Such is the way to deal with bureaucrats of the world—though it is difficult to resist shooting them as they smirk.

While I was busy finding and correcting the recalcitrant shipper, Rork had been on a quieter type of assignment: make contact with our man in Nassau, the one who had assisted in getting Paloma to Saint Augustine. We would meet later for a drink and conversation, Rork reported. I thought perhaps our contact might be able to shed some light on the peculiar information we were gathering along our path. Particularly this 'O' and 'W' business out of Nassau.

Rork agreed, for the man was in a position that enabled him to know things, and to also get things done. Our occupation requires that we assemble a network of such men and women in various ports around the world.

Robert Mason, an importer, property broker, and semi-retired insurance man from Columbus, Ohio, was our man in Nassau. He knew my profession and helped me out of nationalistic pride, along with a nominal fee. A former U.S. Navy volunteer officer during the war, he'd moved to Nassau for his health in 1880. Mason had been my contact in the Bahamas for five years and was rather successful in providing subtle routes in and out of nearby Cuba for Rork and me, and some of our friends. In addition to knowing how to get things done, Mason also had that rarest of abilities—knowing how to keep his mouth shut.

Rork, Mason, and I met at the old blockade-runner lair of the Royal Victoria Hotel, just east of Government House on Hill Street. The Victoria is a four-story ornate lodge that caters to winter tourism at Nassau, including the most elite of the elite of London and New York. The barroom was open for the local trade but empty of patrons, the tourist months being long over.

It was glaringly hot outside and stuffy inside, with an ambience of neglected importance, like a theater diva backstage caught without her rouge and powders. In wintertime the place was different. Victoria's bar would be filled with the buzzing chatter of New York City's well-dressed industrial barons, escaping the arctic air up north with rum punches and gin flips in the comparatively sultry air of Nassau's finest hotel.

During the Civil War, millions in British pounds sterling, Spanish gold, and Confederate cotton were exchanged during genteel haggling in that very bar. Blockade running made Nassau rich. Tourism in recent years had had a similar effect upon the place, but nowadays, the barons discussed bank transfers regarding railroads, iron, and coal.

An afternoon thunderstorm was kicking up some wind outside, and a merciful gust came through the verandah doors as I signaled for another round from the lethargic barman. I'd already explained to Mason our current off-duty mission during the first round. We'd also covered some items regarding Paloma. Mason had an ongoing role to play in that situation: he facilitated communications with one of my operatives in Havana.

I turned to the subject at hand and asked Mason if he knew of a Captain Kingston and a schooner named the *Condor*.

"Yes, I remember that name of the ship. She was in awhile ago for supplies. Must've been the middle of May, I think. Ran into some of her passengers ashore. Right here, as a matter of fact, in this bar. I was here with one of the colonial office men, discussing American tariffs. Only other people here were *Condor*'s passengers. We got to talking with them. They were business fellows down from New York City. Playing tourist in the islands, as I recall. Spent two or three nights here in the hotel while their boat was being provisioned. Left the hotel afterward."

"Did you see a boy with them? Ship's boy?"

"Never saw any of the crew."

"Did the businessmen say where they were heading from here?"

"They talked about heading south from here. But not all of them. Three were returning home to New York on the next steamer out of Nassau. Had enough of the tropics, they said. The heat down here was getting to them. Only one of them was heading off with the schooner, to the south. Had a bit of a row about it among them. The three were angry their friend wasn't joining them and going home. Said he was being a foolish old man, off on a wild goose chase. Called him 'childish,' as I recollect. That got his dander up."

"Where was this lone fellow headed?"

"Mayaguana, maybe. No, it was Great Iguana. Or was it Exuma? Oh hell, Peter, I'm not really sure, except it was south of here." He shook his head. "Someplace with treasure."

"Treasure?"

"Well, rumors of treasure."

"Anything strange about them?"

"No, they were like any other tourists. Except for the time of year. We don't get tourists in May."

"Did they describe their main reason for being in the Bahamas?"

"Fishing and treasure hunting. They hadn't found much of the former and none of the latter. Put away a fair amount of spirits that day. Enjoyed the rum and even paid for mine, too. I told them about some of the legends I've heard about pirate gold. The man heading south was very interested in those. Oh, I wish I had a greenback for every Yankee that came down here for pirate gold."

"Do you know Captain Kingston?"

"Vaguely. Comes into port maybe three times a year with cargo. Uncommon name for his vessel—*Condor*. Big bird from South America, I think."

"Is he shady?"

"Not that I know of, but he could be. A lot of the skippers carry stuff on the side, as you know."

Yes, I did. Sometimes they did it for Mason and me.

"Are there any Frenchmen around here, Robert? A Frenchman was in Morgan's Bluff a couple of weeks ago, asking about *Condor*.

Came from Nassau on the mail boat. Sophisticated, moneyed kind of man. Middle-aged. Pierre somebody. He was asking the locals about the passengers aboard *Condor*."

"Well, yes, there is one fellow in town from France. Paris, I believe. I met him at one of the governor's social affairs. Don't remember the name. Slick sort of Frenchy, very polished, upper class. Arrived not long ago—early July—on the packet steamer from London. Has enough money to get immediately known to the society crowd here and invited to the various parties. Of course, there aren't many in the summer. In fact, I think he's still around. Not sure where, though. Might be here at the Victoria, actually."

"I want to meet him."

Mason paused, thinking. "I imagine he'll be at the Emancipation Day parade tomorrow afternoon, and at the celebration ball tomorrow night at Government House. It's a full day, and evening, of social events."

"Are you going?"

"Yes. I always go." He shrugged. "It's expected."

"Can you get me invited to the events the Frenchman will be at?"

"As a U.S. naval officer? Yes. As *Delilah's* schooner captain? No. Schooner skippers don't frequent those circles."

I didn't have a uniform aboard, but I did bring a suit. A plain suit, but it would have to do. "It'll have to be something else, Robert. I don't have a uniform with me and I'm not here in an official capacity. Besides, something tells me it's better if the Frenchman doesn't know about my profession, or about us looking for *Condor*."

"Want to be a rich New Yorker?"

I laughed at that. "No, I can't pull that off. Just make me out to be an American businessman from somewhere boring, like New Hampshire, looking around the Bahamas for investments. Tell them I heard about Chamberlain's new endeavor in Andros and I'm thinking of starting one on Grand Bahama Island. And please include Mrs. Saunders in the invitation, if you would. She can be visiting to ascertain if a stay in the Bahamas can help her ailing father. I'll be her escort."

I'd included Cynda in an effort to displace her somewhat maudlin demeanor since our arrival at Nassau with some social stimulation—that, and the fact that I thought her manipulative skills might assist in obtaining information useful to our endeavor.

Mason stood. "Very well, Peter. If I leave now, I can get to the colonial secretary's office before they close and obtain official invitations for you and Mrs. Saunders. We'll meet at the corner of the Anglican cathedral at George and King streets tomorrow, just before noon. A parade at noon starts the day's events, with the dignitaries viewing the show on King Street. At two p.m. there is a service at the cathedral. At four p.m. there is the presentation of cards up the hill, at Government House. At six comes dinner and at seven-thirty there is the ball. That will end at ten o'clock. You'll have several hours to gauge and meet the man."

"Thank you, and please find out all you can about the Frenchman, and about Captain Kingston. Oh! And by the way, do you know of any Russians around here?"

"*Russians?*" Mason looked quizzically at me. "No, Peter. There aren't any Russians around these parts."

The letter came to mind. 'W' would be a common initial, but the other wouldn't. "Know anyone who just arrived here with a surname starting with an 'O'?"

"Sound's Irish. Fella named O'Connally runs an iron shop out on the east end of town. But he's been here for years."

"No, that wouldn't be it. Never mind."

17
Emancipation Day

Christ Church Cathedral
King and George streets
Nassau, Bahamas
Wednesday, 1 August 1888

The center of Nassau transformed overnight. The sleepy languid atmosphere of the prior evening, where no more than two dozen people were on the streets, had become a bustling accumulation of thousands of black residents that filled every thoroughfare. From the deck of our vessel we watched and listened to brass bands, African drums, patois chants, and wildly euphoric dancing. The festive environment gained intensity as the morning progressed—an amazing exhibition of raw, uninhibited, exotic jubilance. It was impossible to hear and see it and not have your spirits lifted.

At eleven o'clock, all hands from *Delilah* went ashore for the festivities—after I hired a sober watchman to stay aboard—and elbowed our way up George Street to the cathedral. The day's breeze on the harbor didn't circulate in the center of Nassau, and the white-washed buildings created an intense ovenlike effect. Every tree had people bunched in its shade. It was beastly hot.

The white population was gathered near the entrance, in their resplendent finery in spite of the heat. I got the distinct impression that most of them couldn't have cared less about the emancipation of their colored fellow islanders. Barely tolerating the noise and seething masses, they attended the event because of societal obligations. My companions and I were regarded with open curiosity by everyone—we were strangers visiting town in August.

As Mason handed me Cynda's and my invitations to the events for later on, a trumpet called our attention to the street. The passionately raucous native crowd around us silenced immediately and craned their heads around to peer west, down the street. The parade, commemorating the forty-forth anniversary of emancipation, was about to start. It was led by the troops of Her Britannic Majesty, Queen Victoria, but you would be hard pressed to know that by their uniforms.

Mason explained. "Not your typical redcoats, are they? The Second West India Regiment is made up of soldiers recruited in western Africa, mostly from the equatorial Gulf of Guinea, from the Gold Coast to the Congo. They have no affiliation to the people of the places they are stationed—the Bahamas, Antigua, Barbados, and Jamaica.

"Their uniforms are a bit different," he said with a grin. "The French African Zouave influence is apparent, with the white turban, blue pantaloons, and white leggings. The short red open tunic is the only British effect, along with the Enfield rifles, of course."

"They're huge," offered Corny.

"Yes, they are recruited for their intimidating size."

"Their headquarters is where?" I asked.

"Regimental headquarters is in Jamaica. There's only a company of about eighty men stationed here at Fort Charlotte.

They're from the Third Battalion at Jamaica. Junior officers are billeted at Dunmore House and the senior man is at Graycliff House, next to the governor's mansion."

"And the officers, what of them?" I asked as the company marched past us, arms swinging high in the British tradition. Six young white men in regular army khaki, subalterns and lieutenants, were ranged across the front of the company. In front of the junior officers strode a tall white man in the Zouave uniform, like that of the enlisted men.

"The officers are Brits from the regular regiments. They are seconded for two or three years to the West India outfits. The commanding officer here in Nassau is that fellow in front, Major Rupert Teignholder. He is, by all accounts, an odd duck. Prefers to wear the exotic Zouave rig for ceremonial occasions. Solidarity with the troops, I imagine."

"These lads have fightin' experience?" asked Rork.

Mason nodded. "The men you see here fought last year at Sierra Leon, in west Africa. Accounted themselves well in quite adverse conditions, according to the press. Teignholder led them. This unit's only been at Nassau for six months."

Next came a small military band. Behind it, the line, composed of civilian groups in their best attire, stretched for half a mile. Mason explained the groups represented the major islands in the archipelago, and the "friendly societies" of New Providence. A friendly society was the traditional African tribal association formed for mutual benefit during slave times and carried on into modern society. The most well-known was the Grantstown Friendly Society, which received a substantial cheer from the onlookers.

Mason leaned close to me and pointed to a distinguished-looking black man marching in the procession. "There's Mr. David Patton. He runs the Union Livery stables on Bay Street and knows everything that happens on the waterfront. I asked him early this morning about *Condor* and Captain Kingston. He knows Kingston. Said Kingston acted queerly the last time here.

Usually he's drunk and loud. This time he was quiet and guarded. Patton thought he might be up to something illegal. Smuggling, maybe in or out of the Spanish islands."

Smuggling? With tourists aboard? Hmm, well, the more I thought about that, the more it seemed feasible. Businessmen passengers would provide a perfect veneer of respectability. What would he smuggle? Most smugglers in the West Indies carried rum, fancy goods, or people past the customs officials. Perhaps I had completely misunderstood. Possibly *Condor's* passengers weren't businessmen from New York City.

A tug from Cynda brought me back to the scene around us. Each civic group had solemn-faced elders in front, carrying the Union Jack. They were followed by a younger set, who danced slowly as they played various instruments, most of them African in origin. In contrast to the jubilation of the morning, the procession was more akin to a coronation. Measured, serious, proud.

Once the parade had ended, we entered the Anglican house of worship, the largest church in the Bahamas. Rork, as is his preference, stayed outside. Christ Church Cathedral's bells rang two o'clock as we sat down five pews back from the front. Above us was a shadowy dark wooden ceiling—in stark contrast to the white walls and pillars. Stained-glass windows, brightly illuminated by the sun, surrounded us.

The service was a high mass of the Episcopal Church, a two-hour ritual with which I was familiar, having grown up in that denomination in New England. The impressive pageantry was made seemingly much longer, however, by the overheated condition of the sanctuary, densely jammed with bodies. Mason scanned the assembly but said the Frenchman wasn't there, suggesting that perhaps the man was Catholic.

A Reverend Swann presided and preached a sermon on "Providing things honest in the sight of all men." The meaning of that was lost on me, but then the rising temperature and odor probably interfered with my intellect. Little paper fans flitted like butterflies in the hands of the ladies, who sat there and baked, glistening with perspiration. The gentlemen's suits formed dark patches, spreading larger as the reverend went on, confirming I was not alone in my misery.

Mason, like the other upper-society people, was apparently unbothered by it all and sat there as if nothing untoward was occurring. I found their serene behavior extraordinary and was myself sopping wet and rather ill-tempered when we emerged into the glaring sun for the next social obligation of the day.

Rork and the others from *Delilah* were off to their own devices for the rest of the afternoon as Cynda, Mason, and I joined a collection of the privileged on the walk up the hill along the shady side of George Street. We passed through the gates to the governor's grounds and up the steps to the Columbus statue, then across the lawn to the large portico of Government House where an honor guard of soldiers awaited. The view of the town below was nothing short of beautiful, but brief, as the line of guests continued their pace inside.

Not anticipating any of this sort of thing back at Patricio Island, I naturally had no *carte visite* for official presentation to the governor's staff. This breech of protocol was glossed over by the fact that Cynda and I did have invitations. Engraved ones, I might add; Mason did have good connections. Of course, other than Mason, I knew not a soul among the locals assembled for the annual audience with the man who ruled Her Majesty's Crown Colony of the Bahamas—one Sir Ambrose Shea.

According to Mason, Shea was a seventy-three-year-old career politician and administrator who had done good work in his native Newfoundland. Knighted in 1883, he was given the Bahamian governorship in October of 1887 by the queen.

Sir Ambrose had the respect and admiration of the islanders, both black and white, and was a courtly specimen of the old school of British etiquette. Meeting me in the receiving line, he barely shook my hand and paused long enough to say, "Welcome," before turning to the next person. He was noticeably more cordial to Cynda, ahead of me, but then again, what man isn't? Shea may have been old, but he certainly was not dead.

Mason explained later that like most Canadians from the Atlantic coast, Shea was more than a bit negatively influenced by the fishing dispute of the previous year. It had erupted into rather bellicose talk between the United States and Great Britain, protector of Canada. I had some inside knowledge of that sad affair, as ONI had been given the task of ascertaining Canadian defenses during the crisis. My commanding officer, Commodore Walker, led a personal covert reconnaissance of the Royal Navy base at Halifax. Not one of our prouder national moments, in my opinion.

But I have regrettably digressed and must now return to the tête-à-tête that ensued within the elegant confines of the ballroom, where the governor's guests had settled after enduring the receiving line. Cynda and I met various personages, including the attorney general, the chief justice, the postmaster, and the chief inspector of police. Smiling and saying inane things to people who couldn't care less—especially in a hot room while wearing a stifling collar, tie, and coat—is my idea of slow torture.

Cynda, however, was made of sterner stuff. With admirable prowess, she targeted her wiles on the chief inspector, asking him about summer tourists in the islands.

I began moving toward the table of chilled fruit juices, hoping to discover a small supply of rum and invigorate the day, when Mason deftly steered me away. With a sly grin, he walked me to the far end of the room and introduced me to Pierre Jean Roche.

The Frenchman.

Roche was tall, thin, and handsome, in his late thirties to early forties, with long dark wavy hair. Below prominent cheekbones and a strong nose, he had one of those pointed goatees and a moustache that was perfectly trimmed. His smile seemed genuine. His handshake indicated resolve. Mason spoke to him in French, and I noted that Roche's reply was in the classical form, devoid of slang or contraction. Upper-class, refined. A graduate of one of the polytechnic institutes, I guessed. Possibly with some military experience, gauging by his stature. He was dressed in a simple but well-tailored satin dinner suit. Pierre Jean Roche was the epitome of a European gentleman, a modern Frenchman of the Third Republic.

But it was his eyes that one's attention was immediately drawn toward. They were narrow, almost oval, and absolutely black, like drops of shiny onyx—beautiful and frightening at the same time. Roche had the habit, probably cultivated over time, of turning them on you and not blinking. Intense. Waiting for your reaction. And most alarmingly, I could not discern any emotion in them.

Mason departed, hailing a friend and discreetly leaving Roche and me in the corner alone. I decided to forgo insulting the man with my mangled French and spoke English.

"Good to meet you, sir. I've heard you are the only Frenchman in Nassau. I regret to say my French is not fit for public intercourse, much less for this august soirée, and so I must beg your pardon and speak English."

He smiled slightly. "And I must ask for your forgiveness about the state of my English. It should be better, but I fear it is lacking substance."

"What brings you to Nassau, sir?"

The eyes surveyed me for a moment. "Tourist, seeking the tropics. I am here with some friends, but only temporarily. We are en route to the south, to the Caribbean proper. And why are you here, sir?"

I glanced over and saw Cynda engaged in conversation with a clergyman. I continued with Roche, very aware that he was evaluating me. This would require, as the French would say, a certain *finesse*.

"Me? I'm here looking for business endeavors that have potential for investment." Remembering what the *Condor's* passengers told Mason, I added, "And what a coincidence, I'll be heading south, also. To the southern islands of the Bahamas. Tell me, Mr. Roche, have you seen much of the Bahamas?"

"No, I have only been in Nassau. I will be leaving soon."

Only Nassau, eh? Hmm. Lie number one. "And where in the Caribbean are you headed?"

The smile again, this time not so friendly. "I do not know, yet, Mr. Wake. It is a decision I will make this week though. There are several possibilities among the French-speaking islands."

I looked him in the right eye and said, "You could try Kingston, over in Jamaica. I hear there are unique birds there. Condors."

There was a split-second delay as he weighed my *double-entendre* before he answered. "You do not appear to me as merely a businessman, Mr. Wake. I observed you during the parade today. You stood like a soldier when the British national flags passed by. Now you speak obliquely, like a diplomat. An unusual combination of behavior."

The smile again. This time definitely not genuine. "If you will kindly forgive me, Mr. Wake, I must go. I see that there are several ladies present who are in need of some refreshment. We French have a duty to assist whenever we see such a tragedy occur."

With that he was gone. I was convinced we would meet again.

Dinner was predictably boring, with a speech by the governor pontificating about the equality of Her Majesty's subjects, the rule of law throughout the realm, and the glory of the Empire. The drone was total hogwash to my way of thinking—I'd seen several parts of the British Empire.

Roche sat with some colonial bigwigs near the head table, animated in discussion. Occasionally I saw him glancing over at me. Cynda and Mason and I sat at the end of the farthest table from the speakers. That was fine with me. Like most sailors, pomposity bores me at the very least, and angers me frequently.

The most intriguing part of the entire Emancipation Day events began for me at nine forty-five—fifteen minutes before the formal end of the evening. Mason approached me with none other than Major Rupert Teignholder in tow. He was still in his Zouave uniform, which are colorfully menacing when worn by an African, but ridiculously cartoonish on a Briton. Didn't he ever look in a mirror? What did the governor think?

After introductions, Mason suggested we retire to the garden for cognac and cigars. At the last minute he veered off, joining Cynda in taking a tour of the mansion with the governor's wife. The major and I walked out into the night alone.

18
Quid Pro Quo

Government House
Nassau, Bahamas
Wednesday, 1 August 1888

The air was warm and humid, but at least it was in motion. Overhead, the stars carpeted the sky like patterns of diamonds scattered on crepe. Around me, coconut and date palms waved their fronds amid small torches flickering in manicured flower beds. Anchor lights twinkled in the harbor and lanterns glowed in the streets below. To the south, the black settlements showed only a few lamps. The muted strains of the final revelers could barely be heard. The contrast was symbolic and real. The emancipated people were down there, but the governing class was up on the hill.

Here and there in the park around me, gentlemen in the black and white formal dinner dress of the upper class strolled the garden while speaking thoughtfully of politics and trade in low whispers. Trailing clouds of smoke, they puffed along their way, resembling slow locomotives. You could sense that this was the place where decisions were influenced and made—after going through the motions of civility inside.

Teignholder wasted no time.

"I understand you are interested in our French visitor."

How did he know that? I wondered what Mason had told the soldier about me.

"I am, sir. His behavior appears most intriguing."

"Oh, really? In what way, Mr. Wake?" Teignholder said it like he knew the answer already.

"His inquiries about Russians in the Bahamas. Aboard a schooner called the Condor that disappeared back in mid-May, somewhere in these islands. A Frenchman asking about Russians aboard a ship that disappeared in the Bahamas? I find that highly unusual, Major."

Oh, yes, he knew, all right. The Brits and the Russians were currently facing off in Afghanistan, but that wasn't the only place where tensions were heightened. Eastern Europe was in turmoil, fomented by the Russians, who had also recently taken on the Turks. There had even been a Russian invasion scare in Australia, of all places, a few years before.

If he hadn't previously known of Roche's queries about Russians in the Bahamas, Major Teignholder would've shown surprise at the news of the possibility of Russians in the Bahamas. But he didn't react in that way. Instead, he changed the subject—going to the heart of my appearance in his area of responsibility.

"And what exactly is your interest in the disappearance of this ship?"

Dealing with foreign authorities over the years, I've learned that there are times to be circumspect and times to be candid. I judged by his manner that Teignholder wanted to help, but that he also wanted honesty.

"Mrs. Saunders—the lady you met tonight—has a son who was a ship's boy apprentice on that schooner. Fourteen years old.

His name is Luke. She believes he is still alive. My friends and I are helping her search for him. We started in Key West, then headed for the Bahamas. We know the Condor was at Morgan's Bluff, then in Nassau, and subsequently departed for the islands of the southern Bahamas. We don't know exactly where. That's our next area to search."

I paused. Teignholder nodded for me to go on.

"I know that Roche was at Morgan's Bluff a few weeks ago, inquiring about Condor. He asked the locals if there were Russians aboard. He lied to me tonight when he said he'd only been in Nassau."

"Why was Condor here in the Bahamas?"

"Pleasure excursion for some New York City businessmen, evidently. I've been told they were on a treasure hunting lark. I don't know of any Russian or French connections, other than Roche's inquiries."

Now that I had bared my soul, I waited for some return information from the British army. I got it, with a surprise.

"Commander Wake, I think you've happened into something far more complicated than the disappearance of a ship's boy and his schooner."

He wagged a finger. "Before you say anything, allow me to explain that I know all about your recent visit to Andros Island, both at Red Bays and at Morgan's Bluff. Thus, I know of your profession, Commander Wake, and your efforts to find the youngster, and also the criminal complaints issued against you within the Crown Colony."

The Major let that sink in, then said, "I am responsible for the defense of this colony. That means keeping apprised of what is happening, particularly concerning foreigners, like Roche. And you."

I held up a hand. "Major, I am not here as a naval officer. I am on official leave and here as a friend of the lady. We're looking for a lost boy."

"You are here under some rather strained circumstances, I'm afraid, Commander. The governor knows about you, as does the attorney general and, of course, the chief inspector of the police here. They are not amused, I assure you. It would appear that you are on thin ice, as they say in Canada, in your legal capacity as captain of the Delilah."

I didn't like the way this was going. Somehow the topic had shifted, in a decidedly unfriendly tone, from Roche to me. "Listen, I am chartering Delilah once the cargo is discharged, which will be tomorrow. I sent a letter to the owner from Key West, explaining my assumption of command and had the mate co-sign it. Yesterday, I sent off another letter to the owner, giving an update. He'll not complain. I'm keeping his vessel working and bringing in money."

A bell rang out. Major Teignholder turned toward the mansion, then back to me. "I see they are signaling the end of the affair, so we must return inside and say our goodbyes to the governor and Lady Shea. I have more to discuss with you, however. Meet me on the front balcony at Graycliff House, in one hour. Alone."

He said it not as a social request, but as an order. I was beginning to dislike Major Teignholder. "For further interrogation, Major?"

"No, Commander—for some intelligence about the gentleman who is evidently after the same thing you are, but for different reasons. I'm speaking of the one who currently goes by the name of Monsieur Pierre Jean Roche."

An hour later, at eleven o'clock, I walked up George Street alone, having explained to Cynda and the others aboard Delilah what had transpired and that I would return to the schooner in a while. Rork was upset with that; he has a nose for action, so I made it an order—everyone was to stay aboard.

At Duke Street, I made a right and followed it around the governor's mansion until it met with Cumberland Street. It was quiet in the town, only the wind in the trees making a sound. No lights shone and I navigated by the dim shine of the stars above. At the intersection of West Hill Street and Cumberland, on the southwest corner, stood Graycliff House.

It was an imposing place. A former private mansion built in the sixteen hundreds by a successful pirate turned leading citizen, it had been an inn since 1844. Other than the Royal Victoria, it was the most exclusive hotel in the town. Like many buildings in Nassau, the outer walls were a sun-faded pink. I walked through the entry port of the surrounding wall and into the front garden.

Graycliff had a military component in its history. During the American revolution, it served as the home for the commander of the American occupation force in Nassau. In 1888, it provided quarters for the senior officer of the regiment's detachment stationed at Fort Charlotte—Major Rupert Teignholder.

Above me was the second-story balcony, where I saw a small lamp. Ascending the steps to the first floor, I passed lavender bougainvillea illuminated by a lone post lantern. Crossing the wide verandah, I entered the darkened house through open double doors.

As I walked in, the only sound was the floor creaking beneath me. Several public rooms opened off either side of the main hallway, but all were vacant. A voice—not Teignholder's—called down. "Up here, Wake. Go down the main hall and come up the stairs to the next floor. Meet us on the upper verandah."

I caught a whiff of cigar, the clink of glasses. Two men were on the second floor porch speaking in low voices. Uneasy, I climbed the stairs slowly and walked down the upper hallway toward a dim glow. Double-doors to the outside were latched open, allowing a clear view of the verandah where Teignholder, now sans the garish costume, was seated at a table with another man. Both were in shirt sleeves with open collars.

Three small glasses and a bottle surrounded the small lamp in the center of the table. The other man was older, gray-haired, and balding. His stern face exhaled smoke from a cigar.

The breeze was stronger on the second-floor verandah, rushing through the palm fronds, which clattered like chattering teeth. I felt the wind brush my face as I emerged onto the verandah and entered the glow of the lamplight. Though the air was warm, that wind felt chilly to me.

Teignholder half rose from his rattan chair. "Commander, this is Inspector Geoff Randall, of the Metropolitan Police Force in London. Inspector, Commander Peter Wake of the American Navy."

We shook hands all around and I sat in the proffered chair. The drink was Mount Gay, a decent British rum from Barbados that I enjoy. I accepted a glass and asked the soldier, "So this is where you live? Nice billet."

"Yes, my room is here, in the front. Best room in the house, called the Woodes Rogers Room, after the famous pirate-turned-governor of the Bahamas. He was rather successful in both careers, capturing a fair amount of Spanish gold in the Pacific and later converting the other remaining pirates here into good citizens. Sometimes through inducement, sometimes through coercion. Rumor has it he stayed in the same room I do, one hundred-sixty-years ago."

The major chuckled. "A pirate turned governor. Ironic, isn't it? Ah, but then again, people in these islands aren't always what they seem to be, or what they used to be. Still true now, just as then."

Randall nodded grimly at the soldier's remark, then poured more rum in his glass. Once that was done, he looked up at me with pity in his eyes, like he felt sad for me.

"Are you talking about Captain Kingston and the Condor, Major?" I asked.

He nodded. "I am. And I think you come under that category

also, which is why I wanted to talk to you here, away from the crowd. I get the impression that you are used to . . . shall we say . . . amorphous situations. It takes a certain aptitude to function well in such conditions. I think you have that ability. You can adjust to a changing state of affairs."

What the hell did that mean? And why was Randall, a senior policeman from London, present at our little talk? "You've lost me completely, Major. Maybe I'm not as adjustable as you think."

Teignholder chuckled. "Oh, you'll understand soon enough. The inspector and I believe you can be of assistance to us. In return, we can be of assistance to you."

I shook my head. "Sorry, but we're leaving tomorrow, after the cargo is offloaded. Heading south to search for the Condor, or her wreck. I can't see how I can help you."

Teignholder drained his glass and held it out for Randall to refill, then turned to me. "You are taking the Frenchman with you, together with his two associates. Along the way, you will ascertain his true name and background, the real motive for coming here, any contacts he has in the colony, who the Russians are that he is looking for, and exactly where he is heading next. You will also take along the inspector here."

Well, this had certainly become interesting. The Frenchman must have really excited the Brits. Or more probably, scared them.

I looked at the policeman. "I presume you followed him all the way from England. Why?"

"He's an odd sort. A bit shady in his manner, but we don't know why. Don't really know anything about him, so I was sent along to find out."

That reasoning sounded very anemic. He was definitely holding something back. The Brits wouldn't send a senior man on a long-shot surveillance like that. And I still couldn't fathom why they thought I would go along with their request, one that sounded an awful lot like a command.

"And why would I do any of this?"

Teignholder sighed. "Because, quite regrettably, if you don't, a communiqué from Delilah's owner, back home in Britain, will be delivered from its temporary delayed-in-transit status to the proper colonial authorities. Specifically, to the Honorable O.D. Malcolm, Her Majesty's Attorney General for the Crown Colony. I believe you met him earlier this evening. The communiqué says that you are not authorized to command or charter Delilah, and it further requests that the vessel be seized and held for the owner's agent, who will be designated once the vessel is found. The message is a forwarded telegram that came in today on the steamer from Jacksonville. I happen to have it in my pocket, as a matter of fact."

The major chuckled again, an evil little grunt. "Naturally, once the authorities receive that message, several events will be set into motion. First, Delilah will be seized. Second, you will be arrested—charged with the five outstanding criminal complaints filed by your former cook. Third, your president—I believe his name is Grover Cleveland—will receive a formal protest about you from the foreign secretary of Great Britain. The protest will be about an American naval officer engaged in maritime commerce within this Crown Colony, a position wholly unauthorized by the colonial office. Some of the more uncharitable blokes at Government House might even see it as an infringement of our territory and our national honor."

Teignholder paused for a sip while Randall coughed slightly, a studied nonchalance that sparked an aggressive urge within me. The major continued. "Fourth, I'm afraid the press lads on Fleet Street in London will learn of this entire affair. Somehow they always seem to find out about these things. Coming, as it does, close upon some inopportune posturing by the American government with regard to the violation of fishing rights in Canadian waters last year, my impression is that it will provide some excellent fodder for a reciprocal spate of patriotic posturing by British politicians. After all, it would appear that the Americans are arrogantly dismissive of our imperial waters, no matter where they are, Canada or the Bahamas. And, of course, there are always those who might think you a spy.

"Oh, I know all that is inaccurate, of course." Teignholder shrugged. "But really, what can one do? The press are like mad dogs once they sink their teeth into a story. Can't tell how bizarre it will get. Patriotic zeal, and all that. Quite annoying for Her Majesty's ministers, and even more embarrassing for the Yanks, I should think. Probably will end up being called 'The Wake Affair.' Not very good for one's career, even in your American version of a navy."

I sat there, seething. The whole damned thing was trumped up. "Blackmail is against the law, Major Teignholder, and rather low behavior for an officer of the British Army."

"Quite right, my new American friend. But this isn't blackmail. Oh, no. It is simply the bureaucratic wheels of justice slowly grinding their way incessantly toward a conclusion. Might take a year to clear you. Well, at the very least a year, I should say. Witnesses, statements, hearings, sworn testimony, that sort of thing. Wouldn't you agree, Inspector?"

The policeman was right on cue, shaking his head sadly: "Oh, yes, Major. It does seem to take an inordinate amount of time, especially out here in the colonies. Dealing with transport between islands and tracking down witnesses and all that."

Teignholder nodded, seemingly sympathetic with my plight. "But, needless to say, all that is in the future. Your decision is now, here. Actually, my request is such a simple one, easily accommodated. And the consequences of your refusal are so dire, I would think it an obvious choice."

The smile left his face. "Would you *really* care to test my resolve, Commander?"

He had me. It was the kind of thing I would expect from a tin-pot despot, not the British military and police. And to think it started with Blackstone. That thug had given them just enough to provide leverage over me. Courtesy of a disgruntled and incompetent sea cook and a distant ship owner, Teignholder had the ability to ruin our search efforts for the boy, embarrass my country, and destroy my career. He hadn't mentioned that he knew what I did for the navy, but by that point I had to assume he did.

"And if I agree to help you?"

Teignholder beamed at Randall. "You know, Geoff, the Royal Mail is a frightfully inefficient government operation, especially way out here."

Randall shook his head again. "I've heard they lose mail all the time. These staff wallahs out here in the colonies just aren't quite the best of the British civil service, are they? Ah, yes, it would be such a travesty of justice if that message from the ship's owner went missing, Rupert. Not to mention the criminal complaints from Andros Island. Just think of all those things that *wouldn't* happen."

They'd thought this whole damn thing out, but I still didn't understand one part. "How do you even know the Frenchman *wants* to go to the southern Bahamas?"

With a smug grin, Teignholder explained. "Because for some reason, he's looking for the *Condor*, just like you. And tomorrow morning, in the bar of the Empire Club down on Bay Street, he will hear what you will hear from me now. The *Condor* headed to Great Inagua Island two months ago so an American tourist could search for the treasure there belonging to Henri Christophe, King of the Haitian Africans. From that location, the *Condor* and all aboard disappeared. I have a brief report from our local man there. It was nothing that unusual at the time—now it seems extraordinary. Once Roche hears of it, he'll want to go there."

"They went to Great Inagua? You're sure?"

"Yes. When we heard an American and a Frenchman were asking about *Condor*, we had the records searched again. A clerk remembered the report from the commissioner in Inagua. I've just read it. Routine report. The schooner put in there, then left. Not seen again."

So now we had a destination. "Yes, but why will Roche want to come with me on *Delilah*?"

"At the same time he learns of *Condor*'s sighting at Great Inagua, he will learn that the mail boat for that area has been unfortunately reassigned to the Abacos in the northern part of the islands. Roche will also hear that *you* are fortuitously heading right where he wants to go, leaving with the tide tomorrow. He seems to be in as much of a hurry as you, so I'd wager he'll very nicely ask to take passage with you. You will accept and take him, his two friends, and Inspector Randall along with you. And here is some good news for you—you can make them pay!"

"No, that won't work, Major. Roche and I already met tonight. He doesn't like or trust me. I could tell. He won't ask to go with *me*."

"No choice. You are the only way to get there. He'll swallow his pride all right—the French are quite good at that. He'll ask. You'll agree. Then you'll get to go search for your lady's boy, free from any worry over legal unpleasantness. And we get to discover what this fellow is actually up to. See how simple this is? No worries, dear chap."

"So I do this in exchange for the fabricated legal problems disappearing? A *quid pro quo*?"

"Precisely, Commander."

"How do I know you'll hold your end of the bargain?"

He puffed up. "Why, Commander—I am a commissioned officer in Her Majesty's imperial forces. You have my word of honor!"

He managed to say that with a straight face. I shook my head. "After knowing you for the last few hours, I'm afraid that doesn't resonate much with me." I exhaled slowly to control my temper. "But, God help me, I'll do it. There's no alternative."

Teignholder said to the policeman, "You know something,

Geoff? I think our American is much smarter than most I've met. Grasped the concept straightaway." He cast Randall a mock look of reproach. "And *you* said he wouldn't get my meaning. Oh ye of little faith . . ."

The inspector continued the sarcastic charade, his eyes alight with mirth at my expense. "Oh, I *do* stand corrected, Major! Our Yankee cousin here is much quicker than I thought." Randall then looked at me with what he probably thought passed for sincerity. "Commander, thank you for your kind invitation to sail aboard *Delilah*. I accept."

Teignholder laughed, then grew serious. "Oh, by the by, before I forget . . . there is one more thing you should know. A native boy found the body of a white man in the harbor, about a week ago. Apparently drowned after a night of heavy drinking. By all appearances an accident, with no sign of foul play. He was a Jewish German fellow named Gerhardt Wein. Wealthy intellectual sort from Hamburg. Arrived at the end of the tourist season in April and never returned to Europe. Decided to retire here, I'm told. Not really part of the local social circles."

Wein. The 'W' in the letter? I tried to not react. "So what's that got to do with me, Major?"

"His drinking companions that night were our French visitors—your new passengers."

Quite a pair, those two. Though I've always held great respect for the British, there is a side of them which tarnishes the carefully upheld image.

Perfidious Albion, indeed.

19

Who Is Who?

Nassau
New Providence Island, Bahamas
Thursday, 2 August 1888

After breakfast on the main deck the next morning, I held a consultation with our entire company, explaining what I'd learned, and how I'd been blackmailed. I wanted everyone to understand the details so they could be on the lookout for signs from the Brit or the Frenchman pointing to Luke's location. Rork was not in favor of taking on the additional passengers, suggesting the British would divert our effort for their own agenda against the French. A grim Cynda told him, "No, Sean, the Frenchman's been the only substantive evidence we've gotten, so we'll do what we must, with whom we must, in order to find my son."

In addition to the political intrigue, we had another factor: time. Rork and I only had four weeks of leave left before we had to be back at naval headquarters on the second of September. Corny and Dan also had to return to Washington. Initially, I thought the search would be concluded by early August. Now I had no idea of where we were eventually heading and when we'd return.

Later in the morning, as Rork and I were walking on Bay Street from the shipping broker's office—he'd managed to find a crew of stevedores to unload *Delilah*'s cargo at the Deveaux Street dock at noon—I noticed a man emerging from the sponge exchange and strolling along behind us. He was the same man I'd seen in the shadows of the Vendue House when I'd walked back to the harbor front the previous evening. Short, dark-complexioned, and clean shaven; wearing the same gray coat and wide-brimmed black hat.

I was being stalked, but by whom? Why? He didn't dress or act like a local, for his gait was too energetic and his clothes too heavy. The locals wore cotton or linen, usually white. Could he be 'O'? Rork instantly perceived my vigilance and studied the man peripherally.

"Ooh, he's followin' astern o' us, all right. Eyein' us close. Looks like a bit o' a ruffian. Think he's a local copper, or one from London?"

"No idea, Rork. Might be one of Roche's men. Or Kingston's. Or Randall's. Or maybe he's a Russian, for all I know."

"I can tack 'round an' have a wee discussion with him in that alley o'er there. Take maybe ten seconds to get the measure o' him an' have the bastard singin' like a bird."

I was tempted. Rork can be extremely persuasive in obtaining information from men of ill intent. However, with the other legal issues hovering over me, I didn't want to add fuel to the fire. Especially should the man be a member of the police.

"No, Rork. This time we stay nonadversarial—for now."

I make correct decisions just often enough to retain my self-confidence. This turned out to be one of those times. Thirty seconds after I spared the stranger from meeting Rork the hard way, the man approached us.

"*Hallo. Capitaine* Wake? *Excusez-moi.* I am Henri Billot. I wish to speak with you."

The man was the converse of the refined Roche. Billot was coarse-looking, awkward, his voice raspy and halting, with difficulty in English.

"Yes, I am Captain Wake." I pointedly did not introduce Rork, who stood to one side and glared at the man. "What do you want?"

"Passage on your ship for my employer, myself, and another person. To go to Great Inagua Island, in the south."

So Major Teignholder and Inspector Randall had carried it off. Still, I decided not to make it easy, just to see how interested the French really were. "I'm not taking on any more passengers."

For a moment, Billot looked troubled, then said, "My boss, he sent me to procure passage, sir. He will pay to go."

"Who is your boss?"

New self-assurance inflated his tone. "Monsieur Pierre Jean Roche, of Paris."

"Does he have enough money to persuade me?"

Billot nodded. "He has enough money to pay, *Capitaine*."

"Tell him to be at the Deveaux Street docks at noon today. The price will be one hundred gold sovereigns. The accommodations aboard will be basic, but I will hear no complaints. Take it or leave it."

Billot was taken back a bit by my fee, which was far beyond exorbitant, but he bowed and said, "We will be there, *Capitaine*."

After Billot left, Rork whistled a low version of "God Save the Queen" and opined, "Well, well, I'm duly impressed. Methinks you've a bit o' larceny in yer heart. A hundred sovereigns is nigh on to five hundred dollars. This merchant sea captain business is agreein' with ye, ain't it?"

"I just wanted to see how well funded this Roche fellow is." I winked at my friend. "And that will pay all of our expenses on this journey, with a nice lump to go to the ship owner to keep him happy."

"An' off our backs! Well done, sir. Sounds like this Frog is damn well funded. Expense account?"

"Exactly what I was thinking, Rork. A pretty *large* expense account. The next question is—who's funding it?"

I had the schooner around to the dock at the appointed hour. The stevedores arrived late, as I expected, but they were well on the way to diminishing *Delilah*'s load by the time Roche, *et al*, finally sauntered down the dock. There weren't three men coming aboard, as I had assumed. It was to be two men and a woman.

Roche, looking cool and calm as ever in a white linen suit, and Billot, clearly harried, were accompanied by a woman of an indeterminate but not young age. My first impression of her was that of a prosperous camp follower. The gentlemen have already been described in detail, so let us turn our attention to this female.

She was *petite*, as the French say, with longish blonde hair done up in a single braid, held by a tortoise-shell comb. At an earlier point in her life she must have been quite fetching, but now her heavily rouged cheeks and crimson lips contrasted with pasty white skin and black mascara to produce a tawdry comical effect. To complete the disagreeable impression, the woman's scowling mouth spewed forth epithets in both French and English at the hapless minions behind her.

No less than five black porters struggled, in between kowtowing to the female, to unload at least a dozen pieces of her baggage from a landau. Rork and Corny, barely containing their amusement, looked in my direction for the effect all this had upon me.

It had a considerable effect, for earlier that morning I had planned to put the three paying guests, who I had presumed would be men, in the forward cabin and move my friends out on deck. That way Cynda and I could maintain our privacy aft, and the passengers could have the illusion of a cabin of their own. I thought it the least I could do, since the Frenchman was paying about ten times the regular amount for a three-hundred-mile passage for three people. That was until I saw the woman. My hopes for resuming a bit of discreet privacy with Cynda disappeared.

A bad mood began to develop in my mind but was interrupted by Roche stepping up to me. With the slightest of bows, he said, "Ah, Mr. Wake. We meet again. Last night you were a businessman. Today you are a sea captain. I look forward with great anticipation to seeing what you will become tomorrow."

My tone turned as sour as my mood. "You brought the money? Passage is paid for in advance—*before* you or your baggage goes aboard."

He didn't blink an eye. "Why yes, I have it here. One hundred golden sovereigns of the British Empire, as you have required of me. You drive a hard bargain, Mr. Wake."

I took the bag of money and opened it. While counting the coins I asked, "Why do you want go to Inagua?"

He waved a hand dismissively. "I am growing weary of these islands. They are not lush, and certainly not cultured, like those further south, in the French West Indies. Inagua is on the way to where I want to go, Mr. Wake. I hear that steamers call there for salt. Hopefully I can find one bound for the part of the Caribbean I am looking for: Martinique, Guadeloupe, Saint Martin, Saint Barthélemy. *Civilized* tropical places, where a gentleman of France can be truly comfortable."

He was smooth all right. I decided to be blunt.

"I was going to ask you a question at the governor's soirée, but you left before I could. Why were you asking about the schooner *Condor* at Morgan's Bluff? And why ask about any Russians aboard?"

No hesitation. "Oh, just curiosity. I heard there is good fishing there. Also a rumor of Russians, a people I find interesting, in the islands. And then a ship disappears in the same area? How very intriguing. Two unusual events, but merely coincidental, as it turns out."

"How did you hear about Russians in the Bahamas?"

"At a party in Nassau, I think. I cannot remember for certain." He shrugged his shoulders. "Idle gossip, nothing more."

No point in stopping now. I had the weather gauge on him, and he knew it. "And why did you lie to me at the governor's house and say you hadn't been anywhere but Nassau?"

Roche's smile got broader. He laughed loudly for those around us, as if I had made a great joke. "Did I say *that*? I must have been mistaken in comprehending your question, Mr. Wake. You know, my English is not so good. I miss some of the nuances of the language. And we must remember the wonderful effects of the governor's champagne, of course."

Standing in the glare of the sun on the dock, we measured each other for a few seconds. I knew he was lying, and he knew that I knew he was lying. But an onlooker wouldn't have been able to tell that anything was amiss. Pierre Jean Roche was one very imperturbable fellow. With the style of a practiced gambler.

I switched subjects. "What's the woman's name? I need it for the log and manifest."

"Oh, how very impolite of me! Allow me to introduce the lady, please." He beckoned her over. "This is Mademoiselle Claire Fournier, my dearest of friends, originally of Avignon, in the south of France. *Ma chérie*, this is Mr. Peter Wake, the American *businessman* I met last night, that I told you about. He has many talents, including being the captain of this boat. He will be taking us south, to a place where we can get passage toward the French islands."

Claire curtsied theatrically, making sure I got a good view of her large bosom, its prominent eruption out of her bodice apparently made possible by a substantial corset. For a fleeting moment, I tried to imagine the engineering needed for that effort. Quite considerable. A brace like that must've hurt, I remember thinking.

"Very nice to meet you, Captain. Will it be a calm voyage?"

Her English was fluent, but there was a tremor in her voice. She was obviously scared, which, in addition to the broiling heat, might have been why her powders and paint were succumbing to gravity, sliding in rivulets down her face. Her carefully done-up countenance was changing from clownlike to grotesque as the colors mixed. My estimate of her age increased, and I felt a twinge of pity for her. She was desperately trying to act like a lady in front of me, under very difficult circumstances.

"This is the calmest time of year, ma'am. And I will do my best to make it a pleasant voyage for you."

Corny sidled over and took her hand. "*Bonjour, madame.* Allow me to introduce myself. I am Doctor Cornelius Rathburn, an ethnologist at the National Museum in Washington. I would consider it an honor to assist you in any way to make this voyage through the tropic islands as pleasurable as possible."

He lifted her hand and brushed it with his lips, his eyes never leaving hers, which then commenced to flutter in appreciation. "Thank you for your kindness, monsieur. You Americans are so *galant* to a lady."

Corny displayed his most innocent and heartfelt look as he murmured, "*Enchanté d'avoir fait votre connaissance, madame.*"

As basic as my French is, I knew he was merely saying that he enjoyed meeting her, but Claire's reaction to my friend's flawless rendition of her language was positively gushing. Giggles, batting eyes, blushing cheeks, and a full curtsy were the joyous results of his efforts. It was all a bit much for my taste.

Roche, I saw, was ignoring the show, but Billot was less detached. The little man was staring at Claire and at Corny. Then he walked away.

Absalom walked by and I called for him. "Ab, put the French gentlemen's gear in the forecabin and the lady's baggage in my cabin. Another passenger, a Brit, is coming, too. He'll be in with the Frenchmen. Dan and Corny are joining you and Rork on deck. Tell Cynda that she and the lady will stay in my cabin. I'll move my gear into the mate's cabin."

Claire still stood there, so I smiled and said, "Now, if you will excuse me, ma'am, I must attend to my duties. Absalom here will show you to your cabin when it's ready."

I was rewarded with a smile and another bosom-displaying curtsy and turned to see how Rork was doing with the stevedores. He was almost done with the task of offloading *Delilah*'s cargo, but my eyes keyed in on another person, standing stiffly in the background. Cynda was watching me from twenty feet away, with pursed lips and folded arms, and a very determined face. She'd heard everything. Executing an about-face, she marched up the gangway to the main deck and proceeded down the ladder to her now *former* cabin.

At that moment, to round out my very good reasons for a foul temper, Inspector Geoff Randall walked up, bag in hand and innocent grin plastered on his fat red face. He went around introducing himself to the passengers and crew, then ambled over to me. "Geoff Randall," he said, as if we'd not met. "Methodist missionary from the Society to Spread Christ's Word. Bound for Great Inagua to save souls for everlasting life. I believe I'm on your passenger list, sir."

It was quite a performance. "Yes. You are," I replied unenthusiastically.

Randall looked around at the menagerie. "What a truly eclectic yachting party."

He leaned forward and lowered his voice, while raising his eyebrows conspiratorially. "Should be entertaining, don't you think, Commander? This is much more interesting than mucking about with the dregs of London."

"You didn't tell me Roche had a woman with him."

"Didn't want to spoil the surprise!"

"What else about them do I need to know?"

Randall allowed a sly smile. "Nothing at this time, Commander." He then left me and hailed Claire in terrible French, explaining how much he'd always loved her country.

We got under way at four in the afternoon. This was after waiting for Roche to make his final goodbyes to new good friends at the Empire Club on Bay Street, Claire making Absalom run back to her hotel room for a missing hat box, Billot returning from an errand for Roche, and Randall having me occupy Claire's attention while he searched through her baggage for incriminating evidence.

With all plain sail set, we close-hauled our way east through the harbor with the assistance of an ebb tide, tacking through the various anchored and moving vessels. By five o'clock we were clear of the eastern end of the harbor. With a moderate breeze from the northeast and Absalom up at the crosstrees guiding us, *Delilah* took her departure from Fort Montague, charging toward Porgee Rocks, southeast of Athol Island.

Once at Porgee Rocks, we bore off to the southeast and roared our way toward the notorious Yellow Bank, where a swash channel would allow us to traverse the coral-studded bank and gain an eventual overnight anchorage on the lee side of Dog Rocks, just north of Ship Channel Cay, in the Exumas.

Our European passengers lounged about the main deck, looking at distant cloud formations and joking among themselves. Clair and the "clergyman" were by the foremast. Roche and Billot were aft of the mainmast, sitting on the starboard side of the cabin top. We had barely avoided a giant mound of coral near the surface, with much swearing in Gaelic by Rork, when a new facet emerged in the mystery of exactly *who was what* aboard the schooner.

I had the helm at the time, with Corny beside me. The Frenchmen were speaking in their native tongue quietly, but the few words I understood translated into "message received in Paris" and something about someone named "Philippe Dru."

Corny, historian and international ethnologist, is fluent in the major languages of Europe and knows the basics of several others. While steering, we compared whispered opinions of the topic of the French conversation and settled on it probably being about the person who funded their journey.

Then, suddenly, Roche shook his head and glared at Billot, growling out, "*Elle ne me plait pas!*" I knew that meant *I do not like it!* The surprise was what happened next. Billot recoiled from his boss's wrath and blurted out, "*Prahsteetyee. Ehtah nyeh lyeekhko!*"

Roche instantly snarled back, "*Durak! Vyehrnyeetyehs' nahzahd k frahntsooskee!*"

Following his outburst, Roche backhanded Billot across the face, knocking him off the cabin top to the deck. Rising quickly, Billot went to the leeward main shrouds and stared bitterly out to sea, one hand on his swelling lip, the other holding on to the shroud.

Catching Corny and me staring at him, Roche muttered a quick, "*Excusez-moi,*" then stormed off, heading forward.

"Well, that little tirade wasn't in French, was it, Corny?" I asked.

Corny confirmed my suspicion. "No, it surely wasn't, Peter. That was *Russian.*"

"That's what I thought. Do you know what they said?"

"When Roche said, '*I don't like it*' in French, Billot answered in Russian. I think he said, '*Excuse me. It isn't easy!*' Roche answered, '*Idiot! Go back to French!*' Then he smacked him."

Corny held up a hand. "Peter, I'm not that good, and it's a damned tough language, but it sure sounded to me that both of them spoke Russian like natives. So now I'm doubting if these boys are French at all."

He gave me a questioning look. "This whole mess has gotten a lot more complicated, my friend. Do you have any idea just what—and who—have we gotten involved with here?"

At that point, my mind was reeling with possibilities. None of them were good.

"No, Corny. I don't."

20
Great Inagua

Matthew Town
Great Inagua Island, the Bahamas
Tuesday, 14 August 1888

At last we made Matthew Town, main settlement of Great Inagua Island, famous for its enormous salt industry. The journey wasn't easy. Of the two weeks it took to transit the 300 miles south to Great Inagua, we spent six days holding on at anchor in the lee of Deadman's Cay on Long Island, courtesy of yet another hurricane moving across our path. When the wind and seas subsided, we made our way to the southern end of Crooked Island and its infamous Mira Por Vos Passage. Absalom, who knew the Bahamian archipelago better than any other man I've known, before or since, counseled anchoring for the night under the eastern lee of Castle Island, famous for its 130-foot light house. From there we departed for Inagua, crossing in light air and confused seas.

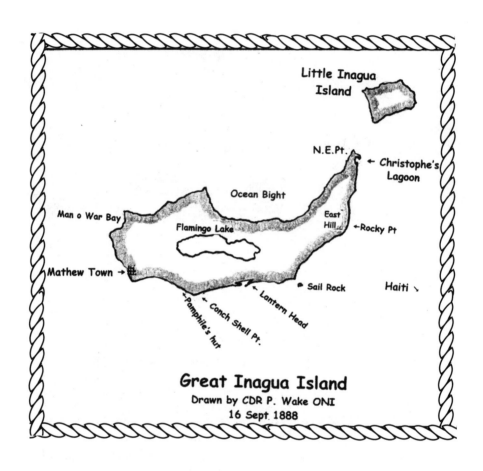

Little Inagua
Island

N.E.Pt.

← Christophe's
Lagoon

Ocean Bight

Man o War Bay

East
Hill

Flamingo Lake

←Rocky Pt

Mathew Town →

Haiti ↘

● Sail Rock

←Lantern Head

←Pamphile's hut

← Conch Shell Pt.

Great Inagua Island
Drawn by CDR P. Wake ONI
16 Sept 1888

By this point in the narrative, I'm sure the reader is wondering about the state of affairs between the guests aboard. Perplexed by the Frenchmen's intimate knowledge of Russian, I passed along that intelligence to the Britisher, but he merely smiled, as if I had confirmed a prior notion. Inspector Randall then asked if Cynda had befriended Claire enough to obtain information from her.

I replied that Cynda was not disposed to befriend anyone at the moment, including me. Randall nodded politely. The policeman—alias preacher—did not know of the depth of my relationship with Cynda, or of our habitation arrangements before his arrival aboard.

Even though I had terminated our rather tactless daytime lovemaking, we had still enjoyed very discreet romantic interludes in the evenings. Those ended when we left Nassau, and Cynda was still upset over the loss of our privacy by the arrival of a woman aboard—a woman she was forced, by *me*, to share a cabin with, and whom she deemed nothing more than a dim-witted and badly dyed concubine of Roche and Billot. Cynda vehemently shared her views with me belowdecks, two hours after we departed Nassau, and our relationship had grown colder since. Alas, it's been my sad experience in life that once a woman has made that particular determination about another of her sex, there is no changing her opinion.

Rork, who's never been shy about providing me his opinion, provided his assessment of the situation aboard while we were riding out the storm at Deadman's Cay. He was even more animated than usual.

"Methinks ye got swindled by that Limey redcoat major, an' swindled good. None o' them're real Froggies, sir. Nary a whiff o' garlic or wine about 'em. By God, I can tell a Froggie a mile away, especially upwind, by the smell o' that garlic. Comes out o' their skin, it does."

He was on a roll, but paused for a breath before resuming his lecture. "An' that Rooskie stuff is a bad omen, too, I tell ya. *Rooskies* in the *tropics?* Who ever heard o' that? An' none o' the bloody lot o' 'em 're using their real names. Damned imposters, I say. Aye, they's all as fake as that trollop's face. A bad bunch that'll give us nothin' but trouble, mark me words."

"You're probably right, Sean. And somehow they're involved with the missing boy. But damned if I know how . . ."

Rork raised his false hand to make his point. "Oh, they're in it to their friggin' eyeballs, an' a lyin' bunch o' bastards too. Aye, mind me words here an' now—the Devil's in here somewhere with those foreign bastards, that much's for certain."

The French, which is how I kept thinking of them, kept to themselves all this time, plainly frightened by the sea. I heard no more Russian spoken and very little French. Evidently, they knew they'd blundered and were determined not to repeat the mistake.

Randall did his best to act his part, praying over us in the storm, attempting to ingratiate himself with his fellow passengers, all the while periodically nipping below and surreptitiously going through all of their things. Rork observed him in the act several times and reported it to me. The Brit didn't share the results of his investigation with me, instead regarding me with amused condescension, like a superior regarding an upstart. My dislike, and extreme distrust, of the inspector escalated. The sooner I was rid of all of them, the better.

During our several days at anchor off Matthew Town, I managed to accomplish several things. First, I divested myself of the French people and the Brit, who were installed ashore in a boarding house. Second, I obtained provisions for *Delilah*. Third, and most importantly, before Roche or the others could do so, I asked Mr.

McGregor, the local magistrate, about the missing schooner, explaining that my friends and I were searching for the missing boy. McGregor, one of the few black magistrates in the islands, was a dignified gentleman and deliberated over my question for several seconds.

"Yes, *Condor* visited the island, three months ago. I remember her well," he said.

"That would place her here in late May. Did you interact with the passengers or captain?"

McGregor nodded. "Yes, I duly noted *Condor's* arrival in my journal. Later, ashore, I had occasion to speak with Captain Kingston and learned of his passenger's standing. I then arranged for a dinner at my home, visitors of such high strata being a rare occurrence here."

He said that the dinner was attended by Kingston and the New York businessman, Jason Hobart Vanderburg. The crew, including Luke, stayed aboard *Condor*, which was anchored directly off Matthew Town, as we were.

McGregor and his wife saw nothing indicating duress from Vanderburg.

"Quite the contrary, he and the captain seemed gay and excited, for they were going the next day to search the eastern end of the island for the hidden treasure of King Henri Christophe, the black king of Haiti. They had already looked about at other islands for treasure. Henry Morgan's loot at Andros, I believe.

"Mr. Vanderburg vaguely indicated that he'd had some sort of falling out with some companions earlier and they'd gone home from Nassau. He said he was heading home also, after hunting around Inagua for the Haitian treasure."

McGregor never saw them again. Later, when he got word the schooner was no longer anywhere in sight around the island, he got to thinking it over and sent a routine report to Nassau reporting *Condor's* visit to the island. Until we arrived, he hadn't thought again about Captain Kingston and his passenger.

When I asked about the actual legend of the treasure, McGregor smiled and said, "I think it's untrue, a quaint romantic myth, but there are many here in the Bahamas, and in Haiti, that do place credence in it. In fact, I know one man on Great Inagua who knows more about it than anyone else."

The magistrate suggested I visit Victor Pamphille, an elderly ex-Haitian retired to a modest dwelling on the south shore of Great Inagua after a life spent commanding island schooners around the Caribbean. It was still light out, so we walked the mile or so to Pamphile's home, just west of Salt Pond Hill. McGregor asked the man to tell me all he knew of the treasure, that a boy had gone missing while searching for it. Leaving me there with the old man, the magistrate began to walk home.

McGregor was a man who took his responsibilities seriously, so before he left, I decided to alert him to some of the oddities regarding my former passengers, who were now under his accountability.

"Mr. McGregor, there are some unusual aspects of my passengers that I think you should be aware of. Pastor Randall is actually a British policeman, who has been surveilling the French people all the way out here from London. And there is some speculation that they are not really French, since they speak Russian quite well. I've discovered that Roche, the tall Frenchman, had been inquiring about the *Condor*'s visit at Morgan's Bluff, up in northern Andros Island. He is connected in some important way with all of this, but I don't know how. What he did tell me were lies. Perhaps if you do learn anything about them, you could share it with me. It might help in my search for the boy."

"Hmm, how very interesting. I'll have to keep alert." He stopped abruptly, looking at me with doubtful eyes. "And what about you? Should I be alert around you also, Captain Wake? What are *your* secrets?"

I feigned humor. "Oh, nothing nearly that interesting, sir."

McGregor wagged his head and said, "I hope so." Then

he sauntered away, toward the mango-colored sun setting over Matthew Town. I don't think he believed me.

Pamphile was getting frail in body, but his mind was still taut as a main sheet in a gale. The best short description of the old man across from me at that table was that he was *weathered*, like old teak railings that could still perform their function. I estimated his age as seventy-five, at least. He didn't know himself with any certainty. Educated at a seminary in his youth, Pamphile had developed an aptitude for the European languages of the Caribbean, a skill that helped his maritime career. He spoke English astonishingly well in a steady bass voice, with a schoolbook British accent.

He invited me inside his hut, consisting of coral stone walls and a thatched roof. In the shadowy dwelling, he poured rum into two smudged glasses and we sat down at a hatch-cover table. After establishing our bona fides as veteran seamen, we laughed and exchanged stories of ports and storms and women around the West Indies. It is a necessary prelude among sailors, enabling reciprocal trust.

He grew dramatic, solemn, holding up a hand and saying he needed more rum to tell me what I needed to know. While I waited patiently as Pamphile rummaged his home for another bottle, I surveyed the scene outside.

An opening in the southern wall looked out over the ocean, a hundred feet away. The sun had gone, dusk was gathering quickly. Offshore, Molasses Reef broke the swell in a ragged slash of white foam. The sea itself was indigo dark, blending with the sky, except for that reef with its mocking break in the liquid rhythm.

My host returned and plunked down another bottle of rum, the sort with no label. He filled our glasses again and sighed. Then, with yellowed, watery eyes, Pamphile began to tell his tale.

"The story of Henri Christophe is a long and fascinating one,

Peter. But there is no reason or time to tell it all tonight. Here is the part relevant to your quest for the missing schooner and the little boy. Sixty-eight years ago, in May of eighteen twenty, when I myself was a young boy in the village of Port a l'Ecu, my sovereign, King Henri Christophe—the former slave turned king of northern Haiti—was fighting off insurrection within his kingdom. It was stirred up by General Boyer from the south, at Port au Prince, where the famous Petion had ruled. Then Boyer invaded the border area of Christophe's kingdom. At this same time, my king was a sick man, with serious ailments inside his body.

"While faced with these crises, Christophe received a visit from his close friend, Rear Admiral Sir Home Riggs Popham, Commander-in-Chief of the Royal Navy's West Indies Squadron from eighteen eighteen to eighteen twenty. Popham had been trying to mediate an end to the civil war in Haiti, but to no avail. Boyer knew Christophe was sick and his military was weakening and would not compromise. Why should he? Death was in the air."

With the setting of the sun, it had grown dark in the hut. Pamphile stopped his narration with a curse, then lit an ancient oil lamp, its grimy glass shade casting a weak light that barely reached the walls. Above us the thatch ruffled in the wind, which moaned through the glassless windows. The scene, and Pamphile's ominous story, made me uncomfortable. The old man, seeing my disquiet, topped off our glasses and held up a bony finger.

"Yes, it is a dark story of treachery, but here comes the interesting part, Peter. Admiral Popham was visiting his friend Henri for the last time, at the royal palace at Sans Souci. Popham himself was also very sick, having had two slightly paralytic strokes in the previous four months. At age fifty-eight, he was five years older than the king and going home to England. Both knew this would be their last meeting. Historical records say that they discussed the civil war and reminisced about past glories, but legend says another, more impassioned, matter was discussed."

As Pamphile spoke, I had little difficulty imagining the great African king of Haiti, his ebony face like that of the noble man before me, conferring with his British naval friend by the light of a similar flickering lamp more than three score years earlier.

"The legend says that the king, anxious for his family's safety and financial security when the inevitable should happen to him, asked his dear friend to take several trunks of valuables with him upon his departure. Popham was to hide them at the closest British territory, a mere day's sail downwind from Christophe's kingdom on the north coast of Haiti. That place is right here, Peter. Great Inagua.

"In this way, the king's family would have an easily accessible and safe cache of treasure, on which they could live for the rest of their lives, in comfortable exile. Christophe asked this as a matter of honor between gentlemen. How could a man like Popham refuse such a request?

"Five months later—exactly one month after his friend Popham died in England—and as the external enemies from the south of Haiti pressed closer and closer, the men of Christophe's own personal guard regiment revolted. Six days after that, on October the eighth, in the year eighteen twenty, fate arrived. In his royal apartments at Sans Souci Palace, King Henri Christophe, the first native monarch in the New World, shot himself through the heart, using a silver bullet he kept for that very purpose."

My host slumped, exhausted by the passion expended in the telling of the tale. He poured more rum. It was his seventh glass since my arrival. I waited, digesting the story, forming my questions.

"Victor, does the legend say exactly where Popham buried the treasure?"

Pamphile's mouth creased slyly, those eyes studying me for trickery. "Why, at the place *named* for my king's treasure, Peter. At Christophe's Lagoon. We all know where the treasure is, we just have not found it yet."

"Did you tell this story to some white men from a schooner

called *Condor*, back in May?"

Suddenly, he changed, slurring his words, lapsing into Haitian Creole. Was it the rum hitting him or was he alarmed by my question? I wasn't sure.

"I told some *blancs*, yes, but I do not remember their names or the name of any *bato*. I mean ship. They looked, but not very hard. *Bitsi bitsi*. Little bit here and there. But *anyen*. Nothing. I did not think they would find it—they are *blancs* and do not have the proper understanding. I left them there, after they paid me, of course."

"Do you remember a white boy in the crew? His name was Luke."

"*Oui*, there was a boy. He helped them search."

"Where did they say they were going next?"

"They did not say. But they looked *fatigué* . . . tired, when I left them. As I am tired now. I thought at the time that they would sail home, but no one saw them again. You know, Peter, my new friend, I am old, and the *wonm* . . . *excusez-moi*, *le rhum* . . . the rum, it has weakened me . . ."

I was losing him. It was no act. "Victor—stay awake! Has anyone ever found any of this treasure?"

He rolled his head to one side and stared at me. "*Non, mwem zanmi*. No, my friend. Though many have tried."

"Does anyone live out there, at the end of the island? Could they have come in contact with the whites?"

"Oh, yes . . ."

"Can you take me there?"

"In three . . . days . . . when the wind serves. I am . . . tired . . . now."

Pamphile slowly lowered his head to the table. Seconds later I heard snoring. Walking back to Matthew Town by the light of a half moon, my mind turned to the immediate future. The end of the island was the last place I knew that *Condor* was seen by anyone. Maybe I could find a witness. One who was sober.

21
Unlikely Allies

Matthew Town
Great Inagua, Bahamas
Saturday, 18 August 1888

By now we were eighteen days into the sweltering month of August. The previous three days saw the weather resume its summer norm—light to moderate winds from the east and south, with the occasional afternoon thunderstorm. During that time we prepared *Delilah* for a further voyage, which I assumed would be to search the Ragged Islands archipelago to our northwest, and then return back to Nassau.

Once there I would relinquish the schooner. Rork and I would then take a steamer to Key West, sail *Nancy Ann* back to Patricio Island, and subsequently take train passage to Washington and our naval life. I calculated that the timing would be close, but with luck we could make it.

The former passengers, meanwhile, had been to all outward appearances as languid as the atmosphere and people of Great

Inagua. Randall told people at the local church he was thinking of heading to the Caicos Islands to preach there. Lounging around the boardinghouse, the French passed the word they were waiting for a southbound steamer.

McGregor, as I had hoped, shared with me what he had heard.

"Your man Roche has been discreetly inquiring about *Condor*, and particularly about her people. Asked about Russians aboard and where the schooner was headed next. Billot has been trying to get someone to take him out to the eastern point. He hasn't talked to Pamphile yet, but I imagine he will. The French woman has been asking about Haitians here on the island and their communications with Haiti.

"Mr. Randall finally came to me with his true profession. I am not, of course, at liberty to discuss that subject any further. But you were correct, Captain Wake. They are an artificial lot."

"Well, they are *your* lot now, sir."

His face crinkled into a grin for a moment. "Not for long. With any luck at all, the monthly steamer should be here any day now."

My companions had changed during the journey thus far, and not for the better. Cynda was growing more morose and hostile each day. Our affection had yet to recommence. After the French woman vacated the stern cabin I returned there and Cynda resumed her place in the mate's cabin. But the moment for love had evidently passed. She was still polite, and sometimes playful, but mostly sad and distant, as if she knew the search was nearing the end, knowing she would have to confront reality soon and admit that her son was dead.

Though they maintained polite loyalty, Corny and Dan were no longer optimistic supporters. The twists and turns of the expedition had drained their positive hopes and energies, and now even they showed subtle signs of doubt in my leadership, or in the wisdom of continuing the mission. It didn't help that Corny's suave attempts with Claire had been for naught, since she was obviously attached to Billot.

Tensions mounted. Our guide Absalom respectfully expressed a desire to head back to Andros. And Rork, my stalwart friend, was clearly nervous about our official leave ending in two weeks. He doubted we would make it back to headquarters in time. Unfortunately, neither of us were strangers with disciplinary repercussions in our careers. Rork reminded me that we didn't need any further problems of that sort at naval headquarters.

Early that Saturday morning, three of us embarked on the final step to find definitive evidence of Luke Saunder's location. Rork, Cynda, and Dan stayed aboard *Delilah*. Absalom, Corny, and I walked to Pamphile's house, where we all launched his small boat out into the surf line and sailed east along the twenty-mile southern side of the island. The old man, who was doing this for a payment of one bottle of rum—*afterward*—and two dollars, still had the skills of a good sailor, keeping the boat just off the line of reefs the whole way. It took all morning to pass Lantern Head, Sail Rock, and Rocky Point, until we reached the far end of the island.

Once there, Pamphile sailed the boat over the reef into a circular cove where he rounded her up triumphantly into the wind. He swung his arms about him and proclaimed, "Christophe's Lagoon. This is where the king's treasure is. Somewhere here."

We, of course, were not there for treasure, and he knew that. My idea was to search for any islanders who lived nearby and possibly had had contact with the men of the *Condor*. Maybe they could give me insight as to what had happened here, and where the schooner was heading next. Pamphile said there was only one family who farmed the area.

Half the circumference of the cove was a serrated line of barely submerged reef, the other half a low shoreline of sandy beach. The depth was perhaps ten feet in the middle, with a shallow opening to the northeast. Because of her draft, I surmised that *Condor* had probably anchored just outside of that opening, on the narrow ledge of sand and coral bottom fringing the island, before it dropped off into the ocean deep.

I assigned each man a task. Absalom would walk inland and look for the farming family. I would walk west along the beach, Corny east and north, both of us searching for any debris from *Condor*. Pamphile would watch the boat and examine the cove itself.

An hour later, Absalom approached me with a young native boy, who informed me in a rapid-fired thick accent that, yes, he had met white people looking for the gold in May.

I eagerly interviewed him. "Did you see a boy of fourteen with them? He was in the crew. Please speak slowly, so I can understand you."

That was obviously an effort, but he complied. "Yes, the boy had a Bible name. Luke. He helped the old men look, but they didn't find anything. No one does, you know. They were only here one day, until just before the sun went down. After they talked to my father and heard what he said, they left."

Corny and Pamphile joined us as I asked the boy, "Where is your father now? I want to speak with him. I need to know what was said."

"He's gone to Abraham's Bay, up Mayaguana way. But I know what he said. It's same as what he says to them all. He told them this is only the little treasure, the big one is that way. . ." He pointed southeast. ". . . It's still back in Haiti, at the big fortress."

"What happened then?"

"They left in the boat. That way, toward the big treasure."

He pointed to the southeast again. Toward Haiti.

I turned to Pamphile, who shrugged. "The boy is right. The main treasure is still hidden in Haiti. It never got out."

"Why didn't you tell me that?"

"You only asked about the treasure here. When I left the white people here, I thought they would return to Nassau. I did not know they headed toward Haiti—a very foolish thing to do."

Foolish maybe, but understandable. Haiti is close to Great Inagua. I quickly estimated how long it would take us. "There's no time to waste. We need to go there too."

Pamphile took a breath and shook his head slowly. "No, no, . . . Captain. The treasure there is in a haunted place. At Laferrière, atop Bonnet l'Eveque, the bishop's cap. A place of death and despair."

"Where the hell is that?"

"The fortress of King Henri Christophe, inland from Cap Haitien, on the north coast."

Corny stepped forward. "Isn't Cap Haitien close to here?"

Absalom nodded and said, "One hundred miles. An overnight passage in this light easterly wind, but it won't hold light. It will pipe up soon. And when the trades build up, it takes a week against the wind and current."

"The land of *voudou* . . ." Corny intoned solemnly as he gazed across the ocean toward Haiti. "I studied some of that, years ago. Remnants of it are still around in the States, especially Louisiana. I'd be interested in seeing the home of it all."

Pamphile snorted in agitation. "No, no, no! *You* people should not want to go there. If your boy is there, then he is dead. Let it be."

He was becoming upset, but I was invigorated by this decisive intelligence of *Condor's* whereabouts. It made sense. Civilization was to the north, and *Condor* hadn't been seen that way. So maybe they headed away from civilization, on one last desperate try to find treasure, in a place few visited. Wrecked on the shore, they could be waiting there. We were provisioned and ready to go. *Delilah* could be under way as soon as we got back to Matthew Town.

The old Haitian's chest was heaving in anger at being ignored. "*Do not* go there!"

"And why is that, Victor?" I asked him gently, as the island boy backed away, alarmed by Pamphile's outburst. The boy ran off from us.

The old man pointed a shaking finger inches from my face. "Because you are all the wrong *color*, Captain Wake! You do not—cannot—understand the ancient ways."

The yellowed eyes came closer, no longer pitiful, but intense, almost crazed. He

grabbed my wrist in a surprisingly strong grip, and squeezed it for emphasis.

"*Les blancs* do not survive in Haiti . . ."

We arrived back at the dock at Matthew Town an hour before sunset. Loading last-minute goods into the dinghy at the wharf and absorbed in the minutiae of getting a ship under way, I didn't notice Roche's approach.

"May I have a private word with you, sir?" he asked.

His deferential tone stirred my curiosity. We walked over to the corner of the nearest salt warehouse, while Absalom, Rork, and Corny finished stowing the supplies in the boat.

The Frenchman surprised me. "I know you are sailing to Cap Haitien tonight. Pamphile just told my man Billot, who ran to tell me. My assistants and I need to go there also and want to take passage on *Delilah*. Our baggage is being assembled and will be here in ten minutes."

Oh, no, you don't, thought I—no parasites or idlers on board my ship now.

"This isn't a pleasure trip, Mr. Roche, and Haiti is not a tourist destination. I have no more time for passengers."

I started to walk away when he held my shoulder and said,

"I know that you are an American naval intelligence officer, Commander Wake, not a businessman or a merchant schooner captain. And though I will pay you fifty gold sovereigns to cover our expenses, we won't go as passengers on this journey."

I stopped. "My profession is of no consequence here. And you are correct—you won't go as passengers, or anything else, even for money."

His voice had military authority in it as he said, "We will be your allies-in-arms. You have need of us as allies, Commander. Especially *me*."

I was mightily tired of British and French pomposity by this time. I've had my fill of it around the world. "Oh? And pray tell me, why in the world would I need *you* right now?"

Roche's tone softened. "Because I think I know the area where Luke Saunders is, who he is with, and why he is there. And I further believe that you do not have the remotest idea of any of it."

More than his words, it was his grim confidence that compelled me to wait, to let him explain. "Very well, I'm listening."

"He is in the mountains of northern Haiti, somewhere near the fortress Pamphile spoke to you about, at the redoubt of a Russian émigré who has been engaged in a criminal enterprise there. We will need each other, Commander, to reach this place and take action once there."

He didn't seem to be an escaped lunatic, but his wild comments certainly gave the appearance of one. I surveyed him closely, this apparent European swell, stuck on a poor black island in the tropics. Was this a ruse to get off a boring island? Or perhaps an effort to flee the closing noose of the British police? Only desperate people went to Haiti. Why was he desperate?

In the past, I've had to make instantaneous judgments about people. Sometimes I've been wrong, but this time I didn't think so. Roche had the ring of truth about him. That alarmed me, for if what he had indicated was true, Luke Saunders was involved in some very perilous stuff indeed.

"I think we'd better start over, Roche. We'll begin with the first question in my mind: just who the hell *are* you?"

"A man who is compelled by circumstances to trust you, Commander. A man with a background and responsibilities very much like your own. I cannot say more on that. The situation is precarious but simple—you must trust me and what I tell you. Together, we can accomplish both our missions, and save lives in the process. Separately, neither of us will be successful—and many men will die because of it."

"Go on," I said, wary of the theatrics.

"It is a long story and we haven't much time, sir." He looked to the south. "We must make this passage before the trade winds from the southeast start up again to prevent a fast voyage. I suggest we continue this conversation aboard *Delilah* while en route to Cap Haitien. What I have to confide with you at that time will change your mind about me and my present urgency. My colleagues will be here to board at any moment. Please, let us make haste now."

And so it was that I said the words I couldn't have anticipated only ten minutes earlier: "All right, Roche. I'll do it. I'll trust you. Get your peoples' gear aboard. I presume Randall isn't coming."

Roche raised an eyebrow and grinned. "No, Commander. There is no requirement to notify him, and no need for a policeman, or a pastor, where we are going. The culture there is quite beyond the point where those professions would be useful."

He walked away and I returned to my comrades. True to his word, ten minutes later, the French entourage arrived on the dock in the gathering dusk, this time carrying a minimum of baggage.

Claire explained to Absalom. "We will not need the more fashionable clothing where we are going."

Right then, I didn't know how very true that statement was.

My conversation with Roche at the Matthew Town dock was the exact pivotal moment when everything changed for me that summer. The noble quest to find out what had happened to

Luke Saunders was about to abruptly transform from a general exploration for information into the focused pursuit of an evil man and his fantastic enterprise, the likes of which I had never imagined in my rather complicated life.

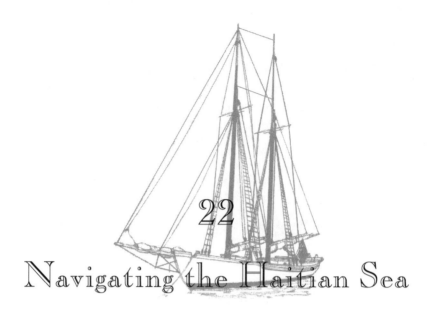

22
Navigating the Haitian Sea

Aboard the schooner Delilah
Bound south in the Sea of Haiti
Monday, 20 August 1888

The wind was already beginning to pipe up when we put to sea. It was coming directly from our destination at Cap Haitien, so the closest we could steer on the port tack was for Cape Nicholas, seventy miles to leeward along the coast, at the western end of the upper pincer of Haiti's clawlike shape. The stories of sailors being taken west by the wind and currents along the coast were legion, and that was my primary fear.

At ten that evening, once we had gotten everything stowed properly and settled into the uncomfortable routine of a ship pounding to windward, I called all hands aft to where Rork was steering. I wanted everyone to hear what Roche had to say, and therefore be as prepared as they could be for what we would confront in Haiti. With our newly found intelligence and the decision to head south to Haiti to exploit it, there was a perceptible rise in my companions' spirits. At last, for fair or foul, we were doing something that might lead to our goal.

By the glow of the binnacle, the circle waited for Roche to finally shed his pretenses and tell us what he knew. When he did, it was beyond anything we'd imagined.

"I will be succinct. I have confidential information, the origin of which I cannot share, that there is a Russian émigré from Paris currently residing in the remote mountains of northern Haiti. It is a land of various warlords with an imperfect authority over their domains, which has allowed him *carte blanche* to engage in building an army of filibusters that will eventually embark on a mission to return to Europe, probably France.

"Once there, they will join certain revolutionary organizations across the continent and function as a military cadre, with the greater aspiration of fomenting chaos and disruption to bring down what they feel are antiquated political systems of oppression. The Russian's name is Sergei Alexandrovich Sokolov. He has been in Haiti for about three years, assembling his mercenaries and equipment."

He waited while a wave crashed into the bow and spray covered us. I asked the first of many questions that sprang to mind.

"Why are *you* interested in this man?"

"Because my work in France is to keep a check on these types of organizations. I was sent here to ascertain Sokolov's capabilities."

"Oh, so you work with the Deuxième Bureau, under its commander—I can never remember his name . . ."

"Colonel Sandherr. You know him?"

Correct answer. Colonel Jean Sandherr was the commander of French military counter-intelligence—the Deuxième Bureau. Roche still wasn't telling us everything about himself and his colleagues, but now that I understood his profession I didn't expect him to. Instead, I went on to my second question. "What does any of this have to do with the schooner *Condor* and Luke Saunders?"

He glanced at Cynda, then back to me, "We heard a rumor

that Sokolov was running out of money, that he was going to turn to crime to finance his operation. We knew that Captain Kingston and the schooner *Condor* brought him smuggled weaponry over the past year, through the port at Cap Haitien and other smaller places on the coast nearby. So I speculated that Kingston might be used for seagoing robberies to build the Russian's finances."

"Piracy . . ." muttered Dan. Cynda's eyes widened at that word. She moved beside me and her hand reached for mine.

Roche nodded. "Exactly. They would have to be against targets that carried cash or easily convertible things of value. And that meant private yachts."

Straining at the wheel as a gust hit us, Rork said, "Yachts don't go anywhere near Haiti. Too bloody dangerous."

"But the Bahamas has 'em in spades," offered Corny.

This wasn't adding up for me. "We've not heard of any piracy, though. Yachts go to the Bahamas mainly in the winter, not in the late spring and summer. And why would Kingston take on a load of fancy passengers if he was going to go on a piracy plundering expedition?"

The moment I said it, I knew the answer to my own question. It was so damned obvious, now that I had the rest of the information. Roche registered my obvious enlightenment with a nod and continued.

"I had the same questions, Commander. Then, after I reached the Bahamas and began my inquiries, I realized that Kingston did not have to go about the islands searching the sea for victims—he already had them aboard his ship."

"He *kidnapped* the passengers?" asked Dan. "Then why take them on a treasure hunting caper through the Bahamas?"

Cynda's grip on my hand tightened. Roche shrugged. "I have not deduced that part yet. This is only my theory."

It was a plausible theory, and I had an idea why Kingston had taken the victims on the treasure hunt. "No, Dan. They *weren't* kidnapped yet. They were willing passengers. People have seen them ashore, remember? The businessmen could've gotten help at Andros, Nassau. Recall Vanderburg at Inagua. All the way to Mathew Town, he thought he was eventually going home and told people as much.

"No, Kingston took them southbound through the islands, ever closer toward his ultimate destination in Haiti, with the *façade* of a treasure hunting expedition, keeping them happy. It would make it easier for him."

"But three left in Nassau," said Corny.

"Yes, Kingston lost three of them at Nassau, but he still had Vanderburg. Then, once they had examined Christophe's Lagoon, Vanderburg heard about the biggest treasure of them all, only another couple of days away, in Haiti. It was the perfect way for Kingston to get his victim all the way to Haiti with no trouble, no attempt at escape, no injuries. He just fed the fantasy of finding treasure. The victim sailed to his captor in Haiti of his own volition. Brilliant plan, really."

"What about my boy . . ."

All eyes turned to Cynda. Tears streamed down her cheeks. My heart melted and I embraced her, supplying the best interpretation I could conjure for Luke's safety.

"Darling, he's just a cabin boy, a steward. Brought along to care for the passengers. Most likely ignorant of Kingston's plan. Once they got to Haiti and continued the treasure hunt ashore, he may have been left at the port by his captain to fend for himself. We'll likely find him sitting on the wharf at Cap Haitien, bored out of his wits and very happy to see his mother again."

Cynda mumbled something in reply as *Delilah* thumped into another larger wave, knocking everyone off balance and drenching us thoroughly. Lurching from handhold to handhold along the cabin top, Claire came over and put an arm around Cynda's waist.

"Come, *ma chérie*, we should go into the cabin and change into something dry. Women are so much smarter than men. Let these dismal brutes stay up here and have this wet weather."

When they'd gone below, Dan asked Roche, "So there is a possibility that the passenger aboard *Condor* went ashore unknowing of his future capture?"

"Certainly. If my theory, and that of the commander's, is correct, then the businessman would not discover he was a captive until deep within the interior of Haiti. Then the trap would be sprung and what could he do? But I must remind you, all of this is but an assumption, gentlemen. Until we get to Cap Haitien, we won't know."

"What are your plans, once we get there?" I asked him.

"Find Sokolov's lair."

"And what then?"

"Determine with my own eyes what he is doing, and how far along he is in accomplishing it."

"Just the three of you?"

Roche gave a Gallic shrug. "Well, I was hoping you gentlemen would accompany me."

"I don't think so, Roche. We're here to rescue young Luke. Not to get involved in some European operation against some crack-pot mercenary scheme in the middle of the Haitian jungle. That's not our fight."

My friends vocally agreed. Roche shook his head, holding up a hand in objection.

"Ah, but what happens if your Luke Saunders is one of the kidnappers or the mercenaries? What if he is one of the hostages? What will you do then, Commander?"

That took me aback. "I don't know."

The Frenchman wagged his head in sympathy. "We shall all see what to do when we find out what has happened. I am afraid that there are no certainties in this affair, Commander, except those that we make happen."

A thought came to me. "Do the Brits, Inspector Randall and Major Teignholder, know about any of this?"

Roche raised an eyebrow. "My dear friends the British do not have any idea about Sokolov, or Kingston's connection to Haiti. As for the good Inspector Randall, who incorrectly suspects me of some anti-colonial motives and was, I believe, about to try to thwart my passage, my trail just grew cold."

"And what did Pamphile tell your man Billot about the treasure in Haiti?"

"That it was guarded by powerful African mysteries, ancient and understood only by the tribes in Haiti and Africa. And the old man said that we Frenchmen would find certain and agonizing death while seeking it. That is to be expected. You see, Commander, for very good reasons the Haitians distrust and dislike all whites, but they have reserved a very special hatred for the French. I do not blame them, of course. There were things that were done, unspeakable things, to the slaves that rebelled. One shudders to think upon it."

I'd seen slavery myself and was aware of how deep the scars and lust for revenge could go. What we were about to experience I could not predict, but everything Roche told us sounded possible, even probable.

I had been to Haiti before and had no fondness for the place. Just after the war, in '66, I'd patrolled the southern coast during one of their many internal wars. This was a time when the United States was considering leasing a Haitian port as a coal depot. To our credit, and my personal relief, we demurred from that negotiation. Four years later, I'd chased a renegade American pirate across the Caribbean, Rork finally killing him at Henne in the Bay of Gonave. In 1873, I'd visited Port au Prince by warship in a successful effort to deter depredations against American citizens there.

It is a bizarre culture, more Africa than New World, with startling dignity and compassion, and absolutely shocking brutality. The dark-hearted pagan character of its primitive religion, the infamous *voudou*, is augmented by the obscure mysteries surrounding its rituals, which few white-skinned outsiders have been allowed to observe. To say that Haiti is completely indecipherable to our American sensibilities is no exaggeration. To suppose that any of us can understand it is naive folly.

Sailors of the West Indies know that you can smell Haiti long before you see it. Its mountains rise to considerable heights close to the sea, and from them the charcoal smoke from thousands of cooking fires drifts far out over the ocean, obscuring the horizon in a sweet gray haze, making landfalls there dangerous. This odorous cloud is one more exotic effect of the place, enhancing foreigners' curiosity about the legendary black republic. Some of the more romantic among the whites call this phenomenon the "The Shroud of Haiti," though I've never heard a Haitian say that.

So it was when we approached from the north. This expanse, the water surrounded by the giant island of Hispaniola, the colony of the Bahamas Islands, and the colony of the Turks and Caicos Islands, is known by local seamen of the area as the "Sea of Haiti." It was so named on our chart. The hard winds, unpredictable currents, and that incessant smoldering murkiness make it a uniquely dangerous place to navigate a ship, above all a sailing vessel, which is far more at the mercy of the natural elements.

My worry increased in proportion to our distance gained. We'd departed Great Inagua Saturday evening against a small southeast gale, sailed on a southward tack all day Sunday, then the next sunrise fought that wind and current to get easting. Now it was dusk on Monday evening and we were drawing near Haiti. The sun, burnt red in the dirty sky, had sunk, leaving us alone on the sea. The slate-gray ocean melded with the smoke-laden haze, eliminating the horizon altogether. The closer we got, the thicker the cloud and the lesser our visibility ahead.

Somewhere out there was Portugal Point, the eastern end of Tortuga Island, which parallels the coastline for twenty miles. The mountains of the island stand right at the edge of the deep-water shoreline. One could literally sail up and hit those rock walls in the dark with no warning from shallowing water, no sight of land ahead in the haze. To make matters worse, infinitely worse, the wind and current raced westbound along the Haitian mainland's coast—right toward the dagger of Portugal Point. I had *Delilah* heading southeast, but knew we were sliding westerly to leeward at an unknown velocity.

Though I understood the south and central coasts, I had never visited Cap Haitien and the north coast. Neither had anyone else aboard, so the geographic knowledge of our destination was limited to a chart twenty-eight years old, covering the entire Gulf of Mexico, Florida, and upper West Indies, with no large scale details of the coast.

In my navigation, I tried to overcompensate for all of these factors and make a landfall to the east of Cap Haitien. I thought I'd taken *Delilah* far enough to the east on our offshore tack, in order to be able to go about and bear off, giving the schooner a good run south. Thus comfortably progressing under reduced sail and speed on broad reach, we could pick up the beacon flashing from the hundred-forty-foot-tall lighthouse at Pointe Picolet, the entrance to the channel into Cap Haitien. I had seen plenty of fog in my time as a young schooner man in New England and was sure the lighthouse's flash could cut through the smoke as well.

Now I had my doubts, however, and because of the squared appearance of the waves around us reasoned the current was stronger than I initially estimated and we'd drifted too far west, near that vicious Portugal Point. *Delilah* was thus close-hauled with all plain canvas set in twenty knots of air, sailing fast as night fell brusquely, as if someone had rudely turned off an electric light. The stars refused to show themselves and the rising full moon, which would've been invaluable, had decided to be faint-hearted, a mere distant pale blemish in the dark.

Noting the period of time that had passed since our last tack, by thirty minutes past eight o'clock in the evening I was relieved that we'd missed the primary danger in my mind, Tortuga Island. There would be another ten miles before we'd come up on the Haitian mainland. Well over an hour to go.

The reason for this rather involved explanation of my navigational efforts will become readily apparent to the reader in the next paragraph. And so, because of the combination of the various aforementioned factors, and the attending result, at precisely eight forty-one p. m., on Monday, August twentieth, 1888, our heretofore good luck completely changed its character, in what I later determined was four seconds.

That was when *Delilah* smashed full speed into a cliff face—one hundred and forty feet below that lighthouse at Pointe Picolet.

23
Mother of the Twins

Pointe Picolet
Near Cap Haitien
North coast of Haiti
Monday, 20 August 1888

I will take the liberty to pause here and praise the men of the Albury family of Man O War Cay in the Abaco Islands of the northern Bahamas, who created *Delilah* in 1864. That I am alive to share this account is because of them. *Delilah* was the toughest ship I've ever seen, the epitome of the shipbuilders' art.

She was completely destroyed, of course, by the rock bastions of Haiti, but not before she performed the impossible. A miracle if ever there was one.

Rork was at the helm. I stood beside him, scrutinizing the folded chart in my hands for the thousandth time, trying to perceive some new bit of wisdom that would help me figure our position. I remember checking my pocket watch for the time, to measure the period until our next tack.

There were two sets of eyes on lookout: Absalom at the foremast and Dan next to him, clinging to the port foreshrouds as our ship fought the seas. Corny was below in the gyrating galley, washing the dishes with Cynda after the evening meal. Billot and Claire were seated on the windward side of the cabin top, trying to displace their seaborne fears by shouting into each other's ears above the wind about their favorite Paris theaters. As usual, Roche stood alone aft, hanging on to the mainsheet and staring off to windward.

Spray filled the dark air, rigging moaned, the hull rumbled, and the sails' leaches rattled as we lurched, slid, and rolled our way through the seas. Looking back on it, I do seem to remember a brief inkling that the seas had changed direction and were choppier. Sitting here in the comfort of my bungalow at Patricio Island writing this narrative, I now know those waves were reverberating off the rocks. But at the time, I couldn't complete that deduction, for that was the moment when it all happened. By the grace of God, no one was in the forward cabin when we hit.

My first realization was the crack of thick timbers breaking.

At the same instant, I and everyone around me were propelled forward through the air as the entire rig—masts, topmasts, gaffs, stays, shrouds, sails, sheets, halyards, blocks, crosstrees—flew apart and descended upon us. The schooner did not stop at first impact, but drove up and over a line of boulders in the water. She was still moving when the rock wall of a cliff stopped her with dead finality. *Delilah* shuddered for a fleeting moment as her bow crushed into the cliff, then she fell away onto her starboard side.

Under the pile of ripped canvas, tangled rigging, and splintered spars, I gradually came to my senses and saw I was wrapped around the twisted deadeyes of the starboard foreshrouds. A few feet away, Rork was similarly draped around the stump of the foremast. He wasn't moving.

Delilah's body convulsed violently as her transom was hit by more waves. Every few seconds the deck would jolt, then cant over even more. The extent of my vision within this mound of debris was perhaps six feet. Beyond that I could hear but not see. The sounds were horrifying in the dark.

The unremitting thunder of surf and shrieks of shredding wood overwhelmed my brain, making it useless to help me grasp the situation. In an attempt to disengage myself, I moved my left leg. Pain spread itself like fire throughout my body. I lay there, terror heaving my chest, and tried to assess what to do next. A larger wave staggered the hull, which crunched sickeningly for a second, then fell even farther over. That left leg, independent of my brain's command now, fell off the gunwale and hung in space. My mind and senses went blank.

How long I lay there, I do not know.

Ultimately, my unconsciousness was pierced by human sound. I heard voices out there, somewhere beyond my vision. Proving that I still lived, those words imprinted themselves in my mind to this very day.

A boy nearby yelled, *"Granpapa! Batoo fraka! Batoo fraka avèk blancs!"*

I caught some of it. *Batoo* . . . like *bateau?*—"a boat." *Avec blancs?*—"with whites." Someone was speaking French? I was trying to process that when someone else, an older man farther away, shouted in panic, *"Mwem Bondye! Voye chèche èd. Rele houngan!"*

That particular lingo was beyond me. But I was lucid enough to realize that somehow during my oblivion, *Delilah* had remained intact long enough for a band of natives to make their way down through the jagged cliff wall to the wreck.

Under the command of an elder, several young men were climbing aboard to see if anyone was alive. One of them, holding a torch with flames whipping about in the wind, leaned over me, shaking my shoulders. I woke to see a wild black face in the dark, inches from mine.

"*Ou vivan?*"

It sounded French, like the other, and I interpreted it as his asking if I was actually alive. I made the mistake of trying to answer likewise in French and implored him to send for help.

"*Appelez . . . aide . . .*"

He shrank back and yelled to his comrades, "*Franse! Franse!*"

Then I remembered where I was and what Roche had said. "No, no! *Américain, Américain!*"

That did the trick. He came close again and lifted the fore gaff off my left thigh, immediately alleviating the pain I felt there, then brushed the hair and blood from my eyes. He tapped his chest and said, "*Mwen Adolfus. Kijan ou rele?*"

His name evidently was Aldolfus. I took it that he wanted to know mine. Not wanting to incite problems again by using my admittedly bad French, I parroted his phrase and said, "*Mwen Peter.*"

Two of them were huddled over Rork. By the light of Aldolfus' torch, I could see my friend was covered in blood and still not moving. One of the Haitians used the word "*mouri*" and shook his head sadly. The worst had happened. Rork was dead. After all we'd been through on five continents, my dearest friend died because I'd failed in seamanship on a routine voyage in our home region. My heart went still, emotion filling my eyes as I cried out, "Sean! Please Sean, get up. Dear Jesus, not him."

Adolfus began throwing debris off me, hurried by another lurch of the hull. When the pile was cleared off, he pulled me along the deck to a section of planking that had been broken off. I was laid on it and from somewhere another man appeared. They lifted me up and a third man lashed me to the makeshift litter. Seconds later I was passed over the gunwale to other men on the rocks, who then gave me to still others, passing me up a line of men along a narrow path through a jumble of large rocks, up the cliff face.

Torches illuminated the area of the wreck below, allowing me to see others of my party being transported in a similar fashion. Coming up the path behind me I saw only three litters and tried to remember how many had been aboard. Was it eight? No, it was nine. None of bodies on the litters were moving. Instead, their heads rolled with the motion and limbs down hung limp. I rose on one elbow and searched for Cynda. By the flickering light I could tell which one was her by the blue cotton print dress. Her body lay inert, a clump of clothing on a board.

God help me, they were all dead. . . .

Adolfus put me down in a shallow cave, maybe twenty feet up the cliff from the wreck. Across the walls crude emblems were painted in white and blue; the graveled floor contained piles of papers, simple sketches of faces, and pieces of clothing. Scattered on the floor around me was a white powder in the vague shape of a cross. In a far corner, I saw a bottle surrounded with tiny lit candles, the kind one sees at Catholic churches. The candles cast a dim dreamlike gauzy light, illuminating facets in the rock, casting nervous shadows. It was an other-worldly scene.

Aldolfus gestured around the space and said, "*Gròt Manman Jimos yo.*"

I had no idea what he meant by that. "What did you say, Adolfus?"

He ignored me and left. I lay there, alone, still tied to the planking and unable to move. I called out, "Hello? Does anyone here speak English?"

From the shadows—the cave was deeper than I'd thought— came a woman's voice, deeper than most, deliberate, with a patience about it, as a teacher would have.

"Adolfus said to you that this is the Cave of the Mother of Twins. *Gròt Manman Jimos yo.* People come here to get help with their troubled relationships. And yes, there are a few of us in Haiti who speak some English. Missionary school, when I was young."

I craned my head around but could see no one. The voice was disembodied.

"Where are you? I can't see you."

"You do not need to see me, for you would not—*you cannot*—have the power to believe what you would see. I am the *mambo*, the woman shepherd, of these people. It has pleased *Agwè*, the *loa* of the sea, to save you. Therefore, our duty was clear. You will be safe for now."

I couldn't fathom her statement, or the strange words within, but then I wasn't in a mystical state of mind. "Thank you for your help, madam. Will you please get someone to untie me?"

"Yes. They are coming now with the other *blancs*."

I heard him before I saw him.

"Thank ye, lads, but me legs're workin' now an' I can walk fine enough. Me shipmates'll need yer help, though. Oh now, boyos, I can do it—let me walk."

I felt my body literally inflate with joy. He looked dreadful, but Sean Rork was far from deceased as he peeked cautiously into the cave.

"*Sweet Jesus, Mary, an' Joseph!* I was thinkin' you were dead an' washed away to sea. Peter Wake, you'll be the death o' me yet, scarin' me such as that!"

Rork limped in to me, followed by a Haitian carrying our seabags and Dan Horloft on a litter carried by Aldolfus. When he saw me, Dan muttered, "Nice landfall, Peter."

His short sarcasm struck straight to the core. Rork glared at him, but Dan was right. It was my fault.

Adolfus unlashed me as two other Haitians lugged in the litter carrying Cynda. When they put it down I saw her eyes were open. Tears blinded me. "Thank God above. Darling Cynda, where are you hurt?"

"Everywhere . . ." she croaked out. Moaning as she rolled over, she held out a hand, which I smothered in mine.

Adolfus reported to the *mambo* in rapid Haitian, which elicited a lengthy reply, more like orders than conversation. Adolfus and the other Haitian men immediately headed out of the cave in response.

Corny Rathburn hobbled in, favoring his right arm, and sat by Cynda. "I'm afraid your dear lady broke my fall down in the galley, Peter. She's got bad bruises and sprains, but no breaks, I think. I do apologize, Cynda, for being such an oaf."

She sounded stronger. "Corny, you're not an oaf. Thank you for carrying me out of the cabin. You hurt your arm?"

"Well, I do fear my drinking hand has been wounded. I'll be limited to smaller glasses."

He was rewarded with a faint giggle from Cynda. "Oh, Corny, you're a saint, aren't you? You've made me laugh in the midst of all this."

Absalom entered, carrying the front end of a litter containing Roche. The Bahamian was bleeding heavily from his forehead, but walking with only a slight limp.

"Ab! Damned if you don't amaze me," exclaimed Dan. "I saw you fly through the air like a bird. You didn't hit a rock?" He rubbed his knee. "I sure as hell did."

"Yes, sir, I did. But I came to my senses in the water. I must have bounced off a rock and back into the sea. Praise the Lord."

Rork took a breath, which I could see hurt him, and returned to his role as my number two in command, reporting, "Two didn't make it, sir. Billot and Claire're dead. Hit a big boulder on the port side. Roche made it, but he's hurt bad. Ribs and legs, me's thinkin', by the sight o' him."

Roche hadn't uttered a word to this point. He rolled to his side, facing me. Through gritted teeth he told me, "Claire . . . Henri . . . gone."

"I know, Roche. I'm sorry. How bad are you?"

"I am here and alive . . . will walk. Just need a little time . . . to get . . . my strength back."

197

Claire's body was brought in on a makeshift litter. Massive head wound from the rocks. Horrific to see, but a mercifully quick death. One of the Haitian men covered Claire's head with cloths from the pile on the floor. Billot was laid next to her. I forced myself to shake off my despair. There would be time for pity and accusation later. I needed to calculate what should be done now.

"The ship—did you get a look at her? What's left to salvage?" I asked Rork.

"Hull and rig're done for. *Delilah's* skin and bones're falling away fast. Maybe some provisions an' belongin's can be gotten out. I had them get your and my stuff out. By the way, sir—where the hell are we?"

"I don't know exactly, but I think we're close to Pointe Picolet."

"Then where's that damned lighthouse?" said Dan. "I was on lookout and didn't see *anything*."

The *mambo's* eerie voice echoed out of the shadows, startling my cohorts.

"The lighthouse is right above us, on the top of the cliff. President Salomon had it built ten years ago to warn *blanc* sailors of this point of land. It is iron for strength, has the most modern light mechanism, and will last a long time. Salomon wants to modernize Haiti, you see. To encourage trade, to make us like the other countries. He is, of course, a foolish dreamer."

"We didn't see any light."

A little laugh came back to me as she uttered, "But of course, *monsieur*. This is Haiti. Salomon's lighthouse has not been lit for years. No need for it—*we* know the location of Pointe Picolet."

She waited, then said, "It is time for you all to go. We have done what *Agwè* desires. You will be taken to the fort and turned over to the authorities. They will meet you there."

I called out to the dark corner, "We must get the rest of our personal things from the ship first, madam. It won't take long."

The voice that replied was almost a snarl. I'd never heard a woman sound like that. "The contents of your ship belong to us now. Some will be returned to *Agwè*. Others will be given to the deserving. Do not come back to this place, *Capitaine* Wake. Yes, I know your name. You will go and take your dead with you. It is not for you to be here. Any of you, even the Bahama *nwa*."

Absalom's eyes widened and he said something to Corny, the two of them turning their attention to me. Sitting up by then, fully alert and vexed by the dramatics, I peered into the gloom from where the voice emanated. I still could not see her, though she must've been just outside the cast of the candles' light, not more than fifteen feet away. "And just how do you know my name, madam?"

"*Agwè* knows your name and told me. Beware, *Capitaine* Wake, for the *loa* of the sea has told *Kalfu*, he who controls the crossroads, too. And *Kalfu* will be watching you closely while you are in this land of Haiti."

I was about to ask for an explanation of all this *Agwè*, *loa*, and *Kalfu* business, who I supposed to be tribal chiefs or some sort, when Corny leaned over toward me, a worried look on his face.

"Don't say a word, Peter. Just do as she says," he whispered. "I'll explain later. But we need to go. Now."

24

Chanm Mouri Nan

Pointe Picolet
Near Cap Haitien
North coast of Haiti
Tuesday, 21 August 1888

We formed a column outside the cave. Rork, Adolfus, and I in front. Corny, Dan, and Absalom followed immediately behind. Roche and Cynda were carried on litters. In the rear were litters carrying Billot and Claire.

The route was even more treacherous than before, a series of ever-ascending stepping-stone boulders with deep crevasses between. Boys with torches were stationed along the way, so that the *blancs* could see the perils of uncertain steps. Other boys waited to help us at the worst places, one of which involved stepping over a small stream plunging down into the sea. Aldolfus led the way, periodically conversing with me in his language, none of which I could decipher beyond his tone, which was attentive for our safety.

No, actually it was beyond mere concern—the man was

visibly scared that we would be hurt. I'd seen that look in the Orient. It was as if he had been made personally responsible for us, at his own peril.

We finally made it up to a level place with wind-bent stunted trees, perhaps ninety feet above the crashing waves, and rested there. We *blancs* fell in exhaustion, massaging legs and ankles. I didn't think I, or any of us from *Delilah*, could go much further on foot, but there was no place a wheeled vehicle could have traveled. The Haitians stood around nervously, exchanging comments and watching us. It was clear they didn't want to linger there.

"What time is it?" I asked Corny, who had his watch out. We were sitting together on a rock ledge, the sea surging below. A torch nearby showed how little room there was.

"Little after three o'clock. Another three hours till daylight."

"So what was it you wanted to tell me back there?"

"You were angry, Peter. I needed to stop you before you got that *mambo* woman annoyed to the point of ordering her men to do something violent."

"I didn't like her threat, Corny. We're shipwrecked seamen. Human decency dictates that civilized people help us, allow us to retrieve our belongings, not threaten us with mumbo-jumbo from their petty tribal warlords."

Corny lowered his tone. "These people *are* civilized, Peter, but it is a very different kind of civilization than what we're used to. And she wasn't referring to human warlords, she was referring to spirits."

"Oh, for God's sake, Corny. Not you, too. I expect this sort of drivel from young Absalom, and Rork, but you're an educated man—"

"—who has studied exotic cultures, including this one. Peter, we're not in the Western Hemisphere anymore, culturally. Make no mistake about it, my friend. We are in Africa and what she was talking about is *voudou*. Every Haitian's soul is purest Africa. Their *voudou* is not magical entertainment—it's their religion from

Africa. If we violate that, or dismiss it, we do so to our mortal risk. *Agwè* is a powerful *loa*, or spirit, here—the patron saint, as it were, of sailors and the sea. They think he saved us. Don't make light of their beliefs."

Absalom joined us, listening as Corny continued his elucidation. "And *Kalfu* is the *loa* of the night. He is one of the most powerful and sadistic of their spirits, the guardian of the crossroads from one world to another. Most of all, he controls the evil forces of the night. Her warning about him was very real. She was upset."

"One of his signs is the moon," added Absalom, who shifted his gaze upward. Above us to the west, the full moon began to shine through a thin area of the charcoal haze hiding the stars. Several of the Haitians were pointing it out to Adolfus.

Corny exhaled loudly. I noticed his hands trembling. The man was seriously worried. "So Peter, let's just be very cognizant that the Haitians believe in this, and let us try not to antagonize them. When we get to a city, we'll probably find sophisticated Christian people that will help us. Until then, we need to go along with whoever we find in charge."

"You agree with this?" I asked Absalom.

"I am a Christian like you, sir. But, just as I said at Andros Island, there are some things we can't explain. The *obeah* of the Bahamas is like this *voudou* in Haiti. Christians in the Bahamas do not make light of it."

After a short rest, we started up the cliff again, my crew barely able to move at this point, tottering stiffly along in line. When we reached the top, Adolfus stopped and pointed with his right hand toward a higher outcropping set back from the edge. A boy ran off with a torch and halted fifty yards away, illuminating an object.

It was the lighthouse. Made of an iron cylinder with thick

support braces and a checkerboard black and white paint scheme, it poked above the surrounding trees and faced north, across the sea. A useless silhouette in the dark. Seeing streaks of rust in the paint, I wondered how long Salomon's lighthouse would remain standing.

We tramped inland, now moving on a real path through ever thickening foliage. The ground was relatively level, a bit easier to negotiate. At a wide part of the path, after hearing his charges in constant pain, Adolfus proclaimed another rest stop, gesturing for us to sit along the path. My people did so, groaning with the effort.

Rork nudged me and walked fifteen feet away, to the edge of the torch light, where he sat down and leaned against a tree. I joined him, apart from everyone else. The Haitians gathered in a group on the far side of the path from us, much more agitated, and glancing around into the dark for some reason. Several looked our way, and none too friendly.

"Methinks we're bein' led somewhere evil, sir. The native lads're getting' a might testier the farther we go, like they're knowin' what's acomin' for us. We'd better be ready to fight."

"Yes, I've perceived that, too. But it'll be a damned short fight in our condition. Where are our seabags?"

We had our personal weapons in the seabags, but Rork pointed out that the bags were over next to Adolfus and his men, who had been carrying them. Thus they weren't within reach. Then he had an idea. "We could get some deadfall limbs to use for cudgels. If it looks like a fight, we bash 'em over the head, grab our bags and get the weapons out. Until then, we use 'em as walkin' sticks."

"Good idea. Let's find some and pass them out to our men, along with the word to stay alert. But don't let anyone know about our pistols and shotguns."

I surveyed the ground around me, seeing off in the dark a good five-foot-long branch. It was straight and would serve our purpose well. While bending to get it, I caught sight of a radiance, indistinct and barely discernible, in the woods perhaps forty feet away. I thought it maybe a village, the light deflected by a trick of jungle shadows, where we might find some government authority. The Haitians were having an animated discussion among themselves, so I beckoned Rork and we walked toward the curious glow.

Halfway there, we saw that it came out of a fissure in the ground, a crack perhaps four feet wide and twenty long. We exchanged glances. I looked back at our Haitian escort—they were still engrossed in conversation. "Let's see what this is," I murmured to Rork.

We cautiously trod to the very edge of the fissure, where a bamboo ladder led down ten feet into a cavern eroded into the rock. It was a large space, the volume of a ship's launch. The light came from candles like those we'd see in the *mambo*'s cave, but that is where the similarities ended, for her abode was positively benign compared to this place.

The candles shared space on a crude table with bottles and animal parts and feminine personal belongings, but the most bizarre item was centered in the middle of the cavern. It was the decaying body of a black woman in a white dress, the grinning face of whom was a frightening vision of decomposition. Her hands, folded across her chest, held something, though I could not tell what without descending to get closer, something I felt no urge to do. In fact, I had to fight the urge to flee in panic.

"Oh, Saint Michael an' Saint Patrick, don't fail me now! Me's ne'er seen the likes o' this," Rork said breathlessly, mesmerized by the gruesome sight below us. "Ah, sir . . . methinks 'tis time to return to our shipmates, straightaway."

"My thoughts exactly, Rork. Now I know why the natives had us stay on the path to rest."

We headed back but were too late.

"*Rete! Pa bouje!*"

The furious shout came from Adolfus. He stood arms akimbo on the pathway, glowering at me. I dropped the stick. Four of his men ran over and seized Rork and me by the wrists, dragging us back to the path and into the torchlight. They then backed away, leaving us standing there alone, as if afraid to be associated with the transgressors.

His eyes fierce, Adolfus indicated where I'd been and growled, "*Chanm mouri nan! Blanc ensolan!*"

Corny quickly stood, held up his hands in submission, and blurted out, "*Non! Sivouplè, Mesye Adolfus—adon! Padon. Nou regrèt . . .*"

Adolfus was so angry he was shaking. He flung his arm forward and marched down the path, his men pulling the whites up off the ground and pushing us along behind him.

"What the hell was all that about, Corny?"

"I'm no expert on this language, Peter, but it's a version of French. I think what he said was that you and Rork saw something outsiders shouldn't: *Chanm mouri nan*—the Chamber of the Dead. He also called you insolent. From what I remember of my studies long ago, the *voudou* people have a place their deceased go before burial, where prayers and offerings are made to ensure a peaceful afterlife. You violated that place, though unintentionally."

"What did you say back to him? You spoke the lingo pretty good."

"Based on my French, I've picked up some basic Creole words tonight, so I begged his pardon, saying that we were sorry."

A truer statement was never made.

~~

We arrived an hour later. Fort Picolet was a four-tiered stone and brick fortress perched on the cliff at the very end of its namesake point. As we entered on the second tier, by the light of our torchbearers, I saw a row of century-old French 32-pounder cannons mounted along the parapet. Around us, the interior buildings—barracks, officers' quarters, cookhouse, guardhouse, et cetera—were in a dilapidated condition, none of them having so much as a roof. The entry port was guarded by an impossibly young Haitian in a quasi-French uniform from the previous century. His musket was a contemporary of the cannon. He gave the impression of a theatrical chorus member, rather than a military man.

Adolfus, whose attitude had reversed completely from attentive to hostile disregard, motioned contemptuously for us to wait within a bricked ruin, uncovered like the others. He and his men then disappeared, leaving us one sputtering torch to see by. There we assembled—the living, the wounded, and the dead, from *Delilah's* wreck.

It appeared that, like many small countries, the Haitian army did not garrison the fort, for that would take a thousand men. Instead, a small lookout detail was posted there. The boy soldier had two older comrades stationed on the uppermost tier of the fortress, overlooking our place of rest. They spent what was left of the night sitting on a parapet above us, discussing the bedraggled visitors. Most of their attention was directed at me and Rork. Word, it would seem, had already circulated about our transgression.

True to his nature, Rork at once began building a pile of small rocks, for use as missiles in defending our miniature stronghold, should the situation deteriorate. Dan and Absalom assisted. Even Corny, the previously ever-optimistic member of the crew, joined in. Meanwhile, our seabags were once again in our possession, and as the others were piling their stones, I checked the readiness of our weaponry inside. Cynda, still on the litter, lay there staring at the torch, her only sound a forlorn moaning.

I am sure that at this point the reader can well imagine the thoughts occupying each of our minds right then, so I will forgo that most depressing description and forge ahead to the next phase of our odyssey.

Now that our immediate defense was secure, my primary task was to find shelter, food, clothing, and medical care. After that, we would push on to find Luke. In order to accomplish any of that,

I would need to meet, and get the support of, some Haitian in a senior official position.

Instead, I met a man who was to prove far more valuable than all the senior officials in Haiti, combined. His unique name and background were a great amazement to us, but those characteristics formed only a small part of an exceptional individual.

As the reader will soon understand, *Sergent-Chef* Vladimir Noel Yablonowski was a soldier who knew how to get things done. No small feat in a place like Haiti.

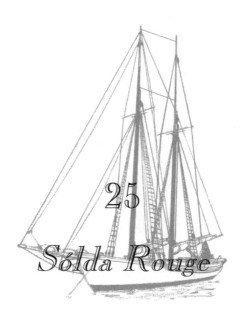

25
Sôlda Rouge

Cap Haitien
Northern Haiti
Tuesday, 21 August 1888

The sun peered over the fort's entryway when Rork roused me from a cramped slumber. Rising from the pile of stone ammunition, the solar rays seared my eyes, stunning me into temporary confusion as to my exact locale. I looked around, remembered regretfully where we were and proceeded to stretch my body. A searing throb in my back reminded me of the previous night's wreck. That damned leg also protested when I attempted to stand, making me stumble onto Cynda, who lay next to me. She let out a cry of pain and swore a most unladylike oath.

Dan stood next to Rork, scowling at a figure approaching at the head of a line of men in uniform.

"Company's comin' an' methinks it's official," Rork advised me.

"All right, get everybody up."

Dan went around and woke the rest of our number, so that by the time the man and his detail of soldiers arrived at the doorway to our decaying quarters, he faced an expectant group of six white faces and one black. Unlike the other Haitians we'd encountered, this one didn't seem fazed by our appearance in his country.

He was attired in a uniform that showed its French antecedents by the red trousers and blue cutaway coat with brass trim, topped by a black shako with red plume. His sleeve had the three thick chevrons of a senior sergeant. The other soldiers were coatless and wore simple faded fatigue uniforms that probably were once dark blue. Two of them had rifles—old Springfields from our Civil War twenty-five years earlier. Modern for Haiti.

"I understand that you are Americans, so I will speak in English. I am Sergeant-in-Chief Vladimir Noel Yablonowski, second assistant to the aide-de-camp to General Florvil Hyppolite, commander-in-chief of the Department of the North. I want you to know that you are safe and under the personal protection of the general, who sincerely laments your tragedy."

To say I was shocked is beyond an understatement. Not only did Yablonowski have a decidedly un-Haitian name, but he was speaking in fluent American-accented English. His face was in shadow at first, then he turned toward the east and I could fully study it, which only added to my surprise. The sergeant's skin was not the dark-black of Africa, but coffee-colored, and unlike everyone we'd encountered so far, he had deep blue irises set in oval eyes, along with the high cheekbones of his Slavic ancestry. Under his kepi was not the black nap of a Negro, but curly brown hair.

I spoke for the crew. "Sergeant, please accept our heartfelt thanks for the assistance. We are in dire need of decent food, water, clothing, and medical attention."

"And a bath," added Cynda.

He smiled. "We will all travel into the city of Cap Haitien now. Regrettably, there is no road from Fort Picolet worthy of the name, so we must go by foot along the coastal path until we get to the road at Fort St. Joseph, where we have wagons waiting. At Cap Haitien, you will be taken to the hotel for rest and food. Clothing will be arranged. A doctor has been notified."

"So how do you speak English so well?" asked Dan, rather too bluntly.

Yablonowski executed a half left-face, looked at Dan, and said, "Baptist missionary school, years ago, sir. Unlike many, I am a true Christian."

"Baptist?"

"No, that was just for school. I am a Catholic."

Roche, sat halfway up on his litter, looked coldly at Yablonowski, and uttered, "*Dobrahyee ootro.*"

The sergeant's head swiveled to Roche. "Thank you, sir. Good morning to you, as well. But I am not Russian. I am one of the *Polish*-Haitians. It is a long story and we do not have the time right now. Come let us get going before the sun gets too strong."

Roche grunted something and lay back down. Corny shot me a dubious glance. At that point Cynda spoke up softly. "Claire and Henri need to be buried."

Yablonowski bowed slightly. "Yes, of course. We are very sorry for your loss, madam. I thought you would appreciate a burial in the Christian cemetery in Cap Haitien, rather than a place like here."

He said the last with contempt, so much so that I inquired, "What exactly is this place, Sergeant?"

"This fort is very old. Adolfus put you in these ruins of the old French commandant's quarters. His decision to put you here was bad. This spot has been used for the last sixty years as the *hounfour* of a *malfacteur*—the *voudou* place of a practitioner of evil doings. Over there is an altar to *Ogoun*, the warrior *loa.*"

He pointed to a small bottle in a debris-filled corner. It was surrounded by short knife blades and pikes. Red patches of clothing were scattered among the blades. Red powder was everywhere. When we'd arrived, I was dog-tired and had missed it in the dark.

"So the man was trying to send us a message?" asked Dan.

Yablonowski frowned.

"No, it was not a message to you—for you as *blancs* cannot really understand this. Adolfus either had too much to drink last night and did this as a joke to himself and his friends, or he did it as a gesture to the *malfacteurs* to show them the objects of his anger, which would be you. *Ogoun* the warrior is associated with the revolutionary war against the French, and sometimes now invoked against all *blancs*. And up there is the home of *L'inglesou*, the *loa* of wild places, who kills anyone who offends him."

He gestured to the parapet above us, where the two soldiers had been perched, watching us in the night. "It is where the *bokors*, the sorcerers, conjure their concoctions."

"What about *Kalfu*? Is he around here?" asked Corny. "The *mambo* in the cave by the sea mentioned him last night. She said that *Agwè* had told *Kalfu* about us and that he would be watching us."

Yablonowski slowly let out a breath, looking none too happy with Corny's remarks. It was obvious that the sergeant had been given personal responsibility for the *blancs* who suddenly arrived out of nowhere, probably because he spoke English. Now that task had become far more difficult.

"*Kalfu* is everywhere in Haiti. Everywhere you may go, people will have already heard that *Kalfu* is watching you." His tone became more insistent. "You will be fine if you please do what I say and do not stray away from me. We will make arrangements to get you all out of Haiti as soon as possible on the first ship available."

I judged it best not to tell the sergeant at that moment of our search for a missing fourteen–year-old—or of my infringement of the chamber of the dead the previous night. It appeared that I had inadvertently made quite an enemy in Adolfus. I am a

Christian and therefore his pagan notions held no sway over me, but I did wonder if he would elevate his animosity from notions to actions.

Yablonowski, insistent to get under way, began issuing orders to his men, who then gestured to my people to get up and going. The soldiers had canvas army litters, and soon had the wounded and the mobile formed into a line. Ten minutes after the sergeant's arrival, we walked out of the old fort.

As we walked east into the rising sun, none of us expressed regret that we were leaving Pointe Picolet, with its malevolent air and bizarre inhabitants.

The coast east of Picolet trended around to the south, toward the anchorage at Cap Haitien. The ship channel followed close inshore, where two more forts, obsolete batteries, really, covered the seaward approach to the city. St. Joseph was a small battery of half a dozen old French cannon, not maintained or guarded. We climbed onto three carts there, with a fourth carrying our dead. Passing the third battery, Fort Maydi, composed of equally ancient mortars, we rounded the final point of land and saw Cap Haitien stretched out before us.

It was a tropical sprawl with a touch of Old World elegance. A collection of formerly sophisticated stone and brick buildings, constructed with European architecture, extended along a curving coco-palmed shoreline for a mile. These crumbling structures were predominantly a faded whitewashed gray, appearing like a line of old men bent over by age and infirmity.

As the town's suburban tentacles crept up a steep green mountainside, it changed from stone buildings to small wooden ones, some painted in the Caribbean's ubiquitous pink, blue, and green pastels. At the upper edges of the place, physically farthest from the sea and symbolically farthest from the French cultural influence, were hundreds of thatched hovels, blending into the ever-present jungle.

Among the rooftops in the center of town, three church spires pierced the sky. A large blue and red national flag drooped in the airless humid morning from a tall mast in the center of the city, near the tallest spires. It reminded me of a corpse someone forgot to take down after a hanging execution.

The brownish-sand shoreline before us was a gathering point for careened native boats, scattered flotsam, piled cargo, draped fishing nets, rubbish, and lounging people. At the center of Cap Haitian's waterfront curve stood a length of stone seawall, from which jutted a long planked wharf into the bay. A substantial building stood at its base, with another Haitian flag hoisted high. The only steamer in port was anchored just off the wharf. I couldn't see it clearly, but spotted a strange apparatus at the stern, where a British red ensign hung.

Yablonowski proudly informed me that I was looking at the customs wharf. The steamer was a cable-laying ship—the company was finishing up the completion of a telegraph line that would connect northern Haiti with the world, another project of President Salomon. The apparatus was a cable drum. The ship lent a certain sense of industry to the otherwise bucolic scene.

The city's quaint impression wilted rapidly upon closer familiarization. A strong stench first disabused my notion—a very unquaint combination of sewage in the streets and rotting fish on the beach. But we continued onward to our lodgings, located near the central plaza. When we arrived, Sergeant Yablonowski bowed and flourished his hand as we were helped down from the wagons.

"Welcome to your accommodations while here in Cap Haitien. They are the very best available, and I am certain you will find them to your liking. The account is being taken care of by the general as a gesture of our national goodwill toward the United States."

Hotel Colon, otherwise known as the Travelers' Hotel, stood at the corner of two streets. A run-down wood frame affair, it had seen its best days fifty years earlier. After what we'd been through, however, it looked like Eden. It was administered by a man we learned was famous in Haiti, of whom I'd never heard. With wild hair sprouting in confusion from his head, Oswald Durand was a politician and poet when he wasn't busy being the general manager. Welcoming us graciously at the front door, he and Corny—birds of a feather if ever there were—became instant friends.

Durand, colorfully attired in a blue silk suit with an outlandish white cravat, gushed in cultured French his condolences at our loss, his delight in our survival, and his hope that we would enjoy the hospitality of the city—all in one sentence. Obviously, not everyone in Haiti despised the French and their ways.

Not to be outdone in the oratory department, Corny proclaimed in fluent French our admiration for the culture of Haiti and undying appreciation for Sergeant Yablonowski, General Hyppolite, and Oswald Durand. Too tired to muster up my own French, I just kept my mouth shut. Corny was doing fine without me.

In the resulting air of *bonhomie*, Durand sent fruit and chilled juices up to our rooms, arranged hot baths for all hands, and promised new clothing and a visit from a doctor later that morning. Promises are never expected to be kept in the West Indies, but, most notably at this hotel, they were actually fulfilled. The stench and local suspicion of us at Cap Haitien were off-putting, but there was no denying the general's, and Durand's, sincerity. To be fair, all the people of substance we had encountered within the city were uniformly accommodating to our needs, leaving us with a pleasant impression of middle and upper Haitian society. By noon, the entire contingent—fed, clothed, and medically ministered to—had fallen into bed.

Except for me, of course. With the exchange between him and Roche still in my mind, I cornered Yablonowski in the lobby and asked about his background. My suspicions that, despite what he said to Roche, he was in fact Russian turned out to be unfounded.

The sergeant enlightened me on the subject. It seems that when Napoleon sent forty thousand troops to recover Haiti from the rebelling slaves in 1804, they included over five thousand men in the famous Polish Legion. That veteran army was led by General Wladyslaw Franciszdek Yablonowski, the good sergeant's great-great-grandfather, by way of a Haitian servant woman.

During operations in Haiti, eighty percent of the Polish Legion died of wounds and disease. The general himself died of yellow fever. By the end of the conflict, four hundred Poles, disaffected with the French, elected to join the revolutionary side and became Haitian citizens. Within a year, that had dwindled to 240, who intermarried and settled in five towns across southern Haiti, where their descendants still lived. Those Poles were the only white people allowed to become citizens and to own land in the new black country.

They were known as the *Moun Rouge*—the light-skinned people. The sergeant was commonly known as the *Sólda Rouge*—the "light-skinned soldier." Yablonowski candidly explained that his general valued his inherent military skills, his lack of blood affiliation with anyone in the north, and his disconcerting appearance to the local population. Not to mention his language ability. "I am useful in unusual situations," he said with a slight smile.

I learned from the sergeant that the American consul was in Port au Prince due to some political troubles there. I asked about sending a cable to Washington, my intention being to explain to my superiors the probable delay in returning from leave, but was told the new telegraph line was malfunctioning. Worried about my commanding officer's reaction to us overstaying our leave, I wrote a letter to Commodore Walker explaining our predicament and asked Durand to post it. It may be fairly questioned why I didn't send a letter to *Delilah*'s owner, explaining her loss. The candid answer is that I was exhausted and forgot. A regrettable omission, as I would later realize.

Finally, I requested to see the head man in the area, General Hyppolite, to present my appreciation for his, and his countrymen's, generosity to us. Yablonowski went off to deliver the request in person, returning an hour later with an approval. I was to be guest of the general at breakfast the next day. Thanking the sergeant again, I wearily climbed the stairs to my bath and the ultimate refuge of that glorious bed.

26

Hyppolite's Decision

Governor's Residence
Rue Penard and Rue Consuiel
Cap Haitien, Haiti
Wednesday, 22 August 1888

Compared to his fellow citizens, Florvil Hyppolite lived in magnificent luxury. We shared breakfast in the interior courtyard of a one-hundred-fifty-year-old mansion that once belonged to a slave-owning Frenchman. Surrounded by verandahs overlooking the estate's tranquil gardens, the whole protected by a ten-foot-high wall, it was a world removed from the impoverished reality of the city. The historic Gallic architectural accents and Haitian servants padding around silently told of the old times, but my host, as African as one can be, brought the impression up to date. He was a senior general of the Republic of Haiti, second longest independent nation in the Western Hemisphere.

"Captain Wake, we will get you home as fast as we can," the man offered pleasantly in very good English as he sampled a slice of pineapple. "Most fortuitously, a passenger-carrying cargo steamer should arrive tomorrow or the next day from Port au Prince. They are heading for Havana. We will prevail upon them to take you and your passengers away. Sergeant Yablonowski will arrange everything."

General Florvil Hyppolite was an impressive man. Sixty years of age and of medium frame, he had the patrician's unlined benevolent face, like a bishop comfortably entrenched in an affluent diocese. His chocolate skin and black moustache, receding carpet of snow white hair, and small shock of white goatee gave the man a grandfatherly air. Clad in his blue and gold dress uniform that morning, he projected something more than aristocratic poise, however.

Life and death were his to dispense. Florvil Hyppolite was the most powerful man in northern Haiti, and his intense large brown eyes, the only incongruous part of the image, showed that he knew it, and demanded that you respect it. They looked right through any veneer you might erect.

He clearly wanted these newly arrived Americans and Frenchmen out of his area as soon as possible. That much was obvious, despite the flowery talk that had occupied our breakfast so far. Unexpected, and requiring far more effort than we were worth, my companions and I were an annoyance he could do without right then, for he had larger issues to deal with. Unfortunately for the general, I was about to make his day worse. Although I would try to be as pleasant about it as he had been to that point.

"Your Excellency, thank you again for the wonderful kindness and compassion shown to me and my companions by the gentlemen of the Army of the Republic of Haiti. The inhabitants of this city have been wonderful. No nation in the world could do more than you have, and it is profoundly impressive and appreciated. Until this moment, I have not had the chance to explain why we were coming to Haiti, so allow me to explain—"

He stopped eating and interrupted me with a displeased tone. "You were intentionally coming to Haiti? Why?"

"To search for a missing fourteen-year-old boy named Luke Saunders, who came here several months ago on a schooner called *Condor*. Her captain is named Kingston. Do you know of him or the vessel, sir?"

His answer was far too quick. "No."

"The lady in our group, Mrs. Saunders, is the mother of Luke, who was a ship's boy on that schooner. The ship and boy are missing now but were last seen heading right here from Great Inagua Island. The lady is convinced her son is alive. I am convinced he is here in Haiti. The other gentlemen aboard, important men from Washington and Europe, are also convinced Luke is in this part of Haiti."

I paused to gauge his reaction. His jaw set like stone during my last sentence about Washington and Europe. The next part of my presentation would be delicate. If Roche was telling the truth and there really was a criminal called Sokolov in this area, the general might very well be one of his cronies. Hyppolite focused on me. He didn't fidget or delay his reply.

"I know nothing of a missing white boy around here."

I judged that Hyppolite was lying about *Condor* and Kingston—but truthful about his ignorance of Luke. Now came the main proposition.

"I think the boy got lost in Haiti and is residing with a Russian man named Sokolov, at some sort of farm up in the mountains. I intend to go there, retrieve the boy, and go home to America. But, of course, General, I need your help to do so."

Hyppolite leaned back in his chair, all signs of amiability leaving his face. Folding his hands in front, he inspected anew the audacious Yankee who had disturbed his domain by crashing into it.

"*Sólda Rouge* was wrong," he grumbled, more to himself than to me.

"Sir?"

"He said you would be gone in three days. On the steamer."

The general shook his head slowly, his eyes never leaving mine. "I think Yablonowski and I have completely misunderstood you, Captain. As a military man, I have learned that misunderstandings can be fatal. I do not make a habit of such mistakes. Now I must re-evaluate you, and the situation at hand."

He stopped me from replying with an upstretched hand. Then my host seemed to rise slightly in his chair and lean forward, the more to allow his total authority to emphasize itself upon me.

"I presume you are about to ask me to approve your travel to this man Sokolov's farm and also to provide an official escort on the journey to ensure safety. Alas, death is part of life in Haiti, Captain Wake, and I fear your presence in the interior would tempt the darker forces that inhabit men's souls—and those more violent *loa* that many believe live in the air around us. Not that I believe in such things, needless to say."

He let all that weigh on me for a moment, employing the old technique of transforming a guest into a subordinate. The performance was neatly done, I must admit, and probably enough to frighten the wits out of the average *blanc* who found themselves within the zone of his displeasure.

I, however, most assuredly did *not* fall into that particular category. No, indeed, for I knew certain things and had some unique leverage to which the dear general in all his grandeur was not privy. You see, I knew what Florvil Hyppolite was afraid of.

This positive turn of events stemmed from the evening before, when two of our company had not been idle. Following his afternoon rest, Corny went with his new friend Durand to the *Club des Negociants*, the Traders' Club, down on the waterfront, where they met a talkative local businessman named Gourgues. The three *raconteurs* enjoyed dinner and wine and several rounds of *digestifs*.

At the same time, Rork sat with Sergeant Yablonowski for simpler fare at a tavern near the barracks in the center of town. Both Corny and Rork shared a common mission assigned them by me—find out everything they could about Kingston, *Condor*, Luke, and Sokolov. Our conference had taken place later that night in my room.

Corny reported that he learned Kingston and his vessel were occasional visitors to the harbor who excited no undue interest. *Condor* had last been at Cap Haitien in late May. The schooner stayed only overnight and departed the next morning, after the tourist aboard, an old rich man from America, made his way ashore with Captain Kingston. Once on land, they were met by some Haitians and immediately proceeded out of the city. The rumor was that they were en route to a place known as the Citadelle, on a mountain peak called Laferrière—the fortress built by King Henri Christophe. The same place Victor Pamphile had told us about.

Rumor further had it that they were either amateur archaeologists or treasure hunters, which made sense to the locals, as Haitian legend had it that there was a cache of treasure hidden within the fort. No one had seen them since they'd left for the interior, and Durand thought the *blancs* might have forged their way farther south to Port au Prince, an arduous journey. It was ninety miles as the crow flies, but over a hundred fifty by road. The hotelier knew of no young white boy. He had heard of a Russian émigré, however, who was running a cattle ranch in the northeast part of Haiti, but he did not know names or details.

Then Corny briefed us on the political situation, which was in flux. The president of the country, seventy-three-year-old Lysius Salomon, a progressive from the south, had been in office since 1879. Over the years, his administration had increased public education, decreased the national debt to France, reorganized the army, established a national bank, joined the International Postal Union, fought down numerous rebellions, and contracted with a British company to connect a telegraph cable from Cap Haitien to Cuba—hence the ship in the harbor. In 1883, Salomon had sent two offers to the United States: naval base leasing rights at the island of Tortuga or at Mole St. Nicholas, in return for American protection. Both were rejected, a development I remembered well, for the rejections were my suggestion.

The situation had dramatically changed in Haiti in the last several weeks though. Salomon, tired and ill, resigned from office on August tenth; a special executive council of various personalities in Port au Prince had ostensibly taken over the government as of August eighteenth; rebellion by bands of *cacos*, peasant revolutionaries, was spreading throughout the land; and on the nineteenth, the U.S.S. *Galena* had entered Port au Prince harbor to protect American citizens. That explained why the local consul went to Port au Prince.

No one was in real control in the capital and anyone might seize command of the country at any time—except in the north, which was under the firm control of Hyppolite. Rumor had it that General Hyppolite was about to march on the capital and form a national government, by force if necessary. Everyone in Haiti was pondering what side to take when that happened.

Rork reported that Yablonowski had heard of Captain Frederick Kingston and the *Condor*. He did know that a party of white people had headed into the interior, looking for French ruins. He'd personally seen them leaving the city—with a young white servant. None of them appeared under duress. He also knew of the Russian with a cattle ranch in the remote mountains east of the Chaîne de Vallières mountains, near the border with Santo Domingo. He said the local word was that the Russian was building up the ranch stock with an eye to eventual export of the beef around the Caribbean.

Both Rork and Corny reported that none of their companions knew anything of a man whose name began with an 'O'. No one knew of the Russian doing anything illegal. And no one had seen the missing captain, tourist, or boy since they'd left town.

Thus, as I watched General Hyppolite regard me as an old tomcat would a cornered mouse, I knew that inside that emotionless exterior he was uncertain as to his own longevity at the hands of his compatriots; and most importantly, uncertain about what the United States thought of *him*. No doubt, he was probably waiting nervously for a U.S. Navy warship to come around Pointe Picolet any day now. Ah, yes, surmised I—this was no time for a Haitian leader to be harming, or even threatening, Americans in Haiti.

And right then was the moment to let him know precisely that.

"General, there are only the two of us in this room, so let us not waste time. I will be very blunt. This is what I need: a decent map of the region, a letter of introduction from you to whomever I may meet, Sergeant Yablonowski assigned as my guide, some sturdy pack animals, and a dozen *good* soldiers for security. It will take a week, maybe two, then we will leave with the boy. Our journey will be subtle in nature and not disturb the peace of the people, that I can assure you."

He began to shake his head, but I said, "No—hear me out. Let me finish. What *you* need is *this*: someone to find out what Sokolov is really up to out there in the jungle; and secondly, someone with influence to speak on your behalf to the American military when they arrive here, probably next week. As you well know, the U.S. Navy has already arrived in Port au Prince and their guns cover the city."

I counted internally to ten after that rather salient point, then continued with my discourse. "The United States can be a valuable ally or a formidable foe. The French, British, and the Germans will also probably arrive with warships within a week, to protect their people and investments.

"General, you are poised to be the supreme leader of the Republic, to realize your destiny and become the most famous of your country's presidents. Now is the time to safeguard your political flanks and rear with the support of prominent foreigners who can and will persuade their governments to support your efforts. You know that I, and the gentlemen of my expedition, can quite efficiently satisfy that need."

Thankfully, no one in Cap Haitien knew my real profession, or things would've gotten really complicated. Most of what I'd said was pure bluff. The ensuing silence lasted a full thirty seconds—a long time when you are staring eyeball to eyeball with a man who could very easily have you taken out and shot, or worse. It began to appear as if he was considering that very thing, until he finally spoke.

"I will give you the letter, the sergeant, some pack animals, and some men. You will write *me* a letter, copied four times, right now. This letter will be addressed to any captain of any warship from Europe or the United States. It will say that General Florvil Hyppolite is a professional military man of honor and should be accorded all of the respect and privileges such a man deserves. It will also say that I am the primary government executive in northern Haiti and all matters regarding foreign people and money will be referred to me and decided through me. And when you return to Cap Haitien from this journey into the mountains, you will privately brief me about this Russian and his farm project."

I raised my glass of rum-infused orange juice. "It would seem that we are both well-intentioned allies, sir. May I offer a toast? That the future unfold well for both of our enterprises."

I left the general's residence in the late morning with Sergeant Yablonowski and ten soldiers in tow. The letters had been written and signed. Supplies for the expedition were obtained from the army depot. The map, from the revolution eighty years earlier, had been gone over by Yablonowski and me. All was ready.

My next duty was a sad one—to oversee the funeral of Claire Fournier and Henri Billot in the Catholic house of worship facing the main square of Cap Haitien, the Place d'Armes. The church was a distant echo of France's glory, its roof a hodge-podge of underfunded renovation, the unpainted walls eroding in spots, the pews merely crude benches. But the edifice was still guarded by large statues of St. Peter and St. Paul, set in niches on the outside of the front wall. These two guardians of the faith overlooked the once-great plaza, presently a weedy yard, where once rebellious slaves were tortured in front of crowds of blacks forced to watch the spectacle.

The decayed treasury building, another ancient relic of the French, squatted across the square, perhaps remembering those glory days and quietly brooding its present fate. Around us, the descendants of those slaves shambled unhurriedly on their errands during the heat of the day, oblivious to the fears of this *blanc* in their midst. Their grandparents had exacted a gory revenge upon the French masters, and I wondered as I watched them if that hatred still smoldered. I thought it must. The Place d'Armes was a depressing scene of civilization decayed, of unspeakable horror— the ultimate nightmare scenario of European empires.

Inside the gloomy church, it was a plain service. Roche said a few words about his compatriots, the elderly priest intoned a prayer and I, though I never really got to know Claire and Henri, managed to say something reasonably appropriate. Then, when the talking was done, my limping shipmates carried the two pine boxes to the corner of the churchyard where the few lingering *blancs* in Haiti found eternal rest.

As we exited the churchyard gate afterward, Rork nudged me. Across the side street stood a tall figure watching us from the shadows of an almond tree. Aldolfus's teeth flashed white as he leered at me. Rork growled a Gaelic curse under his breath.

I steered the crew down the street and kept their attention away from Adolfus—no sense in knocking their morale even lower. The melancholy crowd hobbled along back to the hotel and our rooms for a final evening of recuperation. Everyone was nursing severe contusions and cuts, Roche had cracked ribs, Cynda's leg throbbed, Rork and Dan still could barely walk, and Corny's back was a constant source of pain. Even in his agony, though, Roche came alongside me and asked what I'd learned from Corny and Rork's evening with the locals and from Hyppolite.

I replied, "Damned little, Roche. Your Russian's raising cows, that's all."

Cynda and I walked together. Her resentment toward my decisions aboard *Delilah* having faded, our mutual fondness had returned. I think it was made stronger, desperate even, by the maudlin circumstances and eerie surroundings in which we found ourselves.

That was the night that I abandoned all reticence regarding Cynda. We lay under a mosquito net in her bed, lovers intertwined, as a silvered shaft of moonlight crossed the room like approval from heaven. Chastened by our experiences on the search so far, we murmured the hope that, against all that was arrayed against us, in the days to come we would find Luke and return to the lives we once knew.

Quite probably alone for the final time, due to the uncertainty of our coming journey, I harbored no doubts that my quiet affection for her was right. I was beyond caring about reproach by others. And so, my innately world-weary soul relaxed its defenses, surrendered to nature's instincts, and allowed me a night of blissful contentedness. I felt normal again. Love was a word I hadn't used, hadn't felt, since Linda had passed away from me seven years earlier. My heart had been devoid of real romance for years, but that evening I allowed myself the luxury of intimacy and love.

I think Cynda felt it too. Later, touching the scar on my chest caused by an Arab bullet in Africa, she softly asked, "Peter, do you think we could make a life together? A life back in our world?"

I was contemplating the same thing. "Once we've got Luke and are out of Haiti, we'll figure it out."

At dawn the next day we set off.

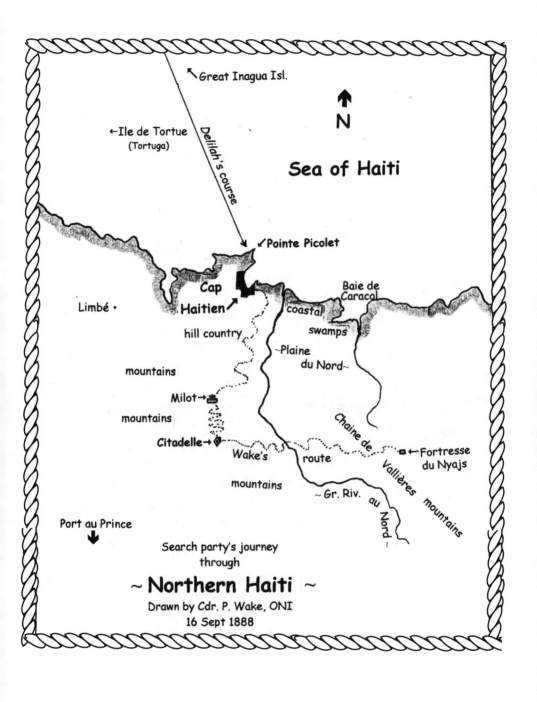

Great Inagua Isl.

←Ile de Tortue
(Tortuga)

Delilah's course

↑
N

Sea of Haiti

↙Pointe Picolet

Baie de
Caracol

Cap
Haitien

coastal

swamps

Limbé ·

hill country

~Plaine
du Nord~

mountains

Milot→

mountains

Citadelle→

Wake's

route

Chaine de Vallières mountains

↞Fortresse
du Nyajs

mountains

~Gr. Riv. au Nord~

Port au Prince
↓

Search party's journey
through

~ Northern Haiti ~

Drawn by Cdr. P. Wake, ONI
16 Sept 1888

27
The Citadelle

Village of Milot
Palace of Sans Souci
Montagne Laferrière
Northern Haiti
Saturday, 25 August 1888

With Saturday's sun still rising, we finally made it to our mountain goal, but it had been anything but an easy trip. The route was only thirty miles to the great fortress where we'd been told the New York tourist was heading—but it took three fatiguing days to get there. Nothing is easy in Haiti.

After starting late the previous Thursday morning, our column stretched out for fifty yards. Each of the eight foreigners had what we were told was a donkey to ride, as did the sergeant. Mine was the smallest donkey I've ever seen, barely supporting the weight of myself and my seabag. Six of the soldiers tended the pack animals while they walked alongside. Two soldiers formed an advance party a quarter-mile ahead, and two formed a rear guard a hundred yards astern. Yablonowski rode in front with me beside him. Rork and Roche were behind us, followed by Cynda, Absalom, Corny, and Dan. Behind them came the supplies.

Rork and I had our pistols pocket-ready, with the shotguns in the seabags stowed behind us on the donkeys' backs. We'd taken great pains so far in the journey to keep these weapons out of sight from our companions, a decision based upon the mutual observation that we weren't quite sure of who was friend and who was foe. All the better to surprise anyone trying to surprise us.

As is the case with most seamen, Rork and I are woefully deficient in equestrian skills, a trait our diminutive mounts grasped at the outset. The ensuing contest of wills provided great entertainment, especially for the curious natives who watched the column plod by. Rork and I finally established command over the brutes, following which they gave us little further trouble. Roche, who huffed condescendingly at our efforts, handled his steed like a cavalry officer from the start.

We left the crowded city and crossed a simple suspension bridge spanning the river Haut du Cap. Soon the road became nothing more than a cart path. Passing a French fort in ruins at Saline, we turned inland down a trail through a broad savannah of fields and swamps, made infinitely more difficult by recent deluges of the rainy season. Within ten miles, the coastal plains inclined into hills that grew in size with each step.

In the midst of yet another downpour Friday evening, we arrived at King Christophe's palace of Sans Souci at the village of Milot, more than a thousand feet in elevation. Yablonowski steered us to the house of an acquaintance. This friendly fellow had the appropriate name of Jolicoeur—jolly heart—and lodged the whole group in several stone dwellings. All hands were thoroughly exhausted and soaked, and we gratefully accepted the meager accommodations without complaint.

Later that night, our local host took Roche, Sergeant Yablonowski, Rork, and myself into the ruins of Christophe's palace and showed us where Kingston and his cohorts had rummaged for treasure. An earthquake in 1871 had laid waste to a large part of the edifice, but it was still an impressive sight—an exact copy of the palace at Versailles, complete with statuary-filled courtyards, colonnaded halls, sweeping entry stairs, ballrooms, and magnificent apartments for the king and the queen at separate ends of the palace. This was no savage's crude copy from a picture in a book. It was an intricate stone manor that was larger than anything I'd seen in America.

A full moon bathed us in silvery gray light, making everything indistinct and gauzy in the ever-present haze. Almost mystical. The scene of such incredible grandeur, reproduced from a hated culture that had enslaved these very people and accompanied by the fearsome sounds of jungle animals at night, lent a unsettling feeling to our tour. Finally, we ended up in Christophe's bedroom and sat down on the edge of a balcony to rest. Below us was the village and a narrow valley that cleaved the mountain. Torch lights flickered here and there, and from somewhere came the sound of drums, beating in a fluctuating staccato.

"A message," said Yablonowski, looking uncomfortable. Jolicoeur regarded Roche and me with open suspicion and rattled off something in the native lingo. The sergeant translated: "The message is about you gentlemen. It is a warning to the people to beware of you. That you are not tourists."

Roche asked, "A warning from whom?"

"*Kalfu.*"

I determined right then to get some answers immediately— by morning our hosts and the others in the town might be muted by fear or loathing of the *blancs* in their midst. Accordingly, Yablonowski translated my questions to Monsieur Jolicoeur and his answers.

Yes, he did recall the earlier visit of the *blancs amerikens* and their servant boy. It was memorable to him, for the foreigners had rampaged through the palace's ruins all night in an alcohol-fueled frenzy to find the old king's treasure. Right where we were sitting, in fact. Jolicoeur pointed to a mound of fresh rubble where they had dug. Naturally, as was the norm by that point, Vanderburg found nothing. This was the cause of an argument with their guide, a white man they referred to as "Captain." The boy was a bystander in the affair, watching from the distance.

The next day, they had gone farther up the mountain to the Citadelle fortress, again searching for loot. They spent the night in the fort, something few *blancs* had permission to do. Beyond that, Jolicoeur knew only that the Americans had descended the mountain by a different route. They headed not back through Milot to Cap Haitien, but down a trail to the east, into the jungle. He knew not where or why. He said he knew nothing of Sokolov the Russian.

As we got up to return to the village, Roche said aloud what we were all thinking. "They were heading *east*, not north back to Cap Haitien, or south to Port au Prince. Sokolov's lair is to the east. This is as I feared. They were heading into a trap."

He let that sink in before adding a statement of the obvious. "And now, my friends, so will we."

As the sun rose to our left—a weird pumpkin orange orb in that smoky Haitian sky—we began the climb to the top of the mountain. From Jolicoeur's place we could see the distant Citadelle, a brooding lead-colored monolith silhouetted against the gray morning sky. The great fortress built by King Christophe clung to the peak above us like an eagle grasping the body of its prey.

Initially, it looked to be an undemanding proposition, for the slope of the path out of Milot was not that adverse. We soon found out otherwise, for a quarter-mile along the path it became a cliffside route only wide enough for one person at a time. On our left side, the mountain plunged five hundred feet or more.

The incline steepened until our donkeys were plodding along at half a man's pace, struggling with the effort. Perched precariously atop the animals, the members of our clan leaned to the right, ready to abandon ship should the mounts stumble and go down. For another mile we traveled like this, each step a gamble for donkey and human. No one talked, no one made a sound. Even the soldiers, normally a chatty bunch, grimly trudged onward and upward along the path, watching every footfall.

At a switchback, Yablonowski halted the column and pointed straight up where a gray stone wall poked out of the bush-covered crags far above us—the base of the fortress. "The mountain is very steep from this point on," he informed us. "The donkeys cannot go farther. We must continue by foot. It is another two hundred fifty meters of elevation up to the fortress."

That announcement was met by a collective groan. It was a death-defying cliff. Corny said something about the mountain and Mohammed, Rork let out an Irish oath that rang off the valley below. Roche absently muttered in French that someone would probably fall off the mountain and die.

Absalom helped Cynda down off her donkey. She looked at me and set her jaw. "If we have to, Peter, we have to. Let's get to it. I can feel his presence here. Luke has been here. I think he's close."

The donkey path was a highway in comparison to our new course, which was literally a goat trail. With the sergeant leading the way, we clambered hand over hand up the rocks. There was no jungle here, we were too high, too exposed to wind. Bushes clung to crevasses and we clung to the bushes, pulling ourselves up, our arms and legs afire with pain, our lungs gasping for air. It was cold at that height. Not cold in a northern sense, but a humid chill aggravated by the wind and by our fear.

After two hours, we made it to the top, falling down in gasping heaps with our limbs twitching in pain. For at least half an hour we lay there, silently taking in the vista while recovering our breath. Around the northern horizon we could dimly see the coast through the haze. Nearer, a range of high ridges, like green waves in a storm, rolled off to the east—the direction Kingston and his party had gone.

Christophe's Sans Souci palace had been magnificent, but his Citadelle made it look miniscule. Never in my life, before or since, have I seen anything that compares to it. It was gargantuan. Half a mile long, its outer parapets towered one hundred and fifty feet above us.

"Thousands died building this fortress," Yablonowski explained as we subsequently made our way around the eastern side to the entrance. "King Christophe was insistent that it be the strongest fortification possible since he always expected the French to return and try to subjugate us again. It was built for four hundred cannons and has enough water and provisions for a garrison of four thousand men to last seven months without reinforcement. But, of course, the French never came back. Perhaps because of it."

After passing a dozen pyramids, each composed of thousands of cannon balls, we arrived at the massive twenty-foot-high double oak doors, where our guide added, "The Citadelle is the largest fortification in the Western Hemisphere. The pride of our nation."

Then he called up to the guards high above us, giving a password and the reason for our entry. Seconds later a thud resonated off the walls as the bolt was withdrawn and the doors slowly creaked opened.

"We will be staying inside the fortress for tonight, for it is not safe to be outside after dark." He didn't elaborate on that comment, but instead lightened his voice and stated, "Due to the fact you are under the special protection of General Hyppolite, we have been granted the privilege of staying in the royal apartment tonight. Please follow me and do not stray away. It is easy to get lost inside."

We entered a dark, casemated room. It was crowded with thirty-two-pounder smooth-bore cannon, aimed to sweep the ground in front of the entry doors. Then we emerged into the daylight, circled around an inner wall of the fort to the opposite side where a moat separated us from another doorway. A drawbridge was lowered and we crossed into the inner fortress, through a wall at least one hundred feet high and thirty feet thick. Another line of casemates watched over this entrance.

Once inside, we entered another dank dungeonlike space and proceeded down a winding passageway to a steep set of steps that took us up many levels to the broad central courtyard. At least a thousand feet long and three hundred wide, it was divided across the middle by a wall, into an upper patio and lower courtyard. The royal apartments were on the western side of the lower. The inner walls had a row of cannon lining its top. There were, undeniably, hundreds of them there, but most were at least a century old. None were modern rifled ordnance. The place was a museum, manned by a platoon, at the most, and commanded by a lieutenant.

The royal apartment had seen better days, but my people settled in for an afternoon of rest. While the others recuperated, Yablonowski and I were summoned to the fortress commander. We found him at the very top parapet. Behind him, the sun was settling down, a magenta orb suspended in the gray curtain. It colored the surroundings in an unreal sepia-rose tone, like a badly developed photograph.

Lieutenant Adrien Laurent was not what I expected from a man given such a prestigious post. A solid sixty years old, he was the color of sienna, with a deeply lined face, snow white hair, and the ropy muscles of a farmer. Yablonowski said he was an old comrade of the general's, a corporal until a year earlier, which is when he'd gotten this assignment as a repayment for some service rendered. By later that night I was able to surmise just what kind of service that had been.

The lieutenant wore the same fatigue uniform of his men, and

I could see where his former chevrons had been removed upon the promotion. Though he spoke articulately, he had the look of a peasant about him, perched with his legs dangling over the edge of a two-hundred-foot drop, while eating a dinner of some sort of meat stew. Obviously not impressed by our arrival at his fort, he rudely motioned for us to sit down. We sat dutifully beside him, our own legs dangling in air. I tried not to look down, instead concentrating on the man before me. The conversation was brief and Laurent started it, with Yablonowski, as always, translating.

"Why are you *blancs* here?"

My reply was equally succinct. "Searching for the white boy who was with the white men that visited here in late May. I know they were here."

He mumbled something.

I forged on. "Did any of them appear to be under any coercion?"

"Coercion?" He harrumphed at that notion. "They were under the influence of *rum*, and acted arrogantly, looking for the king's treasure and desecrating his memorial place in the courtyard, until I stopped them. Because they were ignorant *blancs*, I did not kill them. Instead, I let them stay the night, with the intention of making them leave in the morning. Yes, there was a boy with them. He was drunk and stupid too."

"Where did they go after leaving in the morning?"

"They didn't wait until morning. At midnight that night a couple of Bizango men arrived and asked for the leader of the *blancs*. He was expecting them."

He chuckled, a wicked sound. "After meeting with the Bizango men, the leader—he was a sailor captain, like you—talked to his own people, an old man and the boy. I do not speak *amerikan* but it appeared that the sailor told them he had found the treasure and had guides to take them to it, that it was a day's walk. He lied. Then he let the Bizango lead them all off into the night through jungle that way." He pointed east.

"Where did they go?"

"There is nothing that way for a foreigner, except the crazy old Russian who tries to raise cattle on a mountain. He buys thousands from around the area but sells none. It takes five days' walk, far past Grand Rivière du Nord, to get to his farm at Montay San."

"Have you been there? Are there other *blancs* with the Russian?"

"No, I have not been there. I hear things, though. Yes, a few other *blancs* live with him. They act like they were once soldiers, but I think it must be a colony for foreign lunatics. They put together strange things in a barn but do no real work. To work and guard the farm, the Russian brought in forty, fifty Bizango men from the south. The Bizangos keep the local people away from the farm. They hate the Kongos and Efiks, and the feeling is mutual."

I was about to ask for clarification of that last part when Laurent's mouth curled into a leer as Yablonowski translated the lieutenant's next comment. "The two Bizangos that arrived that night were *bourreaux*."

He turned his eyes to Yablonowski. "You know how those Bizango *bourreaux* are. I think your lost *blancs* who went with them are already dead, or wish they were, by now."

I noted that both times Laurent said the word *bourreaux,* Yablonowski's eyes widened. "Sergeant, what does all this mean? What's a *bourreau?* What—?

He stopped my inquiry with a sharp glance. The man was visibly shaken. "I'll explain later, sir. Later!"

Having accomplished frightening my companion and baffling me, Corporal-turned-Lieutenant Laurent stood abruptly and glared down at me. "That is all I know. Except for this: the general ordered me to let you stay a night, and you shall. But in the morning I order that you leave. I do not want you here. I have heard how you have already humiliated the *mambo* of Picolet and displeased the *loa*."

He leaned over close to me and spoke almost in a whisper, his strange African-sounding language losing none of its vehemence in Yablonowski's translation: "Little *blanc* sailor man, you are just like all the arrogant others who have come here and disrespected our ways, defiled our monuments, tried to steal what little we have, and treated us like the slaves we once were."

Laurent straightened up and gestured around him. "Ah, but Haiti has a way of dealing with you, all of you—from the French monsters in my grandfather's time, to the *amerikens* now. Oh, yes, I can *smell* the anger of *Kalfu* around you and see that the color red is everywhere in the air. Death is in your shadow."

Such was the first time I saw Lieutenant Laurent, but not the last. A few hours later his sinister prediction came true.

28
Revanj avék Pwazon

The Royal Apartment
within the Citadelle
Montagne Laferrière
Northern Haiti
Saturday, 25 August 1888

I called a conference that evening to brief everyone on what Sergeant Yablonowski and I had learned from Lieutenant Laurent. We filed into the royal apartment's dining chamber and sat around a cherry wood table lined with silver place settings that would've done justice to French nobility. In fact, I was informed by the Haitian sergeant that it *had* done justice to French nobility and was looted after their dismemberment following the slaves' revolution. Such was the acquisition process for much of Christophe's wealth.

The room had a strange character about it. The thin veneer of French sophistication reigned amidst a surrounding atmosphere of African malevolence, all of this placed within walls thirty feet thick, built to repel the mightiest army in the world. But was it a place of safety or a prison? It felt like the second to me. We were, for all purposes, very much like the French ninety years earlier—a foreign garrison besieged by an enemy beyond our capacity to comprehend.

Three tarnished silver candelabra mounted on the paneled walls, assisted by a larger one at the center of the table, provided the light. Rork, stationed at the door, gave us a semblance of security, but I cautioned everyone that we had to assume the walls might have passageways, and thus unfriendly ears. Outside, we heard those night drums again, an unsettling background to discuss the latest disturbing intelligence.

Dinner was being prepared for us, but until then we were given *clarin* to drink—out of cut crystal goblets. Priceless Hungarian goblets, Corny observed dryly. *Clarin*, for those fortunate enough not to be familiar with it, is the Haitian version of rotgut sugar cane liquor, and definitely unsuitable for the faint-hearted. There was no need for me to counsel caution on that point, we were all too nervous to imbibe more than a sip or two.

I explained to the circle of anxious eyes that Yablonowski and I had met with the Citadelle's unsympathetic commander, who informed us that Luke Saunders and the others had been at the fortress and left of their own will, heading east into the jungle with Bizango men. Then I turned it over to the sergeant for some background information about the culture of Haiti. Taking a deep breath, and averting his eyes away from Cynda, Yablonowski began.

"Haiti is Africa. The Haitian word for Africa is Guinée—and it is a large part of every Haitian's core to this day. Remember, when freedom came to us less than nine decades ago, the majority of the slaves here had been *born* in Africa. They remembered their homeland and the old ways of their tribe very well. Slaves in Haiti came from many tribes in Western Africa. Some of those tribes were enemies back there. When they arrived here and were put into the plantations, they naturally tended to stay with their own people. Because of distrust and to protect against enemy tribes on the plantations, the slaves formed secret tribal societies based on the ones back in their homeland. The societies also preserved their ways of life, their culture.

"Some of that culture is a religion, called in Haiti *voudou*. Most of it is harmless and a relatively positive influence on the lives of the people. But some of it is what Christians, like me, consider evil. To most Haitians, however, it is simply the everyday conflict between the good and bad sides of a man's soul—his desires and his conscience. The secret societies are part of this *voudou*, operating at night and keeping their people in fear by intimidation. And that is why Haitians stay inside after the sun goes down, unless they are in a society or have the protection and permission of one."

He cleared his throat, obviously uncomfortable explaining this to foreigners, and particularly to the sole woman in the room whose son was now in the jungle with the Bizango. His pained expression reminded me of Victor Pamphile's impassioned plea for us not to go to Haiti.

"As you know, I am half-European and half-Haitian. The Haitian half is of the Mende tribe, from what the Europeans call Sierra Leone. The Mende people have a secret night society here called the Poro. The Kakonda people from farther down in Africa have a society called the Bizango. It is one of the largest in Haiti, very powerful, feared by other tribes.

"The Bizango are mainly in the central and south parts of Haiti. They have a reputation for being very violent to people who refuse their orders. They do not like the people of the Kongo and Efik tribes because they consider them traitorous to the African slaves. Efik lived along the coast of Africa and captured slaves inland, then brought them out to the coast and sold them to the whites who came by ship from Europe. Many Kongo slaves were given good jobs at the plantations, easier jobs, sometimes as foremen over the other slaves.

"In this area of northern Haiti there are many Kongo and

Efik. That is why the Russian man is using Bizangos for his guards and workers, because they intimidate the local people."

Yablonowski swallowed hard, looking at Cynda. He then explained what Laurent had told us about the whites getting drunk and leaving with the Bizango men.

The assembly gasped and it grew very quiet around the table as Yablonowski continued, bringing up the point I was about to inquire upon. "There is another factor. Laurent said those two Bizango men were *bourreaux*."

"Oh, my God," uttered Corny, his head jerked around to see my reaction. "That's the French word for *executioners* . . ."

"Yes, Dr. Rathburn, it is," observed Roche. "But remember our hypothesis: the passenger from *Condor* is probably a hostage. There is no reason for Sokolov to kill him. He'll need him alive to get the ransom."

"If that is what he's really up to," said Dan.

Cynda, silent until then, cried out, "My son is with savages in this jungle! We have to get to him. Now!"

Yablonowski, who had not been privy to Roche's theory, or any of our knowledge about Sokolov and Kingston, studied us carefully as Rork asked me, "When do we get under way, sir?"

"At sunrise," I replied. "We're not going out there in the dark and wander around aimlessly. For right now, we eat dinner and try to get some rest. I want everyone ready to leave the fortress as the sun comes up."

Cynda started softly crying as I told the sergeant of our suspicions about Sokolov. He simply nodded and said, "I hope you are wrong."

Dinner, described by Yablonowski as *diri ak djon djon*, consisted of rice and mushrooms in grayish gravy, scattered with red beans and bits of meat identified as chicken. Two young barefoot soldiers of the garrison functioned as servants, their eyes watching us fearfully as they set the plates down. I imagined they worried about our affiliation with General Hyppolite and any repercussions of our displeasure.

The meal was bland but filling, and my famished companions soon finished. Yablonowski departed to bunk in with his men at the enlisted barracks, two levels down in the fort. His final words to me were, "I do not like this situation, Mr. Wake. It is far more complicated than I was told back in Cap Haitian. There is too much we do not know. We must be very careful when we leave here in the morning."

To say the least, thought I.

As everyone headed off to their beds in an attempt to rest for the night, I posted a guard detail at the entrance to the apartment. I couldn't define why, but didn't like the look in those servants' eyes. Laurent was no friend, Yablonowski was too far away for immediate help, Roche was still an unknown quantity to me, and Absalom was too young, so I used only the men I trusted fully— the Americans. Rork would take the first two-hour watch, I the second, Dan the third, Corny the last. Of course, only Rork and I were armed, but no one else knew that. The men dispersed. I went to my bed and lay there by the light of a tiny candle, thinking.

Ten minutes later it hit me—gradually at first, then accelerating rapidly.

I felt light-headed, dizzy, as if drunk. My mouth filled with saliva, and my face started to swell. The saliva began to dribble down my lips. Was I drunk? I couldn't be, for I'd only had half a glass of the *clarin*. I decided to rise and try to find some coffee, but my limbs were sluggish and I fell back. Rolling out of the bed I dropped roughly on the stone floor, but registered no pain. It was then that I realized my heart was pounding faster and faster, and I tried to call out for Rork, but my voice was a slurred moan.

Was what happened next serendipity or Divine intervention? I think the latter. There was a rustling in the hallway and Cynda opened the door.

"Peter, can I stay with you tonight? I'm so scared, and . . .Peter? Why are you on the floor? Dear Lord, what's happened!"

I couldn't tell her, for my tongue had ceased to follow commands, as did my arms and legs. I lay there drooling and groaning, looking up at her in the shadowy light. The look of absolute fright on her face did nothing to improve my morale.

Fortunately, she understood that I was not drunk and rushed out to get help. It arrived seconds later, when the men lifted me into bed and peppered me with questions I was unable to answer, for my voice was completely gone now, not even a moan was available to me. It was beginning to be hard to breathe and suddenly it all became clear to me. I was dying slowly, while wide awake and paralyzed. Oddly, I could still hear the conversation, but I wasn't looking up at them anymore, I was looking down at them, and my body, from the ceiling.

Absalom was the first of them to ascertain the problem. "Poisoned. A *voudou* poison. But what kind?"

Then Corny shouted, "The beans! We ate beans and rice for dinner. They must've given him Calabar beans in with the rest. They're a West African poison. I read a paper about it years ago, written by a Scottish missionary in Calabar, Africa."

"An' what'd be the medical remedy, then?" demanded Rork, grim-facedly inspecting my body for wounds.

"I'm trying to remember. It's been *twenty years ago* that I read it, Rork. Jesus above, I just can't remember! Well, the antidote was another plant, I do know that."

Rork ordered Absalom to fetch Yablonowski. They returned in what seemed an hour to me, but was probably only minutes.

The sergeant reported to Rork, "Most of the fort's guards have left. One of them still here told me that the lieutenant is Efik—and a *bokor*, a sorcerer, with the Leopard Society. He would know what to do, but I've searched and Laurent is nowhere to be seen. I have my men looking for him now. Only a *bokor* knows the method to reverse a *Revanj avék Pwazon.*"

"Revenge with poison?" asked Roche, translating it into French, then English.

"Yes. There are many different methods of a *coup poudre*, a poison powder. Lieutenant Laurent would know the proper cure, if we could make him tell us."

"Hell, Laurent's the bastard what did this. He'll not help us a wee bit," Rork growled at the Haitian. "You're a local lad. Don't *you* know what to do?"

Yablonowski shook his head quickly. "I stay away from these things. I am a Christian. I'm sorry, Mr. Rork, but I do not know."

"We at least have to get him to vomit," Corny remembered. "Peter has to vomit as much of it as he can, get it out of his body, before he goes into deliriums and convulsions. Is there any ipecac around here? Is there a medical kit? There should be some in a medicine chest."

The sergeant wagged his head. "There is no money for regular medicines. We use bush medicine here in Haiti. Plants. But I do not know which one causes vomiting."

"Buttonwood broth is what the *obeah* use in my islands," Absalom offered. "But we're too far from the coast. It doesn't grow up here. What about snakeroot? They use that in the Bahamas to get people to vomit. There should be some here. It grows in the forests."

"I have heard of that, but do not know its appearance," said Yablonowski. "But one of my men might."

"Get some fast, lad," Rork told the Haitian. "An' take Ab with ye."

Cynda was still holding my hand and stroking my sweating forehead. I couldn't feel her hand. My stomach was cramping so badly it made my body jerk and tremble uncontrollably. My head was on fire and she felt it with her wrist, tears streaming down her face. "He's burning up. We need to do more than just make

Peter vomit, we need that antidote. Corny, please calm down and think—what was the plant antidote to Calabar beans? The plant was . . . ?"

Corny slammed a fist down on the bedside table. "Belladonna! That was it! A solution in sugared water, made into a broth. You put it in the eyes and down the throat. There's atropine in the plant and it restores the nervous system, but too much can kill. You have to get it right. The solution was . . . yes, six grains of atropine of belladonna to one . . . drachma of sugared water. Hmm, we'll have to approximate."

Rork grabbed Dan by the shoulder. "Aye, get yourself down to Sergeant Yablonowski an' tell him to detail some men to find belladonna too, an' get it back up here straightaway."

He turned to Corny. "Get some water boilin' an' ready. We've got to get the water cleaned up for makin' that broth."

Then Rork pulled the lever-action Winchester shotgun out of his seabag. Holding it in his good right hand, he pulled back his jacket to reveal the Navy Colt in his waist and said to Roche, "Guard that door. Tell me if anyone other than our lads is comin' an' then stand out o' the way."

The Frenchman nodded, smiled slyly, and removed his hand from a trouser pocket. It held a small revolver. His other hand produced a cylindrical object that he clicked and a stiletto blade appeared. "I have my own weapons, Mr. Rork. Please allow me the honor of the first shot against any enemies that may appear. I admit to having some experience at it."

I vaguely remember how smoothly he said it—that even then, in the middle of a desperate situation, Roche was polished and blasé and ready for anything. Imperturbable. A very dangerous man. I wanted to warn Rork to watch him thoroughly. Of course, I couldn't.

Cynda called for sugared coffee. To keep me from unconsciousness, she said. I thought that pleasant but wanted to tell her it was too late, for the scene around me was fading into nothingness. Seconds later, I slid beyond awareness of my last senses, the ability to see or hear.

The pain ended. Fear disappeared. A great release of tension came over me. Then there was nothing but darkness. I was amazed that it was so easy. Anticlimactic, really. Almost pleasant, there at the end, floating away. The reader may be shocked at this, but I wasn't anymore. It was suddenly all understandable.

I was dead.

29

Dosye Lanmò, Longè Lavi

The Royal Apartment
within the Citadelle
Montagne Laferrière
Northern Haiti
Sunday, 26 August 1888

What happened next, I do not know. But Rork remembers it well.

Cynda began shrieking when she recognized I was gone. Corny came in with the boiled water and examined me, looking for a sign of a pulse or respiration. A few minutes later Dan, Absalom, and Yablonowski breathlessly came in with snakeroot and belladonna leaves, having run all the way through the fortress from the jungle. The Haitian sergeant had formed his men in a picket line in the courtyard and on the parapet, so there was an outer perimeter prepared to defend the area of the apartment. Laurent's men were nowhere to be seen, apparently having fled with their leader.

Corny could find no sign of life in my body but declared, "This doesn't mean he's dead. The poison slows down the body's metabolism to the point where it's difficult to find a pulse or a breath. He may still be alive."

He started issuing orders to the others. Cynda, still sobbing, prepared the sugared water. Dan, Absalom, and Yablonowski pounded the snakeroot and belladonna into a powder, taking great care as it was poisonous in large quantities. Meanwhile, Roche and Rork maintained a watch on the supposedly loyal Haitians guarding us outside.

Corny cautioned everyone, "I don't know exactly how to do this with an unconscious man. I'm now thinking that we don't put it in the eyes—that's for another poison. This one goes in the throat and nose. I hope I'm remembering this right. Look, we've got to be careful not to accidentally drown him. Be ready to turn him on his side if I tell you."

Corny then slowly poured the solution of belladonna into my mouth from one of the silver spoons on the dining room table. It didn't work. They tried again, but I remained slack, a dead weight, the fluid running out my lips. That was when Absalom started praying aloud in his Bahamian-accented school-learned English, joined by the Haitian sergeant. They kept repeating the words of Jesus in Mark 16: "*Whoever believes and is baptized will be saved, but whoever does not believe will be condemned. And these signs will accompany those who believe: In my name they will drive out demons; they will speak in new tongues; they will pick up snakes with their hands; and they will drink deadly poison, it will not hurt them at all; they will place their hands on sick people, and they will get well.*"

Absalom and Yablonowski placed their hands on my shoulders, continuing their prayers, tears falling from them, their voices getting more desperate with each reiteration. My body did not respond.

"We try again!" yelled Corny. Rork came and held my head steady as Corny reached inside my mouth and wedged my swollen tongue away from my palate. Then he dripped in more solution, this time getting it past the obstruction and down my throat.

"It's in. All right, now for the membranes—a drop under the

tongue and one in the nasal passage."

They were rewarded seconds later with a twitch of my eyes. Evidently the atropine from the powdered plant somehow roused my internal organs into action. The second symptom of life in my body was a tangible pulse, followed quickly by a shallow breath. A faint moan arrived as the fourth evidence of life. Thus, I am very happy to report that the initial impressions of my heinous demise turned out to be, quite understandably (and, of course, obviously), a misdiagnosis.

Amid the subsequent cheering, Corny shushed everyone. "Listen—we've got to get that original poison out. I'm going to try something here. Not sure it will work, but I'm trying to reach the soft palate. If I can reach it, that involuntary muscle might get Peter to react."

My throat dutifully constricted slightly when he touched it, the gagging reflex being stimulated. Corny called for Cynda to pour snakeroot broth into me, then they rolled me over to allow a route of egress for vomit.

I gagged and coughed, to the accompaniment of more cheers and "Thank you, Lord!" in French, Creole, and English. But no vomit.

"Again!" Corny commanded.

It took three times, but my body at last acted upon its mechanical instincts and followed Corny's wishes, purging the contents of my stomach. Some of the broth was poured into my nostrils, and that was what finally procured my system's cooperation—I sneezed into a semi-wakeful state. Snakeroot is a highly unpleasant weed and will, as one now knows, get the attention of the dead.

An hour passed until a more definitive indication of recovery was seen. I opened my eyes and tried to talk. I am told by several of the witnesses that my first slurred communication was less than profound. "I . . . sick."

Over the ensuing days, I was interrogated *ad nauseum* by my companions about my experiences of the afterlife. Of course, they were searching for a cosmic meaning, a discovery of the Creator's grand plan, with a view toward their own futures. That was completely reasonable. I was trying to make sense of it, too. Sorely tempted to create an eloquent account to satisfy their needs, my honesty compelled me to report truthfully that I had no memory of that period. Spreading a deceit, no matter how kindly well-intentioned, about the interaction of earthly life and that of the hereafter, and therefore possibly incurring the displeasure of the Almighty, is far beyond my level of courage.

But what happened during that space of several minutes is a subject that Rork cannot abandon and occasionally still brings up, usually under the stars, usually after several glasses of rum. But, alas, my mind and memory are lamentably mute. The great mystery of life remains unsolved by me.

Sergeant Yablonowski summed it up best of anyone the next day.

"*Dosye lanmò, mwen zanmi, andedan un longè lavi. Mèsi ou, Bondye!* It was a brief death, my friend, within a long life. Thank you, God!"

My recovery took four days. The second day I was eating and walking, and by the third I was ready to go, but Rork refused, insisting on remaining another day for me to get stronger. In those four days we gathered food and provisions from the kitchen and storerooms, maintained a constant guard, and readied ourselves as much as we could for whatever might await us. Conversation revolved around three main topics: finding Luke, discovering Sokolov's plans, and exacting revenge upon Laurent.

One pleasing discovery was that Yablonowski's ten men were loyal to him and demonstrated no ill will or hesitation toward their white retinue. They were mainly Kongo people, I learned, with eight of the ten of them true Christians, and thus had no affection for either the Bizango culture or the *voudou* religion.

Rork and I examined the primary question in our minds—why did Laurent do it? He harbored strong racial animosity, yes, but was that enough? Or was he under orders? From whom? By this point I had to assume Sokolov knew of our presence and motive. Did he control Laurent, through the Bizango men? Laurent owed his promotion and plush assignment to his old comrade and boss General Hyppolite, so would he do harm against a person under the protection of the general? Or was he following the order of the general? Were we allowed into the interior of the country so I could die an apparent accidental death by tropical ailment, so the others would be frightened and flee, going back to America? If so, did that mean the general ordered it? Was his aide Yablonowski part of the conspiracy?

Such convoluted thinking is part of my profession, for events are frequently never what they first seem. But it leads to a certain ambiguity of analysis and ultimately, decision-making, for the potential combinations of motive and capability are always unending. Rork thought Hyppolite the master of this drama, but I thought not. My money was on the Russian. I determined to move forward in our mission, presuming Yablonowski was loyal to me and the general, that the general wished us no harm, and that Laurent was under the control of Sokolov.

We were now well past the point of return anyway; the bonds among our multi-ethnic members having been forged by the death of Claire and Henri, Luke's undeniable peril, Laurent's treachery, my mortal escape, and the all-pervading terror of our environs. Those bonds were translated into a thirst for action, a determination to see this through and get it done. And, I must report, the inability of Laurent to kill me had boosted my image among the Haitians.

So, at sunrise on Thursday, the thirtieth of August, 1888, we walked out of the giant fortress. Leaving the Citadelle, we saw a ridge to the east, as tall as the one the fortress occupied. I picked a gap in the ridge as our first transit point and we entered the dark forest. Immediately we became as wet from perspiration as the trees from the rain. Thirty seconds after leaving the open space around the fort, we were enveloped by the tangle of foliage, descending a steep slope into a valley, and only able to see thirty feet ahead at the most. The path was an overgrown animal trail, barely discernible.

With the soldiers chopping a way through, our procession of eighteen blacks and whites became a tiny organism snaking its way into an alien region of the country, which even our Haitians hadn't visited before. Yablonowski and I took the lead, his crude map and my pocket boat compass our only guides. We'd left the modern nineteenth century behind upon departing Cap Haitien. At the fortress we had entered the eighteenth. Now, as we slowly fought our way east toward an imprisoned boy, we crossed into a primordial world, where time was forgotten and nature ruled without compassion.

Everyone felt it. We were being watched, and were very much on our own.

30

Suh Ghul Wasa!

Mountains of the Chaîne de Vallières
Northern Haiti
Sunday, 2 September 1888

The pace was excruciatingly slow and painful for the next several days. After crossing the Grand Rivière du Nord, we stopped and made camp on the fourth night. My dead reckoning indicated we were approximately twenty rhumb-line miles east of the Citadelle. Of course, actual course over ground was probably closer to fifty or more.

Having slung our hammocks—no one sleeps on the ground in a jungle if you can help it—we were about to settle into a circle and partake of a fish dinner from the river when one of the soldiers on guard came running to report to his sergeant. A couple of men were approaching down the trail. One was white.

As this was being translated for me, we heard a deep voice echo through the canopy of trees. The words were angry but unintelligible to any of our party: *"Suh ghul wasa! Wo dar di kona."*

It wasn't French, Russian, or Creole. Was the white man part of Sokolov's gang? The advance section of an attack on us? Any man other than my present companions I considered an enemy.

We heard it again, a disgusted tone, someone obviously cursing.

"*Suh ghul wasa!*"

"Everyone get away from the camp," I ordered. "Set up a defensive line over there," pointing to a thicket of bushes. To Yablonowski I said, "We'll make an ambush. Get your soldiers on each flank. Roche, Rork, and I will hold down the center."

Now I suppose that it is incumbent upon me to reiterate here that the sergeant knew nothing in detail of my or Rork's background, or Roche's for that matter. He thought Rork and I were merchant seamen and the Frenchman an acquaintance of ours, all of our party engaged from the start to find the boy.

So how did he respond to my commands? Well, I have discovered over the years that the human instinct is to herd together in times of danger and follow the lead of anyone who shows decisive guidance. Yablonowski did as told, like the others in our group. Our position was thus formed into a concave ambuscade. The campsite and cooking food served the role of bait, and consequently, the killing ground.

It gets dark in the jungle fast. We were losing the last of the light when I saw movement on the trail. Then it stopped—they'd caught a whiff of the cooking fire. Slowing their advance to a step-by-step reconnaissance, they were within twenty feet of the fire when one of them, he looked light-skinned, stumbled on a ground root and uttered yet another of those strange curses, this time as a whisper.

I checked our line. The soldiers were aiming their muskets at the white man. They looked nervous and about to fire, but I hesitated to give the order. Rork and Roche had the second in line calmly centered in their sights. It would be over quickly. But apparently it wasn't an attack, there were only two of them. Probably scouting for a larger body behind them. Or maybe they were really alone. What if we could capture and interrogate them?

Rork glanced at me, his face showing impatience with the delay, but at that instant I thought I recognized the white man. But it couldn't be—it was impossible.

"Woodgerd?" I called out. "Is that you?"

"Who the hell is that out there?" the shadowed figure replied in unmistakable Midwestern American English. He had a pistol in his right hand, leveled at the sound of my voice. I focused on the build, then the face. It was him, all right.

I called out to my companions, "Everyone put down your weapons—he's a friend! I know him." I repeated the word "friend" in French, and also in my recently learned Creole: "*Un ami, un zanmi.*"

They lowered their weapons, obviously perplexed by this stranger and his relationship to their *de facto* leader. To Woodgerd, I said, "It's Peter Wake, Michael. And Sean Rork."

Another outlandish phrase erupted from him, ending in English with, "Good God, what the hell is a squid like you doing in this forsaken friggin' hellhole, Wake? Don't tell me Uncle Sam's navy sent you *here*? You must be in deep trouble with some desk-bound admiral for them to send you to this sewage pit."

I'd last seen Colonel Michael Woodgerd three years before, when he was home in Alexandria, Virginia, from a mercenary stint as a military instructor to the Hermit Kingdom of Korea. We'd initially met in 1874, at Genoa, in Italy, then worked together in North Africa. In 1880, I was on assignment in South America and we'd met again, surviving some perilous times on the run from rather irate Chileans. I'd had the impression that he was currently in India, working for some rich maharaja as a military consultant, living a life of dissolute luxury.

His physique still looked the same—tall, barrel-chested, wide-set penetrating eyes—but there the resemblance ended. Now his trimmed goatee had straggled forth into a salt-and-peppered shaggy full beard, his close-cropped hair into long gray waves tied back into a ponytail. He looked like one of those mad intellectual European artists instead of a professional military man and veteran of the Army of the Potomac's campaigns. He also appeared to have been in the swamps for days, his clothes tattered and filthy. The black man with him was the same.

Rork and I strode forward and shook Woodgerd's hand.

"I'm on leave from the navy, Michael. This is a personal trip to assist a friend."

"A personal trip to *Haiti?*"

"Long story. What about you? You look in bad shape."

He looked grimly at me and said, "Ha, so do you, squid, but I'm damned glad to see you. I need some help, Peter."

"Well, so do *we*, Michael. You start, but first let me tell you who's who here."

I introduced him to my people. The Haitian with Woodgerd was named Lucien Aubrac. He stayed quietly in the background, wary of us. Everyone sat down and listened to Woodgerd explain how he was in Haiti as the meal of salt-dried fish and rice was doled out.

It was quite a tale. It turned out that Woodgerd hadn't been in India. That's where he thought he was headed, but the intermediary had misled him. Instead, he ended up in Afghanistan, northwest of India. Working in the mountains as a military advisor to a mercurial warlord loyal to the infamously tyrannical king of the country, Emir Abdur Rahman Khan, Woodgerd fought the emir's enemies for three years. It was no easy task, and one completely without the norms of war expected by Europeans and Americans. Also without any of the luxuries I'd imagined him having in India.

The violent phrases we'd heard as he approached were Pashto curses he'd picked up from his men during the campaign. *Suh ghul wasa* was a vulgarity that could be more politely translated into "What the hell happened?"

The Afghan contract lasted until the previous January, when he came back to his wife in Virginia and cast about for another mission. Through a friend, he heard of a European on a cattle farm in Haiti who needed a man run security for the place, evidently against rustlers. An easy job for a man like Woodgerd, one of only a few highly reputable mercenaries in the world who can demand, and get, substantial fees to form and lead large military formations. The term of the contract was until October. The tropics sounded good after the cold of Afghanistan, and it was a short-term commitment, so Woodgerd headed south to the Caribbean. He arrived in May and immediately realized this was no ordinary cattle enterprise. The German name of the farmer he'd been given was an alias—the man was really a Russian named Sokolov.

Cynda gasped. I put my hand on her arm, whispering in her ear, "Let him tell the story. Then I'll ask about Luke."

Woodgerd took a breath and continued. "I know you won't believe this, Peter. I was there and saw it and I didn't believe it. Sokolov's farm is a façade for a private military operation that is conducting experiments with aerial warship machines. They're part of a European revolutionary group and intend to use them against the monarchy in Russia, or anyone who gets in their way."

"Revolutionaries," muttered Roche. "It may also be of interest that the word 'Sokolov' means 'falcon' in Russian. Aerial warships. Ironic, no?"

"So what happened with you?" I asked Woodgerd.

"Sokolov and his Europeans heard I left the U.S. Army under a dark cloud during the war, so they assumed I was like them—beyond any sense of honor or affiliation. Wrong assumption. Once I saw what was going on, what they planned, I didn't want any part of it. But there I was, in the middle of this—" He gestured to our miserable surroundings. "—so I figured to string them along, find out what they're doing, and nip out when they weren't looking. I bided my time, doing my job training the guards, sort of a militia force."

Woodgerd indicated the man beside him. "Aubrac here was a sergeant in the guards. They're all Bizango men from another part of Haiti, except for him. Turns out he is a Christian from another tribal group."

"Mandique," said Aubrac. He went on in broken English. "I in south when *blancs* get Bizango men. I have time in army, so *blancs* ask me join too. I need money, so I go." He shook his head. "Bad place. No Christian. *Voudou très mal.*"

Cynda's fingers gripped my arm when he said that, and I asked, "Michael, did any new people, whites, arrive recently?"

He leaned back in surprise at my question. "Yes. They brought in an old man they'd misled to come to Haiti, then captured. Businessman from New York. Fellow named Kingston took this man and his friends on his schooner through the Bahamas. The others got off at Nassau, but Kingston got the last one to come along to Haiti, ostensibly to find some treasure the old king here buried. It was a sham, of course. Once they were in the middle of the jungle, the Bizangos ended the pretense, scared the wits out of the old man and put him under guard as a hostage at Forteresse du Nyajs. That's Sokolov's name for his place."

"Fortress of the clouds?" translated Corny.

"Yes," answered Woodgerd. "It's a clearing near the top of Montay San—'Blood Mountain' in Creole. Named for when the slaves butchered their masters and the blood ran down the mountain's river."

"What a quaint place we've found ourselves in . . ." remarked Corny with a perturbed look in my direction. Dan shook his head while gazing at his feet.

"And there was a boy named Luke with the businessman?" I asked. "Is he all right?"

"Yes. I was about to get *him*. Kingston brought him in with the old man. And yes, the kid is all right—doing just fine and happy as a clam, as a matter of fact."

Next to me, Cynda's eyes filled, but Woodgerd missed it and

continued. "The kid's in complete cahoots with Kingston and Sokolov. Luke's in charge of feeding the old man prisoner and taking care of him, and he also plays servant to the Russian. In fact, he lives at Sokolov's bungalow, being groomed as another apprentice terrorist to hate the major powers of the world and destroy them. The kid's already pretty well down that path."

"Did they already send the ransom demand?"

"Not yet. The ransom demand will be a million dollars. The demand'll go to New York by telegraph once the cable line is completed at Cap Haitien, which should be any day now."

Roche and I glanced at each other. His theory was right. Our eyes moved to Cynda, her head bowed in her hands, trying to muffle her weeping as she asked no one in particular, "Why? Why my Luke?"

"That's her son," I told Woodgerd. "We came here to rescue him."

He gave me a *what-are-you-crazy?* look—then regarded her sadly. "Very sorry to be telling you all this, ma'am. He's a strong, smart lad, but he's fallen under the sway of those fanatics. He wants to be just like them."

I changed the subject to the man I now thought of as our main target. "Tell me as much as you can about this man, Sokolov."

"He's unusual. *Very* unusual. Professor Sergei Alexandrovich Sokolov is fifty-eight years old, with quite a history. He is a brilliant engineer, graduate of the top Russian military academy, veteran of the Crimean War in the fifties and the Russo-Turkish War ten years ago.

"Sokolov is sophisticated, intellectual, versed in literature, likes wines and brandy. Prefers French cuisine and French women. In addition to Russian, he's fluent in French, English, and German. Started out life as the illegitimate son of a nobleman named Sedova. Ended up an artillerist in the army, where he spent almost forty years. Studied aeronautic physics on his own time and in eighty-four got himself transferred to General Boreskov's Army

Aeronautical Division. They were working on designing airships.

"But our boy Sokolov wasn't the loyal company man. He got fed up with the decadence of the Russian monarchy during the Turkish War, back in seventy-eight. Said too many Russians died because of royal incompetence, so he secretly joined a group in eighteen-eighty trying to kill the tsar. Gonna rid the country of the bad blue blood. Took 'em years, but they finally pulled it off and killed the tsar. Several got arrested and the rest disbanded. New tsar took over that made the old one look nice.

"Three years ago, Sokolov had finally had enough and deserted the army. Drifted in Germany and France and eventually ended up here, designing and building his dream, an aerial machine that will be invulnerable and deliver death like nothing imagined. His co-revolutionaries were funding him until recently."

"Colonel Woodgerd, do you know when Sokolov was planning to make this delivery of death?" Roche asked.

"Originally going to leave in October. He'd figured out the weather across the Atlantic, in Russia, everything. But now it's all changed. Something happened in May—just before I arrived—that worried them. An enemy group had discovered their location and was coming to Haiti. Not sure if they're other revolutionaries or a government unit or what. *Olamda*, or something like that, is what Sokolov called it. He's gotten very secretive about it.

"His supply man in Nassau, the one who transships large equipment on to Haiti, sent a warning letter to Sokolov about it. Then this Nassau man was killed in July, presumably by this enemy group. Sokolov accelerated the timetable on getting his machine ready for action. It's ready to go now. I don't know where this opposition group is exactly, but Sokolov and his cronies assume they are here in the country already."

Woodgerd glanced around the circle of firelight, then quietly said, "You're in that cloak-and-dagger-business, Peter—ever heard of this Olamda outfit?"

No, I hadn't heard of Olamda. But I remembered the letter to

Kingston from Nassau. *The 'O' is heading for Nassau.* Gerhart Wein was found drowned in Nassau, last seen alive drinking with Roche and his cohorts the night before. Suddenly, it came together for me. 'O' wasn't a person—it was the organization after Sokolov. But who was in it? Roche and his cohorts, to begin with. Who else?

"Don't recognize that word, Olamda," I replied. "But for some reason it is ringing a bell. I'll think of it in a minute."

"*Okhrana.* It is the *Okhrana,* Commander Wake."

Roche was standing at the edge of the firelight, a sly grin spreading across his face. "Do you recognize the name now?"

Woodgerd nodded. "Yeah, that's what Sokolov called it."

Oh, yes, I did recognize *that* name.

I enlightened the others. "The Okhrana is the Russian Imperial counter-intelligence spy organization, headquartered out of Saint Petersburg. But I think this is about the Okhrana's Foreign Bureau, which operates out of Paris and specializes in penetrating Russian émigré revolutionary groups. It works closely with the French authorities."

Turning to Roche, I said, "And I presume that you, Monsieur Roche, are not a French counter-intelligence operative of the Deuxième Bureau, but a senior officer in the Russian Okhrana in Paris. As were your friends, obviously. I must confess, sir—you did have me fooled."

Roche bowed slightly. "A regrettable but necessary subterfuge, Commander. I am impressed by your knowledge of Okhrana. Not many know of our work. And yes, Henri, Claire, and myself are members."

"I also presume that 'Roche' is an alias."

He shrugged. "A temporary *nom de guerre*, yes. Rather uninspired, I know, but what can one do? Of course, my real name is not truly important, especially here in the jungle."

"And since Sokolov prefers French cuisine and women, Claire was to provide him with a little romantic French companionship?"

"It would have been difficult to arrange, of course. However, my dear Claire was an expert in that delicate art."

"You killed the German in Nassau?" asked Dan.

"Henri did that, on my orders. Herr Wein was a dedicated follower of another German—the notorious Karl Marx—and a mortal enemy of my sovereign and my country. This is not about intellectual liberty of expression. This is war. It is as simple as that."

"And Sokolov's revolutionary group in Europe?" I inquired.

"It was mainly in Russia, with a few in Paris. *Narodnaya Volya*—in English it is called 'The People's Will.' Spoiled artists-turned-anarchists. They are no longer a problem for anyone but God."

That was another way of saying they were all executed, a realization not lost on the civilians of my crew.

"I've always had a vague idea of what you and Rork did, but now we find out that all three of you are spies?" said Dan, looking around at Rork, me, and Roche. It wasn't said in admiration.

The Russian's eyebrows arched mockingly. "Spies? Such an unfortunate word, Mr. Horloft. It is not used in our business, for it has unrealistic connotations. More suitable for cheap British novels."

Roche's attention swung to me. "Oh, and speaking of that stalwart island race, Commander, I should let you know that your British friend Randall is not really a policeman. He has been with the Military Intelligence Division of the British army since its inception fifteen years ago. His attempts at surveillance were rather clumsy, however. Completely inadequate. And he did no counter-surveillance at all. A basic mistake.

"If he had any professionalism at all, he would have caught me listening and watching your meeting with Randall and Major Teignholder at Graycliff House, where I was flattered to be the main topic. Randall proved to be such a disappointing adversary. I really expected better of British intelligence than that."

Dan, usually taciturn, was clearly disturbed by the revelations. "What? They're *all* spies?" To Corny Rathburn he said, "Murder, kidnapping, mercenaries, spies? What the hell did we get into here? And just how the hell do we get out of it?"

Agreeing with that assessment, Corny nodded. "Whatever it is, Dan, we're in it now. For better or worse, we've got to stick together."

Roche, leaning casually against a tree with an amused look at the chaos he'd started, inquired of my friend, "Colonel Woodgerd, how exactly does Sokolov think he is going to harm the Russian monarchy with a balloon in Haiti?"

"It's more than just a balloon. It's an aerial warship. He's going to deliver a devastating attack using it against government targets, starting at the Baltic with the naval station at St. Petersburg and working inland to the Tsar's Grand Kremlin Palace in Moscow itself.

"The warship will drop both explosives and some sort of material, clothing maybe, infected with typhus. Also propaganda leaflets to the people, calling for them to take back their country. Sokolov's almost ready to fly the final version of this thing."

The mention of that dreaded word *typhus* brought a gasp from everyone, Haitians, Bahamian, and Americans. To me there was a huge gap in the logic, though. "I don't understand how he's going to get this thing to Russia. It's too far to fly."

"The long distance cable ship at Cap Haitian. Kingston and his crew will capture it in the middle of the night and disappear with it east along the coast to Caracol Bay, just north of here. Sokolov will fly the machine down to the coast and meet the ship. They'll use the cable drum on the ship as an adjustable tow line and steam across the Atlantic to Europe. Look, I know it all sounds far-fetched, but it isn't. I've seen this warship machine. And I know the cable ship is in the harbor. Sokolov's planned this damned thing out pretty well. Kingston has already departed for the coast and I presume he's getting ready now to seize the ship."

Our company, previously troubled by Roche's comments, was now speechless at the enormity of what Woodgerd had just laid out to us. While it did surprise me, I knew that from a technical standpoint what he said was entirely possible.

In my work at the Office of Naval Intelligence, I routinely perused technical reports from our operatives around the world. I'd read the reports on airships coming from American naval attachés in Europe: Lieutenant Benjamin Buckingham in Paris and Commander French Chadwick in London.

Those reports documented the French, German, Russian, and British armies' use of aerial ships, mostly balloons, for observation purposes. The British had used them quite effectively during the Sudan War in the preceding two years. The French used them in Indochina in 1884, a year after I was there, at the battles of Dien Bien Phu and Hong Dha. But balloons weren't powered or steerable. They stayed tethered in one spot or they sailed downwind.

The French army's recent efforts were the most advanced and had gone far beyond simple stationary balloons. They were working on the creation of an aerial warship that could fly anywhere, even against the wind. In 1884, they'd launched an electric-motor-powered military craft one hundred seventy feet long, *La France*. She'd flown through the sky for miles, upwind and down, ascending and descending, and navigating various courses at will. It was just a matter of time until military applications to powered flight came to fruition. The Americans, as usual, lagged far behind, without any current military effort in the field at all.

My knowledge of the advancements in this science was quite basic, but I did know this: If Sokolov actually *had* advanced beyond the French army's aerial warship, he would be absolutely invincible.

"So how and when did you two get out?" I asked Woodgerd.

"Last night we slipped over the wall. My plan was to get to Cap Haitien and warn the authorities. Sokolov knows we're gone by now and probably has men out looking for us. And he'll set his plan in motion right away. It takes time to get the hydrogen generators going, get everything ready, so it'll be tomorrow night at the earliest."

"And his plan is to take himself and his cadre out of there on the machine?"

"Yes."

"With the boy and the hostage?"

"Probably the boy, but not the old man. Now that everything is falling apart he doesn't have time for the ransom idea. No room for the hostage. Weight is the critical factor for the warship. Even I wasn't allowed to go. He told me I was to return to Cap Haitien and get passage home from there, but I figured he'd really have me killed just after he departed. No loose ends that way."

"Then we don't have the time to go back to Cap Haitien. We have to make do with what we have and get to Sokolov's compound as soon as possible. All right, let's break up this camp, we need to get away from the trail in case they come looking. We'll rest for a while over there, in the forest, then get moving again. Michael, you'll lead when we get under way."

Yablonowski came over and sat next to me. "I need to send a messenger to General Hyppolite in Cap Haitien. Tell him about Sokolov's fort and what he is doing there, and about what he plans on doing with the cable ship. I will send two of my men. It will take several days, but I must alert my superiors."

"Excellent idea, Sergeant."

More rain began as we removed our gear from the campsite on the trail. Soaked and sitting on a fallen tree trunk off by myself, mind reeling with the various factors at work, I loathed my inability to come up with a coherent plan of action for when we arrived at Forteresse des Nyajs. There was yet an additional factor that had not yet occurred to me, however—a major one, that both Sokolov and I had neglected to take into account.

God was about to get involved, in a very impressive way.

31

The Monster Revealed

Forteresse des Nyajs
Montay San in Northern Haiti
Tuesday, 4 September 1888

It was sunrise two days later when we arrived, muddy and
exhausted, at the side of a mountain overlooking Sokolov's lair.
I say *overlooking*, but we could not see a thing because the air was
thick with water, for the steady rain had developed into a deluge.

An ocean of water dropped from the heavens, accompanied
by gusts of wind that bent the trees and sent fallen branches sailing
through the air. The northwesterly wind increased by the hour, the
blasts well up into tropical storm force. The Haitians jabbered about
what this meant, the consensus being that yet another hurricane
was on the way. Absalom's opinion was that it had already arrived.
I thought him right.

Rork ventured the notion that we should be thankful, for
the stormy conditions hampered enemy efforts to search for us or
to flee in the aerial machine. And it helped make our approach

undetected. He then suggested that we use the weather to our advantage in our upcoming business, surprise and stealth being our best allies. It was an eminently sound idea, which unfortunately didn't survive the scene we found before us, when we finally could see where we were.

It was noon before a break in the rain allowed a view of our adversary's fortress spread out across a plateau forty feet below us. Between our jungle-covered hillside observation point and the outer wall was a swift-running, thirty-foot-wide, stream called the Rivière San, as in Blood River.

Fifty yards upstream to our left, rocky shoals supplied a potential route across the water, but the river was rising fast. Ten yards from the opposite riverbank was the wooden outer wall. It stretched a long way. The Russian's entire base was huge—every bit of a quarter mile long by two hundred yards wide. Our location was nearest the northern end. Woodgerd pointed out the various features and described them in detail.

The outer perimeter wall was a palisade of palm logs about ten feet high, topped by guard towers every thirty yards. Only one gate pierced the wall, at the farthest end from us. Four of the guard towers were larger and carried deadly Hotchkiss guns, thirty-seven millimeter rapid-fire cannons capable of firing forty-three rounds a minute. Between the outer perimeter and an inner wall lay a barn, paddock, vegetable gardens, and barracks for the Bizangos. Between the walls down at the far end to the south were the officers' quarters.

Inside the five-foot-high inner wall, built of palm logs laid horizontally, lay the reason for the base—the aerial warship's barn, a building fully two hundred feet long, fifty high, and sixty wide. It was surrounded by workshops, and at the southern end, by the armory and Sokolov's bungalow, the only dwelling inside the inner wall.

Rork noted that the men in the guard posts were carrying modern rifles, and seemed to be alert even in the prevailing stormy conditions. Woodgerd said they were armed with the recently issued French army Lebel rifles, an eight-round rifle that used the new smokeless powder I'd heard about but not seen in action. The Lebels and Hotchkiss guns were obtained through Sokolov's contacts in France, stolen from army depots and subsequently sold on the black market in Marseille.

Woodgerd said the hostage was kept in the small barn I could see fifty yards from our position. It had bamboo walls and a thatch roof. The intervening space between us had two barriers: that raging river and the outer wall. An added dimension trumped the barriers—one of the guard posts on that section of the wall contained a Hotchkiss gun, with two men crouching next to it, scanning their sector, which was our hillside.

Earlier, Yablonowski had spread two pieces of canvas hammock between some trees about fifty feet back from the edge of the hill. I ordered everyone to retire to that location, where we'd have at least some shelter from the storm. Rork stayed on watch at the observation point that looked out over the compound below us. One of Yablonowski's soldiers was stationed to watch the animal trail we'd used for ingress.

Huddled under the canvas, the rain an incessant drumroll, I glanced about me to gauge the effect the imposing sight of Forteresse des Nyajs had on my associates. Cynda wore a determined expression. Gone was the demure Southern lady, her eyes now displayed an animal ferocity—we were close to where her son might be at that very moment. Roche, silent as usual, seemed to be grimly designing the destruction of Sokolov's hideout. Dan and Corny were discussing aeronautics and the amount of lift needed to accomplish what Sokolov planned.

Corny was dubious. "He can try, but there is a point beyond which the laws of physics stop you. This is nothing more than a madman's impossible delusion."

Dan is normally reserved in most conversations, but warms quickly in scientific matters, where his mind had a natural affinity.

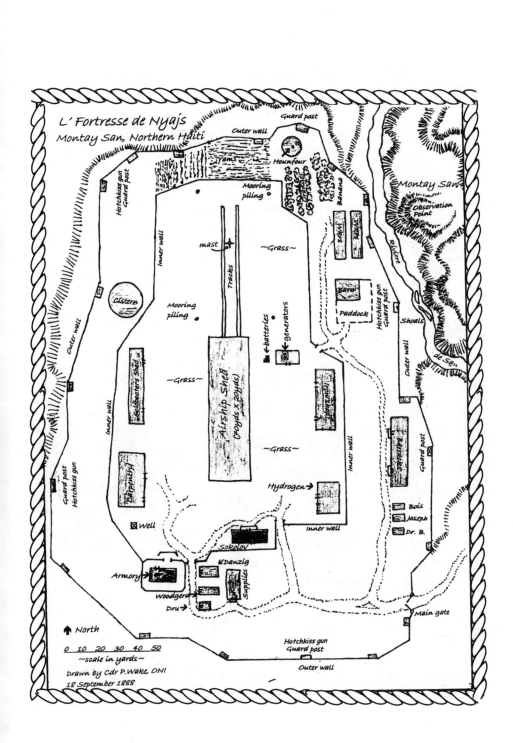

L' Fortresse de Nyajs
Montay San, Northern Haiti

Guard post
Outer wall
Yams
Hounfour
Mooring piling

Montay San
Observation Point

Banana
Sisal

Hotchkiss gun
Guard post

Inner wall

mast
~Grass~
Tracks

Cistern
Mooring piling

Barn
Paddock

Hotchkiss gun
Guard post

Outer wall

Shoals

Rivière

de San

Goldbeaters Shed
~Grass~

Airship Shed
(70 yds × 20 yds)

←batteries
←generators

Hangar

Inner wall

Guard post
Hotchkiss gun

Carpentry

~Grass~

Hydrogen →

Barracks

Guard post

Bois
Joseph
Dr. B.

☒ Well

Sokolov

K'Danzig

Supplies

Inner wall

Armory

Woodgera

Dru →

Main gate

↑ North

0 10 20 30 40 50
~scale in yards~

Hotchkiss gun
Guard post

Outer wall

Drawn by Cdr P. Wake, ONI
18 September 1888

I listened in as he angrily retorted, "No, Corny. You know about languages and cultures and history, but you're completely wrong on this. Sokolov's idea *can* be done."

Dan waved away Corny's coming objection. "You are way behind the science on this, my ethnologist friend. Arthur Krebs and Charles Renard, and the Tissandier brothers, have all built powered aerial ships in France. And flown them repeatedly. Krebs and Renard are using an eight-and-a-half-horse-power Siemens electric motor from Germany for the propulsion, with a nine-hundred-fifty-pound battery for the motor. And that setup got them going at over ten miles an hour through the sky.

"But that's not the latest. I've personally met the men building an aerial ship with a *gasoline*-fueled internal combustion motor in Germany. Karl Wolfert and Ernst Baumgarten are using a new type of combustible engine from Gottlieb Daimler. It was supposed to be flown this summer, but, of course, we've been busy sampling life in paradise down here in the tropics, so I don't know how it went."

"All right, Dan, I give up," said Corny. "The Russian's contraption is possible."

Dan wasn't going to let him off that easy. "Corny, this apparatus is not only possible, it's quite feasible. I've studied the dynamic physics of flight—it's not that far from the dynamics of ships. Archimedes Principle, Boyle's Law, Charles' Law. The primary factor in the air is lift, very similar to that for ships. Archimedes long ago worked it out: the buoyant force exerted upon a body immersed in a fluid is equal to the weight of the fluid displaced. Works the same way in air." He looked at Woodgerd. "They using hydrogen, I believe you said?"

"Yes, sir. The shed over by the airship barn houses the hydrogen generators."

"Very good. Hydrogen will lift about seventy-one pounds for every one thousand cubic feet of volume displaced. Renard and Kreb's ship displaced somewhere around sixty-six thousand cubic feet, so they could lift about forty-seven hundred pounds of weight. That's counting the whole airship and everything in it. Got that, Corny?"

"Yep, I've got it."

I could tell he didn't, but appreciated him not arguing. We were all tired and wet, and I wasn't in the mood for any more quarreling. Besides, this was getting interesting.

Dan was positively enthusiastic now. I'd only seen him this way during the evening philosophy and science sessions, usually enhanced by gin cocktails, at the Celestial Club in Washington. "All right, Corny, so now we go to Boyle: at constant temperature, the volume of a gas varies inversely with the pressure. As the pressure increases, the volume decreases, and also the reverse. Charles' Law works out a companion factor: at constant pressure, the volume of the gas varies directly with temperature changes. If the air gets hot, the gas expands. When it gets cool, the gas contracts."

Dan took a breath and the lecture continued. The man was encyclopedic.

"So my point is this, that the factors involved in lighter-than-air flight have been well known for a long time. Others have learned how to conquer these factors with aerial ships, even handling the critical weight problem. If Sokolov knew of these developments and was able to decrease the structural weight of his machine, while keeping the same capability for lift, he'd be able to build an aerial warship with the ability to carry out his intentions. And if it's bigger than the French ship, with more cubic feet of lift, the Russian's potential would be even more increased. It's a fascinating concept."

"Well, I think it's a depressing concept," huffed Corny. "Good Lord, bombs and typhus infections? This is a violation of the norms of basic humanity and the laws of war. A damnably barbaric machine of death, if you ask me."

Dan wasn't swayed by the ethical counterattack. "And that Hotchkiss gun over there, staring right at us, is pretty barbaric, my friend. But humane notions don't stop science."

I was very surprised at Dan Horloft's knowledge on the subject. He was bringing up things that were in the technical reports I'd read, but hadn't really understood until then.

"I had no idea you were so well versed on the developments in flight, Dan. Where the hell did you learn all this?"

"I was in Europe last year to inspect naval building programs, Peter. Along the way, I met some German aeronauts and heard what the French and Brits were doing." He gestured to our surroundings and added disgustedly, "Must admit I never thought I'd be discussing this in the jungles of Haiti. Or that I'd even *be* in Haiti, for that matter."

"Do you know the operating procedures for these aerial machines?"

He shrugged. "The basics, yes. The crew has to keep all three of those laws of physics in mind all the time for—unlike in the laboratory—when they are in the air, temperature and pressure and volume are constantly changing. Control it wrong and you fall to earth. And there are a lot of subtle nuances to steering one of these things also. The whole operation is three dimensional, not two dimensional like a ship."

Dan then expanded upon the subject of aerial navigation. I saw Roche listening intently and wondered how much he already had known of Sokolov's plans but wasn't saying. He'd told me earlier that he would destroy the machine when we found it. However, as I mulled over what I'd just learned about aerial craft and their potential, another option began to take shape in my mind. A dangerous option, to be sure, but it just might work.

Meanwhile, as Dan's class on the dynamics of aeronautics was unfolding, I noticed our young Bahamian friend sitting off by himself, staring at a tiny jungle orchid and ignoring us. His lips were moving, perhaps praying that he would wake up from his bad dream. Further back in the bushes, Yablonowski was busy explaining the situation in Creole to his men, all of whom had their frightened eyes on that wicked-looking Hotchkiss.

They were young conscript soldiers—uneducated, untrained, ill-equipped, and unmotivated. But even they knew that cast-off thirty-year-old muskets were useless against the modern rifles and machine-driven large-caliber guns in evidence before them. They also knew that an assault on Sokolov's lair would result in several of *them* dying for a cause and people they couldn't understand. I couldn't blame them for looking terrified and ready to run. There was no way I could count on them for any crucial assistance, and from his sad expression, I was beginning to doubt Yablonowski's commitment to rescuing Luke.

We were resting there in a lull from the rain and wind when a large bell sounded deeply five times, coming from somewhere inside the compound. Creeping back toward the observation point, we saw a commotion near the airship barn. A large group of Bizangos were gathering at the north end, straining together on long lines leading back inside the building.

Then out of the open end of the structure emerged the black bow of the object, floating in the air. It was as if a reptile were hatching from an egg. It kept materializing until I could see the forward end was moored to a pair of rail cars on parallel tracks—each pulled by the line of men. It was an enormous balloon ship, inflated to a shape unlike any balloon I'd see. Not spherical, but elongated, cylindrical. Like a fat cigar, more than anything else.

Woodgerd informed us it was fully one hundred eighty-five feet long and forty across. When it emerged completely, a white man walking beside it shouted and lines holding it down to the four rail cars were slacked off. The monster rose thirty or forty feet above the ground, tethered from the bow to a mooring mast. As it ascended, I saw a long boatlike structure dangling beneath it. It was wooden—mostly bamboo framing—with a mechanical apparatus and wide-bladed fan propeller at the forward end. There was a section of woven basketry, twenty feet in length, behind the propeller. A large canvas rudder was mounted aft of a metal device at the stern. The rest of the hull was open framing.

"Ah, I see it's a bit bigger than the French aerial warship," commented Dan. He paused and stared at a leaf-cutter ant on the ground, whispering calculations to himself. When he had finished, he announced, "So let's figure that he has enough cubic feet—eighty thousand would be a conservative estimate—to lift fifty-seven hundred pounds. Ah, just as I thought, he's using the French method of propulsion. Electricity. The German idea of a gasoline or kerosene combustion engine gives greater speed but is too prone to accidental fire."

"Yes, it's electric," said Woodgerd. "He ordered a Seimens electric motor, then modified it to generate ten horsepower. The battery is at the back end, way behind the crew basket, so the weight counterbalances the weight of the motor and propeller at the front end."

Dan rubbed his chin in contemplation. "Hmm, and I see that the front end with the propeller and motor are farther away from the center of effort, the fulcrum, of the ship, which would allow a smaller weight to counterbalance the heavier weight of the battery. Very well done."

Another shout came from the white man, this time toward two other whites inside the hull. Woodgerd told us the man shouting was Sokolov. The propeller began to turn, but quietly. The electric motor made no sound. I immediately thought of a night attack scenario—the monster sailing silently over a city through the dark sky, achieving total surprise. Victims wouldn't even comprehend the source of their deaths.

The propeller's revolutions increased. There was noise now, but not from the motor. It was a constant thumping as the blades thrashed the air, the ship struggling against its tethers. Then it slowed and stopped.

Dan was clearly impressed by Sokolov's design efforts. "So, I would estimate the weight of the propeller assembly and motor at just about eight hundred pounds. The battery would

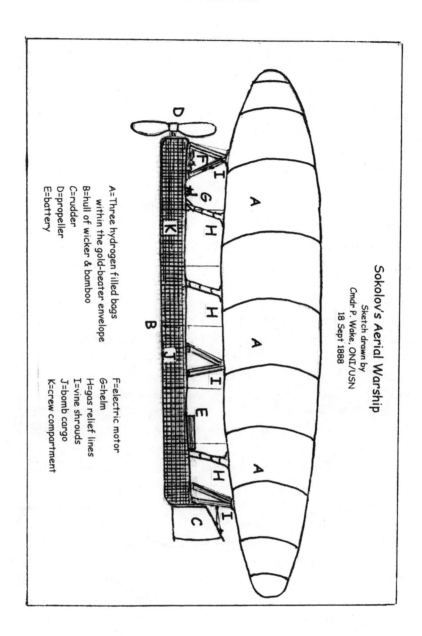

Sokolov's Aerial Warship
Sketch drawn by
Cmdr. P. Wake, ONI/USN
18 Sept 1888

A=Three hydrogen filled bags
within the gold-beater envelope
B=hull of wicker & bamboo
C=rudder
D=propeller
E=battery

F=electric motor
G=helm
H=gas relief lines
I=vine shrouds
J=bomb cargo
K=crew compartment

be a thousand. That means eighteen hundred and fifty pounds for propulsion gear. If he deduced some way to make the entire airship weigh, let's say two thousand pounds, which is quite light for this size craft, then that's a total *fixed* weight of thirty-eight hundred pounds."

Dan rubbed his chin again. "Now, about the variable weight—the Frenchies had a crew of three, if I remember correctly. Colonel Woodgerd, how many does Sokolov plan to run this thing?"

"Four. A helmsman, a gas adjuster, the bomb man, and Sokolov as commander. And maybe the boy—*if* he takes him, which I'm not convinced he'll do."

"Hmm, figure six hundred pounds for the men , without the boy. Now we're up to forty-four hundred pounds. Then there's water, food, and other provisions and supplies—about two hundred pounds, which gets him to forty-six hundred. I'm guessing ballast would account for at least ten percent of the total, or about six hundred pounds. Total is now fifty-two hundred pounds of lift used up. That leaves him five hundred pounds of cargo or weaponry for a total weight of fifty-seven hundred pounds."

I was still doing the mathematics when Dan said, "It's absolutely amazing, Peter. This fellow may well be a demented madman, but he has splendidly managed to master the fixed weight problem. But how, I wonder? The battery and motor are what they are, and can't be diminished. It must have been the ship herself. Colonel Woodgerd, do you know?"

"Sokolov's proud of how he saved weight using native materials he found in the jungle down here," said Woodgerd. "Light and strong. Balsa wood and bamboo for the hull and framing. Hemp that the Europeans use for rigging is too heavy, so he uses native vines. Green liana vines for the long rigging, Monkey ladder vine for the short rigging. The crew basket is woven from friendship vines. Sokolov told me they are half the weight of hemp. The big weight saver was the covering he used for the airship balloon—goldbeater's skin."

"You're joking!" exclaimed Corny. "The old Egyptian technique for making gold leaf? There's no gold on that thing that I see."

"It's the old technique, yes, but not used with gold in this case. It's used on cattle intestines. They're pounded out into extremely thin sheets—you can see through them—then wetted down and plastered together by their inherent adhesion. When they dry they are incredibly elastic, impermeable, and strong. There are two layers of the stuff on there.

"Sokolov told me he learned the British were doing it, so he tried it and it worked well. Much stronger than the doped silk usually used, and much lighter. He trained some of the men here in the technique. Turns out that the local cows' intestines are perfect for it. Took a lot of them, though, to cover that thing."

Dan nodded. "That makes sense. Major Templer, an aeronaut with the British army came up with it five years ago. His balloons in Africa were covered with goldbeater's skin."

"Cows," I mused aloud. "Well, that clears up the mystery concerning the cattle farm. Remember? Laurent told us the Russian was buying thousands of cattle but hadn't sold any."

White lettering was painted along the side of the ship. It appeared Cyrillic, and I asked Woodgerd the meaning.

"It's Sokolov's name for his aerial warship. *Rodinia Voskhod*. I think it means 'The Homeland's Uprising,' or something like that. He wants everyone on the ground in Russia to know that it's time to rebel against the tsar."

Roche corrected him. "*Rodinia* is the ancient name of our Russian trans-continent—the Motherland. In English, this writing would mean approximately, 'Mother Russia Rising.' It is a naive call to the peasants to revolt against their gracious sovereign. I will acknowledge that Sokolov is a brilliant scientist, but he is foolish when it comes to understanding his own countrymen. Peasants cannot read. They do not even want or need to read—their priests do that for them. They just want to be left alone to make babies and work the land."

A squall line appeared over the ridge behind us, sliding down the slope toward Sokolov's base. Hurried shouts set the men to straining again and the behemoth was lowered back down onto its rail cars. When the squall's gusts hit it, the airship heeled over and swung her stern downwind like a ship. The men quickly lashed the mooring lines down to prevent them from running out. After the squall raced through, the thing was pulled back to the rails and returned to its wooden cave.

The wind was from the south now, a good sign that the center of the hurricane had passed to our west. The squalls spaced out more and diminished in strength. Our problem, though, wasn't the wind and rain—it was the torrent between us and Luke. The river was well over its banks and raging its way down to the coast. The rocky shoals disappeared. There was no way we could ford it. The boy was fifty yards away, but he might as well have been on the other side of the earth. That night, I told everyone that we would wait for river to subside.

But we weren't idle.

32

Plan of Attack

Forteresse des Nyajs
Montay San, Northern Haiti
Wednesday, 5 September 1888

The next morning, the first in which we actually saw a sunrise, I called everyone together for a briefing on the strategy of action. The air was fresh and sweetly moist, scented by the jungle muck airing itself out. The sky was the clearest I'd seen so far in Haiti, empty of the usual smoke haze.

The storm had roared off to the west, after washing away half our bags of food, one musket, two canvas shelters, and an alarming amount of our perch on the side of the mountain. However, the most important geographical component to our plan—the river crossing—now seemed possible, for overnight the water had dropped enough to see the rocks. By that coming evening, I predicted it would be fordable. The next obstacle—the Bizango guards—also had a solution, a uniquely Haitian one. I'd been informed of it in the dark, five hours earlier.

Rork had the watch when he woke me from a fitful sleep in the middle of the night. Whispering in my ear, he informed me, "The colonel wants a bit o' a private gam with jes' you an' me. Methinks he's got a wee idea o' what to do 'bout the Rooskie fort. Nice an' quiet-like, if ye please, sir. The camp's asleep."

We met under a bush away from the others. Woodgerd had Aubrac with him. The colonel wasted no time. "Aubrac and I were just talking this through. He has an idea on how to take care of the guards, or at least slow down some of them. They've got a toad here, called the *bouga*, that's got a deadly poison in it. It's as bad as that Calabar bean you told me nearly did you in, Peter. Aubrac's seen several of them hopping around here. Rain must'a flushed them out. He suggested we use them to make a poison, then slip it into the guards' clarin during the *voudou* ceremony they'll have tonight. He knows the recipe for the potion."

I glanced at Sergeant Aubrac, squatting there stone-faced. It was the classic pose veteran army sergeants and naval petty officers use when in the presence of superiors who are talking about them. Rork does it, too, especially when admirals are around.

Woodgerd read my mind. "Yes, I wondered about that, too. Turns out that before he converted, Aubrac used to be a *dokte feuilles*, an herbal healer. He says that after a storm there usually is a ceremony of thanks and everyone gets drunk on this rotgut rum they call clarin. Aubrac will remove his stripes, act like a common guard, and slip into the *hounfour*, the *voudou* temple at the north end of the fort. Once there, he'll add enough *bouga* juice to the clarin jugs to make the Bizangos get sick. He says an hour at the most till they slow down. The locals have a quaint little name for the process: *bouga mange moun*—the poison toad eats the people."

I remembered that initial feeling of pleasant lethargy, just before the terror hit me—realizing my body was paralyzed and slowing down to die, eating me from the inside, and there was nothing I could do. I shuddered as an involuntary gasp escaped me.

"Yes, well, that'll be very effective. Now let's discuss how *we* get inside the fort, what we do once there, and how we escape this place afterward."

Woodgerd used a pencil to diagram the fort on our only piece of dry paper, while Rork held our sole lantern. I asked questions about Sokolov's senior staff and their locations, the aerial craft's supplies, and the location of Luke and the hostage. Rork inquired about the guards' weaponry, ready ammunition storage, and watch routine. Aubrac made suggestions to our list of targets.

An hour later, we had the plan.

It was an interesting study of faces gathered around me. The Americans looked grimly eager to get the deed done. Absalom gazed at nothing and mouthed a prayer—the twenty-third psalm, I believe. The lone Russian, alias a Frenchman, was clearly dubious as he digested what he heard. The Haitian fellows, except for sergeants Aubrac and Yablonowski, showed obvious fear and confusion. The two Haitian sergeants sat there in quiet resignation. I could just imagine what was in their minds: *nothing good ever comes from dealing with blancs.*

I kept my description of the plan of attack simple. At nine o'clock, about an hour after sundown, Aubrac would climb over the northern outer wall, creep through the fortress's farm field, slip into the adjacent *voudou* temple, and taint the Bizangos' *clarin*. At exactly ten o'clock, after the *bouga* potion worked its evil, Aubrac would silently use a cane knife on the throat of the Bizango manning the nearest guard post. He would then signal the rest of us waiting outside the wall with the call of the nocturnal goatsucker bird. On my cue, Aubrac demonstrated the distinctive whippoorwill-like sound.

Upon this signal that the coast was clear, we would scale the wall and enter the fort. Three Haitian soldiers would remain behind at the observation point on the mountainside and act as sharpshooters, waiting to open fire until they heard any gunshots, then concentrate their shots on the nearest Hotchkiss gun. I had no illusions about their marksmanship, but thought their fire might add to the enemy's confusion.

Once the main body of our tiny band was inside, we would separate into two elements. Woodgerd would lead a force to rescue Mr. Vanderburg from the livestock barn at the northeast corner of the compound. Once Vanderburg was liberated, Woodgerd's men would provide cover for the rest of us by killing the Bizangos at the *voudou* temple and blockading those in their barracks, located nearby. His faction would consist of Aubrac, Rork, Yablonowski, and the four remaining Haitian soldiers.

I would lead the second force, consisting of Absalom, Cynda, Dan Horloft, and Corny Rathburn. We would run south through the compound, past the huge airship barn, and rescue Luke at Sokolov's bungalow, located at the southern end of the place. Once that was accomplished, we would secure the main gate of the fort, and hold it until Sokolov's men counterattacked, then we'd rejoin Woodgerd's group. Weapons for my group were in short supply, so scavenging the enemy's would be critical. Fortunately, both Dan and Corny knew muskets, but young Absalom was ignorant of that skill. He would carry a cane knife.

I asked Woodgerd to describe Sokolov's leadership hierarchy.

"Sokolov spends his evenings in his quarters, directly inside the south inner wall. His number-two man is a sadistic Prussian colonel named von Danzig who hates blacks, got kicked out of German Cameroon for abusing them. He'll be drunk on schnapps in his room, just outside the south inner wall, by that time of night. I was the number-three man and my little home away from home was next to Danzig's. The number-four man is a pouffy French naval engineering staff officer, Commandante Philippe Dru, who is in charge of the technical work—the bombs, hydrogen, metalworking, goldbeater's skin. He may be attending the *voudou* celebration at the north end. He's attracted to that sort of thing."

Woodgerd stopped for comments. No one made any, but I remembered Roche and Billot had been talking about a man named Dru just before their angry exchange in Russian on the boat. So Roche knew more than he was letting on, even now.

"All right, that's it for the whites working for Sokolov. There are three Haitian officers in his private army. Doctor Pierre Baptiste is a nasty little bastard. He's in charge of obtaining and keeping the typhus clothing, and the fort's food and medical needs. He dabbles in *voudou*, so he'll probably be with Dru at the north end. Captain Jacques Bois, not so affectionately nicknamed 'the black weasel' by the troops, and Captain Artimis Joseph, nicknamed 'the white snake,' lead the Bizangos. They are what's called *bourreaux*, which means executioners, and they are ruthless. They'll definitely be in the ceremony at the north end. Let's hope they drink lots of Aubrac's potion."

Woodgerd paused, then added, "I think they'll have a minimal guard force on tonight, because of the celebration. Two men at the main gate, and maybe eight of the twenty-one outer wall posts manned, with only one man in each. That means about forty of them at the temple or in the barracks, mostly at the temple—away from their rifles, which are kept at the armory. If we do this quickly and quietly at first, then use extreme violence once an alarm is sounded, we will win. *Do not* show any of them the slightest bit of mercy—they'll use it to kill you."

Roche posed the question to me, "We are killing the Bizangos, but what of Sokolov?"

This wasn't the time or place for timidity. "Kill him on sight."

Roche frowned. "Well, if it would not be too much trouble,

Commander, I would like to have a conversation with Sokolov. I had occasion to work against a friend of his, one Alexandr Ul'yanov, a minor revolutionary leader who attempted to kill our tsar this last year. Ul'yanov is no longer a problem, but I believe that Sokolov has information about Ul'yanov's colleagues that would be very useful to the Okhrana. I promise not to linger too long with him, since our time will be short."

"Very well, you can have him."

Roche nodded. "I appreciate your consideration, sir. One last point, Commander—what of the machine itself?"

I looked him in the eye and lied. "Dan and I will be in charge of destroying it. Right afterward, we all leave over the north wall."

The Russian spy allowed the trace of a smile.

"Then all of our goals will all be accomplished, Commander Wake. You have my compliments, sir, on an excellent plan."

At sundown we commenced, with Aubrac leading the way down the slippery slope to the river. In his *macoute*, a burlap Haitian shoulder bag, he carried gourds of *bouga* poison.

The three youngest Haitian soldiers were chosen to remain on the mountainside as sharpshooters. They solemnly bid us goodbye. Dan grumbled aloud that they'd probably run at the first chance. Yablonowski spun around and confronted him.

"You think Haitian soldiers cannot fight, Mr. Horloft? You are very wrong. I invite you to go to the graves of fifty thousand of Napoleon's finest soldiers at Cap Haitien, and ask them what *they* think of Haitian soldiers."

Dan looked at him hard for a moment, then nodded. "Point taken, Sergeant. I apologize. I'm sure your men will fight well."

Keeping our weapons dry while crossing the river was no easy task, especially for the men carrying the more vulnerable powder muskets. We stepped stone to stone, using our outstretched hands to balance ourselves. Several fell waist-deep into the water, but scrambled back up with the help of the others.

The few guards we could see on the walls had their attention drawn inward toward the *voudou* gathering. Drums heralding the upcoming ceremony had been pounding for hours, the tempo steadily increasing, and now we could hear shouting and laughing—they had begun to broach the clarin. We needed to hurry our pace. Once we arrived at the far side of the river, we crept along the bank, directly under the outer wall and not thirty feet from the muzzle of that Hotchkiss. At the northern end of the fort, we halted and huddled in the bushes as Aubrac dashed off in the darkness toward the wall.

So far, we were exactly on time and in position. Before setting out, I'd made sure Aubrac's watch—borrowed from Corny—was wound and calibrated to mine. We waited. I checked the time. It was nine forty-five by my watch in the moonless starlight. I took a breath. The first part was done. Next would be Aubrac's bird call.

But, unfortunately, that's not what we heard.

33

Bèlantre Mwem Zanmis, a ou Rèv Move . . .

Forteresse des Nyajs
Montay San, Northern Haiti
Wednesday, 5 September 1888
9:57 p.m.

First came a muffled scream, coming from the area where Aubrac was last seen. Then, close by us, we heard a graveled voice I knew instantly. It chuckled sarcastically as it spoke. The words I could not decipher exactly, but the tone was unmistakably sinister.

"*Bèlantre mwen zanmis, a ou rèv move—men li se anpil, anpil, reyèl . . .*"

Woodgerd knew what it meant and muttered an oath. Cynda stifled a cry of fear as half a dozen rifle bolts were rammed shut around us in the dark. Yablonowski translated what the voice had told us.

"It is Lieutenant Laurent. He says, '*Welcome, my friends, to your bad dream—but it is very, very, real.*' We are captured, Commander."

I could hear movement all around us, a platoon at least. There was no avenue of escape. No probability of effective defense. Lamentably, Rork and I were quite familiar with the scenario. Our only chance lay in subterfuge.

To Rork and Woodgerd I quickly whispered, "Hide your weapons under this bush. We'll steal theirs once we get inside. Rork, don't use the spike until we're inside and I give the word."

Seconds after I dropped my Merwin-Hulbert pistol and Spencer shotgun and kicked them under the bush, hands grabbed me roughly, shoving me into a line formed by my comrades. Someone lit a lantern and a face loomed up, inches from mine— Laurent, gloating over his conquest.

"Ah, ha! Le laj blanc fou . . . poukisa ou pa renmen mwen pwas bèls a l'citadelle? Tan sa-a pa se sove!"

I could smell rum on Laurent's breath, his words slurred into gibberish. I wondered if Aubrac had gotten to the clarin jugs before he was caught. No, probably not. No such luck.

"What's he saying to me, Sergeant?"

"He called you the big white fool, Commander. And then he asked why you didn't like his pretty beans at the Citadelle. He says this time there is no escape."

My friends said nothing when they heard that comment, but I could feel their thoughts as we were pushed forward along the wall, back toward the river. I'd failed them again.

To increase his overconfidence, I gave Laurent a crestfallen look, not hard to do in the circumstances. Then I said to Sergeant Yablonowski, "Please tell Lieutenant Laurent the following: You have won the affair, sir. But how did you know where we would be?"

Laurent's gloating response was interspersed with more chuckles. Yablonowski's face was lined with grief as he told us what Laurent said: "Those two soldier boys you sent as messengers to Cap Haitien. The *bourreaux* had a conversation with them. It was easy then to find you on Montay San. We sat near you in the jungle the whole time and heard your plan. The *bourreaux* had a conversation with Aubrac, also, just a few minutes ago, at the wall. He told us everything. The *bourreaux* will soon have a conversation with *you*. But do not worry, it will not require much of your time."

At the main gate I saw that the guard posts were fully manned. Sokolov had known we were out there, all right. It had been a well-laid trap. Once inside the outer wall, we were led past some small dwellings that Woodgerd identified as the white staff quarters, including the one he'd fled days earlier. Then we were through the inner wall and halted between Sokolov's bungalow on the right and the armory on our left. Directly in front of us rose the aerial warship's edifice, enormous and menacing in the flickering glow of the lanterns scattered about.

Laurent's men arranged us in a tight formation. I could smell rum on them, too. Standing ten yards away, some of the Bizangos watched the goings-on. They were distinguishable from Laurent's men by their neat appearance in blue fatigue working uniforms and the modern rifles—Laurent's were dressed in ragged national army issue and carried muskets. The Bizangos exuded confidence and discipline.

The timing for our uprising would be crucial—we had to overcome Laurent's men while they still had us in their custody. Once we were transferred to the Bizangos, it would be too late. I doubted if in our weakened physical state we could fight them in close-quarters combat.

An older white man in a crumpled linen suit emerged from a doorway and strode toward the armory. It was the man we'd seen earlier giving orders to the airship handlers. In the lantern light, I could see a hawk nose separating two piercing gray eyes set deep into a gaunt face. The gray in his eyes was so light-colored as to be almost white, presenting a manifestly frightening countenance.

Sergei Alexandrovich Sokolov stopped when near us, executing a parade ground left turn. In a thick Slavic accent, he rumbled dismissively, "You are intruders, opponents of the people's will, enemies of the revolutionary changes about to unfold. And you will be dealt with accordingly."

Cynda cried out, "You have my boy Luke here—I want to see him! Where is my boy?"

"Your son has rejected the corrupt life you have chosen for him, madam. He is now a revolutionary in the service of the people. A warrior for the future good of mankind, when tyrants are finally deposed and slavery ended!"

Cynda burst into tears. I put an arm around her, while surveying the positions of Laurent's men and the Bizangos surrounding us. Rork glanced at me, an eyebrow raised in query as to the use of his spike. I responded by moving my eyes in the negative. Woodgerd, seeing our voiceless communications, distracted his former employer, by loudly stating, "Sokolov, stop the theatrics and just bring the kid over here so his mother can see him."

The reply was a contemptuous snarl. "You dare to speak! Your turn will be slow, Colonel. Traitors do not deserve quick mercy."

"An ironic statement coming from *you*, Professor," commented Roche in that infuriatingly calm voice of his. "You, my dear Sergei Alexandrovich, are the ultimate traitor to your country, your motherland."

"Ah, Major Kaminski, or should I say Kukov? No, those were your old pseudonyms in Minsk and Moscow. I hear you are in Paris now and Roche is the current alias. Your French toadies must be quite flattered by that. How very kind of you to come way out here to Haiti so I can kill you for what you did to us in Saint Petersburg. It has really saved me a lot of bother tracking you down in Paris."

Sokolov turned to the rest of us. "Well, I have no more time for this small talk, for I am about to depart in my airship. Destiny awaits me. In the meantime, you will be attended to by Captain Bois and Captain Joseph."

He sneered. "They are at the armory this very moment,

preparing a special welcome for their former commander—*you*, Colonel Woodgerd."

It was at this point that Laurent, who evidently understood more English than he'd previously let on, burst into maniacal laughter at our fate, all the while lasciviously eyeing Cynda. The perverted behavior set his subordinates to cackling, pointing at Woodgerd who, comprehending the situation, played the role of humiliated prisoner quite well, complete with disheartened expression. As Sokolov resumed his pace toward the armory, Laurent ridiculed Woodgerd in Creole, causing his mob even more mirth.

The Bizangos weren't joining in the hysterics, but were clearly enjoying their former leader's disgrace. None of our enemies had their fingers on triggers, or even the rifles aimed. It's difficult to be vigilant when slapping each other on the back and jeering your victims.

I judged it the perfect time to end the party.

"Now, Rork!"

In far less time than it takes to read this paragraph, several things happened simultaneously to Laurent's bemused minions. Later discussion with Rork clarified the blur of commotion. My Irish friend whipped off his fake hand and rammed the spike into the temple of Laurent's soldier next to him, then into the chest of another. Woodgerd punched his escort in the throat, dropping him and moving onto another. I brought my foot into the groin of Laurent's corporal, followed by my knee into his jaw when he doubled over. Dan and Corny jumped on their closest opponent and wrestled him down. Aubrac, wounded but ambulatory, threw himself against his guard, both falling in a heap. Roche performed a very deft pugilistic maneuver by hitting two men at once, using one fist for each. Yablonowski proved no slouch in battle either, knocking down a man and rallying his bewildered soldiers with orders in Creole.

Seconds later the tables were turned on our enemies. Those

of Laurent's crew still upright immediately turned tail, their lieutenant in the lead. Having now armed ourselves with the abandoned muskets, we discharged them into the astonished audience of Bizangos, half of whom dropped their Lebel rifles in an attempt to flee.

This gave us some real armament. Yablonowski wisely had his men continue to use the muskets, since they were trained somewhat with them. We foreigners gathered the French-made weapons—even Cynda and Absalom, who proved to be quick studies in working the bolts and firing—and proceeded to mark down the enemy as they dashed for cover.

Unfortunately, not all the casualties were on the enemy side. Aubrac lay dead, two of Yablonowski's men were bleeding, Roche was clutching his previously broken ribs, and Woodgerd had a gash on his left arm.

Yablonowski's soldiers were like lions unleashed. At first they used bayonets and machetes furiously upon their former captors, all the while issuing piercing war cries. Their transformation from prisoners to avengers was instantaneous and stunning—Laurent was run down and hacked apart in seconds by two of our soldiers. Once the initial melee was over, Yablonowski got the rest of his men methodically loading and firing their muskets at the fleeing figures in the dark.

While that very useful diversion was raging on around us, I yelled for Woodgerd to carry out the original plan of attack and meet up later at the aerial warship barn. We thus separated into our two components, minus Yablonowski's musket men, who were otherwise well occupied under the command of a corporal. The sergeant went off with Woodgerd and Rork, north through the compound toward the livestock barn to rescue Vanderburg.

I took Roche, Cynda, Dan, Corny, and Absalom, into Sokolov's nearby dwelling to find Luke. But neither the boy nor the Russian lunatic was there.

34

Chaos in the Dark

Forteresse des Nyajs
Montay San, Northern Haiti
Wednesday, 5 September 1888
10:13 p.m.

If Luke wasn't in the bungalow, I reasoned he must be with Vanderburg. Leaving Roche to paw through the scientist's papers, I ran north through the inner compound. The rest followed and we headed past the east side of the massive central building. Light showed through the cracks in the planking, providing a minimum of ambient illumination in the compound. Moving around the generator shed, I made my way toward Woodgerd's position, where I heard rifles and pistols firing.

The Hotchkiss gun on that side of the fort opened up, a steady pounding sound like someone hammering on metal. The shots were landing somewhere ahead of me at first, then suddenly the shells thudded into the shed close behind. The gunner had shifted target and was aiming for my movement in the dark. I shouted for Cynda and the others to take cover and not advance, as I rushed across the open to an entryway in the inner wall.

Getting down on the ground, I peeked my head around the end of the wall, and looked to the east. In the background was Montay San and the observation point we'd used—all of it inky black in the night. The high outer wall was more discernible, topped by the pounding explosions and staccato flashes of the Hotchkiss gun on the guard platform. I shielded my eyes from the flash to maintain my night vision and continued to search for Woodgerd and his men. Closer in, the livestock barn's paddock fence was only feet away, but that gun was now sweeping the area randomly, each shell slamming into the dirt or wood and bursting into a shower of debris that rained down.

Boom . . . boom . . . boom . . . boom . . . methodical death spit out from the mechanically-driven gun. It wasn't the firecracker sound of a Gatling, but the deeper report of an artillery piece. Between the incessant thumping sound and the sight of it hitting a target, a Hotchkiss was a frightening weapon to behold. One could easily see what it would do to a man—instantly eviscerate him.

Finally, I spied Woodgerd crouched by the corner of the paddock fence, centering his Lebel rifle on the man firing the Hotchkiss. In the lull while the gunner was reloading the Hotchkiss, I heard Woodgerd mutter what sounded like *"Zwani Marg shi!"*

Again the bedlam of noise and flashes erupted from the guard tower. I couldn't hear the Lebel fire, but I saw the recoil as he fired three rapid shots. The thundering Hotchkiss stopped, an eerie void of sound. I ran forward and slid next to Woodgerd.

"Good shooting, Michael," I gasped. "What the hell was that you said to him?"

"Pashto curse: '*Die at a young age!*' He deserved it."

"Were you able to find Luke?"

He turned to me, his angry face inches away. "Oh yeah, I found the worthless bastard, over in the barn. I told him we were here to rescue him. He squealed some nonsense at me, then lit out for the gun." Woodgerd pointed to the guard tower with the Hotchkiss and shook his head. "I was still yelling for him to come down, even though I saw him loading it. Should've killed him then, when I had a clear shot."

His voice hardened. "But I waited too damned long. The worthless little sonovabitch got it working. Killed Yablonowski before I finally stopped him."

There was no time for questions or regrets.

"Rork—where's Rork?"

"Still with the old man, I think. In the livestock barn. Come on, follow me."

The other gunfire behind us was slowing, more sporadic. The Bizangos were regrouping in the southern half of the compound. We crossed the paddock and entered the barn. Vladimir Noel Yablonowski's body sprawled across the doorway. It was mangled into an inhuman mass of bloody meat by the Hotchkiss's thirty-seven millimeter rounds. For several seconds I stood there, overcome by a wave of grief at the horrific death of such a good man.

"Vanderburg's dead an' gone, sir."

Rork's voice brought me back. He was kneeling next to another figure in the far corner. Vanderburg. The old man was laid out in the hay, hands folded on his chest and seemingly asleep in the dim light of a lantern.

"No wounds. Methinks he died yesterday—it's smellin' none too fresh. Maybe the old sod's heart gave out. Or maybe poisonin' did him in, but there's no way to tell fer sure. You know about the kid?"

"Yes." I put a hand on Woodgerd's shoulder. "No blame there, Michael."

"Yeah, thanks," he muttered. "I gave him a chance. He took it to kill Yablonowski."

"So what now, sir?" asked Rork. "Them Bizango buggers'll be counterattackin' soon enough. Once they open up with those other Hotchkisses, this whole place'll be a killin' ground."

"You're right. No time to waste. Michael, we stay with the original plan? How many have we got left now—eight? Without the cargo, I think we can do that. Or do you have another idea?"

"It's gotta be the original plan now, Peter. It'll be dicey, but the jungle'll be crawling with these bastards out to get a *blanc*. There's just too many of them—we'd never make it all the way to Cap Haitien."

The original plan, hatched by Woodgerd, Rork, and me in the dark the previous night, hadn't been divulged to the others, lest they be frightened. In truth, I hadn't really expected it to unfold anyway—too far-fetched and too many people. So I had a secondary plan: flee on foot cross-country to a stream to the east, away from the path back toward Cap Haitien, then float down current to the coast. That was the plan I told the others. But conditions had drastically changed. Now we had a small window of opportunity that *might* make the original plan work, if we seized it immediately.

"All right, Rork, round up everyone and get them to the northern end of the airship building. We've got to pull the damn thing out of there."

"No, we don't," said Woodgerd. "Sokolov's got it pulled out already. I saw Danzig and Dru over there when we got here. They've got the motor running and it'll be lifting up any minute now."

"Good God!" I was already running out the door. *"Then move!"*

As I made it back inside the inner wall a volley of Lebels roared from the southern end of the fort. Regrouped, the Bizangos were attacking in force. Scattered shots sounded in reply. From the northern wall, I registered sporadic rifle fire. Were they attacking from there also?

Above me I saw the monster ship floating above the rail cars, utterly gigantic this close up. Illuminated by lanterns inside the building, the Cyrillic writing ominously reflected the light. The hull dangling beneath it was only two feet off the ground. The thing was straining against its lines, wanting to swing downwind off a hawser from its bow to a mooring post at the northern end of the rail tracks—as a ship swings to an anchor. As I watched, it was released from the cars. Its bow immediately pointed to windward, held only by that hawser. The madman was about to fly it away.

Sokolov and two other whites, the Prussian von Danzig and the Frenchman Dru, were next to the hull. Holding long guns at the ready, they directed men lugging small heavy items toward the hull.

To my left I could see Cynda, Absalom, and Roche running toward us and a mass of movement in the darkness behind them, apparently the Bizangos charging. Corny and Dan were to my right, falling back while engaging the guard posts along the northern wall with rifle fire. Everyone was converging on my position.

Woodgerd yelled to Rork and me, "Attack Sokolov now! He's loading the bombs!"

The range was a mere thirty yards and the three of us fired repeatedly at Sokolov and his two cohorts. Dru and Danzig each got off a blast—their long guns were shotguns—but fired high. Wearing white suits, they made perfect silhouettes in the dim light and all three of them went down when we fired. The laborers dropped their loads and ran to the western wall. We approached at a run as Danzig got up on one elbow. Woodgerd shot him again. Twenty feet away, a bloody Sokolov was trying to crawl away. Woodgerd spun toward him and raised his rifle.

"No!" shouted Roche. "I want him alive!"

I will never forget what happened next. Woodgerd nodded to Roche and, with absolute chaos swirling around him, calmly walked over to the cringing Sokolov and leaned down. I was close enough to hear him say, *"Khudai de wakhela!"*

I later learned it to be a Pashto phrase: *God take you away!* Then my friend turned his back on the Russian and shot a Bizango advancing from the northern wall.

I lost track of Roche and Sokolov when a scream suddenly pierced the air.

"Oh, God—Luke! My baby! My Luke!"

Cynda was over by the livestock barn, collapsed onto the ground, sobbing and wailing incoherently. Her hand stretched out toward the guard tower, where her son lay draped over the edge. Absalom was trying to drag her toward us.

"Corny, go help Ab get her over here," I ordered. "Dan, get in the damn thing and check the helm controls."

Corny ran over to Cynda, but Dan raised a hand in protest. "Peter, you know my calculations were for sea level! We're three thousand feet up and I don't know what the displacement will . . ."

"Just shut up and try!"

The abject terror in my voice must have impressed him, for he jumped up and clambered inside the hull. Seconds later I saw him fiddling with controls at the helm.

Rork and Woodgerd were inside too, unloading the bombs that had been put aboard. They weren't iron-bound, as I'd expected, but three-foot-long cylinders, and leather not silk, like artillery powder charges.

"Incendiaries, Rork—so lay 'em down *gently!* " cautioned Woodgerd.

Sokolov's men were emboldened by the lack of return fire and began charging, led by a frightening vision—a muscular African figure in a gray mask. The mask had large holes for the eyes, a grim mouth, and was topped with massive bull's horns. This was above a black leather chest plate and leggings covered with chalk dust and blood. A similarly attired man was behind him. Both waved cane knives and revolvers, exhorting with animal roars for their men to kill the last of us.

Rork and Woodgerd completed the job and stood beside me.

"Ah, I've been wonderin' where those two were," said Woodgerd. "Boys, meet the *bourreaux* captains—Bois and Joseph.

Looks like they got into their full dress mess for this shindig."

Woodgerd immediately started methodically shooting—felling one of the bizarrely clad captains. Rork dashed over to Danzig's body and returned as several Bizango rounds hit the hull behind us.

"Wanna use yer own shotgun on 'em?" Rork asked as he handed me my Spencer shotgun and Merwin-Hulbert pistol. "Seems them Bizango buggers gave our personal weapons to that Froggie wanker an' the kraut-eater. That was a bit o' a waste, warn't it? Aye, an' now methinks givin' 'em a little taste o' *American* lead'll be right proper!"

Right proper, indeed—the shotguns were the perfect weapon for that massed target crossing an open yard. Rork and I knelt down and began firing, he taking the left side and I the right. The front rank of seven or eight went down, dead or wounded, but it didn't deter the mob. I suddenly realized they were crazed or drunk on something. Screaming epithets in their lingo, they kept coming.

"Bloody friggin' hell an' damnation!" growled Rork as his shotgun clicked empty. I fired my last shotgun shell while Rork emptied his Colt revolver at the nearest enemy.

I scanned to my left, searching for Cynda. They'd made it to the aerial ship. Corny was throwing her up and into the hull like a sack of potatoes, Absalom was already inside, pulling them both in. My mind registered that Woodgerd had stopped firing. I looked but he wasn't there. Was he wounded or dead? No, I saw him vaulting the low inner wall, heading for the guard tower on the northwest side of the outer wall.

I only had the six rounds in my pistol left. At least twenty Bizangos were seventy feet away and closing rapidly. Not enough ammunition. Everybody was out. Not enough time to find more.

There were six of us there, frozen in a tableau of horror, all eyes on the advancing horde. The pistol felt heavier than ever before. One round for each of us—to spare us the certain agony planned for us that would arrive in a few seconds. I wasn't going to let that happen. Cynda would have to be the first. My hand holding the Merwin-Hulbert was shaking as I glanced one last time at the Bizangos.

35
Night into Day

Forteresse des Nyajs
Montay San, Northern Haiti
Wednesday, 5 September 1888
10:19 p.m.

From the western side of the compound I heard strange shouts, punctuated by shots.

"Pyos!" . . . bang . . . *"Pyos!"* . . . bang . . . *"Tyoya mat!"* . . . bang.

Corny heard it too. "Russian cursing. Well I'll be damned." He raised a finger toward the barn and shook his head. "Look at that!"

It was Roche. He was coming from a wagon at the northwest corner of the airship barn. Quickly back stepping at an even pace, a valise slung over his left shoulder and rifle butted into his right, he methodically swiveled and fired at Bizango targets while making his way in our direction. He'd hit Sokolov's men from their western flank unexpectedly, forcing them back away from the airship hull. A temporary respite.

Suddenly I felt arms beneath my shoulders, then saw a right hand reach around my chest and grab a spiked appendage coming from the left side. Rork lifted me up, grunting with the effort. "Get in the bloody friggin' boat, ya daft sonovabitch! Now's no time to be standin' about."

My feet dangled in air for an instant, then I was bodily slammed down in the bilge of the airship's hull. "Damnation, laddie, yer gettin' heavier by the day!"

Cynda was in the bilge too, and reached for me, her face contorted in anguish, but I had no time to console her, for all hell was breaking loose. Dull knocks rattled on the hull and holes appeared everywhere. One round missed Cynda's face by inches. Forward of me, Dan was pulling and pushing some levers and Rork was swearing in Gaelic as he cast off the hawser. The ship at once lost height and bounced roughly along the ground, going astern until Dan moved the throttle forward and the propeller's thrust stopped our sternway.

The ship gathered steerageway forward and we crossed the open yard again until the forward hull—only a few feet aft of the crucial propeller—smacked into the northeast corner of the inner wall, knocking everyone inside off their feet. Dan, swearing a blue streak, leaped up and slacked off on the throttle. The bow fell off from the wind, the aerial ship drifting west once more across the rail tracks.

While this was going on, Roche was trying to stay immediately below us. He was still firing to the south, where the enemy had now taken cover. Corny and Absalom yelled at him to get aboard. Leaning their bodies halfway over the gunwale they clasped his hands at the last minute, straining to hold him as Dan got us higher.

The Bizangos took advantage of our lack of return fire and made a final rush, a dozen of them running across the intervening fifty feet, obviously hoping to bayonet Roche as he struggled aboard with a gasp of pain. I remembered the six rounds in my pistol and shot them into the crowd, but they kept coming as our leeway drifted us across the northwest inner wall.

I could see that our stern was going to crash into the fort's large cistern tower, located between the northwest inner and outer walls. Rork saw it too and dumped bags of ballast sand overboard. Dan frantically opened the throttle again and tried to correct the course. We slowly lifted up, but it was too late and our stern hit at the battery mount, swinging the bow around to the northwest.

A throaty cheer went up from the Bizangos, still led by the last horned *bourreau*, as they jumped over the inner wall—they wanted blood and were about to get it. It was then that the northwest Hotchkiss opened fire from its guard platform, sweeping the ground just below us, missing the bottom of the ship by just a few feet, and cutting into the last of the mob.

Woodgerd. In the pandemonium, I'd forgotten him. He'd stayed on the ground to fight a rear guard so we could escape.

The hull's cockpit was directly over him now—not more than ten feet above—and I watched as he systematically fired four or five round bursts, reloaded, and fired again, hunched over the barrel's gunsights, grimly traversing back and forth. The gun was so loud he couldn't hear our cries to him.

"Rork, lower that line to him!" I pointed to a line by his foot. He coiled it and slung it down to Woodgerd. The ship was past the platform now and the line was running alongside him, about to run out, but he still didn't notice. My shoe snagged on a wrench in the bilge. I picked it up and threw it at Woodgerd, striking him on the shoulder. He looked up, furious, then saw everyone pointing at the last few feet of line near him and nodded. Knocking the Hotchkiss over the side of the tower, he wrapped the line around his fists and held them up in the air.

The next moment, rifle slung on his shoulder, Woodgerd stepped off the guard tower. I heard him groaning as we hauled him up and over the gunwale. As Woodgerd collapsed, blood gushing from his slashed arm, Roche took the rifle.

In agony himself from those ribs, he laid the rifle on the wicker gunwale, sighting along it toward a large wagon by the corner of the barn. It was the one he'd come to the airship from. The wagon had a machine on the cargo bed and a pile of shiny metal tanks stacked next to it.

Roche laughed quietly, "How very careless of the brilliant Professor Sergei Alexandrovich Sokolov. Everyone knows you never put hydrogen near a flame. Ah, well, now he'll get his wish to be a martyr to the people's will."

It was then that I saw what had become of Sokolov. I'd assumed Roche had killed him outright during the chaos, but he hadn't. The scientist was lashed hand and foot to the rear wheel of the wagon. Even at our quickly increasing distance, I could tell he was yelling something at us. Or maybe at the black men now surrounding him. The Bizangos weren't untying their boss. They appeared to be taunting him.

Roche swung the rifle slightly to the right and fired. A lantern on the ground twenty feet from the wagon exploded into pieces, the burning wick igniting the fuel. Flame raced along a trail of oil until it reached the hydrogen generator on the wagon.

A fiery cloud erupted, blossoming out in all directions, covering the building and rail yard in a yellowish-white glare, rising into a luminescent mushroom-shaped form that roiled up into the sky.

Incendiary bombs lying nearby on the ground provided the secondary flash, flaring even bigger than the first and engulfing everything near them that was flammable, including the corner of the airship barn. Solid flames rose hundreds of feet into the air, a giant torch turning night into day, with every aspect of Forteresse des Nyajs in stark detail as the fire cloud lit up the mountain.

We were now well over a quarter-mile away, sailing downwind, but the heat wave reached out to us. For several seconds everyone held their breath and prayed, watching the bag of hydrogen above us, expecting to join the incineration on the ground behind us.

Our prayers were answered. We didn't ignite. Exhausted, stunned, we continued our course northward toward the coast, the thumping of the propeller making the only sound.

In the lone dim light of the binnacle, I surveyed the ship we'd commandeered. The crew compartment of the hull was indeed a wicker, tightly woven from native vines. The open section of the hull was framed in a very light-colored wood.

The rigging that held us below the massive gas bags above was also composed of vines, far thicker than the wicker. From my vantage point below, I could see what was not apparent from the observation point on the mountain—the cigar form of the airship was an outer envelope covering three elongated bags, or balloons, I suppose, inside. The outer envelope was a sheath, as it were, open along the bottom. The hull we were within was suspended by the vines twelve or so feet below the balloons and swung like a pendulum as we pitched and rolled our way through the air.

The barometer on the forward bulkhead should indicate our approximate altitude, Dan announced. But, he added, he wasn't sure of the relative measurement conversion of pressure into elevation, so he periodically looked overboard to try to find the forest tops below. He said he was attempting to stay a couple of hundred feet aloft so he'd have time to maneuver if something went wrong.

The helm was a common ship's wheel, attached in normal fashion by lines and blocks to the rudder aft. Dan also dealt with four levers, one of which I could tell controlled the motor's throttle. Another engaged the shaft clutch. The third operated the short wing structures protruding out on either side, just aft of the bow. They tilted up or down, much like the diving planes on the Peruvian submarine I once had the misfortune to be aboard. I couldn't deduce what the other lever controlled, as it was seldom used.

Behind Dan stood Corny, who was in charge of ballast and several lines that ran up to the balloon. He explained that Dan told him the lines controlled escape flaps to let the gas out of the bags in an emergency. I wondered what that did exactly, but Corny did not look confident—well, none of us did—so I didn't press him on the issue. Absalom stood beside him, gazing ahead to the north, where his islands waited over the black horizon.

Rork and Cynda were aft of me, tending to Woodgerd's wounded arm, a nasty gash that showed raw meat. They were wrapping a ripped section of her petticoat around it to staunch the bleeding, as Woodgerd growled curse words in the various languages he knew. The enigmatic Roche sat at the back of the compartment, staring aft at the receding fire on the side of Montay San.

In a tired sigh, Dan called our attention to a ragged line of white far below us—a line of surf breaking on reefs. I checked my pocket watch. It was four minutes until midnight. By my dead reckoning, beneath us were the reefs off Baie de Caracol. The aerial warship was supposed to meet the stolen cable steamer somewhere in the area. I looked, but could not see the ship below us. Did Kingston and his gang manage to steal her? Were they waiting for Sokolov's war machine on this coast? Could they see us in the night sky?

We'd made just over twenty-five miles in an hour and a half, admittedly assisted by the following wind, but much better than the French had in their aerial warship. I estimated we had another hundred miles until we reached Great Inagua Island. Four hours, maybe five, in the dark.

"Dan, please steer northwest from this point and reduce the throttle a bit so we slow down. I want to arrive at Great Inagua at first light, which should be in six hours. And I think it's time to start a watch system, gentlemen."

Everyone nodded wearily. I again called to Dan, who was bent over, watching the compass swing in the binnacle. "You need a break, so teach Rork how to operate this thing. He'll take first watch and relieve you at the helm."

Dan didn't reply right away. Instead, he gradually straightened up and turned to face me, one hand still on the wheel. His face showed a sickly grin in the faint light. Slowly, his mouth opened and he looked right at me.

"Too late, Peter. I'm so sorry . . ."

I waited for him to finish his thought, but he didn't. Five seconds later, Dan Horloft fell down dead.

36
Dead Reckoning

Off the coast of northern Haiti
Thursday, 6 September 1888

The ship instantly swung to the right and began to fall. Corny rushed to the wheel and tried to correct our helm, pulling the lever for the planes and pushing the throttle. Our motion eased a little, but we were now much nearer to the sea, so close you could smell the brine.

I reached Dan. There was no response, no pulse, no breath. His shirt felt wet, the abdomen swollen and mushy. I pulled open his coat and saw the shirt was soaked by a thick liquid, brown in the yellowed light. I searched and found the hole, just under the right side of his ribcage. The liver, perhaps a kidney, nicked and bleeding into the abdomen, something I'd seen in battle. A Bizango round must have got him as we escaped.

My friend had bled out over the ninety minutes we were in the air, operating this strange machine, knowing he was the only one who could get us out of there. Knowing there was nothing we could do for him without surgical supplies and bright lights to perform an operation. He never let on that he was wounded—stoic New England fisherman to the end—and probably thinking he could get us to safety.

Corny was beside himself with guilt. "I stood here the whole time and never knew! He didn't tell me. Why didn't he tell me?"

I had Rork take the wheel, put Absalom on the gas relief lines to the balloon, and grabbed Corny by the arm. "Because he knew there wasn't anything you could do to help him, Corny. But there is now. You watched Dan operate the airship, so stay here and help Rork figure out how to steer this thing."

"He should've told me . . ."

"Corny, stop it and get your wits together. You've got work to do." An aerial jolt reinforced my request. "Do it."

"Right . . . you're right." He took a breath and said, "Get a rhythm going, Rork, like steering in heavy seas. Anticipate the roll and pitch and correct ahead of it. And I think we need to slow that throttle a bit, the propeller sounds too overworked."

That comment brought something to mind that I'd overlooked earlier. I looked aft to Woodgerd. "Did Sokolov ever tell you how long the battery would last?"

"Oh, hell . . . No, he didn't."

There is a military maxim that no plan, no matter how well conceived, outlives the initial reality of the battlefield. Our odyssey had become a case in point.

At this moment in time, the most inscrutable of our number, Pierre Jean Roche, approached me, contritely asking if I had the time and inclination to talk. I soon discovered that what he really meant was for me to listen.

"I think after all that has happened, we need to be truthful with each other, Commander. You have been more than fair with me and have led us through this treacherous journey to find the truth about your quarry, Luke, and about my target, Sokolov. As a fellow intelligence professional, you, more than others, understand the restrictions I have regarding information about myself and my work. But by now, I think we have proven ourselves to each other. Hesitation is no longer valid."

With the noise of the wind and the propeller, his voice was audible only to me as we sat within the wicker hull. It made for an extraordinary scene—two wary espionage operatives from opposites side of the world, flung together in a precarious situation.

He held out a hand, which I clasped, as he said, "We share a common first name, you know. Peter. My real name is Pyotr Ivanovich Kovinski. I am a major in the Okhrana, the counter-revolutionary section of the Ministry of Internal Affairs, and I command the foreign espionage operations section in Paris. My assignment is to compromise radical émigré revolutionaries in Europe through penetration agents—what the French call *provocateurs*."

Provocateurs. The Russians were known by the murky intelligence profession as the best in the world at that—with the Okhrana as the best of the best. "From what I hear in the press, you are busy these days. There are lots of unhappy Russian émigrés. Are you successful?"

He shrugged. "I am told that I am very good at it."

I thought about his name, Pyotr Ivanovich. Pierre Jean, in French. Not much of a stretch. "So tell me, Pyotr, did you have a *provocateur* here in Haiti that alerted you to Sokolov's activities?"

"Yes, a man passing through the area wrote about an odd Russian with a place in the mountains. The description matched our missing fanatical genius. Later, we sent an operative here from New York to follow up. He confirmed the initial report."

An agent in New York? That was interesting.

"Really? Who was that?" I asked as casually as I could.

"Peter . . . you know I cannot reveal my agents' identities.

Please do not worry, though. Our agents in America are focused on Russian émigrés, not American citizens. We have no quarrel with your country."

I doubted that, but switched subjects. "So you, as the head of foreign counter-intelligence took this mission yourself? This renegade Russian must have been very important to you already. I assume you had been trying to find Sokolov for some time. You knew of his work."

"Yes. His work was pioneering. Then he suddenly left. We found out about his intellectual weaknesses, his true motives, his deplorable treachery. He deceived and used us—to gain knowledge, to expand his evil network, to build his heinous dream machine of death."

Roche, or Kovinski as I now had to remind myself, raised an index finger in exclamation. "Sokolov was judged to be one of our most dangerous enemies. But now, thanks to you, and the others on this expedition, we in Russia can breathe safely again. The fiend is slain."

"And some good people died."

"Yes. And that is why *you* should know that you will always have me, and the imperial House of Romanov, in your debt, Peter. I am genuinely sorry for the loss of your friends Dan and Yablonowski. Henri and Claire knew the dangers, but your friends did not. Everyone aboard has my appreciation."

Later, he let everyone know his true name, which was used from then on. That moment when he opened up to me was memorable, beginning a unique opportunity for me. The Russians were known in the profession for efficiency, ruthlessness, and obsessive secrecy. I now had an entrée into their private world. I thanked Major Kovinski with the assurance that I would be ready to assist him in the future, professionally and personally, should he ever need help.

We honored my friend Dan Horloft at dawn. A born and bred seaman, he would've appreciated the bird's-eye view from higher than any mast he'd climbed. The sun was a sphere of liquid gold, rising through a misty peach-colored sky. Below us was a wave-flecked indigo sea. The panorama was awe-inspiring, perfect for the welcoming of a sailor son home to heaven.

Our resources were obviously limited. I cobbled together a short prayer. Absalom quoted John 14 and the 91st Psalm by heart. Kovinski said a prayer in Russian. And finally, all of us—led by my Catholic friend Rork—sang the first verse from the Episcopal sailors' hymn, "Eternal Father, Strong to Save." Then we let the mortal remains of our companion go down into the sea far below.

Afterward, Absalom, holding one of Cynda's hands and I the other, led a prayer for Luke, an innocent caught up in something he couldn't fathom. Woodgerd closed his eyes like the rest, but didn't mouth the words.

No one spoke for a long time afterward.

We never saw Great Inagua Island, one of the largest of the Bahamian chain, that morning. A distressing development, to say the least. Nervous glances were cast my way by the passengers. Even Rork had a worried look on his face.

Navigation is done by calculating time, course, and speed. I knew the course well enough, and the approximate time by my pocket watch. But I'd never navigated a ship that moved through the air. Once we left the land, I was dead reckoning, guessing really, at our airship's speed and the amount of drift to leeward.

37

Powerless

Southern Bahamian Islands
Thursday, 6 September 1888

In the daylight I found two items in a stowage locker in Sokolov's "navigation bridge"—for lack of a better term—that proved quite useful. The first was a telescope, which I immediately issued to Absalom, who possessed the youngest and sharpest eyes. The second was a general chart of the region. Kovinski, Rork, and I studied it as Corny steered. Woodgerd was aft, resting. Cynda was gazing behind us.

I was going to try to deduce our position but was distracted by marks on the chart. A rhumb line was noted in pencil, emanating from a circled point off Haiti's northern coast, right about where we exited. It progressed across the chart two hundred miles west-northwesterly to a circled point in the tiny archipelago of reef islets south of Ragged Island in the Bahamas. The line then ran straight north-northwesterly to Nassau. A third leg of the line left Nassau in a northeasterly course for a hundred miles, to a circled point out in the ocean, thirty miles from the end of Eleuthera Island. Circled points are used by navigators as approximate position fixes, or as a rendezvous.

Sokolov's plan was right there, before us.

"Well, I'll be damned. His first target wasn't going to be in Russia, gentlemen," I said. "The cable ship would meet him here, then tow him from Haiti to . . ." I peered at the chart. "Santo Domingo Cay, south of Ragged Island in the southern Bahamas. But look, from that place this rhumb line crosses over islands on its way to Nassau, so I presume that would be the course of the aerial warship. It would be launched from the cable steamer and fly north across the Bahamas."

"Attackin' Nassau?" asked Rork. "It's British, not Rooskie. Why there?"

Kovinski nodded. "For practice, Rork. A dress rehearsal attack on Nassau at night, to make sure things worked correctly. No one would know the perpetrator or the method, but everyone would be panicked. Later, after Sokolov attacked Saint Petersburg, people would know who attacked Nassau. He would show the European monarchs his ability to humiliate them, to hit their empires everywhere. Sokolov hated them all, including Queen Victoria."

"Ah, so then after he did Nassau, the bugger'd sail his airship nor'east an' meet up with his stolen steamer at this last place on the chart, out in the ocean. Dicey move, that. Tryin' to find a ship in the dark in the ocean an' get winched down to it."

"Yes, but if the ship shined electrical lights up into the air, like a lighthouse, you could see it from quite a distance at this altitude," I said, adding, "and then, once they get secured to the ship, they steam to the Baltic. But that steamer doesn't carry enough coal to get to the Baltic in one run. He'd have to re-coal the cable ship, and maybe re-arm his war machine, somewhere in the European Atlantic islands. Azores or Canaries."

Kovinski sighed. "I have more work to do. Okhrana must

discover his accomplices in Europe. This came very close to happening. Too close." He looked up expectantly at me. "I must get to Nassau as quickly as possible, Commander, and obtain steamer passage home. So . . . where are we now?"

I had very little idea as to where we were, but one does not admit that to the crew.

"Approximately here," I said, pointing to the area near the Ragged Islands. "We must have gone past Great Inagua in the night, our speed being faster than I thought. We've been steering northwest, but I think the wind must have more easterly in it now and has given us far more leeway than I anticipated. That we haven't seen land in the two hours since sunrise means that we have to be in this area between Cuba to the south, Great Inagua to the east, Acklins Island to the north, and the Ragged Islands to the west. It also means that we should see one of these places soon. Once I get a good position fix, I can alter course and we can then motor to Nassau."

"Aye, an' remember this thing'll surely cause one hell o' a commotion at Nassau," said Rork. "Nary a way ta keep her—o' us, neither—under wraps once we arrive."

It was a valid observation. I hadn't thought that far out in advance. I was beginning to do just that when my cogitation was interrupted by two events.

Absalom shouted out, "Reefs ahead on the port bow. I think it's the southern end of the Great Bahamas Bank, sir. Yes! Look over there where the clouds are clearing, abaft the starboard beam—I think that is Santo Domingo Cay!"

We were at the second circled point marked on the chart. I searched for the cable ship, thinking they might be using this place as a secondary rendezvous with Sokolov. I saw nothing on the ocean, not even a fishing smack.

Absalom came aft and showed me on the chart. "That makes the reef ahead of us South Head. I've sailed the deep water in this area." He shook his head and looked overboard at those razor-sharp coral teeth scattered in front of us as far as the eye could see. "But never up in the reefs. Very dangerous area, sir. Only a few channels through here. Coral heads and reefs are everywhere for hundreds of miles to the west, and for about fifty miles up to the north."

The appearance of fixed objects below allowed me to ascertain our speed and drift. I calculated quickly. Courtesy of Sokolov's motor-driven propeller, our speed was somewhere around twenty knots, faster than the fastest ship in the U.S. Navy. We would cross the fifty miles of reefs in a little over two hours.

"No problem, son. We're above those reefs and will be beyond them by noon." I called forward, "Corny, alter course to due north. Once we get to the Exumas, we'll follow that chain of islands toward Nassau."

Corny replied in a comically false Irish accent, "Aye, sir. Due north's easy to find. Methinks I've got the hang o' this here thing now. Next stop: civilization."

Smiles broke out. For the first time in a long time, I felt optimism. We would make it. And Rork and I would have quite a story to tell, and this warship to show, Commodore Walker and Admiral Porter. That might make them forget we were absent beyond our official leave. The tragedies and heartache we'd endured on the search for Luke Saunders would have at least some mitigation. Our smiles were short-lived, however.

For right then, the electrical motor chose to stop.

"I can't steer!" yelled Corny. "She's going sideways. Won't turn into the wind!"

Kovinski dashed aft and looked at the battery, checking the India rubber–clad cable connections. He held his hands up in a helpless gesture. They were still connected. The battery had expired.

We were a mile past the edge of the reef by then. I studied the saw-toothed coral under us to determine our course and drift. The wind was in control now, blowing us west northwest. We could only steer downwind. Away from Nassau, away from the inhabited islands of the Exumas, and toward the vast desolate stretches of the Great Bahamas Bank.

"Steer as much northerly as you can, Corny. If we can reach the southern end of Andros Island we can find a beach."

"Not many beaches down that way, sir," said Absalom dejectedly. "And no one lives down there, either."

Kovinski, his imperturbability shed, muttered something that sounded like "*Blay.*" I learned later that meant "damn" in Russian, a remarkably benign curse considering our predicament. Rork had no such civility and unloaded a combination of English and Gaelic in the direction of the motor.

"Do the best you can, Corny," I repeated. "Absalom, kindly return to your bow watch and sing out if you see a ship or a boat."

"Too shallow for ships here, sir." Our young crewman was still shaking his head, his tone woefully maudlin. "Won't see any boats either—nobody sails this far into the reefs."

It was a struggle to keep from using some sailor oaths myself. Instead, I calmly said, "Just keep watch, Absalom, and you can forgo additional comments about how deserted this area may be. We fully understand that now, but we've no choice at this point."

Rork put his hand on the youngster and flashed a grin, while steering him forward. "Aye, lad. Now's the time to get *tough*, not sad. This crew ain't done in, nary by a long shot. Oh, me's seen far worse than this wee little setback."

Absalom clearly had trouble imagining that. "Really?"

"Oh, boyo, did me ever tell ya about the time when dear ol' Commander Wake an' me was stuck in a slave box in the middle o' nowhere in the Sahara desert o' Africa? Aye, we was surrounded by the most evil-eyed bunch o' cut-throatin' buggers I ever did see. Now *that* was a dicey deal! No? Well, let's go to the bow, an' while you have a gander at the ocean through that glass, I'll tell ye the tale."

As they moved forward, Kovinski leaned close to me. "Without the assistance of the motor, we have slowed down quite a bit, have we not?"

I checked the reefs again. He was right. "Yes, Major. I'd guess we're doing about ten knots now."

"And those clouds I see on the horizon where we are headed, they are a storm, are they not?"

The clouds around us had gradually been getting thicker and darker. The cloud line on the horizon was black and too big for a thunderstorm. Rork and I had already seen it and knew what it meant, but hadn't said anything to the others. I saw that Absalom had too, but had refrained from scaring anyone.

"Yes, that cloud line on the western horizon is a storm. Looks like it could be a bad one and it's coming this way."

"And it appears that we are losing height above the reefs, am I correct?"

Corny had brought that to my attention, but like the storm, I hadn't mentioned it to the others. "Yes, the bullet holes in the gas bag above us have been allowing the hydrogen to slowly leak out. We've been losing altitude for some time now."

Kovinski's jaw tightened. "Then it would appear we are in extreme peril—and powerless to do anything about it."

"Yes, Major. It's out of our control now."

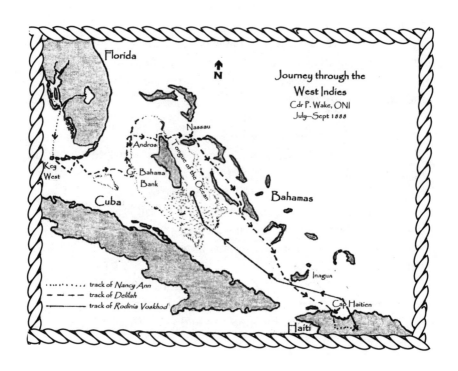

Florida

N

Journey through the
West Indies
Cdr P. Wake, ONI
July—Sept 1888

Nassau

Andros

Key
West

Gr. Bahama
Bank

Tongue of the Ocean

Cuba

Bahamas

Inagua

Cap Haitien

.... track of *Nancy Ann*
— — — track of *Delilah*
—⊢—⊢— track of *Rodinia Voskhod*

Haiti

38

Tongue of the Ocean

Twenty miles east southeast
of Snap Point, southern end
of Andros Island, the Bahamas
Thursday, 6 September 1888

Like the tropical storm we'd encountered in the Straits of Florida two months earlier, this one approached rapidly. The reader may wonder at the unlikeliness, not to mention the unfairness, of having three hurricane storms hit us in just a few months, but at that moment such philosophy was lost on me.

Concerned about our inexorable sinking, I gave orders to jettison the battery, motor, and propeller, with a view toward lightening the ship. We disconnected and manhandled them overboard and the craft instantly rose upward, bouncing in the rough air even more violently than before. Too late, I realized I had jettisoned too much weight, that some was needed to dampen the buffeting, like ballast stone in a sailing vessel. And worse yet, once our initial ascent had ended, we still continued falling. The rate was slowed, but still relentless.

When the storm was five miles away—and we were already fifty miles within the maze of reefs—the wind veered quickly to the southwest, then west. It went from a benign trade wind pushing us, to a Force 6 on our nose. Sokolov's aerial warship was spun around, all efforts to steer were useless, and we now sailed downwind to the northeast, just ahead of a formidable purplish-black, churning cloud that was gaining on us by the second.

Our altitude by then was perhaps two hundred feet—I never could get the hang of interpreting it—and we could quite clearly see the deathly network of coral rock beneath us, the surf breaking into a labyrinth of foam without pattern or predictability. It stretched for miles.

Kovinski spoke the question in everyone's mind. "How long?"

I looked up at the bags of gas, visibly sagging here and there under the weight of the outer envelope. The Cyrillic lettering was buckled, making a mockery of Sokolov's grandiose announcement.

"Once the storm hits us, we'll go down rapidly. I'd say ten minutes at the most until that happens."

Woodgerd stumbled up to us. "Will this thing float?"

"No, not as a boat. The wicker's not tightly enough woven. However, now that the heavy battery and motor are off, the wood and wicker should float as debris, sort like a raft. But we've got to get the frame and wicker hull cut away from the rigging as we go down, or the weight of the balloons and envelope will come down and smother us. I don't know if goldbeater's skin will float, but I doubt it."

Woodgerd, ever the landsman, didn't want to hear that. "Damn it all. You mean I'm gonna end my days flopping around in the water like some squid sailor? Helluva end for a soldier."

There wasn't time for a witty rejoinder. I called all hands together for final orders before our collision with the sea.

"All right, I want a man at each one of these rigging points, port and starboard. Rork, you and Absalom are forward. Kovinski and Corny are aft. Woodgerd and I are midships. Cynda, you'll be with me. Aft will cut away first, then midship, and last the bowmen. When I give the order—*and only when I give the order*—cut the rigging away. That'll be just before we hit the water. I want everyone to stay in the hull. It will fill with water and get swamped, but should float. You must stay *inside* the hull and let it protect you from the coral. Everyone understand that?"

Heads nodded just as a roll of thunder boomed out of the cloud. Woodgerd pointed to flashes deep within the bowels of the approaching dark monolith. "Hydrogen is flammable. How close does a lightning bolt have to get to ignite this stuff?"

"I don't know," I replied. "But we don't have that much hydrogen left, and we'll probably be blown down as the front edge of the storm hits us anyway."

A gust knocked the ship down lower, all aboard falling down. We were now lower than the truck of a schooner's topmast—a hundred feet at most. I could see the individual saw-toothed points on the rocks.

"Get ready!"

"Look—deep water ahead!" cried out Absalom, just as a wall of rain closed off all visibility from us. It didn't matter anymore, we'd run out of time. The airship wasn't going to make it past the reefs to deep water.

Above us the dark cliff had arrived, flinging wind and rain out ahead to give us a taste of its power. The rain pelted us in horizontal sheets, every drop hitting our bodies like birdshot. The wind rose to Force 8 or more—a full gale. Thunder detonated nearby. Everyone held their breath, but the balloons above us didn't ignite.

Cynda's face was within inches of mine, her arms clinging to my waist. Those beautiful coquettish eyes now tragic, pleading, capturing my heart. She was saying something, but in the noise I could only make out her lips forming, *"I'm so sorry, Peter."*

More than anything, I wanted to answer her tenderly, to hold her, to protect her, but the cacophony of sound and motion had dulled my capacity to communicate. I lamely nodded an acknowledgment to her and turned away, forcing my mind to focus on when to give that order.

Just how fast the aerial warship was moving, I do not know. Other than aboard a train, I'd never moved that rapidly in my life, but a rough estimate would be twenty knots below the speed of the wind, so our speed was at least twenty-five to thirty knots. The balloon envelope, and the hull suspended beneath, bucked wildly—pitching, skewing, and rolling. There was no rhythm, no way to anticipate each gyration. None of us could stand, so each knelt or sat in our position, tossed around the narrow confines, blinded by the stinging rain, holding on with both hands to the hull's gunwale.

Six horrified faces watched my every move, waiting for the order.

I tried to calculate the force of impacting the water at that speed, but it was beyond my mental ability, which was overwhelmed by the incredible shrieking of the wind in the rigging vines and the sight of that frothing mess below. I could taste the salt spray and knew we were seconds away. I glanced quickly overboard. It was a vision of watery hell, only ten feet down. Now was time. I pointed to Corny and Kovinski.

"Now! Cut the rigging away now—*aft men first!"*

Kovinski's pocket dagger sliced through his vine. Corny hacked his in two with a Bizango machete. The stern felled abruptly, as Woodgerd and I cut ours with bayonets. The stern hit the water with a tremendous thud, launching everyone several feet in the air. Absalom and Rork struggled to free the bow.

We bounced along the wave tops. Absalom's vine severed, but Rork's didn't for several seconds. Suddenly, the bow section holding the remaining vine rigging tore away and we were down in the water, instantly swamping, my crew swimming within the hull.

"Grab hold and stay inside!" I cried.

Aloft, the goldbeater's skin balloon envelope stayed put for a split second, as if astounded at its new freedom. Then it lifted up and away on the wind, no longer bound by our weight, just a broken toy for the amusement of the tempest. It went higher than we'd ever been, flying broadside to the wind, and was soon a mile or more distant.

For some inexplicable reason, in the middle of all that peril when our lives were about to be consumed in the reefs, my eyes couldn't stop following Sokolov's flying machine of death. I noted that, ironically, it was heading for Europe, and wondered where the giant carcass of plastered sheets of cow guts would finally end up. Rork's beloved Ireland? Teignholder's imperial homeland of England? Perhaps Paloma's motherland of Spain. And what would be thought of the aerial warship when its depleted remains were discovered? Even as my mind formed the question, a flash and thunder synchronized instantaneously to provide the answer.

A momentary ball of fire lit the purple clouds, and the warship was blown quickly into nothingness. Not even smoke remained of the *Rodinia Voskhod*. I turned away and saw that, amidst the maelstrom, everyone had been mesmerized by the same sight.

A swell raised us up and swept the swamped hull forward. I looked around us in the water. There was no surf, no cresting waves, none of the frothing chaos I'd seen below the ship before we crashed. Why hadn't we been crushed into the coral and ripped apart? It dawned on me just as a grinning Absalom pounded Rork on the shoulder and proclaimed the good news.

"We're beyond the reefs. We're in the deep water!"

That we were, without a doubt. That last gust of wind had delivered us beyond the reefs, into a lee of sorts, where the waves were gentler and allowed us a slight respite. The wind still howled, the rain still pelted, but we were relatively safe.

By now, those reading this account fully understand the certain death that awaited us within the vast maze of reefs. But

they may not be aware of just how incredible was our escape. Therefore, kindly indulge a brief discourse on the geography of our location.

Within the middle of the Bahamian islands, there is a maritime anomaly. It is an area of oceanic deep water, more than a thousand fathoms deep, stretching a hundred miles long with a width of fifteen to thirty miles, all of which is surrounded by some of the most treacherous reef systems in the West Indies. It is bounded on the west by the lengthy pastel-colored waters and reefs of Andros Island, on the south by those of the Great Bahamian Bank, with which the reader is now intimate. On the east lie the Exuma Banks, whose reef edge is just as dangerous as that we'd flown over.

This trough of royal blue water enters from the north, reaching around the island of New Providence and probing the inside of the Bahamian archipelago. In a gesture of defiance, it curls back at the southern extremity. The humorously odd shape is easily apparent on a chart, hence its name.

Looking at my bedraggled old friend as he held grimly onto the wicker, I gestured around us and laughed at the absurdity of our deliverance.

"Can you believe it, Rork? We've been saved by the Tongue of the Ocean . . ."

Further ironies were yet to unfold. The wind and waves steadily increased the farther we progressed from the maze of the Banks. With that propulsion our sluggish water-logged raft of wicker and vine made its way northwest across the Tongue of the Ocean. I estimated our drift at two knots, for it seemed we also had the assistance of an ebb tide off those wicked reefs.

Mercifully, there was no sun to broil us, nor was the water cold. Still, it was an arduous day of constant strain, holding on as our contraption slowly worked itself apart in the seas. Our cuts and bruises became inflamed by the salt water, clothing chafed our skin, and thirst dominated our thoughts. Then, in the late morning, the inevitable commenced.

First the twisted after-section, composed of balsa framing with no real hull structure, parted from us. Then the porous wicker section of the hull began to show signs of disintegration. Absalom began praying aloud again, reciting Old Testament invocations of the Hebrew slaves for Divine help. Cynda and Corny joined him, the others of us busy relashing the vines to effect a jury-rigged craft. I guessed we had perhaps another six hours left before it fragmented beyond our meager ability to repair.

The expected happened at sunset, an event shrouded in cloud. The wind had diminished and veered southerly again. Among us, Absalom made the only human sounds as his head rested on the gunwale, lolling back and forth with the motion of the swells. Though his eyes were closed, his lips mumbled in prayer. Everyone else was dozing as best they could while floating within our wicker tub. I was on watch and silently going over plans for what to do when that tub disintegrated completely. All of us would swim ten or fifteen miles to the west, toward Andros Island, which I thought to be the closest point of land.

Suddenly, our piously stalwart Bahamian stopped his mumbled verse and croaked out something unintelligible, his parched throat preventing speech. Concerned about his sanity, I hoarsely whispered for him to calm down. But Absalom's agitation grew. He pointed east and there I saw it. A charcoal line against the lead gray sky.

Finally, he got it out. "Green Cay."

Amazing. The Tongue of the Ocean had delivered us to the infamous lair of the legendary Lieutenant John Newland Maffitt, Confederate States Navy, where he had fitted out the ocean raider

C.S.S. *Florida* with guns and men in August of 1862. Rork and I knew the island well, having been there several times during the war to search for other Rebel raiders. A tiny coral outcropping of the Exuma Banks, it was on the *east* side of the Tongue of the Ocean, twenty miles from Andros Island.

Two hours later, we collapsed on the beach, gasping out a prayer of thanks to God.

I realize that some people, sitting in the comfort of their homes in this scientific age of modern late nineteenth-century America and perusing my words by Edison's electricity-generated light, may think the various fortuitous junctions encountered during this odyssey were mere random strokes of luck—luck that is sometimes to be expected within a system of logical outcomes. They may think me a bit too sentimental, perhaps overcome by the physical and emotional deprivations of the journey within, and out of, Haiti.

I know better, however. I was there. It was no stroke of luck. There was a greater hand than any of ours at work.

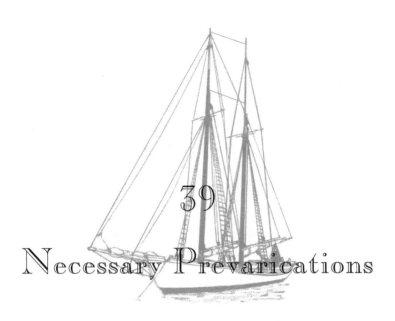

39
Necessary Prevarications

Green Cay
Central Bahamas
Friday, 7 September 1888

Green Cay is uninhabited, so we were on our own. The abandoned salt pan had a hut that furnished us with some shelter but little else. However, there was a bright side to the location. Absalom explained that the monthly mail boat sails past the islet on her course from the Exuma islands to Congo Town on Andros, and thence to Nassau. He also found us succulent cacti to alleviate our thirst somewhat.

Providence shone down on us again the next morning after our landfall, when our Bahamian Seminole native son spied the government sloop on the southeastern horizon, bound for the western end of Green Cay, upon which we stood. Directly, all hands got to work constructing a signal fire out of buttonwood, which sends up prodigious amounts of smoke.

As Absalom and Corny attended to the job of igniting the

thing, the whole while debating whether the Bahamian way or the Navajo method was faster, Kovinski called us together, saying he had something he wanted to tell us. We gathered around the roaring fire—Absalom had won the argument—and listened as the Russian embarked upon an extraordinary speech. He began softly, the suave European gentleman, albeit dressed in rags, preparing his audience.

"After all that we have seen and endured together, I think I am justified in considering each of you a dear friend. Therefore, I will be quick in my remarks."

A pause ensued, followed by Kovinski awarding us an affable smile of seemingly genuine warmth, the first I'd seen from him. Then he turned his attention to the fairest of us, whose grimy tattered appearance was the opposite of when I first saw her at that church in St. Augustine. My mind flooded with emotion. Had it really only been nine weeks earlier? Had we really had a romantic affair during that time? Had I actually fallen in love? Or was it pity? Or perhaps gratitude?

Kovinski's continued speech ended my daydreaming.

"Cynda, my dear lady, I cannot possibly know the depth of your grief, but I hope you know of our sincerest sympathy for your inestimable loss. Your son was a victim of evil, an evil that is insidiously spreading throughout Europe and America. Anarchists, revolutionaries, criminal gangs, terror-mongers, freedom fighters, whatever you call them, they have the same goal—the destruction of all that civilized Christian people hold dear. Sokolov was the personification of that evil. His war machine was the culmination of their work. Thankfully, we stopped him and saved countless innocent lives, both here in the Bahamas and in Europe."

His tone grew husky, emotional, as he fixed Cynda in his gaze.

"Your son, Sergeant Yablonowski, Sergeant Aubrac, Claire Fournier, Henri Billot, and Dan Horloft died so that evil could not spread. Many others have been wounded, including Colonel

Woodgerd here, not to mention Commander Wake's own confrontation with death. Your friends pledged their lives to help you rescue your son. That is over now, and we will all go home. But do not doubt that the menace is still out there. Other Sokolovs still lurk—waiting, watching, learning of our weaknesses, as they continue building their own maniacal strengths. And that is the point of my discourse."

The Russian held up both hands.

"You all know by now that I am an officer in the service of my crown, a service that is devoted to protecting my motherland's civilization and that of modern Christian countries everywhere. I feel it my duty to warn everyone here that we all possess something the evildoers of the world need and will do anything to obtain— the knowledge of how to create an aerial death machine. The knowledge of what Sokolov designed and built."

Woodgerd harrumphed and asked, "What's your point, Major Kovinski?"

"Colonel, it is simple: that we must say nothing to anyone about what we know of Sokolov's aerial machine. Even to those we love and trust the most, for *any* disclosure will eventually lead the information to the press. And we all know how that would end. The press would do Sokolov's work for him, multiplying panic among the public and immensely improving the education of Sokolov's anarchist cohorts in the malevolent art of terror-making. Each of us has a responsibility not to innocently accomplish what Sokolov wanted to happen."

"So we stay mum about Sokolov and the airship?" asked Corny.

"Yes, silent about it all. About the machine, how young Luke died, how our friends died, how we came to be here on this island—about everything that has to do with Sokolov. Am I correct, Commander?"

Eyes shifted to me. I took a breath, looking at Cynda.

"Yes. Major Kovinski is right. We can't allow this scientific knowledge out. It will be used by the Fenians against the British crown, by the Narodnaya Volya against the tsar, by the anarchists in my country against our government. Major Kovinski and I will submit confidential reports to our superiors, but beyond that no one should know."

I cleared my throat nervously, hoping that Kovinski's and my conversation sounded unrehearsed. "I think an appropriate explanation would be that our schooner *Delilah* wrecked on the Haitian coast, that Dan and the others died of disease in Haiti, and that we sailed back to the Bahamas in a native boat that went down, stranding us here. I don't like conjuring up a tale one bit, but I fully agree that the consequences of letting the press get hold of what we know is far worse than the lie we must perpetuate. It is a necessary prevarication."

"Aye, 'tis that," said Rork, who'd not been in the planning of this dialogue, but was loyal to the idea. "Some o' those Fenians are Irish in name only. Their work is death o' innocents, an' I'll not help 'em one wee bit."

I wanted to hear their answers. "So? Do each of you agree?"

Absalom sadly nodded his head. "I don't even *want* to talk about what I've seen and had to do."

Corny sighed. "I see your point, Peter . . . and agree. Will you tell Dan's family?"

I'd been worried about Corny's natural proclivity to liberalism and cocktail gossip. His acquiescence was a worry removed. He would keep his word. "Yes. He had no wife or children, but there was a brother, I think. I'll tell him."

I looked at Woodgerd, who nodded. "Yes, I agree." He certainly didn't need his connection with Sokolov to be made public.

Kovinski knelt before our lady and took her hands in his. "Madam, what are your thoughts on this?"

I watched her eyes fill and wondered if they would ever know joy again. Her voice was barely audible. "My thoughts? I want to remember Luke as he used to be, before this nightmare began. I don't want to think of him with that wicked man. And I don't want my darling husband's legacy associated with it, either. Don't worry, Major. I'll keep quiet."

And so it was that when the mail sloop anchored off the beach and the skipper came ashore, he heard a fable that has been told to this day.

40

An Occupational Necessity

Nassau
The Bahamas
Saturday, 8 September 1888

The mail boat captain kindly altered his schedule and sailed directly for Nassau, landing us at the Vendue wharf that Saturday morning. Our first two hours were taken up by colonial officialdom recording the account, the local Anglican church members providing us with clothing and medical attention, and the Methodists giving us our first decent meal in weeks.

A rather officious doctor with one of those English hyphenated names looked in on Cynda, about whom my concern had grown markedly. Thin, sallow, and weakened by voiding, she looked dreadful, and my worry was a recurrence of malaria or yellow fever, aggravated by the conditions of our travel and the stress of her son's loss. The doctor refused my inquiries after his examination, saying dismissively that it was none of my business, but that I should take better care in the future to have the lady treated as a white woman should be in the tropics. Cynda told me later that my diagnosis was correct, and that bed rest, good food, and decent water would improve her condition.

Robert Mason, my man in Nassau, showed up as Rork and I were enjoying a repast of fried fish and yams in a café near the Victoria Hotel. He had been visiting the other side of the island that morning, but word of our arrival, it seemed, traveled fast on New Providence.

"I've been given three brief messages to present to you, Peter," Mason informed me. "The first came from Leo in Havana in late August: Paloma has disappeared, so has your man Casas." Leo was our secondary contact in Havana.

"That's it? Is it disappeared, as in arrested by the Spanish authorities? Or disappeared and somewhere in Cuba? Or disappeared by fleeing from Cuba?"

"Just those words and no more. That was the last communication I had—there's been nothing more from Leo. I passed it along to ONI by telegraph, with the addendum that you were incommunicado on leave, heading to the southern Bahamas on a private yachting trip."

"Yes, and now Rork and I are a week late getting back to duty at naval headquarters. I'll have the Devil to pay for that. What else've you got?"

"Well, a few days after I passed along the Cuban message, I got the second message for you. It came in from Commodore Walker in Washington: Find Wake and Rork and advise them to return to headquarters immediately. That was it, nothing more. Of course, I couldn't find you."

"I'll deal with it, Robert. Not your fault."

"Major Teignholder's orderly gave me the third message for you this morning. It came in the form of a command, not a request: meet him on his verandah at five. By the way, Teignholder's been asking questions about *me* lately."

"Really?"

"Rather odd inquiries about any connection I may have with the Irish revolutionaries. And Russians."

"He's worried about you and Fenian terrorists? That doesn't add up. Oh, wait. Ah, yep, I've got it—the Russians and the Brits have been on the brink of war several times lately over Afghanistan. They're worried that if that happens, the Russians will support the Fenians in their terror bombing campaign in London. They've exploded several there in the past few years. Stupid tactic. It only makes the British people turn against them."

Mason nodded. "Yes, I think you've got it, Peter. The major knows Rork here is Irish-American. And then there was the Frenchman, Roche, asking about Russians in the Bahamas. In his mind, he sees the connection."

Rork piped up at that point. "Now gents, not all the Clan-na-Gael Fenians're bad men. But let me tell ye, all true Irish sons despise that un-Christian dynamitin' fringe, blowin' up civilians with bombs in London an' callin' themselves Fenians. Those bloody bastards're just like any terrorists anywheres. They're a cowardly bunch o' murderers, they are."

Mason nodded his understanding, unaware of just how close the connections would appear to the British. Mason didn't know, and I didn't tell him, that Roche was actually Kovinski, a Russian Okhrana agent. But in the back of my mind I did begin to worry that maybe Major Teignholder's supposition about the Russians and Fenians might have some validity. The Fenians did have support among the Irish in America; the Russians had agents there. Yes, they could unite and act against the British. It was something for ONI to look at and for me to keep in mind when meeting Teignholder later.

I had one last question for Mason. "Any word of an attack on a cable-laying steamer in northern Haiti? Perhaps captured by bandits, then taken away?"

"No. I just talked to a schooner captain who sailed from Cap Haitien and he never mentioned any such attack. But he did say they have new telegraph connections now through an oceanic cable that was just laid."

"Any word on a revolution there?"

"It's in the air, but nothing's happened yet."

So Sokolov's partners hadn't done their part—Captain Kingston had taken the mad Russian's money and sailed away on *Condor*. Wise move. And Hyppolite hadn't marched on Port au Prince. Time would tell on that score.

I looked at my pocket watch, which in spite of the punishment of the previous three months continued to function. Then I gave Mason his last directive.

"Please send a cable to Commodore Walker through the usual cipher and cover address. Tell him Rork and I are on our way back, via Key West."

"Can't do it now, Peter. The telegraph cable office just closed and won't open till nine on Monday morning." He cast a sly look at me. "You'll be gone by that point—incommunicado once more. Gee, what a shame."

"Precisely, Robert. I'm not in the mood for Walker's wrath just yet."

I concentrated my next efforts on finding passage for my people. I wanted everyone out of Nassau and away from the inquisitive British authorities as soon as possible. Mason, good man that he is, arranged it, including some pecuniary assistance from our operational bank account, normally unobtainable on a Saturday afternoon. It does, literally, pay to have friends in important places.

Absalom Bowlegs was the first to leave—as a crewman aboard an island schooner headed for Morgan's Bluff at Andros. They left with the tide in the early afternoon.

The farewell was tearful. Absalom had become somewhat of

a son to all of us. As usual at such times, promises were given to correspond, to visit when in the area, to continue the bond which had formed. Rork gave him an Irish blessing. Cynda became a sobbing mess. Even Kovinski showed emotion, demanding the Absalom visit him in Paris, where he would be shown "the hospitality that only a Russian host can give a mighty Bahamian Seminole warrior!" He then pounded Absalom on the back and pronounced him "a comrade-in-arms, forever!"

By chance, a Ward Line steamer was in from Charleston, bound ultimately for Havana the following morning, via Key West. It was a perfect opportunity for the rest of us to escape. Kovinski could take it to Havana and get a steamer directly to France from there. We Americans could get off in Key West and make our way north. Everyone went aboard that afternoon, comfortably laid out in the first real beds we'd seen since the hotel at Cap Haitien.

At five o'clock, with one more duty in Nassau before I could be on my way to Key West, my weary body trudged up that slope toward the Government House, turned right at Hill Street, and entered Graycliff House. Just as the daily rain began to fall, I met the Brit soldier on his verandah outside the Woodes Rogers room. He had Randall with him, a *déjà vu* scene, though in daylight this time. Both smiled benevolently, putting me even more on guard.

"Commander Wake, how kind of you to come, especially after the ordeal you've been through. Please have a seat, and some decent Jamaica rum I brought back from regimental headquarters in Kingston. A little different from the Barbados Mount Gay you had the last time here, but I think you'll enjoy it. Many say that Jamaican cane is sweeter."

Major Teignholder gestured to a bottle on the table. It was a special reserve of Appleton's Estate rum. He poured me a glass, which I gratefully took—it'd been awhile and it hit me fast. I resolved to be careful lest its effects loosen my judgment.

Randall, who had nodded a hello, now spoke to me with a grudging edge in his words. "You managed to evade me at Great

Inagua, Commander. Congratulations. That was deftly done."

He tossed down a drink and poured another. "You know, I ended up having to remain there a fortnight and actually play the role of visiting vicar—admittedly, not one of my best. They even had me deliver a guest sermon at the church, which turned out badly, I'm afraid, when one of the parishioners asked me a question about Nahum of Elkoshite. Evidently he's some sort of fellow in the Bible, but I still don't know what his fame is."

Neither did I. But I knew Randall's true occupation. "Well, Captain Randall—our friend Roche, the man you were following, told me you're not a police inspector, but are actually an officer in military intelligence—I thought we were done with each other at Great Inagua, so I left."

Randall raised his glass in salute. "So the bugger saw through my bluff. Oh, well, no more clergy roles for me. But say, old man, you didn't get me my information before you departed. I wanted to know his name and mission and destination. We had an *agreement*. Remember?"

There was no reason to play coy, or withhold *all* that I knew from these men. I handed over my part of the bargain, but only what they needed to know. "Yes, we did. But I didn't find out the information until after Great Inagua. So here it is: Roche's real name is Major Pyotr Kovinski, of the Russian Okhrana, based in Paris. He was searching for a Russian émigré in Haiti who had formed a group and was plotting a revolutionary attack against the Russian imperial government. The schooner *Condor* was thought by Kovinski to be part of that, which is why he was in the Bahamas asking about her. The subject Kovinski was searching for was named Sergei Alexandrovich Sokolov. He and his group have ceased to exist as a problem for anyone."

"Ceased to exist? So they're dead?"

"Yes."

"A Russian with the Okhrana, eh? Hmm . . . And the subject's name was Sokolov," said Randall as he glanced with surprise at

Teignholder, then turned back toward me.

"I hear by the rumors in town that you made it to Haiti, where *Delilah* wrecked. I presume you were there when this Sokolov and his gang ceased to exist as a problem?"

"Yes, I was. It was a Russian problem, not an American or British problem."

"And *Condor*?"

"Disappeared. Her captain—Kingston's his name—is on the run. I think he's probably in the other end of the Caribbean, with a new name and paint for his ship."

"And I hear that the boy you were searching for is dead."

"Yes. Died in Haiti. The mother is distraught and heading home to grieve. Some of my other passengers died as well. Very sad. Everyone is going home."

"Our sincerest condolences, Commander. My superiors will be relieved, however, that Kovinski, alias Roche, isn't up to something against *us*. Is there anything else about these people that we need to know, especially the Russian, Sokolov? No unusual acquaintances or alliances or logistics?"

In intelligence work one sometimes gives nothing, frequently gives a little, but never gives everything. Knowledge is strength. Strength gets more knowledge. The Brits had just gotten all they would from me. The extent of Sokolov's efforts, and of Kovinski's counter-efforts, weren't part of the equation. If our cousins across the ocean were to be made privy, that would be a decision for my superiors, no doubt in a *quid pro quo* of their own. I've found that it is always useful to be able to present one's own commander with that type of leverage.

"Not that I can think of right now, Captain Randall. Kovinski isn't interested in Britain or America. Or Fenians, if that's what you are concerned about. He's headed back to Paris. The Russians have more than enough to occupy them there with the émigré revolutionary groups."

I turned to the major. "And now, gentlemen, I believe a *quid pro quo* is in order, as a result of our earlier agreement on this very spot. I did my part in taking the Russian on board my vessel and getting you the answers you sought. I presume both the complaint of the *Delilah*'s cook, and the negative telegram from the *Delilah*'s owner to the Bahamian government, have been unfortunately lost—am I correct?"

Major Teignholder shook his head and sighed. "Commander Wake, I told you the colonial mail system is frightfully inefficient. I'm afraid no one knows what you are talking about. What complaint? What telegram?"

"Very good, gentlemen. I'll be leaving for Key West on the first steamer, with my fellow Americans. Oh, one more thing, I really hope those messages are never found, for if they are, an unfortunate result would be the exposure of how British army military intelligence failed to identify Russian spies roaming the Crown Colony of the Bahamas and hobnobbing with the Her Majesty's governor, even when the queen's vaunted army intelligence agents followed them all the way from London. That would be red meat for the press boys of Fleet Street, wouldn't it? Especially given the domestic political climate in parliament . . ."

I let that simmer for a moment, then added the crucial component.

"And for my peace of mind, I think that a report should be issued by you, as commander of Her Majesty's forces in this colony, to the Colonial Office, regarding a confidential informant's report you received that detailed the unfortunate sinking of a schooner named *Delilah*, with all hands aboard lost, south of the island of Great Inagua. That way, the owner of said vessel will be pleased to accept the insurance money for his loss and have no living target for legal suit.

"Ah, yes, and one last thing—really, this is the last—a certified copy of that report should be in my hands aboard the Ward Line steamer no later than eight o'clock in the morning, for we steam at nine."

Teignholder's brow furrowed. "Why, Commander Wake, I do believe that you don't trust us. That sounds frightfully like bloody blackmail."

I smiled. "Trust you? Not a bit, Major."

I could hear him exhale quietly. "Cover your tracks well, don't you, Commander?"

"One has to try, Major. An occupational necessity."

It was time to change the tone, which had become rather tense.

"Now, gentlemen, why don't we soldier on to more pleasant topics, shall we? How about another glass of that Jamaican rum? You're quite right in your assessment—it *is* sweeter than Barbados rum."

41
Bridges

Jefferson Hotel, Duval Street
Key West, Florida
Tuesday, 11 September 1888

My daughter Useppa was nowhere to be found when we arrived at Key West. It will be recalled that two months prior she had angrily departed my boat at Pinder's dock after observing her father in a somewhat delicate, and religiously immoral, situation with Cynda.

On the steamer from Nassau to Key West, I thought about that last confrontation and decided that I should try again to explain my behavior to Useppa, in an effort to return harmony to my paternal relationship. Upon inquiring at the Frederick Douglass School on Thomas Street, where she worked, I was informed that she was presently in Saint Augustine at a conference of Methodist missionaries. Ironically, Useppa was at the same church where I and Cynda reunited.

Useppa wasn't returning to Key West for another week. Well,

that presented no problem, thought I. Saint Augustine was but a short deviation from my rail route north to Washington.

Meanwhile, my weary friends settled into the Jefferson Hotel, a three-story inn on Duval Street just down from Front Street. After my longtime favorite, the Russell House, had been consumed in the 1886 fire, the Jefferson became my lodging when on the island. Woodgerd, Kovinski, Corny, and Cynda obtained nice individual rooms on the front of the second story. Rork and I shared one in the back on the third floor, a cramped little place with two cot-like beds that reminded me of accommodations aboard ship, except for the exorbitant price.

Cynda's health was still a concern for me. The improvement in lifestyle had not produced a concurrent change for the better in her appearance. Quiet and withdrawn, she was still thin and pale, subject to frequent bouts of indigestion, and consistently fatigued. There are many diseases endemic to the tropics and I feared she had contracted one of the more vicious, like bone-break or dengue; or perhaps she had become infected with consumption, which is spread widely in the West Indies.

Disregarding my worry, she suggested that her general malaise and debilitation was no doubt a product of the recent good food and drink, which was at odds with the stuff she'd ingested during our time in Haiti. Cynda said her body merely needed to balance itself and assured me she would be her usual gay self in a week or two.

Kovinski was set to re-embark aboard the Ward Line steamer early the next day, Wednesday, the twelfth of September, and head to Havana. The six of us were to dine together in the evening, but we were at leisure during the day, so I determined to assist Cynda's recovery by arranging some exercise and special medicine. She hesitatingly acquiesced and retired to her room to set about her feminine preparations.

Accordingly, we set off in the late morning, before the sun had reached its broiling zenith, to stroll along the lanes to Alicia

Carey's Ice Cream Parlour on Rawson Street. As we ambulated along, I was heartened to see my little plan working. The lady seemed invigorated by the activity, her eyes lighting up for the first time since that awful last night in Haiti. Chatting away about the flowers we passed along our route, she was the Cynda I'd become entranced by, the woman who had penetrated the barriers of my heart. A taste of ice cream would be the perfect prelude for the serious conversation I wanted to have with her, for I had done a lot of contemplation of late. Her future and mine were at a nexus of space and time, and a decision needed to be made.

She chose lime. I chose chocolate. We sat under the awning by a tamarind tree, where a ghost of a breeze brought the earthy tropical scents of salt flats and periwinkle flowers. Cynda held my hand and smiled. The time had come for me to press my case.

"Cynda, I think we need to talk about us, and our future. I know that Patricio Island is a bit difficult in the summer, what with the bugs and storms, but it's a very nice place in the late fall, winter, and spring. And there are some things that can be done to make it even more pleasant, of course."

"I thought it was very charming," she said gently, flashing that demure look at me, making my heart skip.

I took a breath and started again. "Yes, well, as I was saying, dear, my island home is rudimentary compared to what you've been used to at the plantation in Puerto Rico, but I have plans to add to its conveniences. Things that a lady would need, to be comfortable there. You see, I have a little money saved up and . . ."

She stopped me with a caress of my cheek. "Peter, if you are about to ask me to marry you, please wait until I have *my* say. All right?"

That took the wind from my sails. She didn't wait for an answer.

"Peter, my darling, I know that you love me. You've proven that beyond any doubt, proven it more than any man ever has or ever could. And I think you know that I have a love for you, a love that will never end. Our tender moments, in the midst of the troubles and tragedies of these past months, have been the most loving I've ever known."

She stopped. I supplied the word that came next. "But?"

"Yes, there is a 'but' in this. Peter, we are not youngsters anymore, madly romantic and naïve. We have lived through too much life to think that love conquers all. We know better."

"But we do love each other, and I can take care of you, Cynda. I can give you what you need—"

"Stop. No, you can't. I was married to a seaman, Peter, remember? Jonathan was a good man who loved me and left the sea to make me happy. But in the end, he withered in a life for which he wasn't made, a life ashore as a farmer. I was miserable, knowing that I was responsible for that, but unable to change it. I'll not live that way again, forcing a man to be something he's not, and I'll not live a life of waiting at home for a man who has to roam to seas. It's not your fault. I love you for who, and what, you are. But not enough to marry you and change who I am, or make you change."

I couldn't believe she had reduced our relationship, and our future, to those terms. I tried to get her to see my point from a different view.

"Look here, now, each of us has had heartbreak in our lives, Cynda. Our bond goes back to the war, has returned with this journey and became stronger. There are better days ahead. Right now we're at a bridge. I'm lonely, I love you, I need you, and I want to cross this next bridge with you beside me, and live those better days. Please don't make me beg, Cynda, because I will."

Cynda's voice quivered with emotion as she held both my hands in hers, those gorgeous eyes locked on mine. "You want me to cross a bridge now, for better days ahead? Peter, listen to me. It would not work out well. We are too deeply set in our own ways, and to try to change them would kill our souls. I will not do that to you, and I don't want you to do that to me."

"I don't understand why you are suddenly talking like this."

I saw her eyes lose their softness. She withdrew her hands. Her tone hardened. "Then understand this, Peter. You are right—we are at a bridge. There are some bridges you cross, and some bridges you burn. I'm one of the ones you burn."

I reached for her, but she was already standing.

"I'm not heading north with you to your island, or anywhere else with you. I'm not going to the dinner tonight. I've written notes of appreciation to everyone for what they did for me. In the morning I'll be on the Ward Line steamer for Havana. From there, I'll return to Puerto Rico. Do not follow me."

Stunned at her change, I sat there utterly incapacitated as she leaned down and kissed my forehead. "I love you, Peter Wake, and thank you from the bottom of my heart for everything you, and the others, did for me. *Know that*, and know it well for the rest of your life, Peter. Live that life the way you should, as a man of the sea, a servant of your country."

Cynda backed away a step, her final words emerging as a command.

"I am returning to my room at the hotel now—alone. Please allow me my privacy and dignity."

And with that, Cynda Saunders walked out of my life.

Fifteen minutes later, by an obviously over-optimistic prearrangement on my part, Rork showed up to celebrate the announcement of my engagement with Cynda. Right away he knew something was wrong and said, "An' where's the lovely lady? Did she melt away like that ice cream all over your hand, me friend?"

I looked down and noticed he was right. "I'm an idiot, Sean."

He seated himself in her place. "Aye, well, we've known that for a long time, now haven't we? But methinks there's something afoot, an' yer plans're asunder."

"She said no and walked away."

He sighed. "All right then, stow yer oars an' tell me what happened, me ol' friend."

One incident provided a moment of comedy in Key West. Actually, it turned into far longer than a moment. As is a tradition with sailors, my melancholia at the ice cream shop produced a desire for rum, which Rork suggested we quench at E.H. Stillman's saloon, at Duval and Front streets.

Entering the place we found some old friends, none other than that band of troublemaking troubadours known as the Yard Dogs. Former Union soldiers who stayed on in Florida, they play their music at taverns from Tampa to Key West, and occasionally while residing in various jails. For over twenty years they'd been friends and drinking comrades.

The three of them sat at the bar, nursing beers, but they brightened when Rork roared out upon our entering, "Well, methinks the day's gettin' better, Peter—'tis me ol' friends Kip, Brian, an' Charlie, an' they're lookin' in a rum-drinkin' mood if ever there was one. A round for all these idlers an' ne'er-do-wells, Mr. Stillman, for liberty ashore has just begun!"

Now, when Rork orders a round for all hands, one would think he's paying for it. But one would be wrong. Rork never pays for it. He expects *me* to pay for it. And not the cheap swill either. Oh, no, he expects the good stuff.

Since Vicente Ybor introduced me to it back in eighty-six, we've been partial to Matusalem rum from Cuba. It's some of the very best sipping rum around, so naturally, he ordered that.

Years ago, Rork explained his theory of payment within taverns to me: "Aye, now listen carefully. Yer the officer, Peter Wake, commissioned by the high an' mighty Congress o' the United States, an' yer expected to provision yer men with the very best, so they can do their very best, for our sainted country. Me knows this a serious naval duty, an' a matter o' great pride for an officer. An' I'll not dissuade ye from yer duty, nor will I diminish yer pride—no sir, not one little bit. So let's mind the good liquor, an' cast off that rotgut lot."

The rum arrived. When asked why the boys had downcast looks, Stillman the publican, told Rork and me, "Kip just found out his campaign for Monroe County sheriff has sunk. He's not on the ballot—couldn't qualify because he didn't get the required signatures from real voters. All he had was twenty-two former jailhouse prisoners who can't even vote."

"Yep," said Kip, the nominal leader of the trio. "And I found that out *after* I had the posters made up." He pointed to the wall, where a crude likeness had been drawn on a sheet of packing paper. Below his face was written VOTE FOR CHANGE. "Got three of them up around town."

"In the finest bar establishments," added Brian, the rhumba box player.

"Damned shame," said Charlie, the accordion man. "I was gonna be the chief deputy."

I raised my glass in salute to them. "Shame indeed, men. Here's to a short political career, but a long life."

They tossed the sipping rum down their throats, slammed the glasses, and ordered another round. It was going to be an expensive afternoon.

Kip stood uncertainly—I think they'd been there quite awhile—and raised his finger to emphasize his next statement.

"Thanks for the drinks today, Peter. But you should know that my political career is far from over. Nope, it's just *refined*."

"Refined?" I asked.

"Yes, refined. I've discovered I can't win fame through democracy, so we're gonna have a revolution, like the Cubans here in Key West. By God, we're gonna secede!"

"From what?"

"Lee County."

"Kip, you're a bit late. Fort Myers and Lee County already seceded from Monroe County last year."

Another raised hand, this time swaying slightly. He was warming to his subject and grinned like the proverbial Cheshire cat.

"Ah, yes, they did. But we're heading up to live at Harrsenville, on Matlacha Passage. Once there, we'll declare our independence from Lee County. We'll be rebels! Won't be some pissant new county, either. Nope. We're forming our own *country* from the islands in that area. Yes, our own country!"

His companions cheering him on, Kip nodded pleasantly to me. "And because we like you boys, we'll even let Patricio Island join our country."

I couldn't help but laugh. "Thank you for the honor, my friend. And what, pray tell, will be the name of your new country?"

"The Mangrove Republic! And I will be the *prime* minister. Charlie here is the minister of culture. Brian is gonna minister to fallen women. We'll have a lot of those."

"Aye, me likes the sound o' that," offered Rork, gesturing to Stillman for yet another round. Planning a new country is thirsty work. "Any job for an ol' bosun in this Mangrove Republic o' yours?"

Kip attempted to bow grandiosely and nearly collapsed. His recovery was nicely done, however, the product of years of practice. "Why, of course, my fine Irish friend. You, sir, will be the minister of rum. One of the most important positions in the government, I might add. And Peter here, of course, will be the minister of *war*."

And so the afternoon went on.

The *Nancy Ann* was waiting for us at Pinder's dock. We rode a broad-reach westerly that brought us to Patricio Island the following

Thursday afternoon, where Whidden greeted us at the dock. It was a subdued bunch at dinner at my bungalow, weighted by all we'd seen and done and endured. My friends were as surprised as I at Cynda's decision and offered clumsy but genuine sympathy. Their sentiments, and the subsequent atmosphere among us, were as if yet one more person had died on our odyssey. I was heartily sick of maudlin moods by then and ready to get back to my naval work.

By Saturday, the fifteenth of September, the four of us—Rork, me, Woodgerd, and Corny—were aboard the train at Punta Gorda, steaming northbound. Woodgerd, the only married man in the crew, would see his wife for the first time in more than six months. Corny would return to the academic world of ethnology and history, soon to be heading west to study an Indian tribe in Minnesota. Rork would report into the senior petty officers quarters at the Washington Navy Yard, then his desk at the Office of Naval Intelligence.

At the stop in Palatka, I inquired about the Methodist conference in nearby Saint Augustine and discovered it had ended early. Useppa was back in Key West, by way of the steamer from Jacksonville. Thus, my opportunity to explain things to her had disappeared. I didn't see her for sometime after that.

As we continued toward Washington, I went over my plan. My first duty would be to report into Commodore Walker and Admiral Porter and explain the reason Rork and I were late for duty, why and how the Paloma mission had evaporated, what I discovered from Sokolov's aerial war machine about powered flight, and what I'd learned from Kovinski about Russian secret intelligence operations in Europe and America. As a professional intelligence officer, I should have incorporated all of the aforementioned should into a typed report.

But I didn't. The chaotic escape from Haiti had occupied my mind until Nassau, followed by my worries about Cynda's health. My focus then shifted to the romantic notion of betrothing

Cynda, of which I was abruptly disabused. Since that afternoon in Key West, I just hadn't had the concentration to organize the information and apply it to paper.

We would arrive in the capital at seven in the morning on Monday, the seventeenth. By late on Sunday night, as the dark carriage car rolled through the Virginia hill country, Rork quietly nudged me and said, "Oh, thank you, Jesus, that me's just a wee bosun in a big navy. But you, me friend, yer the officer an' the responsible one. Peter, have ya any thought in the world o' how're ye gonna explain all o' this mess to the commodore and the admiral?"

"No, Sean. Not a notion. We're absent without leave, the Paloma mission fell apart and our contacts are no doubt compromised, we've killed foreign nationals in a foreign country, I've acted without permission as a merchant skipper and have criminal complaints lingering out there somewhere about my conduct therein, and we interacted with European intelligence services without the permission or notification of our superiors. At the minimum, we'll be cashiered from the service. I'd estimate the maximum to be about thirty years in prison—for me. Don't worry, you're the junior rank, so you'll only get about ten years."

He shook his head. "I was afraid ye'd say that. Aye, methinks this is one time your silver tongue can't talk our way out o' trouble. Ten years, ya say?"

"Ah hell, Sean, you'll only be sixty-seven when you get out in eighteen-ninety eight—still young enough to bull your way through any bar or squire any girl. But me—I'll be seventy-nine years old when I get out in nineteen-eighteen. You'll probably write a book, make lots of money, and forget all about me, you rascal."

My attempt at humor didn't work.

42
Naval Discipline

Office of Commodore J.G. Walker
Bureau of Navigation
Second Floor, East Wing
U.S. Naval Headquarters
State, War, and Navy Building
Washington, District of Columbia
Monday, 17 September 1888

The morning started at sunrise when I entered the officer's elevator to my office on the fourth floor of the east wing of naval headquarters. The central administration of the U.S. Navy is located in the massive French-copied palace just across the park from the president's mansion, the edifice well known as the State, War, and Navy Building. It is filled with busy people trying to look busier than other people around them, particularly whenever the senior people walk by them. None of them, to my uncertain knowledge, has ever been in the jungles of Haiti, and damn few of them have ever had to make a life-and-death decision in a split second. The place, and most of the people there, bores me.

351

Rork was already at his desk, looking very busy shuffling papers from one pile to another as the unit's yeoman clacked away on a typewriter in the corner. The other two officers assigned to the office hadn't arrived yet. They were on regular hours and wouldn't appear until eight o'clock. Our tiny office was a back room, set off the main area of the Office of Naval Intelligence.

Lieutenant Rodgers, chief of the main ONI effort and an industrious sort who always worked long hours, passed by and noticed my presence. He looked at me like I was a condemned man. "Welcome back, sir. The commodore's been waiting for you for two weeks. I think he's already in his office."

He was referring, of course, to Commodore John Grimes Walker, the legendary chief of the Bureau of Navigation, the senior bureau of the navy. Rodgers and ONI came under the Bureau of Navigation. My section of ONI, the Special Assignments Section, reported directly to Walker, for our work was of such delicate nature as to be thought above the pay grade of junior officers. That was the official reasoning, at least. I knew it was because Walker wanted to have a personal hand in our espionage operations and had done several himself.

"Yes, I thought he would be," I replied to Rodgers in as confident a manner as I could muster. Rodgers departed fast, probably to telephone Walker and tell him the long-lost Wake had reappeared at headquarters. I spent five minutes staring out the window and then made my way to Commodore Walker's office on the second floor, just down the passageway from Admiral Porter's. Rork winked and made the sign of the cross at me before I left, but I felt none of his humor. It was a long walk.

Standing at the straightest attention I'd managed for years, I bellowed out in my quarterdeck voice, "Commander Wake, ONI, SAS, returning from leave and reporting to the commodore, sir."

Walker turned from studying the wall chart of the world and greeted me with more than his usual modicum of dry wit, his long forked beard bobbing below those infamously cold eyes.

"Wake, how good of you to finally return. Please, remain standing at attention."

The commodore sat down at his desk and leaned back in the swivel chair, before continuing in a weary growl. "Now, briefly tell me why the Paloma mission is in disarray just when we need information about the Spanish Navy, and why you are late returning from a private vacation cruise in the West Indies just as this is all occurring."

"Sir, I don't know what happened with Paloma or where he is. I heard about his disappearance from Mason in Nassau last week. As for my being delayed—"

"Absent without orders."

"Yes, sir. Absent without orders. I was not on a vacation cruise, sir. I was on a search for a missing cabin boy, the son of a friend. That search ended up in Haiti. Once there, I happened upon a military operation that has great relevance to our country, and the Europeans as well. It has to do with a new type of aerial war machine—a powered flying warship, even more advanced than the French airships. I attempted to bring it back to the United States, but we crashed and it was destroyed.

"I also became involved in British and Russian secret service operations in the West Indies and have some knowledge of Russian endeavors here in the U.S. That is why I was unavoidably delayed in reporting back in to duty here at headquarters, sir. I'll be writing a full report on all of it immediately."

"I will admit that you have my curiosity aroused, Commander. Continue and tell me more."

That I did, for the next forty minutes, holding back nothing. The commodore punctuated my narrative with sharp questions about the various people I'd become involved with, the political situation in Haiti, and Sokolov's warship. As I told the story, I realized how far-fetched it appeared, even to me. What must it sound like to Walker? At last I stopped, waiting for his reaction.

"Honor bound to help a beautiful woman, Smithsonian academics, running into Russian and British spies, shipwreck, death and disease, wandering in darkest Haiti, and finding a warship that flies . . ." Walker sighed. "You tire me sometimes, Commander Wake. By gumphries, you tire me, mightily, with your explanations."

He waved a hand around the room. "Your penchant for independent, some would say incompetent, inventiveness in the field is well known in this part of the building. Your 'unavoidable delays' in sending reports—and your unique excuses for the same—have become the stuff of legend around here. I imagine your contemporaries think it humorous, but not so your superiors, Commander."

He slowly shook his head. "But this time there is a very serious problem arising with your disappearance from naval intelligence duties while gallivanting around the tropics. That makes it *your* very serious problem . . ."

He paused. I waited—then realized he wanted me to ask the obvious.

"Sir, I presume the problem is: where are Paloma and Casas, and how much do the Spanish know about our espionage mission?"

"Very good, Commander. I see that West Indian sun and rum have not dulled your intellectual powers. Now, what do you propose to do to solve *your* problem?"

I'd thought about that on the train. I had an idea that would solve two dilemmas—find Paloma, and get Rork and me away from headquarters.

"Sir, I propose that Rork and I will go ashore in Cuba, incognito, and establish contact with another of our contacts in Havana, the secondary one called Leo. Leo was very helpful to us in eighty-six. From there, we'll backtrack the whereabouts of

Casas, then Paloma. Then slip out to Key West and report in by cable. All done quietly."

He looked dubious. "How long would that take?"

"Two days to write the full report on the aerial warship and European spy operations, then a week to get down to Key West, charter a Cuban fishing smack and get dropped off on the coast by Cojímar or Matanzas. Probably another week to get in touch with Leo, find wherever Casas is hiding, and determine what happened to Paloma. Then get a fishing boat to Key West. Should be done by October fifteenth, sir."

"That's what I thought you'd say. And it's not good enough. Not by a long shot."

"Sir?"

"We don't have that kind of time. The report about Haiti and all that can wait. You and Rork are rejoining the United States Navy, Commander. You both will be on the train to Norfolk when it leaves at ten o'clock this morning. There, you'll report aboard *Richmond* as supernumerary flag aide to Rear Admiral Luce. Protocol officer.

"That position will enable you to get ashore for longer periods of time. Rork will be your assistant. *Richmond* will weigh anchor immediately upon your arrival and make her way to Havana at best speed. You should be there in four days. Once there you will be posted ashore as an attaché at the consulate, get in contact with Leo and find out what happened.

"Once you discover the answers, *Richmond* will take you back to Key West for a secure telegraph in cipher to me. I expect it by October first. Here are your orders, endorsed by Admiral Porter. Rear Admiral Luce has been briefed and is expecting his orders."

He took two dark blue sealed envelopes from his desk and handed them to me—one for Luce and one for me.

"And *do not* think I've forgotten your violations of several regulations and the laws of various countries. I will make a decision regarding you and them after your return from Havana."

"Yes, sir."

"Now, for reasons you do not—and cannot—know, time is of the essence, Commander. You will enter Havana overtly as a United States naval officer, then get the answers covertly through Leo. Understood?"

Working in *uniform* at Havana, a place where the Spanish intelligence knew and hated me, would make my job much more complicated. Working under Rear Admiral Luce, a man who did not suffer fools gladly, made it even tougher. I didn't like it, not one bit, but I fully comprehended that Commodore Walker wasn't offering me a choice.

Naval discipline took over. "Understood, sir."

"I hope you do. You know Luce and have worked for him before, so stay on the admiral's good side."

Rear Admiral Luce, until recently the head of the Naval War College, was another legend in the navy.

"Aye, aye, sir." I executed an about-face and got to the doorway before he stopped me.

"And Wake . . ."

"Sir?"

"My credibility is on the line with *my* superiors, all of whom vastly outrank you. So toe the line and don't make a hash up of this one."

43

Postcript

Patricio Island
Southwest Coast of Florida
Thursday, 26 March 1896

ight years later, I find myself sitting here at the table on the verandah of my home on Patricio Island. The scene around me is tranquil, with not a malevolent sight or sound—such a contrast to that summer of 1888.

In the late afternoon light, a fishing smack, Cuban by her lines, is sailing by Mondongo Island, toward Boca Grande Passage. Pelicans glide by above me. A porpoise undulates across the bay. Inside, Whidden is whistling the tune "Loreena" while cooking up some grouper in a sauce of honey and orange juice, accompanied by squash and yams with herbs from our garden. I can smell the rosemary and sage. Proud of his all-day job caulking the dinghy, Rork just trudged up the hill to the verandah for our sunset drink.

This morning I finished typing out the last chapter of this

narrative on my thirteen-year-old navy-issued Remington, which has definitely seen better days but, like an old naval officer, still does its duty. At long last, the story of my journey into Haiti and back, with its myriad influences and experiences, is completed. Reliving those times, and those innermost emotions, has exhausted me, bringing joy and fear, laughter and sadness. I was glad to be done with it.

Earlier today, I asked Rork to peruse the story's ending. Following several minutes of furrowed brow, various grunts, and an elongated "ah, hmm," he pronounced the thing not done.

"Methinks the reader'll be needin' to know the consequences o' this whole bloody ordeal, Peter."

"Consequences?" I asked warily.

"Me friend, fer every decision in life an' war, there's a result. An' the results o' that journey're still with us, boyo. Some're good, some're bad, an' some we just haven't figured out yet. Aye, an' the most important result for *you* is yet to come—an' you know what that is."

Reluctantly, I admitted that Rork was right. Yes, the personal side to the story had to be finished, even though to do so brings sorrow.

The account had ended with us ordered to Havana aboard *Richmond* to ascertain what happened with Paloma and Casas. That story begins another narrative, emerging from very intense memories, which will be written someday. It is too much, however, to relate in this limited space. So allow me instead to add this postscript to the tale of that summer of 1888.

I am very happy to report that Absalom Bowlegs is now a husband and father, and through his personal industriousness has become master and owner of an inter-island schooner out of Congo Town, on the east coast of Andros Island. I receive a Christmas note every year from him.

Major Kovinski, with whom I maintain a frequent professional correspondence, continues his secret work against the revolutionary Russian émigrés from his base in Paris. I've become aware, through other means, of several of his operatives in the United States—all of whom, the reader will not be surprised, are beautiful women.

My report on the journey was completed in December of 1888. It still remains in the confidential section of the vault in the Navy Library. Neither the navy, nor the army, acted upon my recommendations regarding aerial warships. However, recent events in Brazil and Europe have rekindled discussion on that subject, so perhaps my observations will be revisited.

The sixth of September, the day Dan Horloft died aboard Sokolov's aerial warship, has become a significant date in my life since 1888. Corny, Woodgerd, Rork, and I, if we are in town, meet on that day for dinner in a private room at the Celestial Club in Washington. We remember Dan, his life's accomplishments, and how he saved our lives by flying that bizarre machine out of Haiti, even while mortally wounded. I also never fail to thank Corny for his efforts in ending my premature death at the hands of Lieutenant Laurent, the Haitian sorcerer.

And we do not fail to remember our black friend, that noble son of Haiti, Vladimir Yablonowski. When I think of Haiti now, I prefer to think of him, a quiet patriot, aglow with dignity and strength.

Colonel Michael Woodgerd still embarks on "military consultation contracts," as he prefers to call them these days. The snobbier description has enabled him to raise his fees and hobnob with some of the world's richest potentates, warlords, and dictators. No more slogging in the mud with common soldiers on hopeless missions for Woodgerd. Now his campaigns are planned and fought in the considerable comfort of foreign parlors and offices, not to mention cocktail parties. My friend, jaded old goat that he is, refuses to admit it, but I think he enjoys the work. In appreciation for my extricating him from Haiti, he presented me with his Martini-Henry rifle from Afghanistan, which is now mounted on the wall at my island bungalow.

Cornelius Rathburn, doctor of ethnology, continues to set off on expeditions for various universities and museums on projects regarding native North and Central American cultures. Recently, he convinced some of his Smithsonian colleagues to come to the southwestern coast of Florida to delve into the history of the pre-Colombian Calusa empire—but that, too, is another tale altogether.

Rork is still Rork. He'll never change, thank the Lord. He's older now, with more scars and ailments, but then again, so am I. For some reason, we bonded all those years ago during the war and have stayed together as comrade and friend, two kindred souls who find themselves in the peculiar position of hating war, but being rather good at waging it. I suppose that is fortunate, for as this nineteenth century races toward its conclusion there seems to be no dearth of threats to our country's peace and tranquility. Global war with Spain is coming. I can feel its inexorable advance and fear that no one, on either side of the Atlantic, can stop it.

And now I must share the most bitter-sweet consequence of that summer. Cynda Saunders returned to her home in Puerto Rico. I subsequently heard nothing, in spite of many letters to her. Knowing the fragile condition of her health upon our parting and anxious for her safety, I asked a friend in San Juan to check with the local authorities at Mayaguez, the nearest city to Cynda's home. The report back was disconcerting: the lady had sold the plantation and departed the island. Her whereabouts were unknown.

Then, six months later, in June of 1889, a letter arrived at naval headquarters while I was away on assignment. It was sent from Cynda's younger sister, Mary Alice, whom I hadn't seen since the war. She was living with husband and family in Peoria, Illinois.

When I finally returned to headquarters sometime later and opened it, I sat at my desk for a long time, distraught and confused. The letter explained so much, but it broke my heart.

Dear Peter,   *June 10, 1889*

I am sorry to convey sad news to you. My sister Cynda died here in Peoria on April 6, two days after her daughter Patricia was born. The baby showed no signs of congenital infirmity, thank God above.

Cynda knew she was dying and insisted that I promise to carry out her wishes regarding Patricia. When she came here from the West Indies, I knew in my heart she would not survive the birth. She was weak and sickly and it was a difficult pregnancy. The doctor said it was due to her age and the stress of losing her husband and son, but I think she also had a long-standing debility from many years of tropical fevers.

My sister wanted me to wait until Patricia had been adopted to send this letter. Yesterday the adoption was finalized and the little girl is now with a loving family, a new life ahead of her. I do not know who or where they are, but am told that they are keeping her Christian name, which Cynda said was in honor of the island where you live. She told me that she spent a lovely night with you there. Her eyes lit up when she said that, and for a few minutes she became a beautiful young woman again.

Cynda wrote out a letter to her daughter, which I delivered to the court to give to the parents. It is to be opened the day after Patricia turns twenty-one, and explains who her mother and father were, and the reason she was given up for adoption. That will be in 1910, a long time from now. If God wills my existence here to continue, I'll be an old lady of sixty-one. Maybe Patricia will find me and let me know how her life unfolded.

Cynda told me to make sure you know that she loved you, Peter, and that she hoped Patricia would someday find a man to marry who is just like her father.

With affection and respect from your old friend,
Mary Alice

That was how I learned that Cynda, the second love of my life, had departed from this world. I had a little daughter, who would be estranged from me until the impossibly advanced year of 1910, well into the next century, when I would be seventy-one years old, if even alive.

Emotions flooded me. At first I was angry at myself, for not insisting more forcefully that Cynda marry me. Other sentiments rose within me: anger at my career, for dominating my life; anger at Cynda, for selfishly assuming I could not take care of my daughter and not even telling me of her pregnancy; and profound desolation at my double loss.

I've remained silent for eight years. Useppa and I regained our familial love, but I've never explained my actions and the consequences of that summer to her until now. Useppa and her brother Sean never knew they had a sister, for the story of how everything came about was too painful, too complicated, to describe.

But Rork's appraisal of the account was right. The summer of 1888 did have important consequences. We saved untold numbers of people from a terrible death from Sokolov's invention. Vital intelligence on secret terror clans was uncovered. Significant scientific advancements were learned. Valuable professional relationships were begun.

And for me? I learned that love is that most unexplainable emotion of the human condition, that it will occur when you least expect it, and that even the merest fragment of time spent in true affection is worth taking the chance.

Rork just looked at the revised ending of this account and smiled. Then he gazed out over the bay, where the sky was a fantasy of color and texture. Sunsets at Patricio Island make up for the heat and bugs and lack of modern conveniences so common up north.

Still facing the sunset, Rork quietly spoke to me.

"Peter, we got into this thing 'cause ye were feelin' honor bound to Cynda. With all we went through—an' the pain still in yer heart—do ye ever wish ye'd nipped out o' the church afore she arrived, that an' none o' this had ever happened?"

"No, Sean—though I could've done without experiencing that death by voudou poison."

Rork grimaced. "Aye, that was a bit too close."

He came over and shook my hand, his eyes serious. "But ye an' the dear lady got to know true love together. That's more'n most get. More'n the likes o' me."

Whidden began laying out the plates and cutlery on the porch table, fussing to get them right, then disappeared inside, soon to emerge with a steaming dinner. It was a perfect scene, but I couldn't shake an empty feeling. Patricio was a bachelor island again. It felt wrong—coarse, devoid of gentleness.

The sky was more vivid now, the sun a dark red boiling mass, the clouds shimmering iridescent gold. Soon it would be night. Rork sounded the conch shell three times, and from the islands around us were heard answering calls.

I gave the traditional naval toast for Thursday evening: "A bloody war and a quick promotion!" The lads echoed it and began digging into the fish. I didn't. There was something more on my mind that needed to be said.

Rork saw my expression and nudged Whidden, stopping him in mid-bite as I raised my glass of Matusalem northward, toward Illinois.

"Gentlemen, a toast to the future of a little baby named Patricia. May she know true love in her heart during her lifetime. And may God grant us the chance to meet her someday. . . ."

Miss Useppa Wake
Assistant Headmistress
Frederick Douglass School
Key West, Florida   26 March 1896

My dearest daughter Useppa,

Admittedly, it's been far too long in coming, but this chronicle is my attempt to clarify what happened that summer of 1888.

Please understand that I make no apologies for my private conduct then. I do not pretend to be perfect, unlike some of the more arrogant hypocrites I see in Christian society. And after all has been said and done, I still savor the gentle affection I found with Cynda during that ordeal. Great joy is in my heart by the wonderful result of our love, your little sister Patricia. I earnestly hope that you, and your brother Sean, will embrace her fully when the time comes.

In any event, I think you've found this story to be more than moderately interesting, as it demonstrates what your father does for a living, even when he's not supposed to be doing it. Such is the call of my uncommon profession.

I am further gladdened by the fact that unknown numbers of future lives were saved by my professional efforts. And lastly, I pray that Sean sees no similar challenge in his private life or naval career, but I fear he may. Many have. Perhaps after reading this story, he'll be better prepared for whatever decision he makes.

> Your loving father,
> *Peter Wake*
> Captain, U.S.N.
> Special Assignments Section/
> Office of Naval Intelligence
> Bureau of Navigation/
> Department of the Navy
> Washington, D.C.

Chapter Endnotes

Chapter One—The Preparation

—The St. Francis Inn, with the corner room on the second floor, still exists. It's my favorite place to stay in St. Augustine. (visit: www.stfrancisinn.com)

—Wake's mission in 1886 in Havana is described in *The Darkest Shade of Honor*. For more about Wake and Rork's time in 1883 French Indo-China, read *The Honored Dead*.

—ONI also used George Eastman's new Kodak camera in its assessment of potential naval stations along the California coast in the late 1880s.

—There were periodic war scares with Spain over Cuba from the early 1870s onward. Until the late 1880s, the Spanish Navy was considered more powerful than the U.S. Navy.

Chapter Three—God's Will

—Wake's perilous exploits inside the Alcázar of Sevilla, Spain, in 1874 are described in *An Affair of Honor*.

—The Methodist church is still at that location, is now named

Grace United Methodist Episcopal Church, and is very much worth a visit for the unique architecture and friendly members.

—The magnificent Ponce de Leon Hotel building still exists and is now Flagler College.

Chapter Four—*Dèjá Vu*

—For more about Cynda Denaud Saunders' relationship with Wake in the Civil War, read *Honorable Mention*. They met again at the beginning of *An Affair of Honor*, shortly after Cynda married Jonathan Saunders at Puerto Rico in 1873. For the story of Saunders' years as a foe of Wake during the Civil War, read *At the Edge of Honor* and *Point of Honor*.

Chapter Five—The Entourage

—For a while in the 1890s, the St. Augustine Transfer Company was the largest cab and short haul company in the nation. The Colee family owned and operated it until 1996.

—The Smithsonian Institution was the U.S.'s national museum at this time. I've found Clay MacCauley's 1884 ethnological report to be a fascinating look at Seminole life. Powell was famous for his work in documenting Native American culture in the U.S. Goode was equally famous in his field. His study of the fisheries in SW Florida illuminated the islanders' way of life. Cushing became well-known in Florida for his work in 1895–96 on the pre-Columbian Calusa civilization along the SW Florida coast.

—Wake's train trip in 1888 generally followed the same route as US Hwy 17 does today.

Chapter Six--Insomnia

—Albert Gilchrist was an interesting man. Born in 1858, he attended West Point but did not graduate, became a civil engineer, served in the Florida Legislature for many years, was a brigadier general of the state militia, fought in the Spanish-American War, and became governor of Florida from 1909 to 1913. He died in 1926.

Chapter Seven—Lightning Strikes
—Patricio Island is part of the Pine Island National Wildlife Refuge, which was established by Peter Wake's friend President Theodore Roosevelt in 1908. The wildlife refuge covers 17 islands and their adjacent waters in Pine Island Sound and Charlotte Harbor. The island is officially closed to the public.

Chapter Eight—In Flagrante Delicto
—Pinder's Store was located just south of the present-day Schooner's Wharf, which is on land reclaimed from the harbor in the 1900s.

—Charles DuPont won the election and became sheriff of Monroe County from 1888 to 1893. He was a most remarkable man and by all accounts a good sheriff. DuPont Lane is named after him.

—The Frederick Douglass School stood for many years on the southeast corner of Thomas and Fleming streets.

Chapter Nine—A Motley Crew, Indeed
—"Key West Billy" was documented in MacCauley's report on the Seminoles and appears to be quite an interesting person. He and Wake will meet again.

Chapter Eleven—Brown's Cut
—Brown's Cut is between Brown's and Beach cays, about a mile south of Ocean Cay, an abandoned mining islet. In the 1880s the cut had nine feet of water, but it has shoaled in today.

Chapter Thirteen—A Most Interesting Time
—The course taken by the *Delilah* in 1888 could be duplicated today, but use caution. Only try it in good light when you can use your eyeball navigation skills to read the bottom. I have sailed the Banks and it can be dangerous in bad weather, especially close to Andros Island.

—The village of Red Bays still exists, as do the descendants of those brave Seminoles who crossed the ocean to reach freedom. It was only reached by road twenty years ago. I suggest reading Dr. Rosalyn Howard's *Black Seminoles in the Bahamas* and *Reverend Bertram A. Newton…Preacher, Teacher and Friend* for excellent accounts of these very interesting people.

Chapter Fourteen—Of Buccaneers and Monsters
—Morgan's Bluff still exists, but the legendary treasure has never been found.

—Stories are told to this day on Andros Island of the Chickchannies (sometimes called Chickcharnies) and the Bosee-Amasee. Obeah is still practiced in some of the islands of the Bahamas.

Chapter Sixteen—Nassau
—The Royal Victoria Hotel was an icon of Nassau in the 1800s. Grover Cleveland's family were investors in the hotel, and his brother Fredrick was the manager until his death by shipwreck in 1872.

Chapter Seventeen—Emancipation Day
—This celebration is still observed. The Vendue building is now a museum. The cathedral exists generally as it did in 1888, as does the Government House.

—I urge my readers to lodge while in Nassau at my favorite place, the 260-year-old Graycliff Hotel (www.graycliff.com). And yes, that is the American way to spell "gray," a sign of the times. Stay in the beautiful Woodes Rogers Room. Ask to see the wine cellar, which the U.S. Navy used as a brig when occupying Nassau during the Revolutionary War.

Chapter Eighteen—*Quid Pro Quo*
—"Perfidious Albion" is the English translation of the old

derogatory French term from 1793 *"Perfide Albion"* about the British betrayal of the French Revolution. It was used into the turn of the twentieth century, most notably by Mussolini in 1935. Albion was the Greek name for Britain.

Chapter Twenty—Great Inagua

—Records show that Mr. McGregor had a distinguished career as a colonial administrator. His descendants are well regarded in the Bahamas.

—It is known that Admiral Popham was an acquaintance of Christophe and met with the king near the end of his reign, just before the admiral returned to England, where he died. Did Popham hide the king's treasure? Very unlikely, but the legends of King Henri Christophe's treasure still surface in the southern Bahamas. It has never been found, but the place is still known as Christophe's Lagoon.

Chapter Twenty-Two—Navigating the Haitian Sea

—This body of water is no longer known as the Haitian Sea, but I possess an 1860 chart on which it is thus named.

—The smoke from the charcoal fires can still be seen when sailing by Haiti. Much of the forest in certain areas has been cut down to make the charcoal—a huge environmental and erosion problem for the country.

Chapter Twenty-Three—Mother of the Twins

—While researching this project, I made my way along the path below the cliffs of Pointe Picolet and saw the cave known as *Gròt Manman Jimos yo*. It is an eerie spot, full of *voudou* paraphernalia even today.

—Salomon's lighthouse is still there. And frequently still dark.

—Loa, like Agwé and Kalfu, are still revered and feared, and very much a part of life for many in Haiti.

Chapter Twenty-Four—*Chanm Mouri Nan*

—I have seen the *Chanm Mouri Nan*. One brave man from my expeditionary party descended partly into the cavern, and quickly came back out. No dead body was there that day, but it's a very ominous place.

Chapter Twenty-Five—*Sólda Rouge*

—Forts Picolet, St. Joseph, and Maydi still exist, and the cannon and mortars are still there. Evening *voudou* ceremonies are still performed at Fort Picolet each week in the ruins of the former commander's quarters.

—Oswald Durand is regarded as one of Haiti's best poets. Hotel Colon no longer exists.

—Wake's description of the Polish Haitians is borne out by the historical records. Approximately 25,000 modern Haitians have Polish blood. It is an intriguing story.

Chapter Twenty-Six—Hyppolite's Decision

—Lysius Salomon is regarded as one of Haiti's best presidents. General Florvil Hyppolite comes down through history as one of Haiti's more effective leaders. He subsequently became president and stayed in office longer than most. He and Wake will continue their acquaintance for many years.

—The cathedral in Cap Haitian you see today was built in 1942 on the location of the old one, most of which was destroyed by fire. The central plaza (Place d'Armes) still exists, run-down and overgrown. For those who know what happened to the slaves there during the French days, it is a sad place.

Chapter Twenty-Seven—The Citadelle

—I strongly urge any visitors to Cap Haitien to make the effort to go inland and see the palace at Sans Souci and the great fortress of the Citadelle. They are nothing short of magnificent. However, I warn against leaving the road and going on the original path up the cliffs of Montagne Laferrière to the fortress—it is a dangerously steep and long climb, and I damned near died doing it trying to duplicate Wake's journey.

—Night Societies, based on African tribal cultures, still operate in Haiti. They are generally not violent—that is in the past—but they are an important part of life in rural Haiti.

—Creole is a remarkable phonetic mix of French and African, and quite easy to learn.

—*Voudou* is considered a religion in Haiti. The old saying, which is no longer true, was that 80 per cent of Haitians are Christian, but 100 per cent believe in *voudou*. It is a complicated and interesting subject, but a detailed look requires far more space than is available within this novel.

Chapter Twenty-Eight—*Revanj avék Pwazon*

—Poisons are very rarely used in *voudou*, but the ingredients are widely available in the tropics. I had intimate knowledge of a *voudou* death in Florida in 1985 that is still scientifically unexplained.

—Bush medicine is widely used to this day in the Out Islands of the Bahamas and in Haiti. In most cases, it works, as it is based on natural remedies known for centuries.

Chapter Thirty—*Suh Ghul Wasa!*

—For more about Woodgerd and his friendship with Wake, read *An Affair of Honor* and *A Different Kind of Honor*

—My research shows there was a cable ship, the *CS Westmeath*, at Cap Haitien when Wake was there and that a joint British-French concern had the contract with the Haitian government to run a telegraph cable to Cuba. It was completed in 1888.

—Wake's description of the Europeans' military experiments with lighter-than-air craft is correct. The French were the leaders in the field, amazingly far along in the use of powered aircraft. *La France*'s original base, Hangar Y, still exists today at Chalais

Meudon, near Paris, one of the few remaining airship hangars in Europe.

Chapter Thirty-One—The Monster Revealed
—There is no record of Sokolov or the Forteresse des Njajs in Haiti.

—All of Sokolov's apparatus portrayed here was available or feasible then, according to what we know today.

Chapter Thirty-Two—Plan of Attack
—The Alexander Ul'yanov to which Roche referred, was executed in 1887 for the assassination attempt on Tsar Alexander III. His younger brother Vladimir, greatly affected by Alexander's execution, joined the revolutionaries himself and later changed his last name. We know him as the infamous Vladimir Lenin.

Chapter Thirty-Six—Dead Reckoning
—The Okhrana did exist and was quite efficient, probably the best at running *agents provocateurs* in European history. The Okhrana's foreign section operated out of modest offices in the Russian consulate in Paris at 97 Rue de Grenelle. The name Kovinski is an alias Wake used to protect the Russian's identity. I have decided to continue that practice. Kovinski went on to a distinguished career, right up to the Russian Revolution. Wake will work with him again in 1905.

—The Russians did employ agents in New York and Washington, mainly to gain contacts with the Fenian supporters in America who might be of use against the British, should Russia and Britain go to war over Afghanistan. In the 1880s, the Fenians were exploding bombs in London.

—The Narodnaya Volya, or People's Will, was a long-time anti-tsarist revolutionary group. By the 1890s, most of its leaders were in prison or executed, the surviving members joining other groups. Many, like Lenin, joined the Communists.

Acknowledgments

The research for this novel involved delving into diverse background data; interviewing experienced people in some rather strange subject areas; and conducting my usual "eyeball recon" at some very unusual locales in Florida, the Bahamas, and Haiti. None of it was dull, some of it was downright scary, and all of it assisted me in understanding the facts and flavor of the places, people, and times in this story. As my longtime readers already know, I have developed a unique global organization I call the Subject Matter Advanced Resource Team, or SMART. Assisting me with detailed information on everything from religion to bush medicine to balloons, many of them helped me on this project.

My academic research information came from the following:

To understand Washington, D.C., and the naval culture in the latter 1880s, I turned to Jeffrey Dorwart's classic *The Office of Naval Intelligence: The Birth of America's First Intelligence Agency*, CDR John Alden's *The American Steel Navy*, Donald Canney's *The Old Steam Navy*, Peter Karsten's *The Naval Aristocracy*, and Charles M. Pepper's *Everyday Life in Washington*. The Smithsonian's *1886*

Visitor's Guide was a rare view into that great institution.

The photo and textual collections of the University of Florida George A. Smathers Library, and that of Gil Wilson, proved very educational about St. Augustine in the 1880s. Gregg Turner's *Florida Railroad History* is the major work on that subject, and he personally assisted me regarding the railroads of northeast and central Florida.

Cantor Brown's *Florida's Peace River Frontier* and *Tampa*, Lindsey Williams' and U.S. Cleveland's *Our Fascinating Past*, Tom Smoot's excellent *The Edisons of Fort Myers*, Angie Larkin's *Old Punta Gorda*, Betty Holt's *Sanibel's Story*, Charles Dana Gibson's *Boca Grande*, and Elaine Jordan's *Tales of Pine Island* and *Pine Island, the Forgotten Island* were instrumental in my understanding southwest Florida in the latter nineteenth century.

Patsy West's article in *The Seminole Tribune* explained the story of "Key West Billy." Raymond C. Lantz's census book, *Seminole Indians of Florida: 1874–1879*, helped me be aware of the clans. Clay MacCauley's *Seminoles of Florida*, an 1884 status report to the U.S. Dept. of Ethnology, was a treasure trove of detailed observations in that period.

My knowledge about Key West was enhanced by Walter Maloney's 1876 *A Sketch of the History of Key West*, Jefferson Browne's 1912 *Key West: The Old and The New*, Consuelo Stebbins' *City of Intrigue, Nest of Revolution*, John Viele's *The Florida Keys: A History of the Pioneers*, and William Rogers' and James Denham's *Florida Sheriffs: A History 1821–1945*.

Nassau, Andros Island, and Great Inagua Island were studied in Gilbert Klingel's *Inagua: An Island Sojourn*; L.D. Powles' 1888 *The Land of the Pink Pearl*; Michael Craton's *A–Z of Bahamas Heritage* and *History of the Bahamas*; Dr. Rosalyn Howard's *Black Seminoles in the Bahamas* and *Reverend Bertram A. Newton: Preacher, Teacher and Friend*; the June 1888 issue of *Littell's Living Age Magazine*; the December 1889 issue of *Scribner's Magazine*; Martha Hanna-Smith's *Bush Medicine in Bahamian Folklore*; Dr. Gail Saunder's *Historic Nassau*; and many journals provided by Mr. David Gates of the Bahamas Historical Society.

Haitian history and culture were illuminated by John Vandercook's 1928 *Black Majesty: The Slave who became a King*, Hubert Cole's *Christophe: King of Haiti*, Wade Davis' famous *The Serpent and the Rainbow*, and Webster University professor Robert Colbert's excellent database. Facts on the French submarine telegraph cable efforts in Haiti were gleaned from Bill Burns' and Bill Glover's outstanding *History of the Atlantic Cable* database. Navigational information for the lower Bahamas and the coast of northern Haiti was found in Jerrems C. Hart's and William T. Stone's 1976 work, *A Cruising Guide to the Caribbean and the Bahamas*, which I recommend to all sailors.

I was enlightened about the fascinating world of aeronautics in the 1880s by the September 1887 issue of *Manufacturer and Builder*, Jules Verne's 1886 *Robur the Conqueror*, the April 1889 issue of *The North American Review*, the November 1884 issue of *Littell's Living Age Magazine*, Octave Chanute's 1894 book *Progress in Flying Machines*, and Richard P. Hallion's excellent history of the early aeronauts, *Taking Flight*. Little-known facets and photos were found at Carroll Gray's database. One of the Department of Defense's experts on Lighter-than-Air (LTA) craft, LTC Michael Woodgerd, U.S. Army (Ret.), provided detailed information and critique on the subject, all while stationed in the very dangerous mountains of eastern Afghanistan. Further information was provided by Norman Mayer, an engineer who has worked in LTA all his life. They did their best to make it simple for me—any technical errors are mine.

The particulars of imperial Russian counter-revolutionary operations in the 1880s were opened up for me by the CIA's Ben Fischer and Rita Kronenbitter (an alias) in their work on the Okhrana, specifically Rachovsky's foreign operations out of Paris. In addition, significant information was found in Ronald Hingley's *The Russian Secret Police*, Stephen Wade's *Spies in the Empire*, Richard Deacon's *A History of the Russian Secret Service*, and from nineteenth-century media accounts in Cornell University's *Making of America* database, which yielded several contemporary descriptions of the Russian revolutionary culture.

During the "eyeball recon" portion of my research, the following people helped my understanding of their locales and cultures.

In addition to answering a multitude of questions, Balloon Pilot Fred Vereb and Ground Crew Chief Hal Blethroad gave me a never-to-be-forgotten hot-air research flight over, and through, the trees of central Florida. I recommend them heartily: www.bigredballoon.com.

In St. Augustine, Reverend Jim Reeher gave me an insider's tour of Grace United Methodist Church, including a scary climb up and down that belfry. Adele Wright was my gracious hostess at the historic St. Francis Inn (www.stfrancisinn.com), my favorite lodging in the United States' oldest city.

In Nassau, Venita Johnson of the Bahamas Historical Society (www.bahamashistoricalsociety.org) helped me on background information. At the National Archives of the Bahamas, Chief Research Officer Lulamae Collie Gray and her assistant Wendia Ferguson searched their considerable collection of colonial records and *Guardian* files to provide important information regarding the summer and fall of 1888. Enrico Garzaroli, current owner of the 260-year-old Graycliff House (www.graycliff.com), helped me understand the history of that wonderful place. If you visit Nassau, you *must* stay in Graycliff's Woodes Rogers suite.

"Eyeball recon" in northern Haiti wasn't easy, to say the least. But that's where friendships come in. Missionary Eva DeHart introduced me to import-exporter Tony Marcelli, who introduced me to Dr. Paul Louis Noisin, the pre-eminent anthropologist of Haiti and president of the Université Roi Christophe. Dr. Noisin lent me his valuable time and intellect so that I could better comprehend Haitian history and culture.

After my research on the north Haitian coast, during which

I traced Wake's steps in the *voudou* caves and along the precarious cliffs of Picolet, an intrepid band of adventurers helped me on an expedition into the mountains of the interior to follow in Wake's track there. Eva DeHart and Rob Irons of For Haiti With Love, the Christian medical, food, and housing mission I enthusiastically support (www.forhaitwithlove.org) helped organize the expedition. Rob was also a driver; Racine Présumé, veteran commander in the Haitian National Police and dear friend, was the expedition's outstanding *chef de securité*, also a driver, and kept things moving along. Charlot Althiery was senior guide at Sans Souci and Citadelle. Jocelyn Morisset was a driver, and both he and Jean Claude Aristil provided security. Roseline Présumé (also of For Haiti With Love) was chief translator/negotiator—no easy task. Rosemarlene Suprevil was admin assistant; Jean Moreau was the column's flute player; Jon, René, and Edward were bearers; and Joseph Calixte was guide at Picolet. Cesar and Michelle, Frenchmen wandering through Haiti, joined the crew at Milot and helped get the vehicle up that daunting mountain to the base camp. René, Edward, and Rob helped me scale the cliff, just as Wake did, and barely cheat death one more time. In total I had fifteen people with me on that trek—a memorable experience that will last a lifetime.

Back here in the U.S.A., several folks helped me in the actual writing of the novel. I began writing this book at Christine and Mark Strom's high-altitude home of Maramonte in the Black Mountains of North Carolina. Mike and Renee Maurer's place in the Florida Keys was another *refuge de plume*. Famous novelist Randy Wayne White helped with good professional advice and decent rum. And, of course, the lovely Nancy Glickman provided constant love, support, ideas, and very valuable critical reading as well. June Cussen, the executive editor at Pineapple Press, has edited all nine novels of the Honor Series. Along the way, she's taught me more than anyone else in the business about the craft of creating interesting books. I am very grateful to have had the opportunity to work with and learn from her.

Most of all, I thank my readers around the world. Throughout the years, you have kept me filled with more than enough élan for each new project. You are the very best audience a writer could hope for, and I am profoundly appreciative of your considerable encouragement.

Thank you all.

A final word
with my readers

Haiti has fascinated me since my first visit in 1983. Her art, music, humor, and most of all, her people's gentle amity, will find their way into your heart. It's easy to be glib about Haiti, until you really get to know a Haitian. Once you delve into their history, you begin to understand how far they have come, against all odds. I have great respect for their accomplishments.

In recent years, the Haitian people have endured hurricanes and earthquakes and starvation and disease. Many have lost everything except their pride and their humor. But somehow, they keep trudging onward and upward, with quiet dignity and courage.

For years now, I've supported a Christian mission at Cap Haitien, in northern Haiti. For Haiti with Love provides medical care, food, and homes for the people in that area. I urge you to visit www.forhaitiwithlove.org and find out what they've been doing for the last four decades to make life more bearable for the people of Haiti. It's quite a story.

Perhaps you will end up like me, captivated not only by Haiti's history and her culture and her people, but also her wonderful potential for the future.

Robert N. Macomber
Twin Palms Cottage
Matlacha Island
Florida

Other Books in Robert N. Macomber's Honor Series:

At the Edge of Honor. This nationally acclaimed naval Civil War novel, the first in the Honor series of naval fiction, takes the reader into the steamy world of Key West and the Caribbean in 1863 and introduces Peter Wake, the reluctant New England volunteer officer who finds himself battling the enemy on the coasts of Florida, sinister intrigue in Spanish Havana and the British Bahamas, and social taboos in Key West when he falls in love with the daughter of a Confederate zealot. (hb, pb)

Point of Honor. Winner of the Florida Historical Society's 2003 Patrick Smith Award for Best Florida Fiction. In this second book in the Honor series, it is 1864 and Lt. Peter Wake, United States Navy, assisted by his indomitable Irish bosun, Sean Rork, commands the naval schooner *St. James*. He searches for army deserters in the Dry Tortugas, finds an old nemesis during a standoff with the French Navy on the coast of Mexico, starts a drunken tavern riot in Key West, and confronts incompetent Federal army officers during an invasion of upper Florida. (hb, pb)

Honorable Mention. This third book in the Honor series of naval fiction covers the tumultuous end of the Civil War in Florida and the Caribbean. Lt. Peter Wake is now in command of the steamer USS *Hunt,* and quickly plunges into action, chasing a strange vessel during a tropical storm off Cuba, confronting death to liberate an escaping slave ship, and coming face to face with the enemy's most powerful ocean warship in Havana's harbor. Finally, when he tracks down a colony of former Confederates in Puerto Rico, Wake becomes involved in a deadly twist of irony. (hb)

A Dishonorable Few. Fourth in the Honor series. It is 1869 and the United States is painfully recovering from the Civil War. Lt. Peter Wake heads to turbulent Central America to deal with a former American naval officer turned renegade mercenary. As the action unfolds in Colombia and Panama, Wake realizes that his most dangerous adversary may be a man on his own ship, forcing Wake to make a decision that will lead to his court-martial in Washington when the mission has finally ended. (hb)

An Affair of Honor. Fifth in the Honor series. It's December 1873 and Lt. Peter Wake is the executive officer of the USS *Omaha* on patrol in the West Indies, eager to return home. Fate, however, has other plans. He runs afoul of the Royal Navy in Antigua and then is sent off to Europe, where he finds himself embroiled in a Spanish civil war. But his real test comes when he and Sean Rork are sent on a mission in northern Africa. (hb)

A Different Kind of Honor. In this sixth novel in the Honor series, it's 1879 and Lt. Cmdr. Peter Wake, U.S.N., is on assignment as the American naval observer to the War of the Pacific along the west coast of South America. During this mission Wake will witness history's first battle between ocean-going ironclads, ride the world's first deep-diving submarine, face his first machine guns in combat, and run for his life in the Catacombs of the Dead in Lima. (hb)

The Honored Dead. Seventh in the series. On what at first appears to be a simple mission for the U.S. president in French Indochina in 1883, naval intelligence officer Lt. Cmdr. Peter Wake encounters opium warlords, Chinese-Malay pirates, and French gangsters. (hb)

The Darkest Shade of Honor. Eighth in the series. It's 1886 and Wake, now of the U.S. Navy's Office of Naval Intelligence, meets rising politico Theodore Roosevelt in New York City. Wake is assigned to uncover Cuban revolutionary activities between Florida and Cuba. He meets José Martí, finds himself engulfed in the most catastrophic event in Key West history, and must make a decision involving the very darkest shade of honor. (hb)

For a complete catalog, visit our website at www.pineapplepress.com. Or write to Pineapple Press, P.O. Box 3889, Sarasota, Florida 34230-3889, or call (800) 746-3275.